CRIMEFEST

CRIMEFEST

LEAVING THE SCENE

CELEBRATING 16 YEARS

NO EXIT PRESS

IN ASSOCIATION WITH CRIMEFEST

First published in the UK in 2025 by No Exit Press,
An imprint of Bedford Square Publishers Ltd,
London, UK

noexit.co.uk
@noexitpress

Collection copyright © CrimeFest 2025
Edited by Adrian Muller, 2025
Advisory Editor Maxim Jakubowski
All rights reserved

All stories © 2025 by their respective authors

ISBN
978-1-83501-424-0 (Paperback)
978-1-83501-425-7 (eBook)

2 4 6 8 10 9 7 5 3 1

The manufacturer's authorised representative in the EU for
product safety is Easy Access System Europe,
Mustamäe tee 50, 10621 Tallinn, Estonia
gpsr.requests@easproject.com

Printed in Great Britain by CPI Group (UK) Ltd, Croydon CR0 4YY

MIX
Paper | Supporting
responsible forestry
FSC
www.fsc.org
FSC® C013604

To the authors, readers, sponsors and publishing industry people who make up our CrimeFest family. Thank you so much for your support over the years.

CONTENTS

Lee Child

Lee Child is one of the world's leading thriller writers. It is said one of his novels featuring his hero Jack Reacher is sold somewhere in the world every nine seconds. His books consistently achieve the number-one slot on bestseller lists around the world and have sold over one hundred million copies. Lee is the recipient of many awards. He was appointed CBE in the 2019 Queen's Birthday Honours.

jackreacher.com

FOREWORD

Literary theory says stories need conflict – old versus new, or one ideology against another, or whatever variation the story-teller chooses to offer. The most basic versions – and often the most satisfying – are good versus bad, and chaos versus order. Crime fiction offers both, in recognisable, human-sized doses. I have never seriously grappled with ideological convictions, or past versus future, but I have had my cars stolen and my houses burgled. And no perp was ever found or brought to justice. Like millions of others, I have lived with the buzz of frustration – never getting closure or satisfaction.

Crime fiction brings us both. You bet my car will be found! You bet the stuff from my house will be recovered! You bet the bad guy will be marched shame-faced into a prison cell! Justice is done. Closure is granted. The sense of consolation is huge.

The precipitating crimes in fiction are sometimes ordinary, sometimes vicious, sometimes even appalling and horrible. They make you wonder how twisted the authors must be. But here's the strange thing – crime fiction authors are the nicest people you will ever meet. They're kind, generous, funny, interesting and full of goodwill. I have spent countless delightful hours hanging out with my peers. Mostly that happens at genre conventions, where readers and writers gather for a weekend. Those conventions are organised by groups of fans and influencers – themselves delightful people.

One of the best such conventions has been CrimeFest, held every year in Bristol, England, under the aegis of Adrian Muller, Donna Moore and (before he retired) Myles Allfrey, all of whom deserve all of the adjectives in the previous paragraph. I have been many times, and always come away with my spirits lifted, and with new enthusiasm for my chosen trade – plus a little apprehension, given the tsunami of new talent chasing after me.

But nothing lasts for ever, and, sadly, May 2025 will see the last Bristol CrimeFest. To honour the occasion, readers and writers from around the world will gather for one last great weekend extravaganza. And to mark the occasion, those kind, generous writers have donated their talents to this anthology, designed to benefit the Royal National Institute of Blind People (RNIB). People with poor or no sight love – and need – stories like anyone else, and the RNIB has long been a powerful force in bringing the two together. I have been a keen supporter for a long time, and can think of no better purpose for the characteristic willingness to help that all the contributors herein display. I hope you enjoy the stories – and I think you will – and I know you will agree the charitable impulse displayed is well aimed. Thank you for your support.

Lee Child
Cumbria
2025

Jeffery Deaver

Jeffery Deaver, author of fifty novels and more than a hundred short stories, is a Grand Master of Mystery Writers of America. He is the recipient of Novel of the Year from International Thriller Writers, and the Steel and Short Story Daggers from the Crime Writers Association. His novel *The Bone Collector* was a feature film starring Denzel Washington, and his Colter Shaw series is the basis for *Tracker*, the number-one TV drama in America.

jefferydeaver.com

TWO DEATHS IN BRISTOL

Jeffery Deaver

'Four hours to go, Robbie.'

'About that, yes.'

'You know you'll be bored.'

'Life is all about taking chances, now, isn't it?' DC Robert Foxworthy looked up from his immaculate desk, the top as grey as his suit and the thin stripes in his red and grey tie. Tall and forever a bit stooped over, he was jowly and had ears that protruded some, but short of adopting a Beatles haircut circa 1965, there was nothing to do about that.

'Dreadfully bored,' DI Thomas Hayden-Smith, big and stanch and keen-eyed, tried again.

The two were in Foxworthy's cubicle in the Avon and Somerset territorial police complex on Valley Road in Portishead. It was a new facility, and large – forty acres or so. Perfectly fine. Foxworthy preferred the old stations, like Bridwell.

Or Fishponds.

The latter for obvious reasons, of course, given his Sunday afternoon passion.

'And what's on the old pensioners agenda, Robbie? Mary have you painting nooks and painting crannies? What *is* a cranny anyway? Perhaps an irritable old woman who minds the children.'

'I will not miss your humour, Tom.'

The man was, in effect, Foxworthy's boss in CID, though he was ten years his junior. Interested only in policing the street, Foxworthy had not taken the normal trajectory: constable to detective constable to swapping a letter and becoming inspector, DI or DS, much less the netherworld of bureaucracy above, supervisor and the like.

At fifty-five, Foxworthy had five years till mandatory retirement – though higher-ups could dawdle for a bit more time, but tended to be relegated to personnel and budgetary issues, and looking triumphantly stern as they made press announcements of arrests with a barricade of cocaine bricks before them like a wall of a grey-white castle.

No thank you.

Foxworthy might also have retired last year.

After the Incident.

The knife stab in the thigh was from the crazed young man raging against the dangers of immigrants and wielding a nasty ten-inch blade his mother had used just that morning to make her signature stew for supper.

Oblivious to the irony that it was *he* who was dangerous, and the festivalgoers he attacked were peace personified, he had touted his 'superior-race' status. First on the scene, DC Foxworthy had approached cautiously and defused the situation.

Up until the point where he was rewarded for not siccing an ARV armed unit on the kid by a sloppy thrust of the mutton blade. At least Mr Aryan had been courteous, or incompetent, enough to miss vital nerves and vessels.

Cliches are cliches for a reason and Foxworthy leaned into

one of then – getting back on the horse. Following medical leave, he returned to doing what he had been doing for decades in Bristol: investigating major cases within CID. Part of his return, though, had nothing to do with overcoming ill ease and timidity about blades; it was about the fact that, as Hayden-Smith had teased, he did indeed have a fierce allergy to boredom. And one thing you could say about policing was that it never was dull.

But now was the time to leave, he was convinced. The aches – leg and otherwise – were part of it. But more, Foxworthy and Mary wanted to travel (to wherever fish streams waited to be fished and pastoral landscapes waited to be painted). Bill and his wife had moved back to Somerset, with Robert, Foxworthy's grandson, and dinners and outings awaited. Foxworthy had an ancient Austin Healy he was repairing and was long overdue for its resurrection.

And then there was his Team.

The DC was among the fiercest of the fierce followers of Bristol City, which had been described in the past, by friend and foe, as a bit of a yo-yo: promotion and relegation, promotion and relegation.

Foxworthy cared not. He exalted in sitting in the stands at Ashton Gate and shouting and waving the colours – red and white, the hues of the flag of St George himself, no less! He liked the tidal wave roar of the crowd, the elegance of the lads' footwork, the fact that the most famous half-centre in all English football played for City. Billy Wedlock, a hall-of-famer, who was not from Spain or Italy or Korea or Brazil. Bristol born and bred, when not on the pitch, he lived and worked in a pub near the stadium.

Being on call so much, Foxworthy had missed far too many games.

That was about to change.

In four hours.

Well, now three hours and fifty-two minutes.

'The boys give you a proper send-off?' big Hayden-Smith asked, examining a framed citation in the box Foxworthy was filing with mementoes. He'd received it for saving a life. Or for something else. He wasn't sure. He had a lot of them.

The DI was wearing a white shirt, starched to perfection. By coincidence, he too wore a tie similarly coloured to Foxworthy's, though with the width of the red and grey stripes reversed.

Foxworthy smiled. 'Went to the Mare. Rollicking time it was.'

Pints, some toasts, cheesy chips and soggy calamari, a recycled speech by Supervisor McDaniels, some sad karaoke, but then karaoke was always sad, in Foxworthy's view. The boss had presented him not with a gold watch but an Amazon gift card.

Far more appreciated, as a new fishing reel had been beckoning.

Hayden-Smith had not been in attendance. He was leading the Lanham task force, whose existence was the reason Foxworthy's party had not been well attended. Fine with him. Over the years, bedtime had been creeping closer and closer with each night, like a determined if confused mealworm.

'Seriously. I joke. I deflect. But I *do* wish you'd stay just a bit longer. There's something about you. You find things, Robbie. No one knows quite how you do it.'

'Your mobile gone missing, Tom? I'll ring it if you want.'

'Ha.'

He nodded at the large white envelope on the desk, the retirement packet from Human Resources and the forms that sat atop it. 'You haven't signed anything yet, I notice.'

'It's ten past seven, Tom. Noon is my official stop time. And I was just turning to the paperwork now.' And, to prove his determination and sincerity, withdrew from his breast pocket the gold pen he used to jot notes in his interviews with suspects and witnesses.

'Ah, well. All right. So be it. But then do a lad a favour? We're knee-deep with Lanham…'

'Any luck, Tom?'

The DI scoffed. 'I've got a dozen constables on the street canvassing. No sign of him. And in the Surveillance Room, ten pairs of eyes—'

'Twenty eyes total.'

Another laugh, but a grim one. 'Scanning the screens. Not a trace of the bastard.'

Bristol did not have nearly the number of CCTVs of, say, London, where the joke was that every woman who gave birth was presented with a Metropolitan Police security camera for the baby on the way out of hospital. But there were enough eyes in the sky – pole mounted and a few drone – to sweep for villains.

In this instance, the subject of the hunt was one Peter Lanham.

The squat, gruff, compact mob boss from Nottingham had escaped from an MI5 and Nottinghamshire police operation. The list of offenses was impressive. He had violated the Criminal Law Act, the Organised Crime Group provisions of the Serious Crime Act, the Proceeds of Crime Act, the Misuse of Drugs Act, the Firearms Act and the Modern Slavery Act.

Oh, and the little matter of murder and kidnapping as well.

An informant had suggested he'd come west, to escape from the country, and Avon and Somerset was considered a possible egress point.

'You want me to join the hunt and watch TV in my last four hours of service?'

'I wouldn't do that to you, would I, now? No, there's an incident needs looking into. An unfortunate accident, it seems.'

Foxworthy was frowning. 'I always wondered why that particular adjective gets limpeted on to "accident"? How many *fortunate* accidents have we seen?'

'I, for one, *shall* miss your levity, Robbie.'

But then that lightness between them, fragile at best, vapoured away.

A body.

A life had become a non-life.

And for whatever reason that had occurred, it was now Foxworthy's mission to determine why, see if a danger still existed, take care of the many arrangements that such an occurrence required. The paperwork alone was daunting.

There was another mission, too: to tell the survivors of the loss and be as comforting as he could.

After all, a death, he had always felt, was like a precious gem pitched into a pond: the loss of the stone was cause for sorrow in its own right, but the waves that resulted would spread out a vast distance and touch family and friends and neighbours and fellow workers and, perhaps, congregants.

'Traffic?'

'No. Poor bloke tripped and fell. St Nicholas Street. Near the bridge.'

'I'll go over there now, Tom. Of course.' Foxworthy rose.

'Thank you. Oh, and Robbie?'

He looked back as he took a raincoat off the rack in the corner of the cubicle.

'And please don't pull a Kelly.' A grim laugh.

A reference to a superstition in the department.

Referring to the unfortunate case of Constable Evan Kelly, killed by a drunken driver on what would have been his last traffic stop, a mere thirty minutes before retiring.

But this St Nicholas incident sounded different in kind from a traffic stop on a busy auto route.

And *unfortunate* trip and fall.

Robbie Foxworthy was confident he would have it all wrapped up, safely, and be back here well within his remaining time on the force of, now, three hours and thirty-nine minutes.

'Sir.'

The uniformed constable was standing on St Nicholas Street in front of the sheeted barricade the medical team had erected to keep the corpse out of view of the public.

Foxworthy nodded. The 'sir' was not because of his rank. A constable and a detective constable, like Foxworthy, share exactly the same technical status within the police department. It would be the age, of course.

The PC seemed a little surprised at Foxworthy's presence. Perhaps he'd heard that this was to have been Foxworthy's last day, and he would, by rights, be sitting in a pub with mates who were singing a goodbye song, a la 'Happy Birthday', if there was such a tune.

'Are you the SIO?

'No, I'm OIO.'

A beat of a moment.

'Oh, the *Only* Investigating Officer.' A smile.

Foxworthy added, 'The Lanham investigation. It's taken everybody's attention.'

The constable, whose name was A. Darwin, his plate

announced, scowled. 'That man looks like a mean porker, you ask me, sir.'

Foxworthy supposed the Nottingham mobster might have done, though he'd never heard the expression – and suspected it wasn't one much in use in the West Country, or any other region of England. Nor did Foxworthy care whether the perpetrator resembled a pig, a thug, or a saintly priest. Over concern with the appearance of suspects could often lead to erroneous conclusions and distractions.

And, accordingly, deflected investigations.

A sin, in Foxworthy's book

'What do we have?'

'Nearly as far as I can tell, sir, he was walking this way on St Nicholas from the High Street. And tripped. Hit his head on that pile of rubble there – not ribboned off, you can see. That'll be a Health and Safety violation for sure.'

'Indeed, it would. Go on, Constable.'

Darwin continued, 'He staggered this way, looking for help, I'm guessing. Got only to here.'

About two blocks from High.

A medical team – a man and woman – stood nearby. Foxworthy stepped to them, and the three nodded greetings. Foxworthy said, 'Thoughts?'

The female medic said, 'Blunt force trauma, and haemorrhaging. COD. Consistent with a trip and fall.'

'Coroner?'

'We've alerted her,' the man said.

'Your recommendation?

The woman shrugged. 'Probably non-forensic PME. But it will be your call, sir.'

Any death that wasn't anticipated – like a heart or cancer

patient – was referred to the coroner for determination of whether the post-mortem exam should be forensic – suspected criminal – or non-forensic, an accident. In a situation like this, where there were no bullet holes or stab wounds, the medical folks would lean toward non-forensic and most police would concur. Foxworthy was inclined to do so, too.

But his nature, as much as procedure, dictated a bit more work was required.

Foxworthy pulled on gloves and booties for his shoes – he always kept them in his pocket – along with evidence bags. He stepped inside the enclosure. There lay a man of about sixty-five or seventy. He was prone on his belly and his right arm was extended, as was his index finger, as if he were pointing at the pub over the road.

'You touch anything?' he called to the constable.

Darwin cleared his throat. 'His neck. To see if he was alive. Only that.'

Foxworthy supposed he got that trick from television. A neck pulse was hard to find and not a good indicator of life. But he was sure the man was dead by the time the constable arrived. The wound to the head was massive, and the stone or whatever he'd struck on his fall had ripped open vessels. He'd lost much blood.

'The person who reported?'

'From a mobile, sir. Wouldn't leave a name. Communications traced the number and it turned out to be a lorry driver. He's in Wales by now.'

'How they hate getting involved…'

'That's the truth, sir.'

But at least he called. Many people would not have.

'He see anything else?'

'No. According to him. Just the body.'

'I'll want the number just the same.'

'I'll have it sent over.' Darwin played with his phone.

Foxworthy crouched, wincing, a double threat, from age and the wound. A fast search revealed a wallet ripe with credit cards and a pocket containing about a hundred and twenty quid in cash. His name was Victor Morrison and he was – had been – a resident of Bristol. There was no phone. Unusual, but not unheard of among those his age.

He called the constable over. 'Darwin.'

'Sir.'

'Take a picture.' He held up the victim's driving license.

The officer did as told.

Foxworthy looked about. 'Go into the pub, and that tea shop.' He nodded to one across the street from the pub. 'See if anyone knows him or noticed him today.'

'Yessir, I will do.'

Foxworthy's eyes followed the constable as he walked to the pub. It was one of the more famous ones in Bristol, and dated to the nineteenth century. The structure was typical of the architecture of that era in this, the Old City, and the pub it was home to was known for fine ale, good food and a unique decor element: four statues on the first-floor façade: four heads, carved from wood and painted. Three were men, and one – the second from the right – a woman, obscured with a veil. To Foxworthy's knowledge, no one knew who the sculptor was, why they had been created and what the significance might be of the fact the woman's face was largely hidden.

He rose with a wince, which he turned to conceal from the medics.

Unsuccessfully.

'You feeling all right there, sir?'

'I'm fine,' he grumbled, reflecting, but not pointing out, that many people grunt when they rise.

Even star footballers.

He looked up, studying light poles and building facades, and then placed a call to the ASP Forensics Department, which was in charge of monitoring the CCTVs. He recognised the woman's voice, that of the director.

'Julia.'

'Robbie! Are you volunteering to play the game?'

'The where-in-the-world-is-the-Nottingham-gangster game?'

'Aye, the very one.'

The Porker...

Julia Hatcher was a young grandmother of six, a one-time contestant on the *Great British Bake-off* and one of the most renowned physical and computer forensic scientists in the world, keeping Bristol in the forefront of the technological war against crime. She said, 'I do love my gangster movies. *Goodfellas*. Have you seen *The Long Good Friday*?'

'Have indeed. Though I preferred *The Krays*.'

'Oh, my, those brothers!'

Ronny and Reggie Kray, identical twins, ran a crime syndicate that generally was regarded as the most dangerous in the history of modern London. They were known for their lethal – and unpredictable – behaviour. They had spent time in Somerset's most famous prison, which dated back to the seventeenth century, Shepton Mallet, now a popular tourist attraction.

Julie sighed. 'You just don't see good psychopaths anymore. Outside of American politics, that is.'

He chuckled. 'But I'm not on the Lanham case, Julia. Hayden-Smith has seen fit to give me a going-away present. An accident on St Nicholas. Near the bridge. I need to know if you have cameras in a couple of locations.'

He gave her the streets and surrounding area.

A moment later she returned. 'The bridge, yes, we have eyes on. But that portion of High and St Nicholas, I'm afraid not.'

'Damn.'

'Just a mishap, you say?'

'Yes, but I like my z's crossed and my j's dotted.'

A breezy laugh. 'I shall miss you, Robbie. Stay in touch now.'

'I will do. You're a dear, Julia. I can't thank you enough for your help over the years.'

They rang off.

He flipped through the man's wallet and found only one *In Case of Emergency* contact on a laminated card. A son. A call that had to be made, and, after several deep breaths, he rang the number.

No gentleness in delay. He jumped right to the point and told the man, sounding in his forties or so, what had happened.

After a pause, the shattered son broke down in tears.

'An accident? A bloody accident? Jesus.'

Foxworthy had made a number of such calls – via phone and in person – and he had learned that survivors would in general much rather their relatives were dispatched by some evildoer – either human or biological, like a virus or clogged vein or renegade cancer cell. At least then there was some logic to the death. The perpetrator had a purpose.

To die by a twist of fate like this, though, was beyond cruel.

After spending some minutes offering his condolences, Foxworthy gave Morrison's son instructions on how to contact the coroner and where the unfortunate man's body would be transported. Relevant phone numbers, too.

'A final question, sir. Did your father have a mobile? And carry it with him often?'

'Always, yes.' The man choked. 'We rang each other once a day.'

They disconnected, leaving DC Foxworthy with the sense he always had under such circumstances: that he would have given anything to do more to ease the pain.

It was then that he glanced down at the corpse once more and, rather than crouching, this time merely bent down and in gloved hands gently manoeuvred Morrison's heavy, inert head upward. The careful touch was not from reverence but from a policeman's innate instinct to make sure the scene was as little disturbed as possible.

Because he had just concluded that this death was no accident at all.

'Crikey,' Hayden-Smith was saying through Foxworthy's mobile. 'Why do you think so, Robbie?'

Foxworthy replied, 'Because, Tom, either after he struck his head, he decided he enjoyed the experience so much that he fell again on purpose, or someone brained him. There were *two* wounds on his head and from different parts of the brick. One, the flat front. The second, an edge. And his mobile was missing – and that had to do with the death. A random corpse picking? They would have taken the money. Cars are here, Tom. Have to go.'

Two patrol cars had arrived and blocked off this portion of St Nicholas Street. This was a weekday and traffic was already snarled – a word that Foxworthy had told Mary news presenters loved to use when referring to congestion. Born and raised in Boston, his wife said that Americans tended to use the word 'jam', which could mean jammed up, of course, but that she, as a girl, thought meant thick as marmalade, a la Paddington. Foxworthy liked her interpretation better.

The gowned crime scene people – looking like space walkers – would soon descend and pick up all the magic bits that they found. Crimes were largely solved by two things nowadays: forensics and CCTV footage. The latter was not helpful here, as Julia had explained. Perhaps the former would be.

Constable Darwin approached. His canvassing had unearthed no obvious answers. None of the bar staff or the servers at the pub recognised him. Victor Morrison was, however, known at the tea shop. A troubled clerk, a young woman with many tats and braided dark hair, took the news hard. She told the constable that Morrison would pop in sometimes during a walk. He was cheerful and chatty and knew everything there was to know about Bristol and Avon-Somerset. He was, apparently, quite the itinerate resident and every morning took a several-mile consti-tutional to the Old City from his home, which she believed was on Oxford Street, about a mile and a half away.

She knew of no reason why someone would wish him harm.

Foxworthy called and requested an officer to get a warrant to examine the man's dwelling.

The woman wiped tears and added that his walks usually ended up here because it took him past St Nicholas Church, which he and his wife, now deceased, had attended frequently.

Foxworthy walked the two blocks to the High Street, then over the road and spoke to a priest at the Anglican church. He was shocked by the news. He did not know Morrison well, but they had exchanged pleasantries from time to time. Like the tea shop clerk, he knew of no reason why anyone might wish him harm.

The church itself did not have any security cameras focused on the pile of rubble or that portion of St Nicholas Street, where the attack would have taken place.

Foxworthy then walked to Bristol Bridge, looking over the Floating Harbor and Welch Back, the wharf dating back eons to the days when the dock was used for trade between the two countries.

He returned to St Nicholas and began to retrace Morrison's logical route – to the site of his attack.

It was curious. He could picture the assailant slipping up behind Morrison, gripping the brick, spinning the shocked man about and slamming the block into his head. He would have readjusted his grip and struck him again. He would have planned on another strike, but something had distracted him, maybe a passing car or some pedestrians. This gave Morrison a chance to stagger further down St Nicholas.

When the coast was clear, the killer hurried to the body, checked that he was dead, and then fled.

Foxworthy's mobile hummed and he took a call. It was from the lorry driver who had spotted the body in the first place. He apologised for not waiting but had a vital order to deliver to Monmouthshire in Wales. A few questions and answers later, the DC concluded he knew nothing more, and they rung off.

The crime scene people arrived and climbed out of the white van and dressing in their matching white moon-walker outfits. He briefed them and displayed the two crime scenes: the pile of rubble and the body.

He then sent Constable Darwin on another canvassing mission, extending the search area to up and down St Nicholas, High Street, the church and Bristol Bridge.

The young man eagerly trotted off.

Reminded Foxworthy of himself at that age. A faint smile broke out before it was summarily suppressed.

Foxworthy returned to the body and stood over it for a long moment, noting the blood, the misshapen head and 'pointing' finger, which was surely not that at all but merely an eerie coincidence.

Death rearranges the body in so many curious and horrific ways.

As he gazed down, several questions rose prominently in the detective's mind.

One: why had Morrison continued up St Nicholas after the blows rained down? Assuming the assailant had ducked out of sight, Morrison might just as easily have returned to the High Street, which was more populated at that time of the morning than St Nicholas and he would have stood a better chance of being seen and aided.

And two: why had he been killed? Robbery, possible but unlikely. A demand for money was one thing, but outright murder? A cell phone and some cash were hardly worth life in HMP Bristol. But other classic reasons to kill? Revenge? A serial killer? An argument gone lethal? A whistleblower? A love triangle? They said sixty was the new forty – Foxworthy hardly felt it – but perhaps he'd stumbled on a simmering soap opera plot.

But Robbie Foxworthy knew that speculation without facts was a waste of time, and so he now resolved to add to his investigative quiver.

Unfortunately, the only way he saw of doing so involved a task he was hardly looking forward to.

* * *

'Tell me about him. If you would be so kind.'

Sitting across from Foxworthy in the DC's cubicle, the dapper man took in the question, nodding. He dabbed at his eyes, red-rimmed and damp. His suit was of a navy-blue shade and a much finer cut than Foxworthy's. Mary was handy with a needle and thread, but those skills did not extend to men's suits, and he wore whatever fit the robots at M&S's preferred fabricators decided.

Morrison's son, Harold, replied, 'Dad wasn't into anything illegal, if that's what you're suggesting. Drugs, or... women or men or whatever.'

'No, no, of course not,' Foxworthy assured. 'I'm merely curious about his life. Every fact, big or small, gets us closer to answers.' His face was draped with sympathy.

Though, in truth, Foxworthy had not in the least dismissed drugs or women or men or whatever. Because people were killed for reasons involving one or more of those factors with some frequency. But he would never openly suggest they were at play here, because a relative like Morrison's son would then focus on his father's defence and, possibly, fail to give up the one vital key to the case. And so he merely nodded and encouraged and remained neutral and attentive.

'Don't try to make it relevant to the case. Anything that comes to mind. Imagine I simply want to know who he was. Which, in fact, I do.'

This was true. A biography made victims real and turned them into something more than just an inert object or a case number.

And that in turn motivated Foxworthy all the more to find those who had injured or killed them.

Slowly a portrait of Victor Morrison emerged.

A retired actuary for an insurance company, he was a widower of twelve years and had never dated since his wife passed away. Harold was his only son, and he and his wife had given Morrison two grandchildren: a boy and a girl. Harold rattled off more details, and Foxworthy was amused to learn that the girl, Penny, shared her grandfather's passion for fishing.

'I shouldn't be telling this to a policeman, but she broke the law, she did.'

'How's that, sir?'

'The Environment and Countryside rules? About using live bait?' he whispered. 'Penny thought worms caught better trout than flies. At ten years, imagine. I shouldn't be saying this. My own daughter. I should have kept mum.'

He might have been joking but Foxworthy gave him a reassuring smile and told him that angler crimes were not within his jurisdiction.

It was here that another officer might have interjected a comment about the coincidence that his grandchild too, Robert, enjoyed rod and reel. But these moments were not about him. An officer should vanish entirely from an interview. He was there to encourage and direct. When he instructed his proteges in the art of interviewing, he found the best approach was not to bluster or threaten but to pretend you were wafting smoke away from your child's face at a campfire.

Victor explained his father was kind and gentle and concerned about the environment and the plight of the homeless, assessments that Foxworthy ignored because those words might apply to anyone from the Pope to the Nottingham organised crime porker, Pete Lanham.

Foxworthy couldn't quite explain what characteristics were relevant to a homicide investigation, but he knew them when he saw them.

But, like panning for gold, you were patient and you swished away a lot of mud before the nuggets appeared.

Victor Morrison was frugal when it came to clothing. He was impossible to buy presents for because there was nothing he wanted and was opposed to a child, even grown, spending money on his father. He helped his daughter-in-law bake Christmas cookies and burnt not a one. He loved Bristol, the city of his birth, and knew enough of the history of the place to be a part-time docent at one of the city museums. Foxworthy recalled the clerk in the tea shop saying much the same of the elderly man.

He enjoyed the British version of *The Office* and *House of Cards*, preferring them to the American. He loved his puzzles – crosswords, Scrabble, acrostics, anything involving words (Sudoku and number games left him cold). He had a reputation for being wickedly clever at pub quiz night and he was constantly in demand to be a partner for the competition (especially by moon-eyed widows). He won a bottle of twenty-four-year-old Macallan Scotch, which sat on his mantelpiece unopened because the man liked trophies but did not much care for liquor. He read biographies, and enjoyed the scandal sheets, while claiming – with a wry twinkle in his eye – to sneer at them. His game was cricket, a sport in which he had failed to interest his son. Harold added with some pride he was a dyed-in-the-wool Bristol City football fan (again, Foxworthy kept mum, acknowledging the comment with a faint nod).

The details unfolded until, finally, the sorrow dammed the flood, and after whispering, 'I'm sorry, I just can't....' he fell silent.

'Not at all, sir. You've been more than helpful.'

'I have?'

'Indeed.'

'But how? A disjointed rambling of memory?'

'That, I can't quite answer yet. But I hope to be able to soon.'

The man's eyes fell to the photograph, one of Foxworthy's favourites, of his wife and son, who was then ten. It was the last decoration that remained out and not in the packing box with the rest of his personal effects.

A wave of bitterness flushed through Harold Morrison's face as he cut his eyes to the DC. 'Maybe if you find him, he'll resist.' A cool, eerie smile appeared. 'And you can shoot the wanker to death.'

Foxworthy had heard this before and he had to explain. 'The Crown Prosecutor'll see that justice is done. We don't carry guns, you know.'

This came as a surprise, it seemed, probably because TV suggested that everyone with a badge carried a six-gun.

He added that very few police the UK were allowed to carry a weapon. 'There's a special unit.'

Harold seemed dumbfounded. 'You go after a man who would kill an innocent victim like my father so brutally – with no gun? Aren't you afraid for your life?'

'It would be very bad form to attack a copper,' Foxworthy assured him. 'Happens very rarely.'

And, coincidentally or not, his words happened to be accompanied by nasty throb from the wound in his leg.

St Nicholas had become a mini tourist attraction.

The death had made the news, of course, and Foxworthy politely rejected the offer from several reporters to be interviewed. Avon and Somerset Police had a press office for that.

The journalists, who needed constant fodder for their airtime and digital columns machinery, reacted with displeasure, but such was the relationship. Like warring siblings on *Eastenders* or *Coronation Street*, the police and press wrestled constantly but would never, ever disappear completely from each other's lives.

Spectators, too, were present.

Among them, selfie takers, which angered Robbie Foxworthy no end. But shooing them off might result in a complaint. There was a large swatch of the countryside that felt the police had no authority to require them to do anything when they were not breaking an explicit law. Some even when they *were* breaking a law…

The yellow tape remained, though Foxworthy was certain there was little need to protect the scene any longer, since it had surely shed all the clues it was going to, like the black snake in Mary's garden doffing its pale crisp skin before hibernation.

He stepped into the taped-off area, minding the dried blood – now the gesture *was* one of respect – and stood with arms crossed, looking about. His eyes swivelled to the pile of rubble, also ribboned off.

The church.

The pub with its odd sculptures of the three men and the solitary, veiled woman.

Memory images were present too, from earlier that day: the body, the bloodstains. The extended arm.

There were answers here, he believed.

You find things, Robbie. No one knows quite how you do it…

He remained unmoving for what seemed to him an hour, though when he glanced at his phone, he was surprised to see that he had been here for only eight minutes.

The time was merely a coincidental fact. He had not pulled out his mobile to check the hour.

His intention was to place a call, and this is what he now did.

As he sat at the comfy table in the window of a coffee house, DC Robbie Foxworthy was thinking that the place had an unfortunate name.

Java 'n More.

Unfortunate because of the botched contraction: the word *and* should have been shorted to 'n' since two letters had been excised. More troubling was the Java reference. The owner of the franchise was likely American, and would accordingly not understand that the term became synonymous with coffee because of the brutal exploitation of Indonesia by the commercial colonial power, the British East India Company.

Although he supposed that many of his fellow Brits might not know the travesty visited upon the native population.

Foxworthy was not enjoying his tea. The barista had not used proper boiled water, but steam from the cappuccino spout on the elaborate espresso machine. He didn't know the engineering aspects of the device but somehow the arrangement imparted a faint coffee-and-milk taste.

The biscuit, however, had been good.

Foxworthy had been sitting here for only five minutes when he noted a tall man wearing an impeccable blue suit – a bit too light for Mary's taste, he observed (Foxworthy had almost bought a similar garment). The fellow's hair was a thing of perfection, silver-brown and sculpted. A square jaw, lipid brown eyes. Mary would have rated him 'right handsome', easily looking past the flaw of the suit.

After he had bought a takeaway cup of coffee, the man turned to leave, but Foxworthy rose and stepped between him and the door.

'Councilman Hyde?'

Displaying his badge and ID card.

A blink.

'Officer.' A squint. He read more closely. 'Constable. How can I help you?'

'Wonder if I might have a word, sir.'

'Aye. Well. Here?'

Three distinct words, Foxworthy noted. 'If you don't mind.'

'Dreadfully busy.'

Though he had time to pop in to order coffee.

Foxworthy said nothing. Repeating requests dilutes them.

'Well, I suppose a few minutes wouldn't hurt. If it's important.'

'It is, sir.'

They sat at the wobbly round table in the window.

Bristol had sworn off mayors a few years ago, in favour of a committee approach. Henry Hyde was one of five councilmen. His bailiwick was city development.

'How did you…' He waved a hand around the room.

'An associate. She checked the CCTVs around city hall and College Green. Seems you come in here every day around this time.'

This slowed the transit of cup to lip. He continued and sipped the coffee he had lost a taste for. That a DC had looked at his whereabouts would be alarming, but he managed to put on a cooperative front. 'So, Constable, how can I help?'

A deliberate excising of the 'detective'? Ah, the games of power people play when they're distressed.

'I'd like to ask you where you were around six o'clock this morning.'

Silence.

The nervous swallow that preceded the sip of coffee was far

more energetic than the one that sent a trickle of brew down his gullet.

'And I'd like to ask why?' Asked with an edge.

Yet the question was reasonable, and an answer would do no harm to Foxworthy's destination at the moment.

'A man was killed on St Nicholas Street around that time. And I have reason to believe you might have been present and know something that pertains to the death.'

Hyde spat out, 'Well, that's mental! Why would I have anything to do with a man's death? I'm a solicitor, a town councilman! I was an officer in the Territorial Army.'

Foxworthy had not, of course, suggested that Hyde had any involvement in the murder, at all. The question could have been directed to a passerby, innocent as a Disney princess.

But since Hyde had brought up the supposition, Foxworthy pushed forward. 'I don't believe you actually struck the man. I think that was done by an associate, but you were involved.'

'Absurd. How can you possibly think that?'

'Because the victim identified you.'

'Impossible. He was…' The man's voice faded.

'Was dead?'

'*You* told me he was.'

'I did indeed, Councilman. But I didn't say *when* he had died. And your reaction just now tells me that you seem to have had some assurance that he was dead after you and your associate left the scene. Perhaps if you, or he, checked his body.'

'Wait!'

But Foxworthy didn't wait. 'Of course, the phone records would have confirmed your location then. But not if a suspect's phone is shut off.'

'You—'

'Telecommunications warrants are so easy to obtain, in the case of homicide, you know.'

Hyde now grew livid. He learned forward abruptly, and Foxworthy had to grab his cup to avoid a slosh. The man muttered, 'You're making a big mistake here.'

And it was clear that Hyde did not mean, as the American expression went, he was barking up the wrong tree.

The words were a threat, pure and simple.

Well, no matter. Foxworthy had been threatened before. And he had the wound in his thigh to prove it.

Inside the coffee shop, the two men rose to their feet, facing each other.

The councilman and the police detective.

Roger Groll had followed the copper, who had a faint limp, from the scene of that morning's murder, and had been observing the get-together from a shadowy spot over the road for the past twenty minutes.

He was curious why the officer had picked a table near the window.

In Groll's line of work that was considered a mistake. You assumed the world was out to kill you – every minute, every day – and you made sure to keep yourself as inconspicuous as you could. You sat nowhere near the windows in establishments (your home, either, for that matter). And you positioned yourself with your back to the wall, facing the door.

Groll followed this rule religiously, and he was still alive as a result.

He was squat and bulky and strong – he did construction when he wasn't hurting people and shaking down businesses.

Well, one man's slip-up is another man's boon.

He now stepped away from the alley and, with a look around to see if he was invisible, moved closer to the coffeeshop window.

The cop's back was to him, and the detective didn't see him approach.

Right, Guv. Keep it that way.

This morning's murder had been via blunt object – the brick he'd picked up from the pile of rubble on St Nicholas Street. It had been staged to appear like an accident, but that, it seemed, had not worked out.

A shame.

So now it had to be straightforward murder.

He drew the Glock pistol from his waistband and stepped closer.

The policeman, back to Groll still, had no idea what was going down.

Ten feet from the window, he paused and lifted the gun. He aimed carefully and pulled the trigger three times. He saw his victim drop instantly to the floor, amid a shower of glass shards.

Groll turned and walked away. Quickly, but not too quickly. He did not look back. He knew the man was dead.

He was a far better killer with a pistol than a brick.

But then, bloody hell, who wouldn't be?

DI Thomas Hayden-Smith stood in Robbie Foxworthy's cubicle in the ASP complex.

He happened to be looking at a picture of Foxworthy and his wife, Mary, and their son, William. It had been taken some years ago, on holiday in the Lake District.

He saw, too, on the desk the white envelope from the human resources department.

The retirement packet.

He closed his eyes, horrified at what had happened today.

You'll be dreadfully bored…

Hayden-Smith should never have—

'You all right there,' came the voice from the doorway.

He turned to see Foxworthy walking into the office.

The DI stepped forward quickly and aborted a handshake, noting bandages. 'What did they say in surgery?'

Foxworthy touched his cheek and left hand, both swathed. 'Glass shards.'

'That's all?'

'Partly deaf. Only temporary.'

'And Councilman Hyde?'

'Three shots close range. To the head.' A shrug. There was nothing to add.

Foxworthy sat behind his desk, and Hayden-Smith in a chair across. Foxworthy looked his boss over and gave a laugh. 'You smack of a worried grandmother. Forgive me, Tom, let's make it *mother*, shall we?'

'I can't stop thinking about how close it came. Inches away. I thought I'd sent you for a Kelly.'

'Oh, I was never in any danger. The shooter was a pro. All he wanted to do was take out a partner who was at risk of developing a loose tongue. Let's be honest, we *do* search for cop killers a bit more diligently than the ones who erase fellow thugs, now, don't we? Besides, it's quite the lucky thing the shooting happened.'

'You *do* look a bit chuffed. What on earth do you mean?'

'You wanted me to find something. And I did.'

'So, Victor Morrison was murdered,' Foxworthy began. 'Considering the *why*, I eliminated all the motives except one. I

31

concluded he must have seen something that the killer didn't want to be seen.'

'Which was what?'

'Still don't have quite the answer to that. We'll have to wait for marvellous Julia, our Forensics Queen, to get back to us. In the meantime, let me tell you about the second question that needed answering in the case.'

'And that was?'

'Why did Morrison turn away from the High Street and stagger up St Nicholas to the exact spot where he lay down and died?'

Hayden-Smith lifted a palm in query.

'And more significantly, was he actually pointing at something with his extended arm and finger, or was that gesture merely a coincidence, a muscle reaction in his last moments? I took the position that there *was* a meaning. He was trying to tell us something.'

'What was he pointing at?'

'The Veiled Lady on the façade of the pub on St Nicholas. You know it?'

'Of course. Excellent food, by the way.'

'I kept asking myself what the message was. No one in the pub knew him. His son said he'd never mentioned it. He wasn't a drinker. The place was closed when the crime happened. Ah, but then I had an idea.'

'You do like your ideas, Robbie.' A smile spread across the DI's face. 'So do we.'

Foxworthy stepped over the compliment and continued. 'I remembered something that his son told me. That Morrison loved puzzles and word games. He wanted to identify his killer but the man had taken his phone. He guessed he had only seconds left to live and couldn't write message in his own blood. Was there something he could use, perhaps pointing out something that could be deciphered into a clue?'

This is what he'd been explaining to the poor Councilman Henry Hyde when the conversation had been so abruptly interrupted.

'He was pointing to the pub, yes, but specifically to the second carving from the right. So I thought I'd start there. I asked Julia to run the words "the veiled lady" through an anagram generator. That produced a surfeit of results, thousands. Who would have thought, from those three short words? Interestingly, "death" and "dead" were among the results. But I don't think Morrison, in his dying moments, would bother to impart those words. His demise was a given. No, he was giving us name.

'There were a lot of them. Dave and Davey and Dev and Adelle, a dozen more. I sent them to his son. None struck him as a possible threat to his father. Then I thought: maybe he didn't personally know the individual; maybe he simply knew *of* him. And so Julia – did you know she plays video games in competitions? And a grandmother, no less.'

'I did not.' Hayden-Smith stared. If Curiosity were a mask in a Greek play, the DI's face would be a model for it.

'Julia used another program to compare the list of names from the anagram against a database of public figures Morrison might know about from the news. And voila: out came "Hal" – a nickname for "Henry", of course – and "Hyde". Was he the killer?' A shrug. 'Probably not. But it was likely he was present at the killing. Oh, a word game was hardly proof, but it certainly was enough for me to have a bad tea with him and put the matter forward. And his response told me he was there.' A shrug. 'I did bluff a bit when I suggested – only suggested, mind you – that there was a warrant that showed his phone was shut off to hide his location. Apparently it was, in fact. I knew I had him then.'

The line about telecommunications warrants being so easy to obtain, in the case of homicide, was more or less true. It simply did not apply in Hyde's case because Foxworthy had not sought one.

A grimace. 'I was going to keep at him till I skewered out a confession. But…' He glanced at his bandaged hand. 'That didn't quite work out.'

'Word games…'

Foxworthy said, 'Did you know that during the war, MI6 ran newspaper ads for a phony crossword puzzle contest to find the nation's best players?'

'No. Why?'

'To send them to Bletchley Park to decrypt the Nazi's Enigma coding machine.'

Hayden-Smith lifted an eyebrow. 'Well, Robbie, if I'm ever on *Pointless* maybe that will be my winning question.' The Greek mask returned. 'A town councilman, a gunman, an early morning meeting in the Old City. We still need to know why.'

Foxworthy's phone hummed with a text. Smiling, he read it and sent a reply, then booted up his computer and turned the screen so that both men could see it.

'That was Julia,' he explained. 'Answering your very question. She's sent me a CCTV video.'

He tapped keys and soon the movie was playing: the wharf near Bristol Bridge, timestamped around six that morning. It depicted Henry Hyde, as well as a broad, squat man in black jacket and jeans.

'That's the shooter,' Foxworthy said, tapping the screen.

'He would surely be typecast for one. Looks like a malevolent toad.'

A third man was present, as well, bundled with cap and scarf and sunglasses despite the predawn hour. Hyde and the Toad helped him into a skiff, which then sped off quickly, heading downriver.

There was yet another person caught on camera, too.

Victor Morrison, the soon-to-be victim, stood atop Bristol Bridge, glancing down at the wharf. He paid no particular mind to the incident and turned away, continuing out of view toward St Nicholas Church.

On the wharf, Hyde and the Toad were glancing up to where Morrison had just been, and had what seemed to be a troubled argument. They vanished from view too, heading presumably towards the stairs that would take them up to High Street – and the murder.

The DI said, 'It was the passenger that Hyde and the thug didn't want seen. Who do you think… My God, was it…?'

'I think so, Tom. Peter Lanham, Nottingham's most notorious.'

'Escaping by boat. He's taking the Avon all the way to the Severn and then to an oceangoing ship, bound for who knows where?' A frown. 'But his face was obscured.'

Foxworthy nodded. 'I imagine one of your twenty eyes saw that very clip. But thought nothing of it, without any facial recognition assist. But Hyde and Toad couldn't take the chance. Ironic: if they'd let Morrison live, Lanham would have gotten away scot-free.'

'That was six hours ago, nearly. Depending on tides, a skiff like the one we saw could be at the Severn docks in an hour, hour and a half at the most.'

Foxworthy was already typing. 'I'm sending the name of the skiff to ASP river patrol, Customs and MI5. They'll have him on camera, find out which freighter he's making his getaway on.'

Like all docks in the UK, Portishead's were encrusted with CCTV and had regular drone surveillance flights, to monitor for terrorism, smuggling and human trafficking.

Lanham would be captured within the hour.

'The shooter at the coffee shop?' Hayden-Smith asked.

'One of Lanham's lads from Nottingham, I'll bet. We'll go through Hyde's phone records and find a number. Or Lanham will give him up to earn points with the Crown Prosecutor.'

'Those people squeal like pigs, to save their own skin.'

Porker...

Hayden-Smith asked, 'But what was Hyde's involvement?'

'I'm guessing he was laundering money for Lanham through the building projects. Overseeing development for the city, he knew all the bankers and builders.'

Foxworthy looked at the clock.

'You timed it well, Robbie. You have eight minutes until retirement.'

'Ah, yes, that reminds me. Here you go.'

He handed over the retirement packet.

The DI sighed and took the envelope. He reached in and extracted the documents, then extracted a pen. His signature was required, too.

He stared. 'They're blank.'

'Changed my mind, didn't I? Quite a lot of questions about Lanham's operations here in Somerset. I feel like digging up some clues. I have forebears in Newcastle, you know.'

'No, I didn't, Robbie. So you come from a long line of coal miners.'

'No. Worked in the brewery, most of them. Two were thieves. But I like the metaphor.'

As Hayden-Smith walked out the doorway, Foxworthy turned back to his computer to write up the report on the Veiled Lady incident.

He paused a moment and reflected that, yes, it was a good decision to postpone retirement. He was confident that trout would still be populating West Country streams a year or two from now, and his Austin Healy would suffer no lasting indignity by remaining disassembled a bit longer.

And, as for football, he had every confidence that Bristol City would admirably acquit itself, despite the absence of its number one fan in the stands at every game – as difficult a challenge as that might be.

Cathy Ace

Cathy Ace writes the Cait Morgan Mysteries (the TV series, produced by Free@LastTV, will star Eve Myles), and the WISE Enquiries Agency Mysteries. Shortlisted for Canada's Bony Blithe Awards, and the Crime Fiction Lover Best Indie Crime Novel Awards, three times – winning each award once. Cathy has also won IPPY and IBA Awards. Her work has been twice shortlisted for the Crime Writers of Canada Awards of Excellence. She migrated from Wales aged forty, and now lives in Canada.

cathyace.com

WAX

Cathy Ace

When the doorbell rang, Helen was in the middle of killing her husband. She froze: no one ever came to the house. Who on earth could it be? And now, of all times.

Rod spoke with his mouth full. 'You'd better get that.' Helen reckoned he sounded pleased about something. When he added, 'Hurry up, love – you don't want your food to get cold,' he laughed. She'd been picking at a salad.

As Helen stood, she examined her husband's plate: Rod was eating particularly slowly, so she revised her initial estimate – she was probably only about a third of the way through killing him. Visualising the way she'd added her own secret ingredients to his mushroom ragout while he was showering, she beamed sweetly, then left the table.

Something dark and globular was visible through the frosted glass of the front door, and she opened it to find herself confronted with a bunch of red roses.

An androgenous face peered over them. 'Mrs Pelling? Mrs Helen Pelling?'

'That's me.' And she'd be changing it back to Helen Greene as soon as she was a widow.

'For you.' The flowers were thrust toward her.

Helen managed a seemingly bright, 'Thank you,' before the figure turned and headed toward a lime green van which informed her that Florrie's Flowers always arrived promptly, and with a smile; she'd witnessed the smile, but had no idea about the timeliness of the delivery. It was sixteen years to the day since Rodney Vincent Pelling and she had exchanged their deeply traditional 'I do' vows, so she supposed this was as good a time as any to receive her first ever official bouquet. She counted the rose heads; yes, there were sixteen. There was a small card: *Happy Anniversary, love Rod xx*

Helen suspected she should feel a pang of guilt, because the man who'd been thoughtful enough to arrange for roses to be delivered to his wife on their wedding anniversary was presently eating a meal that would, inevitably, lead to his death in no more than a few days, and possibly much sooner. She paused, making sure the door was properly locked, to give the matter some thought. No… not even one scintilla of a twinge, let alone a pang.

Rod called from the dining room in a sing-song voice, 'Who was it?'

Helen gritted her teeth, then twittered dramatically, 'Oh Rod, you shouldn't have. They're lovely.' She gave a little squeal for good measure, pinched her cheeks to make them appear flushed with happiness, then rushed into the dining room with the enthusiasm of a tween meeting their pop-idol in the flesh. 'My dinner can wait, I'll get these straight into some water. Don't let your food spoil.'

She did the necessary with the roses in the kitchen sink. When she returned to the table, her crocodile tears became genuinely joyous as she placed the vase of velvety buds beside the plate Rod had now completely cleared.

'I didn't mean to make you cry.' The smile on Rod's face suggested to Helen he was happy that he had, though he did seem genuinely surprised by how overwhelmed she was by the roses. Had she overdone it?

She managed to camouflage her intense desire to shove a fork into his eyeball by pretending to curb her sobs of delight. 'Let me clear that dirty plate of yours, Rod. I don't think I fancy any more of mine, so I'll just put everything to soak.'

She'd already washed the cooking pot in boiling water and scrubbed it. Twice.

Her husband sounded almost gracious when he said, 'Leave the dishes, come and have a sit down with me.'

'No, Rod, love, you go on into the living room and get the telly on. This'll only take me five minutes.' She had to get everything sterilised. 'Fancy a cuppa?'

'Ta.'

She gathered up each item in the kitchen that might have come into contact with his dinner and stuffed everything into the sink, submerging the lot in the hottest water she could get from the tap, to which she added a double squirt of detergent; a dishwasher was a luxury far beyond their means, so she reckoned that two good soaks would do the job.

As she waited for the kettle to boil, Helen stared out of the window at the muddy fields that surrounded the rundown Victorian farmhouse, and felt the familiar rage build. They'd left their lovely little new-build home, that she'd decorated and furnished just the way she liked, to move to this lonely backwater. They'd had no choice, Rod had said. The pandemic had changed everything for them, as it had for so many: they'd both lost their jobs. His parents had left him this place – the old family home – which had been rented out for several months, but Helen eventually had to agree to sell their place and move in here, because the online work she managed to pick up as a bookkeeper just wasn't enough to pay their mortgage.

Her husband's initial assertion had been that the half-acre garden would allow them to be self-sufficient, to a certain extent, but Helen reasoned that Rod must have watched too many episodes of *The Good Life* at an impressionable age – what he possessed in idealistic enthusiasm he lacked in gardening capabilities. His vegetable beds yielded produce a quarter of the size Helen could buy at the shops, and his argument that small, disfigured veggies tasted just as good as large, pretty ones was all well and good, but Helen's strongly held opinion was that endless carrot soup and courgette muffins were not all they were cracked up to be.

The kettle's whistle dragged her back to the present.

As she spooned dried nettles into the pot, Helen reminded herself that she'd soon be able to sell up and buy somewhere just for herself… re-enter the real world, inhabited by real people, and eat real food once again. She couldn't help but chuckle as she recalled that she'd stood in that very kitchen not two months earlier and had denied wanting to do any such thing when Rod's younger sister, Deb, had asked her if she was happy living in what had once been the siblings' family home.

She'd heard herself say, 'It's a classic – such good bones. All it needs is a bit of TLC. Give us a few years and you won't recognise the place.'

Helen had never expected to meet her sister-in-law: Deb had been cut off by her parents when she'd exhausted their last iota of even tough love by the time she'd reached her early twenties. She'd popped up the day before Rod's last birthday. He'd invited her and her new husband to stay for dinner on that occasion, and the two couples had spent a few pleasant times together since then.

Deb hadn't been at all what Rod had led Helen to expect: no devilish horns, no black fleece… just a goofy grin and a bit of a dithery personality. Helen smiled again when she remembered how Deb had expressed deep concern about how risky she thought it was that her brother insisted upon foraging for wild mushrooms. Maybe that was when Helen had started to see a way forward. A way out. She didn't know, really. But Deb had been right, of course; it's so terribly easy to mix up the good mushrooms and the absolutely deadly ones… as Rod's impending death was about to prove.

Helen had been pretending to have a tummy in turmoil for a couple of days, so that Rod would think she'd given him something nasty when he started to feel the same way. Which she would have done, of course… just not the something nasty he thought.

'Here you are.' Helen placed the tea-tray on the rickety table beside Rod's chair. It was one of those reclining things; he'd found it in a charity shop and had insisted upon buying it. The fact that it smelled as though someone had died while sitting in it didn't matter, apparently, because it was 'a bargain'. She'd sprayed it with everything she could think of, but it still gave off a sour smell when it got warm. As soon as Rod was gone, it would be going to the dump.

Rod stirred the teapot, saying, 'You could bring those roses in here. Put them next to the telly.'

'Good idea. What a lovely way to celebrate sixteen years of marriage. I've got something for you, too.'

Rod looked surprised. 'What have you been spending your hard-earned money on now?'

Helen opened a drawer in the sideboard her grandmother had received as a wedding present almost a hundred years earlier. 'Surprise!' She shoved a long cylinder that she'd tried to make look like a cracker into her husband's hand, and stood back to watch his reaction.

He shook it. 'What's this, then?' A puzzled look.

'I don't think you'll guess. I found out that wax is what you're supposed to give for a sixteenth wedding anniversary, and there's a bit of wax in there, attached to… something.'

Rod's face slid into a new shape; he looked… sly. 'You're not the only one to find out about the wax thing, and it's not just flowers I splashed out on. I've got something else lined up for you. Later on.' He winked.

Helen couldn't be bothered to even wonder what he meant, so watched with pretended anticipation as he tore off the three layers of wrapping she'd taped around the cardboard tube.

He fiddled with the plastic cap, then peered inside. 'Is that paper in there?'

'If you put your finger into the middle and just…'

'Yes, yes… I know how to get it out.' For the next two minutes he displayed that he didn't.

Helen remained as patient as a happy, expectant wife should.

With the scroll finally unfurled in his hand, Rod looked completely puzzled. 'There's a wax seal, yes. But why?'

'Read it out loud.'

He didn't. She watched as he made hard work of deciphering the gothic-style lettering, his lips moving silently, and slowly. 'I'm a… a lord? I don't get it.'

'I bought you one square foot of land in Scotland. Now you're the lord of that land. See? There's your title, at the bottom.

And that's your crest, pressed into the wax.' She bowed and pulled at an imaginary forelock. 'M'Lord Pelling.'

Rod actually smiled. 'I had no idea you could do such a thing. And you really shouldn't have spent your money on something… like this. I tell you what, though – I'll take it down the pub with me, tomorrow. See if it gets me a free pint, eh?'

Helen enthused, 'Excellent idea. Nothing tastes as good as free beer, does it?'

'Exactly. Oh…' Rod grabbed at his midsection.

Helen's research had suggested that the initial effects of death cap mushrooms wouldn't start for a few hours after ingestion; it couldn't be happening already, could it?

She forced herself to look appropriately concerned. 'Bad tummy?'

'It's probably just wind. This tea will sort it.'

'Yes, I'm sure you're right.'

Helen knew she had to keep Rod calm: the severe nausea, abdominal pain, irreversible liver damage, seizures and death were hours away. She hoped he'd fall into a coma soon after the seizures started, because she didn't want to watch him suffer too much. They reckoned just half a mushroom would kill, and she'd given him half a dozen; she wondered if that meant his symptoms would start a lot sooner than she'd imagined they would. Ah well, time would tell.

Rod grimaced over his mug. 'I hope I haven't picked up that bug of yours. I can't lie around doing nothing all day. If I don't keep on top of things in the garden, we won't have anything to eat at all. You're up to your eyes in your bookkeeping work… and you're not even a hundred per cent yourself, poor dab.'

'It's probably just a bit of wind, like you said. That rocket leaf salad was lovely, by the way. And the dried tomatoes, too.

But that ragout you made smelled wonderful. It's a shame my tummy wasn't up to it.'

Rod smiled. 'Sorry, love. But you're right – it's best if you keep to plain foods for a while if your stomach's upset. Me too, maybe… given how I'm feeling at the moment. Mind you, they were all free, those mushrooms. You can't beat it. Foraging is the way we should all be going.'

'But it's not for everyone, Rod. As you've always said, you've got to know what you're doing with foraging.'

Rod put down his mug. 'Exactly. You can't be too careful when it comes to mushrooms. But it's worth all the effort of researching them, then hunting them out.'

Helen was only too well aware of that. It had taken her weeks to find those death caps. She'd had to wear gloves when she'd picked them, and then again when she'd cooked them down so Rod wouldn't recognise them when she added them to the meal he'd just polished off.

Helen did the head-tilting thing that she knew made Rod think she was proud of him. 'Nothing's too much trouble for you, love. Not if it's good for us. I know that. How's that tea, by the way? Those were the nettles we got from the field down behind the bus stop. Also free.'

Rod picked up his mug again. 'You can't beat it. Nice of Jeremy to give us that honey, wasn't it?'

'You gave him those eggs, in exchange. Fair's fair.'

'True.'

The next couple of hours dragged for Helen; she wanted to stare at her husband, keen to spot the first waves of discomfort, but she didn't dare. It would all start soon enough… and, short of a liver transplant, there was no saving him now, anyway. Helen told herself that she had to settle to a bit of a waiting game. She'd already thought through how she'd explain it all: Rod was well known, locally, for his mushroom-picking habit – him and Rajesh at the Indian takeaway had a real competition going between them. Helen would never understand men; why did everything become a fight to prove who was best? Why couldn't they just… be?

After the soaps were over, Rod disappeared upstairs. When he'd been gone for almost ten minutes, Helen dared to allow herself to hope that he was hanging over the toilet bowl suffering the first attacks of nausea, but he shocked her when he burst through the living-room door, scooped up the vase of roses and said in a stupid French accent, 'Madame Pelling will follow me, please.'

As he climbed the stairs ahead of her, Helen panicked for a moment that he might have some bedroom shenanigans in mind… until she saw steam billowing out of the bathroom door. He swung it open, and she stuck her head inside: the bath was full of bubbles, and almost every possible flat surface was dotted with lighted candles. The effect was surprisingly romantic. Rod popped the vase on top of the toilet tank.

'Indulge, my love. It's not much – but they're beeswax candles from Jeremy… and there are sixteen of them.' He smiled, and kissed her on the cheek. 'Thanks for everything, Helen. They were good years. Some downs, and ups, but good, overall.'

Helen allowed the hot water, and mounding bubbles, to ease her muscles as she soaked… like the dishes that were soaking – for the second time – in the kitchen below her. Was killing Rod the right thing to do after all? Yes: she wanted her old life back, and getting rid of him was the only way to do that.

Helen and her new-found sister-in-law, Deb, had giggled about how Rod was nothing if not dogged; always had been, said Deb. And even Deb had agreed that, now Helen and Rod were living this lifestyle, he'd never want to go back to the normal ways Helen preferred. They'd talked about how, even though his parents had managed to get planning permission for the house to be extended significantly before they'd died in that awful fire that had torn through their caravan in a matter of moments, the couple would never have enough capital to get any significant work done to the house. So that was that.

A knock at the bathroom door jolted Helen. 'Yes?'

'Sorry to disturb you, love, can I come in? I just want to get something from the airing cupboard.'

She drew more bubbles around herself then called, 'Come in.' He did. He looked a bit peaky. 'How are you feeling now? Any better?'

Rod shook his head. 'Tummy's still a bit wonky. I'll just take that little bucket we've got downstairs with me. The cover could be useful if I… well, you know. I want you to have the bathroom all to yourself for a while.' Helen watched him bend into the cupboard and heard him shift some stuff around in there. He emerged through the steam with the covered bucket in one hand and a brown paper bag in the other.

Helen was puzzled. 'What's that?'

Rod smiled sheepishly. 'It's another treat for you.'

He placed the bucket on the floor, reached into the bag, and pulled out a fist-sized white sphere. 'Surprise!' He dropped the ball into the water… then another, and another, and another.

'Oh, nice. Bath bombs.' Helen reached to roll them around her body. As they started to dissolve, the foamy bubbles in the bath began to burst.

Rod looked sheepish. 'I didn't get sixteen of them – only four… one for each four years, my love. Enjoy.' He left with the bucket he'd retrieved from the floor, and pulled the door firmly closed behind him.

Helen watched as milkiness dispersed, and noted a sweet, light fragrance. Then one of the bombs popped to the surface and really got going, making the bath water fizz quite dramatically. Another emerged to join it – this one rotating from the force of its explosion. The sharp aroma caught in Helen's nostrils… then she started coughing… then felt her throat getting tight… and, with sudden terror, she knew exactly what that smell was…

When Rod closed the bathroom door, he knew he'd killed his wife. The almond oil and almond milk in the bath bombs would be released by the hot water, fill the steamy air, and Helen would go into acute anaphylactic shock because of her almond allergy.

Rod did his best to ignore the thought of his wife thrashing about in the bath above him as he rinsed off the dishes in the kitchen sink, wiped them, and put them all back into their assigned places. Helen was very particular about assigned places, so he made sure to put everything exactly where it belonged; when he phoned for the ambulance, he'd be able to point out how he'd been going about his usual domestic duties and had been oblivious to the catastrophe befalling his dear wife of sixteen years – to the very day, no less.

The candles, the roses, the soapy foam, and even the remnants of the bath bombs themselves that they were bound to find in whatever water remained when he'd drained the bath – the better to 'save' his darling – all pointed to a loving, romantic and happy couple.

They hadn't been such a thing for a few years; not since he'd lost his job. He still couldn't quite understand why that had made him feel so much… less. That said, he'd thrown himself into his new circumstances with as much enthusiasm as possible, and they'd not been doing too badly, even though it meant that Helen couldn't shop the way she'd always done in the past. He'd lost count of how many sets of 'seasonal décor items' she'd had boxed up in the garage at their last place. There certainly hadn't been any room for a car in there. It was just as well they'd lived in a shoebox-sized house, or he couldn't imagine how many more pillows and curtains and table runners and wreaths for the front door she'd have accumulated. But here, back in the home where he'd grown up? She'd spent money they hadn't really had on paint and wallpaper until even she'd realised that more couldn't be done. None of the curtains from the old house had fitted any of the windows in this one, and the front door looked ridiculous – out here, in the middle of nowhere – with one of her 'Welcome to our Home Sweet Home' wreaths on it, so they'd all gone into the bin.

Thank goodness.

Eventually even Helen had to agree that the stuff they'd brought with them from their old life didn't really work well in what was likely to be their home for a long time, so they'd furnished the place in more traditional ways. Which Rod preferred.

She'd been no use in the garden, but she'd managed to bring in a bit of cash with her online jobs. He'd grown blisters in places he even didn't know he'd had as he'd striven to achieve all he could for them; it was hard, slow, and often frustrating work, but he'd managed to provide for the table for the past few months now, and didn't feel as idiotic as he'd once done when he read a packet of seeds, or stood in front of a shelf-full of different fertilizers. He was learning. Even his sister had agreed with that.

And wasn't that a thing… Deb turning up out of the blue, and not being as bad as he'd remembered? That Alan she'd gone and married in a heartbeat seemed steady; construction people were always in demand, so he'd weathered the lockdown quite well, and he and Deb were coasting along nicely now, it appeared. Alan had told Rod that, when he'd met Deb at that grief self-help group they'd both belonged to – he was there because he'd lost his wife in a freak boating accident – she'd still been struggling to come to terms with her demons… exacerbated by the terrible death her parents had suffered. But it seemed she'd just needed a purpose in life, and Alan, to help her start again. And the job she'd got herself at a childcare centre really suited her. They were even talking about having kids of their own – not something he and Helen had ever considered. Well, Helen hadn't, though Rod had always quite fancied the idea of being a dad.

Yes, that was what had got him and Alan chatting, when the four of them had gone to the Farmers' Market in town a few weeks back; Alan was bemoaning the fact that a one-bedroom flat wouldn't be a suitable place to start a family… then they'd met up with Jeremy at his Bee-licious stall, and they'd all talked about how Rod's foraging, and Jeremy's devotion to all things bee-orientated, was the way of the future… then Idris had called them all over to his cake stall.

Rod recalled how delicious Idris's fruit cake had looked that day, and how he'd explained why he had to decline trying a piece. The other men had each enjoyed a slice, both agreeing it was a shame that Helen wouldn't have been able to so much as taste it, not even if she'd removed the marzipan and icing that coated it, and how annoying it must be for him that Rod was also unable to indulge. They'd also agreed that it must be difficult for Rod and Helen to always have to work out if something contained, or had even touched, anything remotely almond-related.

It had been Alan who'd pointed out the almond-based bath bombs on the Scrub Up Nicely stall. Until then, Rod hadn't considered how dangerous they might be for a wife whose almond allergy was truly life-threatening. In fact, if Rod were being honest with himself, until that thought had registered… and after Alan had asked him about how he and Helen were set for life insurance arrangements – because he had a friend in that line… it really hadn't occurred to Rod that he could be a lot better off if his wife were dead.

Then he'd found he could think of little else.

So, when Helen had started up again about how the bathroom needed to be completely renovated and how the kitchen would be so much better if only the wall between it and the dining room were to be demolished, Rod had begun to wonder exactly how those bath bombs might affect her… and he did a bit of googling. Which was why she'd just died, and he was about to become a great deal richer than he had been when he'd got out of bed that morning.

When Deb answered the door, she was expecting the police. Condolences were expressed, then the questions began. She and Alan had rehearsed their answers for hours – not word for word, because that would smack of contrivance, but in general terms. Yes, she and her brother had become recently reconciled, but she couldn't say that she really knew him well, nor his wife; she'd been *persona non grata* within the Pelling family since she'd run away from the second rehab facility they'd got her checked into. She'd been twenty-two at the time; now she was in her mid-thirties, and had managed to turn her life around. She and

Alan had met, married, and were planning to start a family...
soon.

The news that her poor brother had died so tragically was
something she received with what she hoped was an appearance
of stunned resilience. Yes, she'd known about his foraging lifestyle, and of his enthusiasm for using his own 'free' ingredients
whenever he could. She expressed great surprise that something
as seemingly innocent as a mushroom could prove deadly,
explaining that she wasn't really a 'nature' sort of person.

And now to also be informed that his wife had died just the
day before him? And of an allergic reaction to almonds, while
enjoying a soak in the bath, on the couple's wedding anniversary
no less. Deb agreed that it was truly awful that her brother and
sister-in-law had chosen to buy bath bombs that neither of them
knew contained almonds, but she didn't know what more to say
about such shocking news. Nor did Alan. The couple spoke
wistfully about the times they'd enjoyed with Rod and Helen,
and blood was blood, emphasised Deb, after all. But neither
she, nor Alan, had any useful insights to offer about how both
Helen and Rod could have managed to allow circumstances to
arise where they'd each, accidentally, sealed their own fate.

The talk shifted to coroners and inquests and solicitors...
and Deb nodded, tearfully – comforted by her husband. The
police left within the hour. She'd managed to snuffle her way
through the interview quite well, she thought.

Alan had suggested that it should be Deb who took the lead
when it came to enquiring about what it meant to be her late
brother's next of kin, and Deb had agreed that it made perfect
sense. The solicitor she approached quickly discovered that
neither Helen nor Rod had drawn up formal wills, and made it
clear that everything Helen had owned when she'd died had

automatically passed to her husband, and – upon his death – everything he owned would become Deb's. Astonished to hear that she would inherit the old family home, and the savings that Rod and Helen had from the sale of their previous home, Deb and Alan were careful to make sure that both the solicitor and her assistant understood how distraught they were that two such tragic accidents had led to their good – financial – fortune. Yes, thanks to such professional explanations, they understood that the whole legal process would take some time, but they explained they would be only too happy to wait until it reached its natural conclusion. It was agreed that they could move into the old Pelling family home immediately, if they wished, which they did.

When the letter arrived from the probate office, Alan said, 'Good, it's come, like they said it would. Right, let's open that bottle of champagne, Deb.'

His wife was curled up on the settee, watching a quiz, glassy eyed. 'How much did we get?'

'This house and land; seventy grand in savings, all from their old house, I suppose; plus the hundred thousand from Helen's life insurance… and Rod's life insurance was for two hundred grand. The solicitor never said that, did she? Nice. More than I thought, to be honest.'

'We'll be lucky to shift this place.' Deb sounded a lot less enthusiastic than Alan had expected.

'The planning permission your parents sorted make it worth a lot more than you might think, Deb. And all the fields around the place can't be built on, so it'll always have its open aspect. It could go for a lot. We'll be set. We could auction it now… but I'll have a chat with a few mates, because it might be worth holding onto it and getting the work done ourselves. It's what everyone wants these days – a big house in the countryside, with all the mod cons, but a bit of history. And some landscaping could make that horrible garden out there into something worth having.'

'I don't know about that, Alan. I thought you said that shifting it as soon as we legally owned it would be the best thing to do. It's almost falling down around us. And God knows what Helen thought she was doing when she decorated it like she did; it's hideous. If we sell it, we could buy a nice modern place for ourselves.'

Alan had been enthusiastic about the plan to rapidly dump the Pelling family home when he'd come up with it, but that had been the better part of a year ago, and – since then – so much had changed. Deb hadn't worked for the past six months; the pay from his construction jobs had kept them just about ticking over, though things had been a bit tight. But that wasn't the main problem. The worst thing was that Deb had changed so much since she'd given up her job looking after those kids. He was sure she was drinking again: she never smelled of booze, but she'd always been good at hiding things, ever since he'd known her. He'd always thought they could beat her demons between them; now he seriously doubted it. He wondered if she even wanted to.

Now she just sat there, watching the telly and snacking… always snacking. And she did nothing around the house; it hadn't really been too bad when they'd first moved in, but now – Deb was right – there were lots of things, in almost every room, that needed attention. If she kept the place clean it would help… but she didn't seem to care about anything, these days. He was the one who was expected to clear up all the takeaway stuff from the night before and dump it outside before she rolled out of bed, or else she'd complain about the smell.

He felt the disgust crawl up his neck as he looked at his wife's bloated figure when she wobbled up off the settee. She didn't even smile at him any longer. Where had the old Deb gone? That young woman with the great figure… and the suggestible nature. It had only taken him a couple of meetings to pick her out from that self-indulgent group of twerps who thought that talking about grief and coming to terms with it were one and the same thing; she'd been the best mark by far… he'd always known this house could end up being worth a packet. The extra money that Rod and Helen Pelling had added to the pot was just the sweetener.

His wife scratched her back lazily when she said, 'Did you get us something for dinner on the way home from work?'

'Mushroom biryani and onion bhajis.' He knew she liked those.

'No meat?'

'Chicken korma. And I got you some poppadoms. I'll open you a new jar of that spicy chutney that Rajesh makes.'

'Good. I'm going to the loo.'

'I'll put it all on a plate for you. I'm just having one of my special shakes.'

Deb snorted dismissively when she said, 'Still trying to beef yourself up with those protein things? I don't know why you bother. You spend hours at that gym, and you still look exactly the same.'

Alan smiled, fighting to control his emotions. 'I want to look my best. For you. You could come with me, you know. The place isn't full of bulked-up blokes lifting weights… they have classes for women, too.'

Something glinted in his wife's eye. He shouldn't have mentioned women.

She snapped, 'So that's why you're there all the hours God sends, is it? So you can gawk at the young girls posing around the place.'

Alan told himself not to visualise Linda in her workout clothes – nor out of them – and said, as calmly as he could, 'I only have eyes for you, my love. You know that. Since we first met, it's always been us two against the world, hasn't it? And look at what we've achieved together.'

'Look at what us making a concerted effort to get my brother and his wife to bump each other off has got us is what you mean. None of what we've just inherited would be ours if it wasn't for me.'

'I know that, Deb. Trust me, I know that.'

'Good. And don't you forget it. I'll be right back. I want to see that spot-the-killer gameshow thing that's on in ten minutes. Mind you, I don't know why I bother – the killers are always so obvious.' Deb headed toward the bathroom.

Alan called up the stairs, 'Fine… I'll sort your dinner, but let me change the dressing for that cut on your hand before you eat, will you? You managed to slice yourself good and proper with that knife. I warned you that I'd sharpened it, but you had to run your finger along the blade… like you always do… didn't you? Anyway, it'll need a new dressing tonight.'

'Fine.'

Alan walked into the kitchen and pulled on a pair of washing-up gloves before opening the jar containing the concoction of soil-covered garlic and honey he'd nurtured for a few weeks that was now full of what he'd discovered was properly called *botulinum*. He smeared a bit of the gloop onto a piece of gauze. He knew there were many quicker ways to get rid of Deb, but he wanted her death to look as natural as possible. That was always best. The extra time would be worth it, though his patience was wearing thin. Linda didn't just have a killer body, she also had a ninety-year-old mother with a lot of exceptional jewellery, and a four-bedroom, detached house on the good side of town.

Ninety-anything was a good age; that's what everyone always said. Especially at funerals. He was sure he could come up with some way to get the old bird to fall off her perch… once a decent amount of time had passed after he and Linda had tied the knot, of course. He enjoyed the planning stage of things almost as much as seeing the results. And his plans usually turned out well… for him.

Mike Ripley

Mike Ripley is the author of more than thirty books, winning awards for both his comic crime fiction and his non-fiction history of British thrillers. He has written for television, radio, contributed 200 monthly columns to www.shotsmag.co.uk and, for ten years, was the crime fiction critic for the *Daily Telegraph*. He now writes (but happily only occasionally) for the Obituaries section of *The Guardian*.

THE SCALES FROM HIS EYES

Mike Ripley

I had asked for the presence of the local police constable to give the appearance that the proceedings were official, knowing that those who had been summoned would feel more comfortable that way, especially if the face in the uniform was a familiar one.

The English have always had an unshakeable faith in the ruddy-faced 'Bobby' even when the uniform was shiny with age and fitted far too tightly, the wearer being well past the age of military service. He was, of course, unarmed, and because I was not expecting the proceedings to be disrupted, so was I.

From the outset I had stressed that I was holding an enquiry and not an inquest; I was not a coroner and there would certainly not be a jury present. In any case, there was no doubt at all about how Arthur Seddon had died – only why.

I had commandeered the village hall, a shoddy rectangular building occupying a plot of Church land near the tiny Victorian infants' school, for the purpose and requisitioned a folding table and two chairs, placing them in the centre of the large room which had, in happier times, hosted wedding receptions, Saturday night dances and the village's annual fruit and vegetable show.

The constable at the door, enjoying a transient moment of authority, clearly saw himself as a master of ceremonies or toastmaster, and insisted on introducing, in his throaty rural accent, each witness as they appeared nervously in the doorway.

'Mr Lionel Finch, Your Honour!' he announced as if addressing the baying crowds in the Colosseum, his declaration echoing around the empty hall.

'Do not address me as Your Honour, Constable. I am not a judge,' I said, hiding a smile, for that is exactly what I was that day.

The man who approached the table, his rubber boots shedding dried mud as he scuffed across the floor, was a white-haired bull of a man in shirt sleeves, his trousers held up by braces and a thick belt under the bulge of his ample stomach.

'Please have a seat, Mr Finch,' I said, indicating the chair on the far side of my table with my fountain pen.

'I've come straight from work, wasn't given a chance to change,' he said petulantly as he settled his buttocks on the slatted wooden chair, which creaked in protest.

He had, at least, taken off the bloody apron which he wore as a badge of office as the village butcher, a position of some influence these days, which also explained both his attitude and his girth. Finch, I knew, was not the jolly fat man once greeted cheerfully by the locals in the village pub. He was well aware of the power he held over his housewife customers thanks to rationing, and enjoyed their simpering and flattery, for which he was generally disliked by their husbands.

'Don't worry yourself, Mr Finch, this is an informal enquiry, not an official one.'

'Thought it must be, what with you in your smart uniform, Captain.'

'You should be used to seeing uniforms by now,' I said reasonably, 'but I am not a captain. My rank is *Sturmbannführer*.'

I did not expect to gain any useful insights from Finch, but he had known the deceased and had witnessed his death, so I let him talk and noted the relevant points, ignoring the man's crude attempts to curry favour, which were frequent once it had dawned on him that I was never likely to be one of his victims standing in a queue with a ration book.

Lionel Finch had been a member of the parish council, of which Arthur Seddon seemed to have been the permanent chairman, and had also known him through his butchery business, buying beef and the occasional pig from him to sell in his shop. Not that Seddon had been his main supplier (which I suspected meant that Finch's purchases had been 'off the books'), as Seddon's farming business was on a very small scale and unusual, for apart from a few animals and a couple of fields of premium barley, his main crop was fruit – raspberries, strawberries and apples – which he sold to a jam-making concern in the nearby town.

Seddon's soft fruits had consistently won first prize in the village's annual shows in this very hall, something which Finch disclosed in a tone suggesting that this had not made Arthur Seddon popular locally. But I was interested in the other reasons why the late and unlamented Mr Seddon was unpopular.

'Was his farm profitable?' I asked.

'Well, it was,' said Finch with a loud sniff, head bowed, looking at his boots, 'more of a smallholding than a farm and it did provided a good living before…'

His voice trailed off into silence and he only looked up when I completed the sentence for him.

'Before the invasion, you mean.'

Finch relaxed then, the unmentionable having been said, and launched, with some glee, into the story of how Arthur Seddon's farm had been the first local casualty of the invasion. One of our experimental Messerschmitt *Gigants*, a huge transport glider, had landed in Simonds' field of ripening barley, cutting a swathe through his valuable crop before it could be harvested and sold to maltsters and brewers willing to pay top price. The glider's landing was only half the problem, and some of the crop could have been salvaged had not a lone RAF fighter-bomber decided to attack the empty hulk, long after all the troops and their equipment had disembarked safely. It was the resultant fire which destroyed the crop.

The butcher smiled an ugly, cruel smile.

'There's many said Arthur got what he wished for.'

I wrote that down slowly, keeping Finch waiting in silence until I responded.

'And why would that be?'

''Cos he was always on your side, was Arthur, right from the start.'

I asked him to explain that remark, my tone advising him to be careful, and he squirmed on his chair as he did so.

According to Finch, Arthur Seddon had always opposed a war with Germany and had long approved of National Socialist initiatives to deal with mass unemployment, admiring the strength and order of the new regime. He had been an active member of the British Union of Fascists and had helped organise rallies throughout the region aimed especially at agricultural workers (which I knew from our files). When war did come, he had argued to anyone who would listen that England, led by bloated, worthless politicians, could not possibly win, and if a negotiated peace was not possible, then an unopposed invasion would settle the matter and life would return to normal.

The invasion had not been entirely unopposed, but capitulation had come swiftly. Initially, Seddon had welcomed the stationing of a squad of troops in the village – in this very hall – but was perhaps less enthusiastic when he realised their main duty was to requisition his livestock for the *Wehrmacht*, for invaders always arrive hungry.

'Arthur took it on the chin,' said Finch with a sneer, 'kept a stiff upper lip and said things would sort themselves out for the best. He didn't have a family to support, so he thought it was only fair. Mind you, he wasn't too happy when this year's malting barley crop was sequestered to be sent to Germany to make German beer. That must have been a blow to him.'

'Was it enough of a blow to make him do what he did?' I asked.

'Who knows what makes man do something like that?'

'Arthur was a solitary man. Some described him as distant and a little bit cold,' my next witness told me.

I knew very little about Mrs Eileen Loftus other than the information on her *Kennkarte*, which had replaced the National Registration Identity Card. She was thirty years old, had been born locally and was a widow. She was quite attractive in a tired, dowdy sort of way, and held herself well although her coat and blouse showed signs of wear and repair.

'You were Arthur Seddon's housekeeper, were you not, Mrs Loftus?' I began politely, to put her at her ease.

'Yes, for the past two years, after my husband died.'

'He was a soldier?' I asked, although I knew the answer.

'An airman,' she said holding my gaze, 'a navigator. He was

shot down in France. Mr Seddon thought his sacrifice pointless and offered me the job out of sympathy, as I have two children to look after.'

'And did you?'

'Did I what?'

'Think your husband's sacrifice pointless?'

'I thought we were here to talk about Mr Seddon.'

And so we did, as I had no wish to intimidate her unnecessarily.

Arthur Seddon may have been a solitary man – a lonely man – but he had not employed a housekeeper for feminine company. There was never any suggestion of 'funny business' (on that Mrs Loftus was quite clear) and most of her duties were performed whilst Seddon was out of the house, tending his fruit crop or his animals when he had them. Now 'we' had left him with only his soft fruit, she had added with disdain.

'How did he react to the new government?'

'Enthusiastically – at first,' said the woman with a wry smile. 'They say it was his idea to fly your swastika flag from the village flagpole out there in front of the hall. As chairman of the parish council, he was an advocate of law and order, and deemed it important to adapt the new laws of the new order, even the little, niggly ones.'

'Niggly' was not a word I was familiar with, but Mrs Loftus explained patiently, carefully avoiding any judgement on her part. The introduction of reflectors on the pedals of bicycles, for example, had been welcomed by Arthur Seddon as an eminently sensible safety measure on unlit country lanes and would benefit society as a whole. (I did not have the heart to tell her that the patents on those reflector pads were owned by the SS and every compulsory purchase of a set helped fund my very own department.) The campaigns against smoking – following the finding of a link with lung cancer by senior SS doctors – and the recent laws against drinking and driving (a pet project of the *Reichsführer SS* himself) were less palatable to the members of the parish council, but, encouraged by Seddon, they eventually expressed their unanimous support.

'Did they have your support?' I asked and she thought carefully before answering.

'As I cannot drive and do not smoke, those things did not affect me.'

'But other... changes... perhaps they did? You may speak freely,' I said, laying down my pen.

'Well, I did like listening to the wireless and I do miss the BBC now it's gone.' She was wise enough not to mention the so-called 'Free BBC' broadcasting illegally from Lisburn in Northern Ireland. 'I also miss going into town and shopping at Marks & Spencer, now that's been closed because it was a Jewish business.'

'Do many others feel like that?'

'If they do, they keep quiet about it.' Her eyes flashed at me in a quickly extinguished spurt of defiance. 'Mr Seddon used to say we had to accept some punishment for starting the war and restrictions would be eased once things settled down.'

Where there was genuine dissention – which, she added, anyone who knew the English could have foreseen – was the introduction of Hermann Göring's law banning fox hunting by packs of hounds and brightly garbed horse riders.

'Did Arthur Seddon ride to hounds?'

'Of course not,' she scoffed. 'Nobody in the village did, but that's not the point. It was a rural tradition that was being taken away from us; another freedom gone.'

Mrs Loftus stared at me as if daring me to challenge her about freedoms lost, but that could wait for another time.

'Was it the hunting ban which made him angry enough to do what he did?'

'Angry?' The woman seemed genuinely surprised. 'Mr Seddon wasn't angry, he was ashamed.'

I could see my third witness through the open door as he approached the hall, and watched as he paused by the shattered flag pole, now a jagged stump less than two metres high, and made the sign of the cross.

My duty constable proudly drew himself up to attention to announce his arrival.

'The Reverend Brownlee.'

He too was in uniform; the priest's standard issue of dark suit, grey shirt and white reversed 'dog collar'.

'Thank you for coming, Father,' I said as I stood and indicated the chair.

'I was not aware I had a choice,' he said calmly, 'and please do not refer to me as Father, the church here is neither high enough nor Catholic. "Mister" will suffice.'

I pretended to be suitably – politely – admonished and made a single diagonal stroke with my pen on the notes in front of me. The mark meant nothing, and I made no attempt to explain it, but it had the desired effect on 'Mister' Brownlee who sat down meekly, looking far less confident than he had a moment before. In my head I counted to twenty before I spoke.

'I called you here because of Arthur Seddon.'

'Half the village saw what happened,' he said quickly.

'But you knew him well.'

'As well as anyone, I suppose.'

'Then tell me about him.'

I let the vicar talk without questions or interruptions. His kind rarely needed such encouragement.

He had known Arthur Seddon as a churchwarden and from the parish council, but the Rev. Brownlee would never claim to have been his friend. Seddon was a man who kept himself to himself, a confirmed bachelor who seemed to have no need of close friends. Not that he avoided people; he was a fixture in the village church and a regular visitor to the village pub, though he drank sparingly and never stayed late.

Some did not like his politics, especially his views on the war, which he was against and which he felt England had been tricked into. He was called 'traitor' and 'pacifist', but always behind his back, because local people knew him to be a decent man at heart. A lonely one and a quiet one to be sure, who kept himself to himself, but one who never hurt or slandered another soul. Religious? He was certainly a good Christian, who turned the other cheek and always forgave those who cold-shouldered or mocked him over his views about the occupation and the new laws it brought with it.

'Laws with which he fully co-operated, as I understand,' I observed.

'Indeed he did,' Brownlee agreed, nodding his head, 'however unpopular that made him with some people. He thought resistance would be futile and only lead to more suffering. And he himself suffered more than most. He lost not only most of his livelihood because of the invasion, but also his dignity.'

If he expected to get a response from me, he was disappointed. I expanded the silence between us until he continued.

'That flagpole out there,' he waved a hand over his shoulder towards the door of the hall, 'it wasn't Arthur's idea to fly the swastika flag. As chairman of the parish council, he was made to by the local *Wehrmacht* commander. It was a symbolic gesture, in effect a white flag to signify that the village had surrendered. As the nearest thing to a community leader, poor Arthur was made to raise the flag himself.'

'Which might explain *what* he did, but why did he do it *now*? You have been part of the Greater German Reich for over a year. There is no fighting near here and life goes on.'

'But at a cost,' said the reverend gentleman, 'to Arthur Seddon personally. He was shunned in the village pub, even in the church, and the children were encouraged to refer to him as "Herr Von Seddon" or to salute him with a "Heil, Arthur!" – though never when your soldiers were about.'

'That was sensible,' I said.

'And then there was his farm business,' Brownlee continued, 'which he saw disappear before his very eyes. His barley and his livestock were taken from him and some folk said it was poetic justice, as he had welcomed in the very thieves who had robbed him.'

I studiously ignored the vicar's nervous glance and silently made another mark on the paper on the table.

'Did you know he had gun?' I asked without looking up from my scribble.

'This is the countryside,' he blustered, 'and every farmer has a shotgun for rats or foxes or rabbits for the pot, or they used to, before they had to be handed in.'

'How did Seddon manage to keep his?'

He shrugged. 'No one knows. The gossips say it is because he was so well in with… with the new administration.'

'Do you know what would have happened if he had used it on a member of the new administration?'

He held my gaze as he answered.

'Shooting a member of the occupying forces would have resulted in the execution of a hundred hostages. I believe that is the current rate of exchange. But Arthur didn't shoot anyone, did he? He shot the flagpole out there, bringing down the flag you made him fly.'

'And then himself,' I added.

On the day in question, Arthur Seddon had eaten 'a good breakfast' according to Mrs Loftus, but after the village postman had called and he had read the letter just delivered, he had told his housekeeper that she would not be needed for the rest of the day. He dressed in his 'Sunday best' and walked to the vicarage to see the Rev. Brownlee. Then he had returned to his house, left an envelope containing some Occupation Reichsmarks and two five-pound notes for Mrs Loftus, taken his shotgun and some shells from wherever he had concealed them, and marched proudly down the street to the village hall, where he halted at the flagpole from which hung the hated *Hakenkreuz*.

He levelled the shotgun an inch from the white-painted post and pulled the triggers, blowing the pole in two. Several villagers saw the detached half of the pole with its red flag still fluttering crash to the ground; some may even have cheered.

Arthur Seddon did not acknowledge them, and any cheers turned to shouts and screams as he reloaded the shotgun then turned it on himself and blew most of his head off.

'Did he tell you he was going to do that when he called on you?' I asked Brownlee.

'Of course not. I would have stopped him, or at least tried to,' he replied indignantly.

'But he came to tell you something,' I prompted.

'That he had had some bad news in a letter and had to go away for a while. He asked me to look after what was left of his property in his absence.'

'That was all?'

'Yes. He was quite short, very matter-of-fact, and clearly had been affected by the contents of that letter.'

'That I can understand,' I said.

'You've read it?'

Of course I had. It had been sent by an old school friend of Seddon's, a farmer in the south of the county called Adams who also had orchards and fields of strawberries and raspberries. When the fruits were ripe, Adams would, annually, employ families of travelling gypsies to pick them, and the gypsies would then move on to Seddon's farm and do the same.

The letter from Adams had obviously shocked Arthur Seddon as much as it had confirmed my darkest suspicions. There would be no roving gypsies coming this year, or any future one, to bring in Seddon's only remaining cash crop. Their gypsy work-force, along with all the *Roma* in southern England, had been rounded up and were being transported across the Channel to be sent to labour camps 'in the East'.

'It gave me the inspiration for my reading and sermon on Sunday,' said the Rev. Brownlee.

'A sermon on suicide?' I snapped at him.

'Far from it. I took my text from the Acts of the Apostles; the conversion of Saul of Tarsus on the road to Damascus. You know the story?'

I nodded silently, knowing what he would say and allowing him to say it.

'Saul was struck down on the road by a blinding light, and

it was only after he had been taken into Damascus and met with a holy man that the spirit of the Lord made *the scales fall from his eyes* so he could see clearly. I think that is what happened to Arthur, the scales had fallen from his eyes.'

And though I said nothing, I felt they had also fallen from mine.

Samantha Lee Howe

Samantha Lee Howe is the writer of over twenty-five novels and several story collections. She is the author of *USA Today* bestselling novel *The Stranger in Our Bed*, which she adapted for screen. She has won multiple awards including Best Thriller for the National Film Awards. Samantha's latest novel, *The Soul Thief*, published in December 2024 by HarperCollins, is a supernatural thriller. She is currently writing a new post-war series for Bedford Square Publishers, which she describes as cosexy.

samanthaleehowe.co.uk

THE GARDEN

Samantha Lee Howe

'What do you think?' I asked as we stood in the garden over-looking the view.

'I think it's got potential,' Rosie said. 'Beautiful views. Great piece of land, but the house isn't great.'

I glanced back at the building. A four-bedroom former farm workers' cottage, it had been left to the elements for a long time: leaking roof, bathroom and kitchen so dated there was barely any amenities. Even though the estate agent called it 'cosy', it was a long way from being that, or even being liveable.

Even though we were both working and had been saving for years, we still couldn't afford a house in the city, which was why we'd begun looking further out. If we bought this house, we'd have a longer commute, but we'd finally be on the property ladder.

'There's so much needs doing,' Rosie said. I knew she wasn't that keen, but I couldn't keep the love for the garden from my face and in true Rosie fashion she saw what I was feeling and gave me what I wanted. 'But we can do it up. It'll be a project, Jake, won't it?'

I was beaming from ear to ear then. The house really didn't matter to me at all. We could knock it down and rebuild if I had that garden to look at every day.

'We'll have to do some number-crunching,' I said, forcing myself to be sensible.

'Yes,' said Rosie, and I could hear the relief in her voice.

'We'll have to keep the flat going… come here at weekends, until we make it habitable,' I said.

Rosie turned full circle in the garden and looked back at the house.

'It looks lovely from here. Gorgeous old stonework.'

'Can we do it?' I asked, watching her because I knew if she made her mind up to do this, we'd be unstoppable.

'I think so. We can do a lot of the work ourselves. But you're right, we need to budget, look at it sensibly, then we don't get any nasty surprises along the way.'

A few hours later, my mother called and told me my grandfather had passed away during the night. We'd been expecting it, but it was still a shock and so the idea of looking at our finances got pushed aside as we became swept up in family issues.

The funeral plans had already been set in motion when Rosie and I returned to London.

'Grandad left you something in his will,' Mum told me. 'It should help with the cottage.'

'You know about it?' I said.

'Yes, Rosie called me. She said you were smitten. Let's get the funeral out of the way and I'll come and see it with you both.'

A few weeks later we returned. The property market was slow, and so the cottage and the garden were still available.

Mum was a little disheartened when she saw the state of the place.

'It's going to cost,' she said. 'But Grandad's money should help. And the truth is, I don't need what he left me, so I think you both should have it. Let's see this place revived.'

'Aw, look at him!' Rosie said spotting the watering in my eyes. 'He really loves this place!'

'I can see that,' Mum said.

We put in a low offer for the cottage on Mum's advice, and with a little bit of bartering we finally agreed on a price that made all parties happy. The garden was mine – the house Rosie's – we'd make both of them glorious between us.

We split our time between the flat and our new home, learning all the problems that the house had before we could move in. It became essential that we stopped spending money on frivolous things, as the roof was worse than we thought it would be, and the boiler went almost immediately and had to be replaced.

Rosie and I ended up taking two weeks' holiday so that we could do some basic decorating and repairs once the roof was sorted.

Then, we spent our first night there. It was both a relief and traumatic, as I remember finding Rosie standing in the small cottage-style kitchen looking deeply distressed.

'Have we done the right thing, Jake?' she asked. 'I just suddenly had a panic about being here. A bad feeling, like we wouldn't be happy.'

I hugged her and promised we would be. And we were for years, and we made the house beautiful, and I fulfilled my dream of growing all manner of plants in the garden. But, by the time we reached our tenth anniversary, the Big C struck. Rosie became very ill, and we learnt, then, that our dream of children was never going to happen. Rosie had a hysterectomy and we went through all the treatments. At the same time, our elderly neighbours on the smallholding next door, realising their own mortality, decided to sell up.

I was too engrossed with Rosie's health to pay much attention to who they were selling to, but then *they* moved in.

It was fine at first. A young couple like us, seemingly nice, moved in with their small daughter.

I noticed how loud they were right away. The wife was always shouting, her brash voice echoed across the few acres between our houses, breaking the peace we had enjoyed up until that point. I forgave the racket because, getting wind of our circumstances, the husband and wife came around and offered to help. They were pleasant and friendly, if noisy, and I had so much to concern myself with that I didn't spend a lot of time thinking about the change that was happening.

Rosie went into remission. Her hair began to grow back. I was so relieved at that point that nothing could upset me.

Two more children arrived next door in rapid succession. It got rowdier, and I started to wonder if they were going for their own football team. The wife, Charlie, got louder. Then they began to accumulate animals: cats, dogs, sheep – the worst was the chickens and the cockerel, that woke us up at the crack of dawn every morning.

Rosie had returned to work, and so our trains into London early every day began to feel exhausting because of the sleep deprivation. I had some new windows fitted in our bedroom to try to offset the noise from outside, but Charlie always seemed to be up stupidly early, and always walking their dogs around the border, and under our bedroom window, and there would be shouting and barking – even at the weekends. It was as if she were fearful that their land would be invaded. She even said words like that, when, being neighbourly, we chatted over the fence.

'We have to secure our borders,' she said frequently. Rosie and I didn't have a clue what she meant or why she was so obsessed with these imagined borders – things like that just didn't worry us.

Now that life was normalising, we began to realise that they were very odd people. We took some small pleasure in laughing at their weirdness. Charlie and Johnny thought they were better than anyone else, for a start. And because their land surrounded us, and ours was much smaller, it was as if they believed that their needs and happiness were more important than ours. They had no understanding of being 'good neighbours' but began to imply *we* were bad neighbours and somehow selfish.

'Perhaps it's time we moved on,' Rosie said one day, when she was weary of the noise. It seemed to us there was all sorts of crazy going on next door, night and day. I worried about Rosie's health and feared that her cancer would return, as this was always a worry.

Rosie and I couldn't understand the many passive-aggressive comments that Charlie, and then Johnny, indulged in at our expense. We were the quietest neighbours anyone could have. It was all so peculiar that, after a while, we tried to avoid any contact with them, because any exchanges always left us feeling like we'd done something wrong.

One evening, I took a picture of Rosie sitting in our garden, the lovely view over next-door's field and the sunset behind her was too beautiful to miss. I shared the picture on social media and was immediately met with a torrent of abuse from Charlie, saying we had no right to take a photograph of *her* view.

We both blocked them from seeing our socials again after that.

'If she can't see anything, she can't get upset,' Rosie said. 'It's the best solution.'

I couldn't argue with this logic, but it just seemed to add fuel to the fire. No access to our lives made Charlie's behaviour even worse. And then the texts started coming. Accusations:

> *You've moved the border and stolen some of our land.*
> *You've fed our sheep something that made them ill.*
> *You're terrible neighbours.*
> *You're selfish.*

The barrage didn't stop.

'She's not right in the head,' Rosie said. 'I've had enough of them both now. All this time, the odd behaviour. The weirdness about borders, it just shows, she's really quite insane. I think she needs help.'

I agreed with her, even though I'd never known Rosie to be so blunt before. I looked at her closely, worried about this sudden change in her normally non-aggressive attitude to life. But Charlie and Johnny had been wearing us down a long time and we were both over it.

Then Rosie came back from a routine check-up with bad news. The cancer had returned, but this time, she wasn't going to get better as it had gone into her spine. She decided that she wouldn't fight it this time. I tried to persuade her not to give in, she was too young at only thirty-eight to even consider that, but she insisted on palliative care only.

I was devastated.

I cut my mind off from our noisy neighbours, but first let them know of our circumstances. Charlie gave me an odd little smile when I told her Rosie's condition was serious, and I politely pointed out that she needed peace and quiet going forward. None of which came throughout my poor love's last months.

I was glad that the medication took Rosie out of the situation, though. There was nothing I could do at that point but try to ignore the neighbours while going through the torture of my wife's last days. Finally, Rosie slipped away in the early hours while we both slept. I only realised she'd gone when the awful screech of the cockerel woke me from an exhausted slumber and I reached out a hand to touch Rosie, finding her stone cold, and not breathing, beside me.

I lay there in shock for a few moments, even though I'd been expecting it. I knew I had to phone 999 and report it, but could barely bring myself to get out of the bed. For a moment I considered taking some of Rosie's morphine myself and floating away with her. But I knew she wouldn't have wanted that. It was too awful to contemplate. And I had to live long enough to make sure all her final wishes were granted, and the funeral she'd requested was organised.

After the funeral, I had friends and family over to the house for a small, intimate wake. We sat around, quietly reflecting on our memories of Rosie. Her brother gave a long and lovely speech about what she was like growing up. I couldn't say anything, I was just too choked. Even though I'd been expecting it, I was hurting a great deal. Life was never going to be the same without my wife in it. And, having just turned forty, I felt that it shouldn't be. How could I move on and live without her?

'You're still young,' my cousin pointed out. 'I think Rosie would expect you to find someone else eventually.'

I was mortified by her words. There was no way I could see this happening, and told her so.

'Don't make promises to yourself that you won't be able to keep. Time is a healer. You'll see,' she said.

After everyone left, I went to bed. It was only eight o'clock, but I just couldn't face sitting downstairs alone and watching the TV when I'd often done that with Rosie. Doing anything routine alone just reminded me of what I'd lost.

I turned the light off and then I heard some music start up, loud and annoying. I chinked the curtain open, looked outside, and saw that my neighbours had chosen that evening to host a party of their own, and they had hired a live band which played into the early hours of the morning.

It was a sacrilege, that today of all days they'd behave so badly, knowing my wife's funeral had just taken place.

When the music stopped, I finally collapsed out of sheer exhaustion. My night was haunted with thoughts of Rosie magically coming back to life in some crazy dream-world that turned her death into a horrible misunderstanding. But the dream made me happy, as it was vivid and I almost believed it to be true, even as I was yanked from sleep with the sound of quad bikes skittering over the paddock, below my bedroom window.

I got up, stumbled to the window, threw open the curtains and stared down at Charlie's laughing face. She was stood, waiting for me, and I knew, then, that all of this had been deliberate. The neighbours, for some reason, hated us and wanted us gone. I began to believe, then, that their constant torture of us had caused Rosie's cancer to come back and was the reason she hadn't wanted to fight it. She'd been browbeaten by these scumbags.

I was going to make them pay.

Rosie and I had been careful when planning for our future, and with sound advice we'd taken on and paid into a life insurance policy that paid out on first death. I'd forgotten about it until that day, when, bleary-eyed, I waded through the mountain of paperwork associated with losing a loved one.

The policy was on the top of the pile, and I knew then that Rosie had dug it out and left it for me to find. The insurance company owed me two million pounds, and a phone call later, followed by proof of Rosie's death, meant that the money was cleared to be paid into my account. It didn't help with her loss, but it meant I had enough money to quit the day job, and I could now take up a new hobby and give myself more time to grieve.

When I gave in my notice, my boss tried to talk me out of it.

'It's a mistake to isolate yourself now, Jake. Better to keep working and be surrounded by people,' he said.

But despite his kind words and promise that I could take some time to recover with a chance to return, I knew I wouldn't be back.

After I worked my notice, I returned to my little cottage and took up my new hobby – my garden. Never having the time to devote to my garden when the house had been our priority, I'd kept it simple. Now I planted a range of unusual plants, I put in a greenhouse and began to grow tomatoes and courgettes. A plot of land came up for sale next door, and when I heard that Charlie and Johnny were after it, I offered ten thousand pounds above asking price and quickly secured it, turning it into allotments that I rented out, much to their annoyance as Charlie hated the gardeners peering over the fence at her.

She sent me a letter demanding that I stop renting the land out immediately. I ignored her, and then Johnny came knocking on the door to 'have a word'.

I was in no mood to play nice anymore. The last days of the love of my life had been spent living with their selfishness and noise, and the party had been the last straw of disrespect that I was going to take.

'Just like you,' I said to Johnny, 'I'll do what I want with my own land from now on. And get off my property. You're not welcome here.'

They complained to the council, but the deeds of the land specified it could be used for agriculture, and therefore, letting people grow food on it wasn't a problem.

After that, I continued to ignore whatever they got up to, but the noise level, now with four screaming brats, big-mouth Charlie and Johnny with his childish skittering around on his quad bike got worse.

I took to using earplugs at night and found myself able to sleep again, getting up in the mornings only when I wanted to. Charlie continued to stand and scream orders at the kids and dogs below my bedroom window every day until her throat was raw and she lost her voice. It was silent for a week after that, and I realised just how much racket she alone created. But once her voice healed, it started again and they grew louder and louder, even to the point that the neighbouring property, some eight acres away, heard them and mentioned it to me.

I hardened myself to them, deliberately not looking for an argument, but feigning indifference, while everyone else, even the hobby-food growers who rented space on my land, had issues with the noise. They wanted peace and time to enjoy gardening and the fruits of their labour; instead, they had shouts and jeers and threats thrown over the fence at them. After that a few of them left and stopped renting the space because of my neighbours.

It didn't matter to me, I had a plan.

I put up some new plants that would eventually grow and

block them off from that field completely, but they would take years to do so. But none of that was the end game. What was important was what I was secretly growing that would see the whole lot of them off.

I grew the plant right on the border, between my garden and the picket fence that they owned. Within a year it had grown a good two feet and was poking over into their garden. I knew Johnny or at least Charlie would notice the invasion of one of my plants soon enough, but suspected that they wouldn't know that every part of this plant was poisonous. It took another year, and two more feet, before Johnny decided to crop it from his side, throwing it back onto my side of the fence.

Using gloves, I kept the remains of the plant stored behind my shed. A few days later, I noticed Johnny beginning to build his yearly bonfire which spewed smoke over the surrounding area for days at a time. He'd been wearing gloves when he cropped the oleander and therefore hadn't suffered any ill effects. I was glad about this, as he might have been more cautious if he had.

As was normal for this time of year, Johnny and Charlie went away for the bank holiday weekend to spend with her parents. That afternoon, I cropped down all the oleander from my side, and using a digger that I'd hired for the purpose, I dug down and removed all the roots, disposing of it in a skip I'd hired for the purpose. The skip was taken away the next day, but I kept some of the tree back and stored it with the rest behind the shed. None of it was visible, or even in my garden after I'd finished. I then planted a cherry tree in the space on the border, watering and nurturing it to make sure it settled in quickly.

While Charlie and Johnny were still away, I snuck across the fence, into their land, and deconstructed the bonfire, weaving in the remnants of the oleander with the foliage he'd cut down. Then I put the bonfire back together just as he had. It was all ready for their return.

After that, I returned to my own house, locked and sealed all windows and doors by taping plastic over every frame. I also let the allotment renters know that I was stopping access to the field for a few days due to work I was doing on the border. It was autumn, so most of the vegetation was gone anyway, and there were no objections or desperate pleas to still attend their crops.

The horrible neighbours and their four unpleasant children returned, and Johnny immediately set about burning the garden waste he'd prepared. Watching, I put a mask over my face for good measure. Oleander, I knew, was poisonous even when burnt. And now, Johnny, Charlie and the four children stood around the bonfire, breathing in the toxic fumes.

Johnny was affected first. He began to cough and wheeze, then one of the brats keeled over right in front of the fire. Charlie was furthest away, but ran up to see what was wrong and she too was overcome. I watched and waited as the fire burnt out and each and every one collapsed. The bonfire slowly burnt itself out.

Then, still masked, I went to bed.

The next day, I opened my curtains and looked out on the field. The whole of the family was still lying on the grass beside the dead embers of their toxic bonfire.

I got dressed, removed all the plastic seals from my windows and doors, and then I rang the police and reported what I could see next door.

A few hours later, when the police and ambulances arrived,

bagged and tagged the bodies and took them away, I was questioned about what I thought had happened.

'I saw Johnny lighting his yearly fire,' I said. 'We all burn waste in the country, so that's nothing unusual.'

'But you only saw the bodies this morning?' the female officer asked.

I put on my most sympathetic face. A task that wasn't difficult, because all I had to do was think about Rosie and my own terrible loss.

'I only saw there was something wrong when I woke and opened my bedroom curtains this morning. I wish I had seen something sooner, they might have been…' My voice broke and I let a tear creep down my face before dashing it away. 'Do you know what caused it?'

'Looks like he was burning something toxic. You were lucky not to be outside. All the animals were affected too. Fortunately for the farm further along, the wind wasn't blowing that way so everyone there is okay.'

'I'm so shocked!' I said. 'What a terrible thing to happen.'

'Indeed. And you were lucky. But if you do feel any ill-effects, please go into A&E immediately,' she said.

After that she told me her name was Carol and accepted my offer of tea. I served up some shop-bought biscuits I'd got in for the occasion. Then, after taking my statement, which told her nothing much at all, Carol the policewoman left.

I was alone, then, with the full weight of what I'd done. I tested how it felt to be a murderer: I tried to feel some guilt for the children – but I felt nothing except an intense relief that the fields were quiet. That they were gone.

A few days later the papers reported the tragic deaths, revealing a suspected accidental burning of oleander, a branch of which they found, where I'd left it, behind Johnny's shed with the remains of other garden waste. The police closed the investigation, and the coroner put the deaths down to 'misadventure'.

I never thought I could hate anyone as much as I'd hated my neighbours, and now they were dead, I felt a freedom I hadn't felt in years.

I didn't regret a thing.

Martin Edwards

Martin Edwards' novels include the Lake District Mysteries and the Rachel Savernake books, most recently *Hemlock Bay*. His non-fiction includes a multi-award-winning history of Golden Age fiction, *The Golden Age of Murder*, the expanded second edition of which has just been published. He has received three Daggers, including the CWA Diamond Dagger, two Edgars, three CrimeFest Keating awards, and four lifetime achievement awards. He is consultant to the British Library's Crime Classics and President of the Detection Club.

martinedwardsbooks.com

THE BUTLER

Martin Edwards

'My dad was a toolmaker.' Cormac Kelleher's speech was hardly slurred these days, Ginny thought. 'Lived in Derry all his life. Working man. Great patriot. Said he'd sooner top himself than set foot in England. He'd turn in his grave if he knew I lived in this mansion and was about to hire a butler.'

'You don't have to call the man a butler, if that's too P. G. Wodehouse for you,' Ginny said. 'How about chief of staff? House manager? Lifestyle concierge, even?'

'For fuck's sake, I hate jargon. Butler is fine. Makes me feel like a lord of the manor.' Cormac gave a throaty laugh. 'Who is Wodehouse, anyway?'

'An author. He wrote humorous stories about an old-style butler called Jeeves.'

Cormac Kelleher shrugged. 'I was never a man for reading. Practical turn of mind, see, like my dad. Always wanted to be doing stuff. At least until this happened.'

He jerked his thumb at the walking stick lying at his feet.

'You're making a fantastic recovery,' Ginny said. 'Not many men would look so spry, after having a stroke and a heart attack in quick succession. Thank goodness you're wiry and always kept fit. Soon you'll be as right as rain.' She paused. 'I never knew about your father. Surely you come from a farming family?'

He smiled, showing neat and regular teeth. A man of thirty, half his age, would be proud of them. He'd had a lot of work done, of course. The best dentistry that money could buy.

'My dad died when I was fifteen,' he said. 'Hard on Mum, she'd already lost my elder brother. But she wasn't soft. A year later she married a farmer with a lot of land. After he died, she inherited. And put me in charge. Lucky me, huh?'

Ginny looked around the room. The décor was minimalist, its starkness accentuated rather than relieved by the bold splashes of colour in the Hockney hanging opposite them. She'd bought it at an auction on Cormac's behalf in her second week as his personal assistant. He didn't know anything about art, he explained, but you can't take it with you, so why not splash the cash? Probably the painting would prove to be a good investment, but it hardly mattered. He had no kids, no close relatives. His mother was long gone and he'd never married.

'I never knew.'

'Ah, Ginny, there's a lot you don't know about me. Probably as well.' He rubbed his neatly trimmed beard. 'Y'know what they say about omelettes? Can't make them without breaking a few eggs? Well, you can't make millions without…' – he seemed to rack his brains for a suitable euphemism – 'treading on a few toes.'

She nodded. 'I imagine so.'

'Aren't you shocked?'

'It takes a lot to shock me, Cormac.'

'I bet.' He studied her, searching for clues to what was in her mind. Her clothes, like the rest of her appearance, were businesslike yet elegant. Like her pleasant features, they gave nothing away. 'Remember what I said the other night? We're two of a kind, you and me.'

'About the other night.' She bowed her head. I want to apologise. I shouldn't…'

A shrug. 'Think nothing of it, Ginny. You got the wrong end of the stick about what I meant, that's all. No harm done, eh?'

'You're very kind, Cormac.'

'Not always.' He smiled his impish smile. 'So what about this butler, then?'

'He has a military background.'

This amused him. 'Oh yeah?'

'It's supposed to be a plus in that line of work. You need someone with plenty of discipline. Well trained, good admin skills. That's what it takes to run an estate like this.'

'You could do the job instead. You're a smart girl and you've not done badly this past six months, considering you dropped so unlucky. I never had a day off sick in my life until… well, I don't know how I'd have managed without you.'

She smiled. 'It's smart to know your limits, and I've realised mine. You need someone to run things for you. Making sure everything goes smoothly in a place this size takes a lot of doing.'

'If it's about your salary, I'm happy to…'

'No, no, I'm not angling for a rise. My salary is more than generous. Probably more than I'm worth.'

He shook his head. 'Not a bit of it. You're a modest English lady who learned her manners at a posh public school. I'm just a rough and ready Irish farmer, but working with someone I trust means the world to me. Can't have been much fun, taking a job and then seeing your new boss crippled within a fortnight.'

'You weren't crippled,' she said. 'The medics and the physio have worked wonders. Anyway, the truth is, the responsibility is too much for me. It keeps me awake at night. You employ more than a dozen people, counting the gardeners, cleaners, and people who help Anichka in the kitchen. They all need managing, quite apart from the office stuff. Dealing with your stockbrokers, accountants, bankers, lawyers. The flat in Chelsea, the houses in Provence and Florida. Plenty to keep me fully occupied.'

'Okay, okay.' He gave a theatrical sigh. 'You win. So I need a butler.'

'Shall I draw up a shortlist of candidates? The agency can send over three or four people, so you can pick and choose.'

'Waste of time. If this guy looks like he fits the bill, we'll see him first. What's his name?'

Ginny checked her phone. 'Peter Vardey. Want to look at his CV?'

'Sure.'

She leaned closer, holding her phone in front of him. A photograph of a man in his early thirties filled the screen.

'Good-looking feller,' Cormac murmured.

She scrolled down to reveal the details of Vardey's career. Nine years in the army, four as co-owner of a bar in Spain. Since coming back to England, he'd worked for several wealthy principals. Most recently an Asian businessman based in London, and a Spanish footballer with a mansion in north Cheshire.'

'References okay?'

'The agency sent over a note from the businessman. Singing his praises. Still waiting to hear from the footballer.'

Cormac grinned. 'Deserves a yellow card for wasting time. Okay, I'll see Mr Vardey. What do you think, start with an online interview?'

She shook her head. 'Something as important as this, you need to meet him face to face. See if you like the look of him.'

'Oh, I like the look of him,' Cormac said softly. 'But you're right. I need to see him in the flesh.'

'So tell me about your last employment,' Cormac said, leaning back and putting his arms behind his head. 'Working for a Premier League striker, eh? Fascinating.'

Peter Vardey smiled a non-committal smile. His features were regular, his grooming immaculate. He hadn't over-dressed for the interview: the navy blazer was well-cut, his tie unobtrusive. Ginny thought he'd judged it right. She found it hard to picture him in the dust and the heat of Helmand Province. But she had no doubt that he'd remain cool under fire.

'I always enjoy my work. Though obviously I can't talk specifics. I signed an NDA.'

Cormac nodded. 'Discretion assured, huh?'

'I'm sure you and Ms Brown would agree, confidentiality is vital in this kind of situation.'

'This kind of situation?' There was a touch of frost in Ginny's voice.

Peter Vardey turned to face her. 'Lately I've worked for several Ultra High Net Worth Individuals like Mr Kelleher. I find they value their privacy. There are a lot of troublesome people in the world. Stalkers, obsessives, activists. Even would-be kidnappers. You have a guard on the main gate here for a reason, I'm sure.'

Ginny crossed her legs. 'In this day and age, any wealthy person is something of a target.'

'Exactly,' Vardey said. 'My job is to make my employer's life easier. Not more difficult.'

She frowned. 'You make it sound very simple.'

'Keeping things simple is hard work, Ms Brown. But I don't mind that.'

There was a brief pause. They were sitting on a vast L-shaped sofa, easily big enough to accommodate another three or four people, in the room Cormac called 'the office'. Despite the presence of a large desk and a laptop, the emphasis was on comfort rather than functionality. Just a vase of fragrant roses and a scrawny male nude painted by Lucian Freud scowling at them from the wall. A door gave onto Ginny's office, while full-length windows overlooked gardens and a lake in the shape of a crescent.

'Care to take a look around outside?' Cormac asked. 'When we come back, you can see how you like the leisure suite.'

'If you don't mind, Mr Kelleher, I'd be glad to get a sense of the estate.'

Cormac nodded. 'Guided tour coming up.'

He pressed a button and the glazed doors slid away. Peter Vardey moved forward to inspect them.

'Steel shutters, I see. Electronically controlled?'

'For every window,' Cormac said. 'Can't be too careful, see?'

'Naturally, this is a smart house,' Ginny said. 'Heating, air con., security, lighting, all controlled by a single app.'

Vardey nodded. 'Is there a panic room?'

Cormac picked up his silver-tipped walking stick. 'I may be an old feller who's not so steady on his feet these days, but do I look like I'm one to panic?'

Vardey allowed himself a ghost of a smile. 'Can't say you do, Mr Kelleher. What are your requirements in terms of dress code? Some form of livery, or are you happy with slightly less formal attire?'

'This isn't fucking Buckingham Palace.' Cormac gave the man's lean frame an appraising glance. 'I may be many things, but nobody could ever call me a snob. Smart casual is fine by me.'

The three of them moved out into the grounds. 'Ten hectares, plus twelve in parkland,' he said. 'Not another property in sight. Reminds me of the Emerald Isle, that's why I bought it.'

Vardey nodded. 'This is a quiet part of the world. Endless rolling countryside. The taxi from the station brought me through two or three villages in the space of seven or eight miles.'

'Too cut-off for your liking?' Cormac gave a sly smile. 'Not like some of the places you toured as a soldier?'

'After that, believe me, I'm all in favour of peace and quiet.'

'Sure. Anyhow, there's a good pub four miles away. They call it the Jolly Thresher. Ages since I've been there, but they serve real ale, if that suits you.' Cormac waved his stick. 'Over there is the whatsitsname…'

'Arboretum,' Ginny said.

'Yeah, clump of trees. Behind them is the farm. Jerry, the tenant, works hard, but he's set in his ways and takes a bit of managing. To make sure the revenue stream keeps flowing.'

Vardey nodded. 'Can't take anything for granted.'

'Too right.'

They pottered through a rose garden and reached the edge of the lake. Ginny seemed to think it was time she spoke.

'Underwater lighting, computer controlled. On a clear summer's evening, the colours are spectacular.'

'I can imagine,' Vardey said.

'Most of the live-in staff have rooms on the top floor of the north side of the house,' Cormac said, pointing. 'The plan is for the butler to occupy the lodge close to the gate. I had it kitted out when I moved in, but it's lain empty ever since. Ginny preferred to be in the main house and her apartment is on the south side.'

When they reached the leisure complex, Cormac came to a halt. He was breathing hard.

'Not as fit as I was. Massive heart attack, see? A stroke had softened me up for it. Felt a pain in my arm, next thing I knew, I woke up in some hospital bed. Thought I was done for, but the medics saved me.'

Vardey considered him. 'They did well, I'd say. You look in pretty good shape to me.'

Cormac gave a shrug. 'I'm not dead yet, for sure. But right now, I'm knackered. Why don't you go for a swim?'

Vardey raised his eyebrows. 'I didn't…'

'Bring your trunks? Don't worry, nobody will disturb you. Fresh towels in the changing room. Make yourself at home while Ginny and I sort out the paperwork.'

'Paperwork?'

'Your contract of employment.' Cormac thrust out an age-spotted hand. 'Congratulations. You got the job.'

The moment they were back in his office, Cormac said, 'What's up, Ginny?'

'What do you mean? Nothing's up.'

'Come on. You've gone quiet. It's a giveaway, you're not happy. Isn't he your type?'

She frowned. 'It's nothing personal. I just think you should look at other candidates. Weigh up what everyone has to offer.'

'You said yourself, he fits the bill. A guy who is tech-savvy and good at valeting. You think he's too good to be true?'

'Not necessarily. I like his idea of drawing up a manual for the staff. Operating procedures for every part of the house and estate. So each member of staff knows exactly what to do. We don't want a young farmhand jamming the woodchipper again. Or a new maid cleaning the Hockney with washing-up liquid. But a businesslike process would…'

Cormac said tersely, 'Listen, Ginny. I never gave a fuck about process. I only care about results. Business is one thing I understand. I was making big money before you were born. And I cut plenty of corners along the way, believe me.'

The rebuke made her flinch. 'It's not like you to make an impulse buy, that's all I'm saying.'

He shrugged. 'I trust my instincts.'

'Very well. Any offer should be subject to satisfactory references from the footballer and the other people he's worked for.'

'You said the businessman was happy. That's good enough for me. Anyhow, I trust my own judgement. Not other people's.'

'So your mind's made up?' He nodded. 'What do you want to pay him?'

He named a figure high enough to make her blink.

'Well,' she said, not quite managing to stifle a sigh. 'It's your money.'

'It surely is.' He grinned. 'I'm raising your salary by ten per cent while I'm at it. Well deserved.'

Her eyes opened very wide. 'I said the other day, there's no need…'

'There's every need. You've done a lot for me. And don't worry. I won't let him put your nose out of joint.'

'Cormac! It was my idea to bring someone else in, remember? I'm not—'

He waved away her protest. 'Peter is a clever guy. I'm sure he's up to the job. And if he isn't…'

99

'Yes?'

He made a throat-slitting gesture.

'I certainly didn't expect to be joining you at table this evening, Mr Kelleher,' the new butler said. 'In my previous positions, I usually saw my principal for no more than a couple of hours a week.'

'Yeah, well, they'd be busier than me. As I recovered from the heart attack, I got into the habit of eating dinner with Ginny most evenings. Nice to have company. When she's not out gallivanting, that is.'

Cormac grinned at his PA. The three of them were sitting round the dining table. Olena, the waitress whose sister Anichka was the cook, had served stewed fish, cooked to a recipe from their native Ukraine. Cormac always looked after the wine himself, and he'd poured each of them a glass of Chablis. Below the kitchen sprawled an extensive wine cellar, climate carefully controlled so as to avoid damaging fluctuations of temperature.

'Cormac likes to imagine that I have an exotic private life,' Ginny said.

'And do you?' Vardey's manner was polite rather than flirtatious.

'If only. No, he's wide of the mark for once. Not that I mind. As you can see, he's a generous host.'

Vardey toasted his employer. 'Your very good health. Even in these liberated times, not many principals would want to eat with their senior staff.'

Cormac shrugged. 'What else am I to do? I've lived alone for years, except for the people who work for me. In a house as big as this, I rattle around like a marble in a tin.'

Vardey tasted his wine. As if emboldened, he leaned over the table and said, 'Forgive me if it's an intrusive question, but do you have a family?'

'There was someone I was close to,' Cormac said. 'But they died. I have cousins back in Northern Ireland, but we're not in touch anymore.'

'I'm sorry. I didn't mean to pry.'

'No problem. We didn't see eye-to-eye on a lot of things. And they saw farming as a way of life. To me, it's a business. A means to an end. Making enough money to do exactly as I please.'

'And you made a great success of it.'

Cormac indicated their surroundings with an airy wave. 'I worked hard for all this. The stroke came out of the blue. Hell of a shock.'

'If you don't mind my saying so,' Vardey said, 'you look in pretty good shape to me. Those daily sessions in the gym are paying dividends.'

'Bruno is okay.' Cormac exhaled. 'Though he's not quite as encouraging as his predecessor, who I had to let go.'

'Oh yes?'

Ginny said, 'As Mr Kelleher says, Lukas was an excellent trainer. But he… overstepped the mark.'

Cormac drank some wine. 'You're a man of the world, Peter, you know there need to be red lines. Lukas was stupid. He fiddled his expenses, when I'd happily have given him the money. I can't bear people who betray me.'

'Fair enough,' Vardey said.

Cormac put down his glass. 'Not that I'm one for formality. I've never seen the world as divided into masters and servants. I'd rather we all called each other by our first names. Ginny and I have done that for ages when we're alone together, haven't we?'

Vardey turned to look at the PA. She gave a sheepish nod.

'Same with Kenneth, the chauffeur. As for Lukas, it was a shame. He… well, let's just say he forgot who was paying his wages. You know what I'm saying, Peter?'

Vardey nodded. 'I understand… Cormac.'

'What do you make of the new butler, then?'

Cormac had invited his PA to join him on a stroll around the grounds. He was, Ginny thought, moving much more freely these days. His recovery had gathered a lot of momentum. To think that only a few weeks ago she'd wondered if he'd make it through the summer.

As they approached a cluster of brick outbuildings, she considered how to phrase her reply.

'He's… very efficient.'

He threw her a quick glance. 'You don't like him?'

'No, no, I find him perfectly pleasant. A little dull, perhaps, but that may just be a hangover of army discipline. It's just that… well…'

Her voice trailed away.

'Not like you to be lost for words, Ginny. What's on your mind?'

A shake of the head. 'Nothing.'

'I can tell you're not entirely happy.'

She gave a wan smile. 'You read me like a book.'

'Come on. Spit it out.'

'It's simply that… I can't help wondering if there's a risk he might… get above himself. Start taking advantage of you.'

'What do you mean?' His face darkened. 'The man's a professional. To his fingertips.'

'Yes, yes,' she said hastily. 'I'm sure I'm worrying over nothing.'

He took a step towards her. Menace flared in his faded blue eyes. 'Are you saying you don't trust Peter?'

'No, I'm probably being quite unfair. It's just that you seem to be guided by his opinion so often. Even on stuff that you know like the back of your hand. Like running the farm. Buying new equipment, all that. Surely he doesn't know as much about cattle troughs and woodchippers as you?'

'I value his advice,' he said coldly.

'Yes, of course. But you've had a terrible health scare. For a time, things were touch and go. An experience like that is bound to knock your confidence. You don't want to become dependent on… a butler.'

'I'm not dependent on anyone, Ginny,' Cormac said softly. 'Remember that.'

Peter Vardey extended his hand. Cormac took it as he clambered out of the swimming pool.

'Four lengths,' the older man gasped. 'Best I've managed since…'

'Too right. You kept up a very good pace.' Vardey withdrew his hand and scanned Cormac's features. 'No dizziness or double vision? You don't feel nauseous?'

A shake of the head. 'Bit breathless, that's all.'

'Only to be expected. Bruno says he's impressed with your progress. I can see why.'

'Not so long ago, I could manage thirty lengths without breaking sweat.'

'You're doing fine. Getting your strength back takes time. Like the doctor said, you have to take it step by step.'

'I've always been impatient,' Cormac said. 'One of my vices.'

He smiled at Vardey, his eyes feasting on the man's lean, muscular frame.

'Life is short,' the butler said. 'Got to make the most of it.'

Cormac laughed. 'You're a man after my own heart, Peter.'

He rested his hand on the butler's shoulder. This time, Vardey didn't shrug it off.

'Happy birthday!' Cormac said as Vardey walked into the office.

He raised himself cautiously from the L-shaped sofa and advanced towards the younger man. Something was gripped in his right hand.

'How did you know it was my birthday?'

'I asked Ginny to check,' Cormac said. 'Thirty-five, eh? If only I was thirty-five again.'

Vardey allowed himself a smile. 'In spirit, you are.'

Cormac grinned. 'Anyone would think being good for my morale is in your job description.'

Vardey said easily, 'It's true.'

'I wish. Anyhow, I wanted to give you a little something to mark the occasion.'

He opened his hand to reveal a fancy vehicle key, painted metallic green.

'What's that?' Vardey's expression seldom gave much away, but his lips were parted in evident surprise.

'Key to your new car.'

'That… isn't that the Porsche badge?'

'Spot on. I got you a 718 Cayman. Kenneth assures me it's a first-rate drive.'

Vardey gazed at his employer. 'It's extraordinarily generous. I don't know what to say.'

'Thank you is fine.'

The butler shifted uneasily. 'I mean… are you sure about this? I've only worked for you for six weeks. It doesn't seem…'

'Not like you to be lost for words, Peter,' Cormac grinned. 'Think I don't know my own mind?'

'A *Porsche*, though…'

'Who else would I spend my money on? In case you're wondering, who do you think paid for Ginny's Alfa and Kenneth's own runabout?'

'Your generosity is breathtaking,' Vardey murmured. 'I… I simply don't know how to thank you.'

'I'm sure you'll think of a way,' Cormac said gently. 'Meantime, don't you want to take a look at your new toy? Kenneth has brought it round to the front of the house. It's a sunny day. Maybe we could go for a drive?'

'You look hot and bothered, Ginny,' Cormac said, putting his head round the door of her office. 'What's up? Laptop still on the blink?'

'No, I fixed that.' Her tone was flat and she didn't make eye contact.

He folded his arms. 'What, then?'

'Nothing.'

'No need to be sulky with me, Ginny. You said once, we may be boss and PA, but we can always talk straight to each other. If there's one thing I hate, it's people who beat about the bush.'

She took a breath. 'Okay, it's about Peter.'

'I wondered if it might be. What about him?'

'I don't mean to…'

'Tell me.'

'Don't you think…?' she began, evidently taking care over

her choice of words. 'I mean, do you think he's beginning to take one or two liberties?'

'Such as?' Cormac's tone was icy.

'Yesterday, he knocked off work two hours early. I saw him swanning off in his swish new motor. He never told me he was leaving early.'

Cormac shrugged. 'Does he have to?'

'It would be a courtesy. What if a member of staff had an urgent issue?'

'You can deal with anything that crops up while Peter was out. He wouldn't complain. He isn't the… territorial type.'

'I'm sure he wouldn't complain. That's not my point. The fact is, he strikes me as rather lazy. And if you turn a blind eye…'

'It's not a question of turning a blind eye,' Cormac interrupted. 'Peter told me he had some business to sort out. Legal stuff, to do with some compensation he's due from the Army. I said fine, take a couple of hours off. So he had my express permission to leave the estate, if that answers your question.'

'All right,' she said gruffly. 'I'm sorry I raised it.'

'Me too, Ginny.' He unfolded his arms, softened his tone. 'Look, all I want is for you and Peter to get along. You're both good workers. He's an easy-going guy, there's no cause for you to be jealous.'

'I'm not jealous! As for easy-going, that's your word, not mine. But you're the boss.'

'That's enough, Ginny.'

The old man's breathing was laboured and irregular. He put a hand to his heart.

'Cormac! Are you all right?' It was almost a shriek.

He was bending over, his breath coming in short gasps.

'Shall I call a doctor?'

'No… no, it's all right. Just a… just a twinge, that's all.'

Slowly, he lifted his head, making an obvious effort to calm himself. She reached out impulsively, putting her arms around him.

'Are you sure you don't want…?'

He shrugged her off. 'I'll be fine.'

Their eyes met.

'That's all, Ginny.' She knew him well enough to realise he was making a huge effort to control his temper. 'And no more of this nonsense about Peter, eh?'

'How are you and Ginny getting on?' Cormac asked after Vardey had talked him through the latest set of accounts from the tenant farmer.

'Fine. Why do you ask?'

'Just wondered. The work you do overlaps a bit with hers, that's all.'

'She's a first-rate PA.' A cool smile. 'And I'm a half-decent butler. Two very different roles, so no need for us to tread on each other's toes.'

'Attractive girl.'

'Certainly.' After a moment, he added, 'Though in case you're wondering, she's not my type.'

'No?' A puckish grin. 'So what is your type, Peter?'

Vardey pursed his lips. 'Ah, that would be telling.'

'So where is Ginny this evening?' Vardey asked as the waitress put the venison in front of him. 'Thank you, Olena.'

Cormac shrugged. 'She has an aunt she's fond of. An old lady who lives in Leamington Spa. So she's spending the weekend there. Didn't she mention it?'

'I've not seen her today, as it happens. I spent hours at the farm, trying to encourage Jerry to modernise his methods.'

'Good luck with that.' Cormac poured the Pinot Noir. 'He doesn't even listen to me half the time.'

'I'm making progress.' Vardey lifted his glass. 'He's begun to get to grips with the importance of sustainability. I know you're almost as sceptical as Jerry, but take it from me, this is the way of the future.'

Cormac picked up his knife. The blade cut through the venison as if slicing butter. 'I'll take your word for it. Not easy to teach an old dog new tricks.'

'You're not that old.' Vardey considered him. 'Nobody would ever guess that you went through such a rough time with your health.'

Cormac laughed. 'Flattery will get you everywhere.'

Cormac opened his eyes and turned over in bed. In the darkness, the time gleamed on the digital display. Ten to midnight.

'All right?' Vardey whispered. 'You slept like a child.'

Cormac stretched out an arm, found the younger man's flat stomach.

'Sleep of the righteous,' he murmured.

Vardey laughed. 'I'll believe anything you tell me. Even that.'

There was a pause.

'I'm no saint, Peter. I've done some bad things in my time.'

'Haven't we all?' Vardey dropped a kiss on his bare shoulder. 'Want to tell me about them?'

'If I did, I'd have to kill you.'

Another laugh. 'You almost managed that anyway.'

* * *

'Will you give Norman Arnold from Gerrard and Company a ring?' Cormac said. 'I'd like him to come here to sort out a document.'

Ginny jotted a reminder on her phone. 'Any particular time or day?'

'Monday or Tuesday next week? Late afternoon would be good. If he wants, he can stay for dinner.'

'Fine. Anything I need to tell him?'

'He'll know what it's about.'

'Okay, will do.' She smiled at him. 'Anything else?'

Cormac shook his head. 'No, that's the only important thing.'

'Congratulations.' Ginny clinked her wine glass against Peter Vardey's pint pot. 'I knew he'd find you irresistible. Once I figured out I was wasting my time trying to seduce him.'

They were sitting in a quiet alcove in the saloon bar of the Jolly Thresher. Vardey took a swig of beer. 'How anyone could resist you, I can't imagine. Not to worry, we got there in the end. You're confident he means to change his will?'

'Norman Arnold is a specialist in probate. Wills and inheritance. Cormac instructed him last time he wrote a new codicil, cutting out the legacy to Lukas. If he wanted advice on an agricultural tenancy or something like that, he'd speak to the partner in charge of property law.'

'Stupid guy, Lukas.'

'Like I told you at the time, he got too big for his boots. And too greedy.'

He took another gulp of bitter. 'So his loss is our gain.'

'Right.' She smiled. 'So how did Cormac seem once you... put him through his paces?'

'For a few moments, I thought I'd killed the golden goose too soon.'

She laughed. 'It would have saved us some time. And I'd still get my legacy.'

'You've been right all along. It's better for him to fall head over heels for one of us. With any luck, I'll scoop the jackpot.'

'You've not done badly so far. That Porsche!'

'Lot of firepower under that bonnet.' He grinned at her. 'Like someone else I could mention.'

She placed her hand on his. 'Let's not smash the speed limit just yet, huh? One step at a time. We don't want to arouse suspicion. Cormac's no fool.'

'But he's not the man he was. You said so yourself. There are so many pills in his bathroom cabinet, it's like opening up a miniature pharmacy.'

She nodded. 'We won't have to wait too long. Promise.'

'Such a treat, Cormac,' Ginny said.

'My piece of resistance,' Cormac said with a grin. 'I never bothered much with cooking, but I can make a mean filet mignon, if I do say so myself.'

He'd given Anichka and Olena the night off, and donned an apron bearing the legend *If you can't smell burning, it's salad for tea.*

'So what are we celebrating?' she asked.

Cormac winked at Peter Vardey and poured from a bottle of red wine he'd opened earlier.

'This is a rather wonderful and very rare Cabernet Sauvignon from Rutherford Bench in the Napa Valley. I must confess I couldn't wait to taste it myself. It's quite distinctive. See what you two think.'

The butler bent over his glass and sniffed before drinking. 'Lovely.'

Ginny nodded. 'The perfect complement to a fine meal. But you didn't answer my question.'

Cormac beamed. 'I've asked Norman Arnold to come for dinner next week. He's a solicitor, Peter. Handles my personal affairs.'

Vardey drank some more of the wine.

'I decided I should change my will. I needn't go into details, but I told Norman I want to show my appreciation.'

'Appreciation?'

'Of the loyalty you've both shown to me.'

'You pay us more than handsomely.' Ginny sipped from her glass. 'There's no need to—'

'Like I told Norman, there's every need,' Cormac interrupted. 'In a short time, the two of you have come to mean a great deal to me. Anyway, this meal is by way of a personal thank-you for your many kindnesses. Tuck in.'

For a little while, Vardey and Ginny chatted in a desultory way. Cormac refilled their glasses.

'What do you reckon to the steak?'

'First-rate,' Vardey said. 'Anichka couldn't do better.'

'And the wine?'

'Delicious.' Ginny paused. 'You're not drinking yourself, Cormac?'

'No, I feel a headache coming on. How about you two?'

Ginny passed a hand across her brow. 'Actually, yes. I do feel a little muzzy.'

'And you, Peter?' There was a twinkle in the faded blue eyes.

Vardey stared at him, but his gaze lacked focus. 'Yes, yes…'

Cormac smiled.

* * *

'What… what happened?'

Peter Vardey stirred from his slumber, and tried to stretch his arms. But the chains that bound him were too tight. To his horror, he realised he was naked.

'My God, Peter, you've got the constitution of an ox.' Cormac shone his torch into the younger man's eyes. 'I thought you'd be out of it for at least another hour.'

Vardey recognised his surroundings. They were in the largest of the brick-built outbuildings. The windows were shuttered. He had no idea whether it was night or day.

'What's going on?'

'The two of you are very good at what you do,' Cormac said pleasantly. 'But you got careless. Did you not realise the landlord at the Jolly Thresher is on my payroll? Not the one the taxman sees, that's why Ginny didn't have a clue. He knows to tell me if any of my staff turn up in his hostelry. Just in case they're misbehaving, you know? I must be slipping, I never guessed you and Ginny were in cahoots. Since before I met either of you, I suppose?'

'But I…'

'Exploiting my little… foibles, was that the idea?' Cormac's tone sharpened. 'How unkind. And so disloyal.'

Vardey looked around. In the pitch dark, it was impossible to see anything. There was no sign of Ginny.

'Where is…?'

'Your lover?' Cormac shook his head. 'Nowhere, truth be told.'

'What do you mean?'

'I fixed the old woodchipper. Thought it might come in handy someday. Took a while, but she disappeared in the end. She didn't suffer much. Probably never regained consciousness. Even if she did, she soon lost it again.'

Vardey screamed and then threw up.

Cormac waited.

'I suppose you're wondering what's going to happen to you?'

Vardey nodded.

'I have something extra in mind, given the extent of your betrayal.' He pointed his torch at a large metal box.

'It looks old, but it has sentimental value. My dad took great pride in his work. Took me out with him a few times. Sort of apprenticeship, see. He didn't care for British soldiers in the bad old days, didn't care for them at all. Specially not after they killed my brother. He paid them back in kind until a sniper got him. I like to think this sort of makes things even again.'

Vardey tried to speak, but the words wouldn't come.

Cormac unlocked the box and took out a chisel.

'Lovely piece of craftsmanship, don't you think? Fifty years on, just look at that blade. And there's plenty more kit in the box, you'll be surprised. Family heirlooms, in a manner of speaking. Did I ever tell you my dad was a toolmaker?'

Dolores Gordon-Smith

Dolores Gordon-Smith is the author of the Jack Haldean murder mystery series set in 1920s England, the latest of which is *The Chapel in the Woods*, published by Severn House, and two WWI spy thrillers, *Frankie's Letter* and *The Price of Silence*. Married with five daughters, a growing number of grandchildren and various dogs and cats, Dolores has been a teacher, a civil servant and a shaker-out of Christmas puddings in a jam factory.

doloresgordon-smith.co.uk

MIRACLE AT THE MANORBIER STREET MUSEUM:
STREET MUSEUM:
A Golden Age Detective Story

Dolores Gordon-Smith

Jack Haldean looked in appreciative delight at the blue-and-gold enamelled box on the shelf. It stood about eight inches high and was about a foot long. The craftsmanship was exquisite and it was ancient.

Part of him itched to handle it, to run his fingers over the chased gold and glowing enamel, but that, of course, was out of the question. You couldn't handle objects in an exhibition.

It was down to Chief Inspector William Rackham that Jack was a visitor to the exhibition of Medieval Enamel Work (admission one guinea) at the Manorbier Street Museum.

'Do I want to come to what?' Jack asked in surprise when Bill asked him.

'An exhibition of medieval enamel work,' Bill repeated rather sheepishly. 'I know it's not the sort of invitation you'd expect from me, but it's in a good cause, Jack. It's in aid of the London hospitals.'

'And you just want to do the hospitals a bit of all right?'

'Yes. No. Well, I suppose so, but the thing is, I ran into an old pal of mine yesterday. Alan Darracot. Captain Darracot.'

'I've heard you mention him.'

'Yes, he's a sound bloke. He was in the Norfolks alongside us at Passchendaele and we saw quite a bit of action together. I didn't know this, but his family – I had no idea they're as grand as they obviously are – own an enamel box thingy.' Bill frowned. 'What d'you call it? A box to keep bits of saints in.'

'A reliquary?' said Jack intelligently.

'That's the one. Anyway, he's lent it to the exhibition and brought it up to London to make sure it's safely installed. He asked me if I'd like to pop along and see it. I wondered if you'd like to come too. After all, it's a churchy thing and I know that's your cup of tea.'

Jack grinned. He was, in his own opinion, a very ordinary run-of-the-mill Catholic, but that qualified him, in Bill's estimation, to take an automatic interest in churchy things.

He turned away from the reliquary to Bill and Alan Darracot. 'It's absolutely beautiful, Darracot. How old is it?'

'Well, that's an interesting question,' said Darracot. 'We've had it looked at by a couple of experts from the British Museum and, according to them, it's over a thousand years old. It's in the Byzantine style, which was copied in Italy, Sicily and England as far back as the ninth century.'

Bill whistled in appreciation. 'It's never been in your family that long?'

'Hardly,' said Darracot, smiling. 'No. It originally belonged to the Augustinian Abbey at Stalycross in Norfolk. When Henry the Eighth dissolved the monasteries, the Shelton family acquired the house, land and goods, including the reliquary. They owned it until the eighteenth century, when a

Shelton had to sell it to pay off gambling debts. That's when we bought it.'

'I don't know what it was about those Georgian types,' said Jack with a laugh. 'You couldn't seem to prise them away from the gaming tables with a crowbar.'

'Absolutely,' agreed Darracot. 'We take very good care of it,' he added seriously. 'No gambling debts for us.'

'I should hope not,' said Bill. 'That's a mug's game. Er… You called it a reliquary. Is there anyone inside, so to speak?'

Alan Darracot nodded. 'Oh yes. St Odelyn. She was native to Nene Drove, not far from Stalycross. Apparently she was given to levitation while at prayer and was famed for curing what they called the palsy. That seemed to have covered a fair range of conditions. Interestingly enough, we still get a fair few poor souls suffering from Parkinsons and the like, wanting to say prayers in the chapel where we usually keep the reliquary.'

'Does it do any good?' asked Bill, trying to keep the note of scepticism out of his voice.

To his surprise, Darracot nodded earnestly. 'Funnily enough, there have been cures. It doesn't do to be too cynical. We do allow visitors, of course. Historians, you know, and anyone sincere, but we draw the line at mere sightseers. There's some pretty hair-raising legends – folk tales and so on – about what happens when St Odelyn is treated without due respect.'

'You don't believe that, do you?' asked Bill.

Darracot shrugged. 'Why not? Besides,' he added, smiling, 'we don't want hordes of trippers turning up in charabancs. We haven't got room. We do let in the occasional farmer. As well as curing the palsy, St Odelyn was famed for curing diseases of sheep.'

Jack laughed. 'Sheep?'

Darracot grinned. 'Yes. Apparently St Odelyn was a shepherdess. Funnily enough, the Shelton family – the gambling chappie and his relatives – owned a fine flock of Norfolk Horn sheep. They were very valuable. The Norfolk Horn brought a lot of wealth to East Anglia because of the quality of the fleece, but the Sheltons' flock all died off after the reliquary was sold. Our sheep are fine,' he added as an afterthought.

'I'm glad to hear it,' said Bill, turning away.

He drew back. He'd very nearly run into a man standing close behind him. 'I beg your pardon,' he muttered.

'Not at all, sir,' said the man heartily in an unmistakable Irish accent. He gave an apologetic smile. 'I just wanted to see the saint.'

'Of course,' said Jack politely, standing to one side. 'He's an odd sort to find here,' he added in a low voice as they walked round the rest of the exhibition. 'His clothes are clean and neat enough but they don't really fit in, do they?'

'His suit's pretty well-worn,' agreed Bill quietly. 'And his boots are workman's boots.'

'He looked very respectable, though,' said Darracot with a touch of reproof. He wriggled uncomfortably. 'What you've said sounds a bit on the snobby side, don't you know?'

'The entrance fee is a guinea,' said Jack without heat. 'That's a lot of money for someone on a workman's wage. In fact…' he added thoughtfully, looking back to where the man was carefully studying the card under St Odelyn's reliquary. 'Stay here, Bill,' he murmured. 'Don't let Darracot follow me.'

Jack walked back to the exhibit. Bill noticed that Jack's limp, a permanent souvenir of the war, was far more pronounced than usual and he was leaning on his stick.

In a mirroring of what had happened earlier, Jack stood

behind the Irishman, so that when the man turned, he had to draw himself up sharply to avoid bumping into Jack.

Jack gave a sharp hiss and winced to one side, grasping his stick for support. His silver cigarette case, which must have been loose in his pocket, clattered to the floor.

'I beg your pardon, sir,' said the man in sincere apology.

'No – don't mention it,' gasped Jack, his mouth tightening in evident pain. 'My fault. I shouldn't have been in the way.' He glanced down at his cigarette case which had opened in the fall, spilling cigarettes onto the floor.

'I say, would you mind awfully…?' Jack tapped his leg. 'It can be a bit difficult to bend down.'

'Not at all,' said the man.

He bent down, scooped up the cigarettes, replaced them in the case, and, with a pleasant smile and another word of apology, gave the case back to Jack.

'Nicely done,' muttered Bill as Jack limped back across the room to them.

'You saw what I was up to, then?'

Bill grinned. 'Give me some credit.'

Darracot, who obviously hadn't heard what was said, looked at him in concern. 'I say, Haldean, I had no idea your leg was as bad as all that. It looked like it was giving you gyp. Do you need to sit down?'

'No, but thanks for asking. I'm sure it'll be a lot better once we get outside.'

They parted outside the exhibition. Alan Darracot to his hotel, with an invitation to meet up at the club for dinner, and Bill and Jack – his leg miraculously restored to its usual vigour – to Scotland Yard.

'Now then, Sherlock,' said Bill with a grin, once they were

in his office. 'Let's see if there's any recognisable fingerprints on that cigarette case of yours.'

It was the best part of half an hour later when Sergeant Wilcox came into the room.

'We've got a match, sir,' he said, laying the papers on the desk.

Bill rubbed his hands together. 'Have we, by Jove! Thanks, Wilcox,' he added as the sergeant left.

He flicked through the papers in front of him. 'Name, Joseph James Byrne, age forty-three, nationality Irish. Married to Mary Byrne, nee Connolly, with four children.'

'What's he done?' asked Jack.

'He was a cat-burglar,' said Bill. He ran his finger down the page. 'He served in the army until 1918, when he was demobilised with a good record. He was nearly arrested in '20 but disappeared. He turned up in America, came back here in '22, then got nabbed after a busy little spell in '23. He served three years in Wandsworth prison and that, I'm glad to say, seems to have cured him of a life of crime. He's been as clean as a whistle for the last two-and-a-bit years.'

'So what took him to the exhibition?' asked Jack. He took a cigarette from his now done and dusted case and, offering it to Bill, lit one thoughtfully. 'I did wonder if he was casing the joint, as the Americans say, but really, any of the items in the exhibition would be rotten things to steal. I mean, they're beautiful objects, but worth what intrinsically?'

Bill shook his head, frowning. 'Not much, I'd say. Darracot's reliquary, for instance, is a decorated oak box and the others are much the same. Priceless, of course, in one sense, but if you melted down the gold on Darracot's reliquary, it'd only give you three or four sovereigns' worth of gold. No fence would touch it.'

'That's true,' agreed Jack. He shook himself irritably. 'It doesn't add up.'

He sighed. 'Have we got this wrong, Bill? When I stood behind him, waiting to do my bit of acting, I took a good look at him. He was gazing at the reliquary very intently. He said he wanted to see the saint. Given his name and nationality, he's more or less bound to be Catholic. I'm prepared to bet he was praying.'

'That seems unlikely,' said Bill uncomfortably. He glanced at the papers on the desk. 'You're right, though. He is Catholic.'

'And we're all sinners,' said Jack with a grin.

'Granted,' agreed Bill. 'Although it's customary to exclude the present company when making that sort of remark. However, there's enough Catholic churches to pray in without paying a guinea a time to do it.'

'Absolutely. It's a bit of a puzzle, right enough. I'm glad we've got those fingerprints, though. I liked Alan Darracot. Liked him a lot. You know where to start looking if anything does happen to his saint.'

It was before breakfast the next morning that the telephone rang. Yawning, Jack picked up the receiver. 'Hello?'

It was Bill. 'Jack? It's happened.'

'What? Has Darracot's reliquary been stolen?'

'It's worse than that,' said Bill grimly. 'Yes, the reliquary's gone but it's worse than that. It's murder.'

'*Murder?*'

'Yes. Can you meet me at the exhibition? As you were there yesterday, I want your opinion.'

Jack looked at the splayed-out body, crumpled up against the stand which had displayed the reliquary.

Even allowing for the dried blood which coated the left side of his face, the murdered man wasn't an attractive figure. A big man, dressed in thick serge trousers, a collarless shirt and a heavy jacket, he had scraggy grey hair and a jowly, unshaven face. He was, Jack guessed, in his late fifties.

'Who is he?' he asked quietly.

'Frederick Cosby. He was the caretaker and night-watchman. He lived a few streets away from here, in Somerville's Rents. No family – at least I don't have to break the news to a widow – and, from what I've been told, no close friends. In fact,' said Bill, lowering his voice, 'he had a reputation as a morose, grumpy sort of beggar with a foul temper.'

'Yes, he looks as if he could be a tough customer,' said Jack, crouching down beside the body.

He pointed to the walking-stick lying at an angle beside the dead man. It had a heavy rounded end, stained with blood. 'That's the murder weapon, I take it?'

Bill nodded. 'Yes, and a pretty substantial one at that. It's actually Cosby's own stick – he always carried it on his rounds. The only fingerprints on it are Cosby's own, but that's what I'd expect. Even babes in arms know enough to wear gloves these days. As I see it, what happened is that Cosby discovered our thief at work – and, thanks to you, we can probably put a name to the thief – and took him on. And, as you can see, came off worse as a result.'

'Yes, poor devil,' said Jack, straightening up. 'How did the thief get in?'

'Through a window in the attic. It's not such a difficult climb for someone who knows their stuff, and a professional would make easy work of the catches on the window. The method fits our pal Byrne, right enough.'

'So what's wrong?' asked Jack, looking at his friend's expression. 'Something is.'

'The violence,' said Bill. 'That doesn't fit with Byrne's record at all. Like most pros, he avoided violence.'

'Perhaps Cosby didn't give him a choice.'

Bill clicked his tongue. 'He's lost his expertise, if so. He must've heard Cosby coming, with those heavy boots Cosby's wearing.'

'Well, you did say Byrne's been a good boy for the last couple of years. Maybe he has lost his touch.'

'Perhaps.' Bill turned to the stretcher-bearers waiting patiently by the door. 'All right. You can take him away now.'

He waited until they had gone, then drew his breath in impatiently. 'But why steal the ruddy reliquary in the first place, Jack? In fact, come to that, why just steal that one? Nothing else has been touched.'

Jack shrugged. 'Who knows? Maybe the idea was to loot the joint and Cosby joined the party as Byrne started work.'

'Maybe,' agreed Bill morosely. 'Not that any of them are worth stealing. We worked out yesterday that the actual value of all this medieval stuff is a few quid at most, and no fence would touch them with a bargepole.'

Jack, eyes abstracted, said nothing for a few moments. 'It must've been stolen to order,' he said eventually. 'That's the only thing that does make any sense.'

'To order?' repeated Bill.

'Yes. A collector, say? There are some unscrupulous collectors, I know.'

Walking across to the row of seats in the middle of the hall, Jack sat down, his hand to his chin.

'Look,' he said eventually. 'When we had dinner with Darracot last night, he described the chapel where the reliquary is usually kept. I know they allow visitors, and although I didn't say as much, it sounds as if anyone with a plausible tale would be admitted.'

'I thought much the same, but it's been safe for years. What's your point?'

'The point is that it'd be easy – far easier than here – to steal it from the Darracots' chapel. Now *if* I'm right and it's been stolen to order, then my bet is that whoever did order it is visiting this country.'

'That's a leap!' said Bill, startled. 'How d'you work that out?'

Jack grinned. 'Think about it. With the publicity around the exhibition, our collector has only just found out about it. For reasons best known to himself – maybe he has a thing about sheep – he wants it badly. Now, the exhibition finishes in a month. Why not wait until it's safely back home and easily nickable? The answer is that's he a visitor and won't be here in a month.'

'I suppose that's just about possible,' said Bill doubtfully, running a hand through his hair. 'It's not much to go on, though. Any more ideas?'

'Yes,' said Jack with a smile. 'He's a rich bloke, obviously. And I'd also say he's an American.'

'Blimey! Whatever gives you that idea?'

'Because of Byrne's history. Byrne spent time in America. Let's presume he was happily cat-burgling while he was there and met up with this collector chappie in the course of his activities.'

'You're presuming a dickens of a lot, but go on.'

'Now, when our collector fetches up in this country,' continued Jack, ignoring Bill's interruption, 'he calls upon someone he knows: Byrne.'

'It's a whole lot of supposition, Jack. It sounds pretty thin to me.'

'It's an idea, Bill.' He spread his hands wide. 'I might be wrong but at least it's an idea. Say there really is a rich American collector. He could be staying with friends, but on the other hand, he could just as well be staying in a hotel. Claridge's, the Ritz, Browns, the Savoy – any of them would fit the bill and at least it gives you somewhere to start looking.'

'Yes, it does,' Bill agreed reluctantly. 'There's that to be said for it. In the meantime, of course, we've got to look for Joseph Byrne.'

'Don't you know where he is?' asked Jack in surprise.

Bill shook his head. 'No. As far as the law's concerned, he's done his time and he's a free man. As soon as I got the news this morning, I put Sergeant Wilcox and his men onto finding out exactly where we can lay our hands on our Mr Byrne.'

He paused. 'Look, I know I sounded sceptical about your hotel idea, but it's worth a try.'

He tapped his pocket. 'I've got his photograph with me. I showed it to the curator and a couple of the attendants. One did recognise him as being here yesterday but that's it. If Byrne really is working for a rich American, as you suggest, the two of them must've been in touch. We could show it to the staff at the hotels and see if it rings any bells. Claridge's is the nearest. D'you fancy coming and asking a few discreet questions with me? You seem to have a better idea of who we're looking for than I can come up with at the moment.'

'Always willing to help,' said Jack, standing up. 'No job too small. Orders taken, satisfaction guaranteed and families waited upon daily.'

'Idiot,' said Bill with a grin. 'Come on.'

* * *

They struck lucky at the Savoy. The assistant manager, a Mr Andrew Kelvin, picked up the photograph with a startled exclamation. 'Good Lord! Yes, I have seen him. I don't know his name, I'm afraid—'

'We can supply that,' put in Bill quickly. 'His name's Byrne. Joseph Byrne.' He glanced at Jack, who was looking understandably pleased with himself. 'Well done,' he muttered.

'Mr Kelvin,' he continued. 'Did our Mr Byrne just hang about or did he want to see a particular guest?'

Mr Kelvin hesitated.

'It is a police matter,' Bill reassured him. 'A serious matter.'

Mr Kelvin steepled his fingers together. 'As you say, Chief Inspector.' He tapped the photograph on the desk. 'This man – Byrne, you say? – has visited the hotel on three separate occasions. Although always clean and respectable, he was obviously a workman and, as such, stood out. As you imagine, our cliental are not drawn from the labouring classes. We kept a pretty good eye on him,' he added.

'So was he visiting a particular guest?' Bill persisted.

For some reason, Mr Kelvin looked uncomfortable. 'Yes, yes he was.' He hesitated once again. 'You understand, Inspector, that I am anxious to shield the good name of the hotel from any untoward publicity.'

'I quite understand that, sir. Who was the guest?'

Mr Kelvin sighed. 'A Mr Patrick Doyle.'

'Tell me,' said Jack with a pleasant smile, 'is Mr Doyle an American, by any chance? An Irish-American, obviously. Doyle's an Irish name.'

Mr Kelvin nodded.

'And well-off?'

'Immensely so, Major Haldean. In fact,' said Mr Kelvin,

steepling his fingers together once more, 'he's popularly supposed
to be a millionaire. As you can imagine, we were surprised that
Mr Doyle should have the likes of this chap' – he tapped the
photo once again – 'visiting him.'

'We need to speak to Mr Doyle,' said Bill.

Andrew Kelvin shook his head. 'I'm sorry, Chief Inspector.
That's impossible.'

'I'm afraid I must insist.'

Mr Kelvin looked harried. 'No. No, you can't. You don't
understand. Mr Doyle died at four o'clock this morning.'

'*What?*'

Bill and Jack looked at each other in stunned silence.

'How did he die?' asked Bill eventually.

'He had a massive stroke. He was a sick man, Inspector. He
arrived at the hotel just over a month ago. Apparently he'd
been informed that Sir Edward Leitholm of Harley Street was
one of the foremost men in the world for dealing with his
condition. Sir Edward was in attendance when Mr Doyle passed
away. I can assure you, sir, there is no question of anything
untoward.'

Bill shook his head distractedly. 'No. There isn't any suspicion
of that at all. Sir Edward's a very well-known man.'

'What was Mr Doyle suffering from?' asked Jack.

'Sir Edward diagnosed it as Paralysis Agitans.'

'Trembling palsy,' Jack translated slowly. 'Bill! Palsy! It's why
Doyle wanted the reliquary!'

'Blimey,' muttered Bill. 'Jack, you're right. The exhibition was
advertised well in advance. Darracot's reliquary and the story
of Saint Odelyn was featured in the catalogue.'

Mr Kelvin looked understandably bewildered by this exchange.

'I beg your pardon, sir,' Bill apologised. 'We were just putting two and two together. Tell me, did Byrne attempt to see Mr Doyle this morning?'

'As a matter of fact, he did, Inspector. Curtis, the commissioner, reported to me that he'd refused Byrne entry and – although he might have overstepped his authority – told Byrne that Mr Doyle had passed away. To do him justice, Byrne was horrified by the news. According to Curtis, the man was so shaken that Curtis thought he might keel over on the spot. So much so that he let him sit down in the lobby to recover himself.'

'Did he,' asked Jack, 'have a parcel with him at all?'

'Why, yes he did, Major,' said Mr Kelvin in some surprise. 'Apparently he nearly forgot it and Curtis had to remind him to take it when he left.'

Bill sat back in his chair. 'This is game, set and match to you, Jack,' he muttered. 'I think we've found out all we're going to here.'

Standing up, he shook hands with Mr Kelvin. 'Thank you very much for your time, sir. You've been a great help. And, although I can't promise, I'll do my best to keep the hotel's name out of the papers.'

'It strikes me,' said Jack, as they turned onto the Strand, 'that there's something in Alan Darracot's story of St Odelyn taking a firm line with anyone who doesn't treat her with proper respect.'

Bill grinned. 'It's a poor lookout for our pal Byrne if that's the case. Mind you,' he added seriously, 'being nabbed for murder is a poor lookout for him without any saintly interference.'

He glanced at his watch. 'I'd better be getting back to the Yard. I'll let you know when Wilcox gets a lead on Byrne. After that, it's just a matter of making an arrest.' He paused. 'There's nothing really for you to do.'

'No, of course not.' Jack clicked his tongue. 'D'you know, I feel sorry for the poor blighter in a way.'

'File him under "Pleasant murderers I bumped into" if it makes you feel any better.'

Jack smiled briefly. '*Bumped* is the right word. Having him barge into me isn't much of an introduction but I rather took to him. We have got this right, haven't we, Bill?'

'No doubt at all in my mind. And, with any luck, he'll still have Darracot's reliquary. If he's got any sense, he'll have dumped it somewhere, but I'll get the truth out of him. And Jack – before you feel too sorry for him, think of that poor beggar, Cosby.'

It was two days later that Bill rang. 'Jack? You know Darracot said that St Whatsername took a firm line with anyone who treated her with disrespect?'

'Of course I do. Why? What's happened?'

'Byrne's dead.'

'*What?* How?'

'It was an accident at work. Byrne worked as a builder – a roofer. He worked for Blaydon and Platt on the Tottenham Court Road. Byrne lived on Mallerton Street nearby. He went home after finding out the news about Doyle at the Savoy and seemed not at all himself. A bit confused and suffering from a violent headache. However, he went to work and took a dive off the third storey of the house they were re-roofing.'

'Poor beggar.'

'Yeah. You can spare some sympathy for me and Sergeant Wilcox, too. Wilcox got Byrne's address, and when we went round to arrest him we were met with a fine display of grief. It wasn't nice, Jack. His widow seems a decent woman. She was terribly upset, as were the kids. Byrne himself was laid out in a coffin in the parlour. Obviously we had to explain what we were doing there and Mrs Byrne took it as well as could be expected. She said she'd known he'd had something on his mind the past week or so, but she didn't know what.'

'Poor woman.'

'I'll say. She was actually quite helpful. I told her about the reliquary. She didn't know anything about it, but said if Byrne had hidden anything, it'd be in the shed. We didn't find it, either there or anywhere in the house. We looked, believe you me. Funnily enough, I was quite glad in a way.'

'Why?'

'Well, if we had found it, it'd be proof positive that Byrne really did murder Cosby. As it was, I was able to avoid having to make the accusation. Mrs Byrne knew he'd strayed from the straight and narrow on occasion – she said as much – but drew great consolation from the fact he was able to receive the last rites before he died. He's going to be buried with a full Requiem Mass.'

Jack was silent for a few moments. 'That's some sort of consolation, I suppose. Where's the funeral?'

'St Mark the Evangelist in Soho. It's next Thursday. Why?'

'I thought I might go. I can't help feeling a bit guilty. It's a way of saying sorry to the poor beggar. I won't speak to the family, of course, but I'd like to be there.'

'Requiem aeternam donnaeis, Domine.' Jack settled into the pew at the back of St Mark's, mentally translating the familiar words of the mass for the dead. *Eternal rest grant unto them O Lord, and let perpetual light shine upon them…*

The church was fairly full. The family – a large family, supplemented, at a guess, by various aunts, uncles and cousins – were at the front. A solid contingent of soberly dressed men sat on the other side of the church. Fellow workmen, he supposed, the majority of them unsure when to stand, sit or kneel in these unfamiliar surroundings and sobered by the black-cloaked coffin in the middle of the nave.

The mass wound to its conclusion. The pall bearers picked up the coffin as the last prayer started: '*In paradisum deducant te Angeli*'. *May Angels lead thee into Paradise.*

What were the chances of that, Jack wondered. High, he hoped. Despite the chilling sight of Cosby's body and that bloodstained stick. Despite his only acquaintance with Joseph Byrne amounting to those few brief seconds in the exhibition, he'd rather taken to the man.

The congregation departed and Jack followed, pausing at the back of the church, waiting for everyone to leave.

The church newsletter was pinned up on the notice board in the porch.

St Mark the Evangelist, 63, Hob Lane, Soho. Parish Priest: Fr Matthew Croft. Among the list of curates, one name stood out: *Fr Michael Byrne.*

Father *Byrne*! And yes, the celebrant for the funeral was noted as Father Byrne! It was a common enough Irish name, but if Joseph Byrne and Michael Byrne were related, that explained why the funeral was here, in Soho, and not in Joseph Byrne's parish church.

Jack looked at the crowd outside the door. First there was the burial and then the wake, but tomorrow he'd pay a visit to Father Byrne.

Father Byrne, a man about Jack's own age, waved him to a chair in his sitting room in the presbytery. 'Were you at the funeral yesterday?' he asked.

Jack nodded. 'Yes, I was.'

'I thought I saw you. Did you know Uncle Joe?'

Uncle! Jack felt a rush of satisfaction. 'Not really,' he said. 'Let me explain…'

Michael Byrne was an attentive listener. 'It was very sad about Cosby,' he commented when Jack had finished. 'However, I can reassure you, Mr Haldean. Uncle Joe was not a murderer.'

Jack looked up sharply. This could be nothing more than family loyalty, but… 'How can you be sure?'

'I was called to the hospital. I heard Uncle Joe's confession and gave him the last rites. I can't tell you what he said, of course, but he was no murderer. In those circumstances, nobody lies.'

'No,' Jack agreed. 'They wouldn't.' He took a cigarette from the box Father Byrne offered. 'You can tell me one thing, though. How did your uncle know Patrick Doyle?'

Michael Byrne smiled. 'Oh, that's easy enough. They grew up together in the same village. Killybegg in County Wicklow. Patrick Doyle went to New York and became a very rich man. When Uncle Joe found it convenient to leave London, Doyle gave him a few jobs.'

'You uncle was an expert cat-burglar,' muttered Jack.

'He was,' agreed Byrne. 'That's the sort of job I mean.' He sighed. 'Doyle was no saint and neither was Uncle Joe, but a spell in Wandsworth – you said you knew about that – made him a reformed man. However' – he gestured with his cigarette – 'when Doyle came to London, he hoped for a cure. His doctor was the finest, but Doyle had heard about this St Odelyn. Doyle was a lapsed Catholic – *very* lapsed – but he pinned his hopes on the saint. He couldn't get to the exhibition, so he asked Uncle Joe to bring the saint to him. Uncle Joe did it as a favour. He refused to take any money from Doyle.'

Jack stubbed out his cigarette in the ashtray. 'Look. You've told me your uncle wasn't a murderer. I believe you. You can't tell me what he said in his confession, but if I tell you what I think happened, maybe you can say if I'm on the right lines.'

Father Byrne nodded slowly.

'Your uncle was in cahoots with Cosby, the watchman.' Byrne looked startled. 'It's obvious,' said Jack. 'Your uncle was a skilled man. He could've easily avoided Cosby. They were in it together.'

Once again, Byrne nodded. 'Cosby promised to look the other way.'

'But, at a guess, he got greedy.'

'He did!' exclaimed Father Byrne, startled into agreement. 'Uncle Joe was there for St Odelyn, but Cosby wanted him to take more.'

'And so they quarrelled. At another guess,' said Jack, choosing his words carefully, 'Cosby attacked your uncle with that stick of his – he had a bump on his head which made him dizzy – and Cosby came off worse.'

Father Byrne lit another cigarette. 'You're right,' he said slowly. 'Uncle Joe shouldn't have been there but it was self-defence.'

Jack nodded. 'He got away with the reliquary. He couldn't give it to Doyle. If the police found it in the house, they'd take that as proof of murder. As it is, the police have no proof because they haven't got the reliquary.'

No, they hadn't. So what had happened to it? Joseph Byrne knew he was holding the bones of a saint. If he'd dumped the reliquary, it would've been somewhere Byrne deemed suitable. A church? Yes. But that would've been reported…

He looked at Byrne's strained face and decided to back a hunch.

'Have you got it?'

Byrne's startled gasp and expression told him he'd struck gold.

'I couldn't leave it in the shed,' he said. 'It's a holy relic! I knew where he hid things. Aunty Mary knew nothing about the reliquary, but I knew if the police found it, it'd be as you say. His name would be blackened. She and the children would always live in shame.'

He stood up and, walking to a cupboard, opened the door. 'Here it is. What now, Mr Haldean? I can't go to the police. They'd never believe me. No one knows I've got it. I don't know what to do with it.'

His face twisted. 'I feel sorry for your friend, Captain Darracot. I'd like him to have it back. I was at Passchendaele in the war. I know what that was like. He sounds a fine man.'

'Maybe,' said Jack slowly, 'we can think of something.'

Jack called into Bill's office that afternoon.

'Bill, without asking any awkward questions and knowing I'm on the side of the angels…'

Bill looked up warily. 'What are you after?'

'Can you find me a reformed cat burglar?'

Dennis Robins swarmed up the side of the building.

Jack looked on in admiration. That was some climb in the dark and that drainpipe hadn't looked any too secure.

Robbins, seemingly glued onto the high windowsill, took a knife from his pocket. There was a brief pause and then a click.

'We're in,' came a carrying whisper. Moments later, a rope ladder tumbled down the side of the wall. 'All secure, Major.'

Jack, knapsack on his back, started to climb.

He swung himself over the attic windowsill with some relief.

'Thanks,' he said quietly. 'Wait for me here. I'll be as quick as I can.'

Bill, a copy of the *Daily Messenger* in his hand, charged into Jack's sitting room. 'Have you seen this? Look at the headline!'

Jack picked up the paper Bill thrust at him and grinned. '"Miracle at the Manorbier Street Museum!"' he read out loud. 'Yes, I've seen it. "The reliquary containing the remains of St Odelyn, stolen in appalling circumstances from the Manorbier Museum, has mysteriously returned! Rumours abound that St Odelyn, known in her lifetime for feats of levitation, herself willed her mortal remains back to the safety of the museum..."'

'You know about this,' stated Bill accusingly. 'You and Dennis Robins. Jack, we're talking about a murder. Murder!'

Jack shook his head. 'No, we're not.'

'What? Don't try and tell me it's a ruddy miracle.'

'Of course it isn't,' said Jack with a laugh. 'But let me tell you a story...'

Jørn Lier Horst

Jørn Lier Horst is one of Scandinavia's most successful crime authors. A former head of investigations, he brings a unique blend of realism and suspense to his award-winning William Wisting novels, offering detailed insights into police work and media dynamics. With over ten million books sold and translations in more than forty countries, his work has earned accolades like the Norwegian Booksellers' Prize, the Glass Key, and the Martin Beck Award.

jlhorst.com

Anne Bruce (translator) studied Norwegian and English at Glasgow University, before going on to work in education. Anne is now a translator, mainly of Nordic Noir, including crime fiction by Jørn Lier Horst, Anne Holt and Heine Bakkeid. Novels she has translated have twice won the Petrona Prize, twice been shortlisted for LAMBDA Literary Awards and three times been longlisted for the CWA International Dagger. Several have also been filmed as TV series, most recently *Wisting* and *Modus*.

THE PERFECT MURDER

Jørn Lier Horst
Translated by Anne Bruce

Scattered banks of fog drifted in from sea and lay like clouds of steam on the wet asphalt, forming small haloes around the streetlamps.

Alan Brown drove with both hands on the steering wheel. He had worked as a criminal lawyer for more than forty years, and knew how important it was to maintain focus and concentration. Nevertheless, there was one idea he had toyed with from his very first day in the courtroom. When the prosecution's arguments became deathly tedious, or the judge's summing up grew boringly repetitive, he sometimes let his gaze linger on a carafe of water as he asked himself the question: how to commit the perfect murder?

As a matter of fact, the idea had been there long before he started working in courtrooms. He had entered into childish roleplay with greater enthusiasm than any of his playmates, and sometimes strayed beyond the limits of the game. His pockets filled up with odds and ends from the other boys' rooms – Lego bricks, plastic cars and money. From time to time he stole things he neither wanted nor had any use for, but he took them because these items meant something to their owners, or quite simply because it was possible to steal them without anyone noticing.

As a rule, he was found out. Either by his mother, who emptied pockets before loading the washing machine, or by the other children. To begin with, he had managed to avoid recriminations for these thefts by arguing that it was just part of the game, or by blaming the others, but eventually he had realised that these petty crimes were far from worthwhile. He had stopped stealing, but had continued the discussions. He enjoyed taking issue with people, not necessarily because he disagreed with them, but because he liked to find counterarguments and objections.

It was this talent for words that had led him into his role as an advocate, but long before he had achieved success at the legal bench, he had harboured the supressed desire to commit a crime. A perfect crime. And as the years passed, it became clearer to him that any old crime would not do. It would have to be a serious and irreversible act. A murder.

He smiled at the thought. He would commit The Perfect Murder.

The exit road was difficult to see in the darkness of night. He dropped his speed before turning off from the main road and drove onto the crunching gravel. The light from his headlamps swept across the bare, sprawling branches of the trees that stood sentinel along the track.

A fleeting glance in the mirror. The grey eyes in his wide face narrowed into thin lines. No one had spotted him, but all the same he felt his pulse accelerate. His hands were clammy on the wheel.

So far in his career he had defended thirty-eight killers, and they had all been found guilty. But although they had all been convicted, Alan Brown knew he was regarded as one of the foremost defence lawyers in the country. After all, ninety-nine per cent of all homicide prosecutions ended in guilty verdicts. The work of a good defence counsel was to construct a strategy to bring his client the minimum sentence possible. This was what he excelled at, creating a plan and building a strategy. He could cause the prosecution for a premeditated act to end up with a conviction for involuntary manslaughter, or he could convince the court that an intentional killing was actually a case of grievous bodily harm resulting in death. To his clients, the difference comprised several years spent in freedom rather than behind bars.

No, his efforts as a defence lawyer had not been wasted. On the contrary, in fact. He had learned from every single mistake those thirty-eight men had made. Being deprived of his liberty was not something he feared. He had dreamed up a perfect plan, and he would commit a perfect murder.

The old road was uneven, covered in potholes and dirty puddles. It twisted its way forward for three quarters of a kilometre through dense woodland before ascending to a ridge, where he stopped the van and left the engine idling. The moon was still behind the clouds, but the fog had dissipated and he could make out the contours of the black fjord swathed in heavy rain. As expected, the summer cottages lay in darkness. Only the bright beams from the lighthouse out on the headland swept across the landscape.

In time, as his career advanced, the idea of The Perfect Murder became almost an obsession. The plan he had made might seem simple, but it was precise down to the smallest detail, and he had designed it with an enthusiasm and passion such as he could only recall from his first days in court. He had longed for that feeling: the satisfaction of not overlooking anything, of getting everything to work out.

The pure sense of perfection.

Selecting a victim had been the most important aspect. And Ann Ortiz was the perfect choice.

He smiled as the van moved forward again and he began the descent towards the sea.

One consideration had been that he was physically stronger than her. This made the actual killing easier, but she also had all the other characteristics necessary for him to get away with the crime. She was forty-one years old, recently divorced and in receipt of disability benefit because of a back injury. With no children, she had an extremely restricted circle of acquaintances. She lived a reclusive life that meant days, maybe weeks, would pass before she was missed. That was the advantage of his plan. He had observed this in the courtroom, how time worked against the investigators, erasing evidence and giving the perpetrator a head start. The greater the gulf between the actual crime and the point in time when it was discovered, the more difficult the task of the police became. The leader of an investigation had once explained in the witness box how critical the first twenty-four hours are. If the investigation has not found a basis and direction within that timescale, then they are hopelessly on the back foot thereafter.

Following that case, he had placed great emphasis on the time aspect in all the defence work he undertook. A lengthy timespan facilitated the creation of doubt in witnesses. They all became hesitant when confronted by the possibility that the timing of an observation might differ from what the police presumed.

He glanced once again in the mirror as he drove onto the gravel surface of the parking area at the end of the track, before reversing to park with the rear doors facing the path that led to the sea.

The clock on the dashboard edged from 01.23 to 01.24. He felt the pressure in his chest increase – the finale was fast approaching now.

He had learned one thing from all the pathologists he had cross-examined: it was possible to deduce a great deal from a dead body. However, contrary to what is suggested by crime films on TV, establishing a precise time of death is not one of the things for which science can provide an exact answer. Parts of his plan depended on this very fact, that the further a corpse has progressed in the process of decomposition, the greater the uncertainty regarding the forensic evidence.

Yet, even though Ann Ortiz's time of death would never be established with any certainty, the timing nevertheless played an important part in his plan.

There is an unusually low tide on the night between Maundy Thursday and Good Friday, and in thirty-seven minutes the tide would be at its very lowest. Almost ten years ago, an oceanographer had explained the phenomenon in the witness box during a trial against a businessman accused of involuntary manslaughter following a boat accident. 'The Good Friday Low Tide' was the expression he had used, and he had gone on to explain that it was decided at the Council of Nicaea in the year 325 that Easter should be celebrated on the Sunday following the first full moon after the vernal spring equinox. And so the moon and the leaders of the Christian Church are to blame for the fact that Easter does not have a fixed date, like Christmas. The respective positions of the Earth, the moon and the sun at this time of year also mean that tidal water is pulled back by the full moon to an extreme point. Along this particular coast, the difference between spring and neap tides could be nearly a metre and a half.

Successful lawyer Alan Brown stepped out of the van, brushed his jacket sleeve and adjusted his tie before breathing in the fresh tang of salt sea air. He was well aware that both his legal colleagues and his clients called him Mr Perfect when they thought he was out of earshot. He revelled in the nickname, and knew it referred not only to the newly ironed shirts he always wore or the knife-edge pleat on his trousers, but also the way he executed his duties as a defence lawyer. The way he assiduously prepared and never overlooked anything, not even the tiniest detail.

The same applied now. Everything had been thoroughly thought through. He had devised a perfect plan.

He squinted out into the darkness to confirm that the theoretical account of the tides also applied in practice. The sloping bed of the fjord had withdrawn for quite a stretch, and the waves murmured in the far distance.

It struck him that many of his clients had fallen foul of false alibis. This was a trap he would not step into. If he were ever asked at any time about where he had been on the night before Good Friday, he would give the following answer: 'Sorry, officer, but I've a dreadful alibi. I'm afraid I was in bed at home, fast asleep. On my own.' But after all, it was doubtful if the question would ever be posed. It was not that he was reluctant to be questioned when the police embarked upon their investigation, but with the assistance of the Good Friday low tide, he would ensure that the police could never establish a precise time for the murder.

As one of the victim's nearest neighbours, he would be one

of the first to be called in for questioning by the police when Ann Ortiz was reported missing and later found murdered. They would also discover that they primarily had a professional relationship through the assistance he had given her in connection with her divorce settlement.

In fact, he was looking forward to the police interview. His satisfaction at being cleared of suspicion of murder would be even greater if he had been questioned. It was as if there was no point in committing the perfect murder if questions were not asked.

The perfect murder had been the subject of several crime novels he had read. Some writers seemed to believe that a murder that was not discovered – when the victim simply disappears without the police launching an investigation – should be regarded as a perfect murder. In Brown's opinion, this was cheating. His plan involved the corpse being found, and the investigators never being in any doubt that they were dealing with a murder.

He skirted around the vehicle, opened the passenger door and took out his Wellington boots.

The interview would make one thing clear to the investigators above all else, he thought as he changed his footwear. He lacked a motive.

That was a crucial part of the plan. There was no reason for him to have killed Ann Ortiz. If there was one thing he had learned in the courtroom over the past forty years, it was how revealing a motive can be. This is what investigators are always searching for, someone who has something to gain by the other person's death. If they found only one person to direct their suspicions at, then the evidence left in the wake of the crime would be easier to locate.

His plan also included the oldest and most useful defence tactic – directing suspicion at other people. He probably didn't even have any need to draw the investigators' attention. Ann's ex-husband would stand out from day one. Gerardo Ortiz was a temperamental Italian, and exactly the right piece of the puzzle he needed to ensure his plan was perfect. Four years had passed since her ex-husband had moved out, but it had been only in January that Ann had approached him and asked for professional help to have the divorce settlement finalised. Brown had delegated the work to one of his subordinates at the office, but had quickly understood why her husband had dragged his heels with the legal niceties. Gerardo Ortiz earned his living as a used car salesman. He had two bankruptcies behind him, and still appeared to be running his business at the expense of his creditors. In order to avoid their ever-increasing financial demands, he had put all his valuables in Ann's name. This meant that, in addition to their grand villa, she was sole owner of three commercial properties, shares, an apartment in Sardinia and a forty-two-foot yacht.

The preliminary meeting between them was fixed for four weeks' time. It would be difficult for Gerardo Ortiz's lawyer to argue for the sole ownership issue to be set aside, but upon Ann's death, all her assets would pass to the spouse to whom she was still married, at least on paper.

It was the same motive that cropped up time and again in the courtroom: money.

Alan Brown walked around the vehicle, a Peugeot Partner, a small two-seater goods van. It too belonged to Ann Ortiz and would become part of the dead woman's estate.

Even statistics would be on his side. In seventy-nine per cent of all murder cases, the victim and the killer were related. As far as the cases he had defended in court were concerned, the figure was higher still.

It was a cold night, and his breath formed a hazy white mist in front of his face. Brown looked all around before opening the rear doors. The interior light came on, and there his victim lay.

It was part of the plan for him to use her vehicle to transport the body. Finding the victim's DNA in the van would be worth zilch as evidence in a courtroom. Four days earlier, he had borrowed Ann's van, using the excuse that he needed to move an old carpet to the local dump. Actually, it was not very old, but it did not match the new suite he had bought and had to be replaced all the same. Ann's small van was practical, and in view of everything he had done for her in connection with her imminent divorce settlement, she could not refuse.

He had made sure he was seen, and even struck up a conversation with his next-door neighbour over the garden fence as he folded up the carpet and squeezed it into the van. He had also kept the receipt from the recycling centre.

Leaning forward, he took hold of her leg and hauled the dead woman nearer to the opening. She was not completely cold yet.

One of the first things he had decided upon was his choice of modus operandi. He had strangled her, a method that had brought him closest to his victim. He held his hands up in front of his face and stared at them. It almost seemed as if he could still feel the sensation of placing them around her neck muscles and throttling her until he felt life dwindle away between his fingers.

The police would never find the scene of crime. He had gone through with it in her living room, but the place bore no signs of a struggle. There had not been any kind of struggle, anyway. He had rung her doorbell just before ten o'clock and she had seemed taken aback, but had let him in when he explained that he had found out something about Gerardo that she should know. Once inside, she had understood nothing of what was happening, not until he had put his arms around her neck and held her in an iron grip. Initially her eyes had shone with surprise, and then her gaze had changed to fear and panic before it became empty and lifeless.

He moved the body and the dim interior light fell on her face. Her eyes were still wide open and stared stiffly up at him through the clear plastic.

The cling-film he had wrapped around her head was a detail that had struck him only a few days prior to the murder, but it was important to ensure that the investigators would be in no doubt that they were dealing with a murder. The time that would elapse before she was found could make it difficult to establish the cause of death with any certainty, or even decide whether it was caused by an accident or a crime. A pathologist had once clarified the external signs of strangulation in the witness box: fingernails that had punctured the skin, bruises caused by hands or fingers, and pinprick haemorrhaging on both skin and mucous membranes. All of these were signs that disappeared in time. Even a fractured larynx was difficult to discover in a corpse that had decomposed, according to the pathologist.

After having twisted the cling-film around her head, he had tied a strong rope around her neck. No one would be in any doubt that this was a case of what the newspapers would describe as a grotesque murder.

The plastic had another function, too – it guarded against trace evidence. Strangulation leaves no blood behind, but quantities of hair in the luggage compartment could cause the investigators to ask disturbing questions.

Moreover, there was the business of secondary transfer. A former FBI agent had once given evidence on this, describing how hairs from a murder victim had attached themselves to the perpetrator's clothing and been carried home by him. Even though the police had not found DNA at the crime scene or on the victim, a tiny strand of hair from the body on the man's jacket had been enough to link the perpetrator to the victim. Of course, there were a number of simple explanations for hairs from Ann Ortiz turning up in his home – for instance, they could have been transferred from the headrest on the van he had borrowed – but given the possibility of eliminating this risk, it was worthwhile doing so.

He tugged his lapels together at his neck and glanced up at the sky. Somewhere behind those clouds, the Good Friday full moon was hiding.

He drew the body closer to the open doors. Ann's garage was an integral one, with an entrance into the kitchen. He had been able to carry her through the house and straight into the van without any danger of anyone seeing him. Another part of the plan was that the neighbours who overlooked the garage doors were on holiday, and out here the darkness would cover his tracks.

Hoisting the body into a seated position, he leaned it against the inside of the boot. Then he hunkered down, draped the body over his shoulders, and got to his feet using a fireman's lift. He had seen this demonstrated in the courtroom once in relation to a death by wilful fire-raising, and remembered how this simple technique enabled a person to carry relatively heavy loads over long distances and still keep one hand free.

His weekly runs would now pay dividends, he thought, as he jerked his upper body to balance the dead woman comfortably on his shoulders. Jogging and his daily press-ups on the bathroom floor. Being in good physical shape was a necessary requirement to succeed with his plan.

He bent his knees a little, threading his right arm between her legs, grabbed hold of the arm that dangled loosely on the other side and drew the two limbs together. Her arm crossed his chest, almost like the strap on a rucksack.

He took a couple of tentative steps, confirming that the dead body lay surprisingly steady around his neck and shoulders before using his free hand to pick up the thick rope lying in the van – this rope formed the nucleus of his plan.

The crime he was in the process of committing was the result of all the knowledge he had mastered through years of experience in the courtroom. He dwelt on that as he struggled to nudge the van doors shut. The investigators would not find any trace of his meticulous planning. He had not searched for answers on the internet or borrowed books from the library that might disclose his preparations. Everything was down to experience. Years of experience. And the most important point he had picked up in the courtroom was to create the maximum distance in time between the crime and the start of the investigation.

The rope was the solution. The rope and the extremely low tide.

Quite simply, the plan demanded that he carry the body as far out into the fjord as the low tide would allow, find a suitable stone, and tie her tightly to the seabed. When the water level returned to normal in only a few hours, Ann Ortiz would lie concealed beneath the waves.

This critical segment of the plan had fallen into place when the chief pathologist at the Forensic Medicine Institute had given evidence in general terms about a body recovered from the sea. He had explained how the length of time in the water slowly but surely caused a human corpse to decompose. Disintegration in sea water can separate hands, feet and head from the body. This specific case had to do with a severed hand that had been found before the rest of the body had been washed ashore. The pathologist explained that the reason for the hand being torn off while the rest of the body remained intact had probably been that the dead woman had been wearing a heavy bracelet. The currents in the water had caused this to rub a hole in her skin, and later fish and crustaceans had assisted with the rupturing process. Approximately six to eight weeks had elapsed before the hand and the remainder of the body had separated.

Six to eight weeks. That meant it would be June by the time the rope that held Ann Ortiz fastened to the seabed would have eaten its way through her wrist and set her free. For two months her disappearance would be treated as a missing person case, and not until every trail had gone cold would it dawn on the investigators that this was a case of murder.

Alan Brown took the first few steps down towards the beach. A damp wind swept in from sea across the land, carrying tiny grains of salt. He felt a really special kind of satisfaction, like the one he had when he resumed his seat after delivering his closing address in the courtroom. The thought that his plan would reach its conclusion in only a few more minutes sent a jittery feeling through his stomach.

He speculated on what the newspapers would call the murder. They always gave them some kind of nickname, usually after the place where the body had been found. He grimaced. 'The

Langvik Killing' was not particularly exciting. Maybe they would use the modus operandi instead. 'The Woman in Plastic', perhaps?

He had travelled three hundred metres from land and the original shoreline when he began to wonder whether he would have to alter his plan. The heft of the dead body was not really a problem, but the waterlogged sand was giving way beneath his weight. Mud and silt were making his boots stick fast and every step had become a struggle. The perspiration on his forehead felt ice-cold in the biting wind. Maybe he should look around for a spot where he could anchor the body right now, further inland than he had intended?

The beam from the lighthouse skimmed across the landscape, allowing him to look ahead to the white strip where the sea met the land. The distance to this spot was two hundred metres or so, and he forced himself to walk on. His plan was fixed, and he meant to follow it through. He could not let it fail simply because he was not strong enough.

He lowered his neck and stared rigidly down at what had been the soft seabed only a few hours ago. When he lifted his eyes again, he estimated the distance to have halved, but now he seriously began to feel the weight of the dead body. He took longer and longer to shift his feet, with the result that they had longer to sink into the quaggy mud. Sheer determination forced him to stagger onwards.

When he had finally reached the water's edge, the tide was already turning. Exhausted, he dropped to his knees and turned aside to topple the corpse from his shoulders.

Nothing happened.

He jerked his upper body to force the body to slide off, but the stiff corpse was firmly wedged. He pulled on the arm across his chest and tried to disentangle the foot, but the limbs did not budge and seemed securely attached to him.

Fear crept along his spine and he tried to stand up, but his burden was too heavy. Panic made him start to crawl back towards dry land, writhing and bucking like a trapped animal, but he was well aware how useless it was to try to remove the weight from his shoulders. He just could not understand how he could have overlooked this one minor detail when he concocted his plan. He had read more than enough pathology reports to know that rigor mortis affects the muscles of the body two to four hours after death, and loosens its hold only gradually after two to three days.

As a wave rolled in, licking at the lawyer's feet, Alan Brown realised that his plan had been only almost completely perfect.

Leigh Russell

Leigh Russell has sold nearly 2 million books in her Geraldine Steel crime series. She also writes the popular cosy crime series the Poppy Mystery Tales. Shortlisted for two CWA Dagger Awards, and the People's Book Prize, Leigh is Chair of the CWA Emerging Authors Judges panel. She is an Advisory Royal Literary Fellow and a freelance editor.

leighrussell.co.uk.

BEST LAID PLANS

Leigh Russell

Miranda scowled. 'I don't know why you want to visit her after all this time. It must be years since you last saw her. How long has it been? It's not as if you're close to her. She probably won't even recognise you.'

'That's not the point. She's family, and she hasn't got anyone else.'

'Well, why can't you go on your own, if you're so keen to see her? I don't know why you want me to go with you.'

Peter frowned. In his mid-fifties, he still retained the good looks that had first attracted Miranda. Ten years younger than him, she would be the first to admit that she had let herself go.

'We've been through this. It's all planned,' he replied, as though his plans were immutable. 'You may not care about meeting my great-aunt, but this is important to me.'

What's important to you is finding out who's going to inherit all her money. You plan to talk her into leaving it to you. Instead of voicing her accusation, Miranda merely said, 'Well, I think it's very kind of you to want to visit the old lady. Not everyone would bother about a great-aunt they haven't seen for decades. I just don't see why I have to come with you.'

She didn't add that with Peter out of the way, she would be free to spend a few days doing exactly what she wanted, without being constantly hounded by him. She couldn't remember the last time she had been free to enjoy herself without him watching her. Far from relaxing his hold on her, over the years he had restricted her freedom more and more, as though he knew she wanted to escape from him and was determined to suffocate the last remnants of her independence. The thought that he would one day retire and be at home with her all day filled her with dread. Only her lack of confidence held her captive. And her lack of money. If anyone needed his great-aunt's fortune, she did.

'I must say, I don't know why you put up with him,' her friend, Rosie, had said to her the last time they had spoken. She had upbraided Miranda as though it was somehow shameful to remain married after fifteen years.

To be fair to Rosie, she had a point, because it had been a miserable fifteen years. Miranda sometimes asked herself why she had stayed with Peter for so long, but the sad truth was that she didn't know what else to do. She hadn't been apprehensive about the future before she met her husband, but somehow, since her marriage, she had lost her spirit of adventure and found herself feeling anxious all the time. Mostly she was afraid of provoking Peter's temper, which she still managed to do with depressing frequency, however carefully she tried to please him.

'That man treats you like a skivvy,' Rosie had protested, when Miranda had described how she spent her days. 'I think it's a disgrace, the way he behaves. Seriously, Miranda, you can't possibly be happy living with that selfish bastard.'

'He's not selfish,' Miranda had retorted, stung because she knew Rosie was right. 'That's my husband you're talking about,' she added indignantly. 'And as it happens, we're perfectly happy, thank you very much, so I suggest you stop interfering in matters that don't concern you. You don't know the first thing about my husband.'

Miranda had once made the mistake of admitting that Peter did not want her going out to work, and Rosie had never let that go.

'It's the twenty-first century, for goodness' sake. How can you tolerate such blatant misogyny? It's borderline criminal. Honestly, Miranda, why do you put up with it? Don't you want a career, and a life of your own?'

'I'm fine as I am,' she had lied.

She regretted not having walked out years ago, before her spirit had been crushed, but it was too late now. Not having worked for fifteen years, she had no prospect of earning a living and no savings of her own. Peter had made sure of that. Sometimes she almost felt that she might be better off homeless than living in this trap she had entered so blindly. It was hard to believe that Peter's attitude towards her working had attracted her to him when they had first met. When he had asked her to marry him, she had seized the opportunity to abandon her failing career, believing she would be happy to stay at home and escape the pressures of work. She had been happy at first, caught up in the whirlwind of romance, predicated on Peter's good looks and successful career. But all too soon, the relationship had turned sour.

While she no longer had to get up early for a job she detested, she still had to be up early to make Peter's breakfast, and the demands of her dull job were replaced by interminable house-hold chores. Peter's standards of cleanliness were exacting, leaving her very little time to herself. She began to fantasise about coming into some money of her own. That dream was one of her few comforts, since she had lost all hope of having a family. A child would have brought joy and purpose into her life, but Peter had rejected that idea. Although she had no way of knowing, she suspected he had privately taken steps to ensure he never fathered a child. She had confronted him with her conjecture once, but he had flown into a temper and she hadn't dared broach the subject again. If only she could become financially independent, she would be able to escape her life of drudgery. It wouldn't have to be a fortune. Her needs were modest. She would need just enough to pay for a cosy little flat of her own where she could live unfettered, and start to rebuild her life in quiet and reflective solitude, free from fear.

Over breakfast one morning, she had tentatively suggested she might look for a job. Peter had laughed. Used to his rages, she had misread the signs.

'Don't I provide for you?' he had asked softly.

'Yes, but I want to earn money of my own.'

Realising she was serious, he had glared at her with a cold hard anger that was somehow more menacing than his furious tempers. Too late, the subtle flaring of his nostrils and the ferocious glare of his eyes had alerted her to the danger. Without another word, he had snatched her phone from the table, dragged her upstairs and locked her in the bedroom. Shutting herself in the en suite bathroom, she had wept for a whole day, cursing herself for her helplessness. That evening, he had unlocked the door and let her out.

'You're behind with the laundry,' was all he had said when she emerged, red-eyed and trembling.

Neither of them ever mentioned that day again.

Muttering darkly about 'coercive control', Rosie had accused her of being a doormat when Miranda had stopped leaving the house to meet her friend. After that disagreement, Miranda and Rosie had carefully avoided the subject of marriage whenever they spoke on the phone. They had been friends since school, and neither of them wanted to fall out, but gradually Rosie stopped calling. She had been right. Miranda always kowtowed to Peter, even when his wishes were opposed to her own. And so, as she was protesting that she didn't want to go and visit his great-aunt, Miranda knew that she would cave in. She hated herself for being so compliant, but she felt intimidated by her husband. They both knew the power he had over her.

'My great-aunt is bound to think more kindly of us if we both turn up,' Peter said firmly. 'The truth is, you're not completely stupid. In fact, you can actually be quite charming when you put your mind to it, and we want to make the visit as enjoyable as possible for her, poor old dear. She's all on her own now. Anyway,' he went on, 'she's expecting us. I told her we'll both be going and we can't disappoint her. She's looking forward to meeting you, so you're coming with me and that's final. I've planned everything. All you have to do is come with me and be pleasant to her.'

'It's such a long way,' she bleated, but they both knew she would comply as she always did. Rosie's words came back to her: 'coercive control'. Pushing the thought to the back of her mind, she heaved a sigh. 'I'd better go and pack, then.'

Not knowing how long they would be staying, and reluctant to question Peter about his plans, she ended up packing far too much for a short trip. When she had dragged her heavy case down the stairs, Peter suggested she make some sandwiches for the journey. A suggestion from him was as good as a command. She couldn't refuse. With a terse nod, she went to the kitchen. The bread bin was empty.

'Pathetic,' Peter's firm lips curled with derision. 'How are you going to make sandwiches without any bread?'

'I'll go and check in the freezer,' she said quickly.

'Don't put yourself out,' Peter snapped. 'Leave it to me to sort out.' He groaned, as though he was fed up with her for bungling everything.

She nodded. She had recently run down the contents of the big chest freezer, which needed a good clean, but she thought there was still a loaf of sliced bread left in there, along with some frozen peas. Muttering about having to do everything himself, Peter went to the utility room, which was off the kitchen, to search for bread. Miranda rummaged in the fridge, trying to decide whether Peter would prefer cheese or ham in his sandwiches, and deciding to make both so he would have a choice. As she was opening the packets, a panicked yell rang out, followed by a crash that seemed to reverberate round the kitchen. The noise came from the utility room. Startled, she hurried after Peter, wondering what he could have knocked over. He was bound to blame her for leaving whatever it was perched precariously somewhere. She guessed it must have been the laundry basket plummeting onto the hard tiled floor.

But the blue plastic laundry basket was still where she had left it on the worktop, packed with neatly folded clean towels – Peter insisted on his towels being washed after each use. It was completely unnecessary. She suspected he wouldn't have been so fixated on hygiene if he had to do the laundry himself, but she had long ago given up trying to argue with him. For a few seconds she looked around the utility room, puzzled. Something had fallen, making a resounding noise, but she couldn't see anything out of place. She had seen her husband go through the door from the kitchen into utility room a moment earlier, but now there was no sign of him. She started to go back into the kitchen.

As she turned her head, her attention was caught by a hand dangling over the edge of the open freezer. Peter must have fallen in and made a futile attempt to pull himself out by stretching up to grab hold of the edge of the freezer. Hurrying over to look, she was shocked to see him lying crumpled inside it. Presumably he had leaned over, reaching for the solitary loaf of bread right at the bottom, and fallen in. She supposed he had hit his head, knocking himself out, because he wasn't moving and he gave no sign that he heard her calling him. He didn't even stir when she reached down cautiously and shook him by the elbow. The movement dislodged his outstretched arm, which fell onto him with a faint thud, but he didn't open his eyes. Transfixed with horror, she stared down at his ghastly white face, tinged with blue.

Suddenly his eyes opened and a trembling hand reached up to her in a gesture of supplication, or command. Startled, she drew back, her eyes locked on his. She thought she saw his lips part but he made no sound; silence seemed to engulf her, suffocating her.

Abruptly the freezer began to hum loudly. Reacting automatically to the warning sound, she slammed the lid down. The thump as it shut sounded aggressively loud. With an effort, she slowed her breathing and waited until her confusion cleared.

'I'd better get going,' she announced at last, when she had recovered sufficiently to speak. 'I don't want to miss the train, not when your great-aunt is expecting us. I know you put a lot of effort into planning this visit, and I'll do my best to see it's worth all your trouble. Don't worry, I'll make your apologies and tell her you're too busy at work to get away right now. I'm sure she won't be too disappointed, because I'm going to be a great comfort to her. With any luck, I'll persuade her to make me her beneficiary. I dare say I can prevail on her to see me as a deserving relative, if I butter her up enough. At least I'll be there for her. Well, I can't hang about or I'll miss the train.' She paused for a moment, musing. 'It's a pity, but she probably doesn't have a chest freezer. They're such useful appliances. Really, every home should have one.' Stepping away from the freezer, she added, 'I do hope the old lady isn't unsteady on her feet, especially when she's going down the stairs. You really can't be too careful. Anyone can fall over, and the consequences can be dire. But I don't need to tell *you* that, do I?'

Peter Guttridge

Peter Guttridge has written eighteen daft crime novels but is now writing an equally daft two-book eighteenth-century-Sussex-smuggler thing that Netflix are interested in. Who knew?

GO SWALLOW A CANE TOAD

Peter Guttridge

The killing was bloody but not savage. One rip of the throat. Sonny Clark and DS Moon stayed out of the pool of blood and looked down at the man sprawled on his back. The desk chair was on its side close by. Sprays of blood on the laptop on his desk. A bone-handled knife lay in the pool of blood.

'Approximate time of death?' DS Moon asked the Scene of Crime Officer.

'Hard to say yet, sir, except that he's been dead a couple of days. Pathologist will confirm in due course. Cleaner found him.' The SOCO officer looked round the room, piled high with books and papers on every available surface. 'Don't envy her the job, even before this.'

Sonny Clark walked to the window, his plastic shoe coverings making strange noises as he did so. He looked out over the patch of the Downs one floor below. Clifton Bridge was off to the left, hazy in misty rain. Cars queuing to get over it.

Moon was over by one wall of bookshelves. 'A lot of books by a Terry Dean.'

'The dead man, sir. Crime writer.'

'Any good?' Moon asked absently.

'Don't read that stuff, sir. I'm more of a Harry Potter man.'

Moon grunted. 'Have you checked the bedroom?'

'We're working on it. Bed only slept in on one side.'

'Okay, Sun,' Moon called. He looked at his watch. 'Let's leave SOCO to it and go for a conflab.'

Sonny Clark nodded. It was about time for a Rioja.

Sonny Clark's nickname in the force had been 'Cloudy', as his temperament was a glass-half-empty thing. But once he and Moon became an item – in the professional sense only – Sun as his moniker became inevitable.

Moon only went by his last name. Not because he was any kind of Morse with a daft first name, more that his first name – some triple-syllable thing of German origin – was pretty much unpronounceable for an English person. As was the case, Sun once ruminated, with many European names. The rumination was because he and his wife had gone to Ghent only to discover it was pronounced *Hent*. In the same way, he was told, Van Gogh was actually pronounced as if you were clearing your throat: Van *Hhoccc*.

Moon eased himself back in his seat. It creaked.

Sun and Moon took sips of their drinks – Rioja and beer, in that order – and looked at each other. They were in the bar of the Arvon Gorge Hotel, their favourite thinking place – well, that's why they told themselves they went there, but mostly it was because Moon liked their choice of beers.

Although only ten years older than Sun, Moon was old-school copper. Did his stint, as Sun was doing, as a detective constable, took his sergeant's exams. Grammar schoolboy but not a posh one. Beer drinker – old school again – which, combined with a lack of exercise, explained him being... Sun pondered what word could be used to describe him now the f-word had been banned by those on high in the Force as being unkind and cruel. Bulky? Was *portly* allowed? Mycroft Holmes would have been turning in his grave – if he weren't too f… fictional. Sun smiled.

'What's so funny?'

'Nothing – thinking about something else.' Sun looked at his laptop. 'So, Terence Oliver Dean is on the Electoral Register as sole occupant of that address. Sole owner too on a long-ish leasehold, though he'll have to renegotiate with the freeholder in ten years or so if he ever wants to resell.'

'He's dead, Sun.'

'I was talking hypothetically.'

'Very hypothetically. Next of kin?'

'Working on that. Never been married. No kids we know of. The throat cut – left-handed or right-handed, do you think?'

'Don't go all Hercule Poirot on me at this stage, Sun. Let SOCO and the pathologist sort that out.'

'Sir. Do you want to sit on the terrace?'

'I think not.'

Aside from low-level acts of violence, there were not many violent deaths in Bristol each year. Six or so murders, sadly usually of women by their husbands or boyfriends. In one instance by both husband *and* boyfriend.

There'd been an accidental death here a few weeks ago. Australian tourist. Drunk, late at night, he fell off the terrace into the gorge below. He'd signed it off as accidental, but – and he recognised his own ego in this – he had kind of hoped it was murder so he could get the kudos for solving it. Assuming he could. But it put him off the terrace.

And then, a week or so later, another man had tumbled into the gorge – not from the pub terrace this time, further up near

Clifton Bridge – whilst flying his drone in windy weather. Not looked where he was going and lost his footing was the conclusion.

And that was about as exciting as it got for Moon.

'Have you read any of his books?' Moon said, coming back to the present.

'My wife loved reading all this crime fiction bollocks.'

'Would that be your ex-wife?' Sun nodded. 'Would that be pertinent? The reading?'

Sun shrugged. 'You mean because a real-life DC is not as interesting as a fictional one? Maybe.'

'Who did she leave you for – Adam Fawley?'

'Don't know who that is.'

'Latest Oxford detective, I'm told.'

'No – she left me for her physiotherapist.'

'That's banal. Sounds like you're better off.'

'Me to decide that,' Sun said sharply. 'Sir.'

'Sorry. Bit grumpy today.'

'We've just got a murder case, sir! I would have thought that would perk you up.'

'Until a DI takes it over. Besides, one less crime writer in the world is no bad thing, surely?'

'You are in a grump.'

'Sometimes realists are perceived as such.'

Truth was, Moon acknowledged, he was in a very bad mood. He knew why, too. He knew he was something of a joke – overdue for promotion, old-fashioned in his ways and – the no-no these days – overweight.

It wasn't that he wasn't fast on his feet. He was. Well, relatively. But these days, if you weren't down one of the many gyms in Bristol five days a week, you were some kind of loser. Although he didn't think Sun was like that – maybe why he'd taken to him.

Actually, Sun had a home gym. Not much, but then he didn't have much since his marriage split. She had the house, quite rightly, he had the rented flat on an ugly street and a rowing machine, static bike and weights. He kept in shape but wasn't muscular or flashy about it.

Mostly his daily workout was to sweat out the Rioja he'd drunk the night before. Although a nurse he'd briefly dated told him that didn't work. Also, the fact he never drank spirits didn't mean he wasn't an alcoholic. He wasn't. He was sure of that. Alcohol dependent? Maybe.

Was Terry Dean a heavy drinker? No, that was irrelevant. Who disliked him enough to kill him? Unless it was random, of course.

'The Crime Writers League – the CWL – are having their annual fiction festival this weekend in that swanky hotel on the edge of Cathedral Green.' Moon looked at his watch. 'Now, in fact. Let's see what the writers know.'

They meandered along the streets of Clifton, Moon puffing only a little on the inclines and, via a circuitous route Sun didn't quite understand, ended up at the top of College Green.

They walked past the Japanese tourists taking selfies in front of the Banksy on the wall before the row of shops.

The hotel was one of the best in the city. On the plus side, it had a great pool in the basement. On the negative side, all the rooms for attendees were in corridors that were so confusing you needed a satnav to get to your bed. Oh, and Moon had been reliably informed they regularly ran out of booze, not recognising the unquenchable thirst of crime writers and some of their readers.

As they walked – downhill now, thankfully, as far as Moon

was concerned – he said: 'I've arranged a meeting with the chairperson of the CWL to see what else they might be able to tell them. *They* being their preferred pronoun, as they were quick to correct me. Good luck with that in the United States of Trump.'

At reception, Moon asked if they were available. 'Probably at a panel,' said the receptionist with a Belfast accent – Moon was never wrong on accents – and beautiful eyes the shape of which it was not acceptable to describe these days. She – or possibly they – looked at the clock on the wall. 'But try the bar.'

They were sitting by the window when Moon and Sun came over. Moon gestured for them not to rise but they showed no sign of doing so anyway.

'What do you know about Terry Dean?'

'Very little. Don't care for him much. Womaniser. Drinker – though that's not unusual in this bunch. One of those writers who takes a puerile revenge in their fiction on anyone who'd wronged him in real life.'

'That's a thing?'

'Oh yes. He was on a panel here several years ago – "Revenge is a Dish Best Served Fictionally". Very popular panel.'

'Interesting. Anyone know him better than you?'

'I'm sure some people here. Stay in the bar long enough and the whole world passes by. He'll probably turn up, too. Why are you asking?'

'Just routine.' They thanked them and Moon went to the bar and asked for a Rioja and a beer. The beer might be a problem, the barman said.

'It's always a problem during the convention – never get enough put by,' a tall guy standing beside him said. He was sporting quite a black eye.

'You're a regular, then?' Moon said.

'Ten years.'

'Do you know Terry Dean.'

'Not really. I think he's a bit of a dickhead, so stay clear.' He held out his hand. 'Harry Mosby. Known for upsetting people with fiction.'

'Harry Mosby? Like the Gene Hackman character in *Night Moves*?'

'Who?'

'Never mind.' The beer arrived and Moon handed over his card. 'Tell me, Harry – do you take revenge on people in your fiction who have done you wrong?'

'I prefer to do it face to face.'

Moon retrieved his card and picked up the drinks. He gestured at the eye. 'How's that face-to-face thing going?'

Harry Mosby turned away.

Moon plonked down in the chair opposite Sun. The chair seemed to groan in protest. Sun nodded and they clinked glasses. He indicated his open laptop. 'That event they mentioned. It was called "Revenge is Best Served Fictionally". Three years ago. Panellists: Terry Dean, Denise Hunter, Ian Rankin and Fred Vargas.'

Moon flipped through the printed programme they'd been given at reception. 'Denise Hunter is here this year but not the others.'

Sun was reading something on his laptop. 'Fred Vargas is a woman.'

'Let's not go there. Here's a photo of Denise Hunter.' He looked around. 'And there she is sitting on her own. Written six psychological thrillers, the titles of which all feature a man getting killed.'

'Makes a change, sir.' Moon looked at him. 'In real life and crime fiction, as you know, it's usually women who are the victims.'

Moon nodded. 'Judging by the titles – *The Dismembered Man*, *The Headless Man*, *The Castrated Man*, and so on – I'd say she's trying to right that wrong.'

'You think she might have known Dean?'

'He's a womaniser – was – she's a bit of a looker…'

'Sir – not sure you're allowed to say that about a woman. But you're not thinking his death had something to do with something he wrote about somebody?'

'No idea. Just want to meet somebody who might know who had a grudge against him. And this is a weird world, isn't it?' Moon gestured around the bar.

Moon shifted with difficulty in his chair – the chair's fault, not his. Why do they make them so small?

They walked over to Denise Hunter. 'Sorry to interrupt—' Sun began.

'I only sign books after a panel,' Hunter said, without looking up. She was a woman in her forties, fashionably dressed. And, Sun admitted, a bit of a looker.

'We're police officers, and wanted to buy you a drink and ask you about Terry Dean.'

'Why? What's he done?'

'He's died,' Sun said, rather bluntly Moon thought.

'And there's a celebration of his death you'd like me to attend?' She finally looked up. 'I'm sorry – that was a horrible thing to say.' She gestured to the seats beside her. 'Large gin and tonic, please.'

Sun went to the bar whilst Moon sat. 'You didn't like Mr Dean?'

'Perceptive. I took revenge on him in one of my novels.'

'I won't ask which one—'

'*The Castrated Man.*'

Moon nodded slowly. 'What did he do?'

'Betrayed and dumped me.'

'Was that before you did the panel about fictional revenge?'

'After. I would have castrated him on stage, had it been before.'

'Doesn't that kind of thing happen all the time?'

'Castration on stage? Not that I'm aware.'

'I mean relationships ending.'

She gave him a long look. 'Not to me.'

Sun rejoined them. 'Do you know anyone Terry Dean offended?'

'How long have you got?'

'Enough to kill him, I mean.'

Moon sighed. Sun mouthed an apology.

'He was murdered. Well, well.'

'Ms Hunter here would settle for castration.'

'Only fictionally. Look, we're a convivial lot, us crime writers. You know what they say – oh, no, I can't say or I'd be pilloried by the CWL committee.'

'We won't tell.'

'To understand the darkness of the human heart you would need to talk to a romantic novelist,' she said quietly.

'You can't say that?'

'No, that's fine – it's the bit that goes with it. If you want blood on the carpets go to the Romantic Novelists Association.' She drained her gin and tonic and stood.

'Just one more thing, Ms Hunter,' Moon said, getting out of his chair with difficulty. Sun was sure the chair gave a sigh of relief. 'Who did he talk about taking revenge on – in that panel you did?'

'He said nobody had really done him wrong, but he liked to take revenge on those who'd done people he cared about wrong.'

'Did he give any examples?'

'He said in one novel he'd packed off two and crippled for life a third man who'd been terrible to an ex of his. Quite romantic, for him.' She gathered her things. 'Find a romantic novelist he's scorned – there's your murderer.'

They watched her go, head high, almost strutting. Men got out of her way whilst giving her covert glances as she passed.

'This isn't proving very useful,' Sun said. 'We should be looking for clues back in his flat.'

'I'm not sure you're right – about the usefulness of this. We should have asked her which book.'

'We could ask his agent. But you really think that might be something?'

Moon spread his hands. 'As I said: I have no idea, but at this stage the net needs to be wide. Let's talk to the director of this shindig.'

'He's going to be very busy just now,' the receptionist said. 'But I can call through. Take a seat in this lounge. A waiter will be over to serve you.'

No waiter came, but Moon busied himself with his phone and Sun with his laptop. Then the fast clacking of leather-soled shoes across the wooden floor alerted them to the arrival of the festival director. He was a bustling little man suited in a too-short jacket and too-tight trousers, as was the fashion at the moment. Moon, perhaps because of his girth, couldn't understand the short jacket thing. In his youth such jackets were called bum-freezers.

The man sat himself down as they started to rise. 'Matthew Penistone, and I've heard all the sniggering jokes. Pronounced

Pennystone, for your information. How can I help, officers? I'm very busy, as you can imagine – or perhaps you can't. People dropping out at the last minute—'

'We're here about Terry Dean.'

'He is coming, isn't he?' Penistone said with alarm.

'I'm afraid he's dead, sir.'

'So definitely not coming. Bloody typical.'

'Not too typical, I hope, sir, even for a crime fiction festival.'

Penistone looked puzzled.

'He's been murdered,' Moon said.

'I'm very sorry to hear that, but it doesn't help me with the problem he's dumped on me. He's left a big hole in a panel about locked room mysteries. Don't suppose you know anyone who could fill in?' He saw their looks. 'Alright then. What do you want from me?'

'Did you know Dean well?'

'Well, we both live in Clifton, so yes, a bit.'

'Did he ever mention anyone who bore a grudge against him.'

'You mean apart from the women he let down? He got around a bit. And he did get involved with a few intense women. But I wouldn't have thought any of them were *that* intense.'

'Was he involved with anyone at the moment.'

'No idea. Hadn't seen him for a bit. But he was the life and soul, you know, so I can't think who would want to... How did he die?'

'Can't disclose that for the time being, Mr Penistone,' Sun said.

'*Pennystone.*'

'Sorry, sir. I should know better – I've actually got an aunt who lives there, up in South Yorkshire. Another lives in Ramsbottom, which they call Tupp's Arse.'

Moon and Penistone both looked bemused at Sun's sudden attack of logorrhoea. 'Do you know of a romantic novelist Dean might have been involved with?' Moon asked after a moment.

It was Sun's turn to look bemused. Surely Moon wasn't taking that woman's suggestion seriously?

'Not off the top of my head,' Penistone said, which drew the two policemen inexorably to the ill-fitting toupee on his head they had both been trying desperately not to gawk at.

'Did he ever mention someone he'd taken revenge on in his fiction? Name that person or persons?'

'Well, on the panel on that subject he talked of taking revenge on three people in one of his novels – I think it was *Madness in the Method* – but he never said who. You think that might have something to do with his murder? All crime writers do it for a lark and as puerile revenge.

'I can't be certain, but I think it was Ian Rankin who on that panel said he'd once told a bloke in the Oxford Bar who was being a pain: "I'll see you in my next novel, pal." And Peter James did a number on Martin Amis in one of his novels because he'd been really rude to him at some book festival.'

Penistone was on a roll now. 'Most famously, Elmore Leonard – Dutch to me – wrote *Get Shorty* after being kept waiting for a whole weekend in a sweltering New York hotel by Dustin Hoffman, who had expressed interest in doing a film collaboration with him. Hoffman had been mooching around in Central Park when they should have been meeting.'

'Back to Terry Dean, if we may,' Moon said. 'So, no known enemies?'

'Except as I said.' Penistone sounded peeved about being interrupted mid-flow. 'Can I get back to work now?'

'Of course – thank you for your time,' Sun said.

'I don't suppose either of you are knowledgeable about the Brighton Trunk Murder – or any other true crime?'

'Why?' Sun said.

'Got let down by this bloke who was part of the True Crime panel. Nice enough bloke but not always entirely reliable. Late with deadlines and so on. Lost his last book deal because he was late delivering – though I think there was more to it than that.'

'Can't help, I'm afraid,' Moon said.

'Okay.' Penistone started to stand. 'Oh. I did see Terry having a flaming row in the street a couple of weeks ago. Or rather, he was being rowed *at*. Young woman, so I don't think it was the usual woman-scorned thing. I was in a café so couldn't hear anything but saw her stomp off leaving Terry just standing there, head down. No idea who the woman was.'

'What street?' Sun said.

'Useless at street names, but directly opposite the Bun and Bread café.'

When Penistone had gone, Sun looked at Moon. 'What now?'

'Well, I'm going to buy that book – I think there'll be a book room here. See who these three people are.'

Sun's phone rang. Moon nodded and Sun took the call. He listened and said: 'Text it to me.' He turned to Moon. 'Here's a thing. A woman filed a complaint against Terry Dean a few weeks ago for killing her dog.' His phone pinged. 'She lives round the corner. With your permission, I'll go and see her whilst you get the book.'

'Let me get the book first, then I'll go with you.'

It was a narrow three-storey terrace house. A woman in her late fifties, maybe early sixties, answered the door and looked at them suspiciously. They introduced themselves.

'We're here about your complaint against a Mr Terry Dean for killing your dog.'

'Oh – someone has finally decided to take me seriously.'

She led them down a narrow hallway, past a dog basket with heated fleece in it, empty bowls, rubber bones and all the usual paraphernalia of dog-owners.

'As I said to your colleagues, that man murdered my dog.'

'With a broken vase?' Sun said, looking at the notes he'd downloaded. 'Talk us through it.'

'We were just coming back from our walk on the Downs and, as usual, walked along the quiet street because Sonny doesn't like the busy road with all the traffic.'

'Sonny?' Sun said.

'My lovely dog.'

Moon held back a smirk at Sun's slight discomfort. 'Carry on,' he said.

'He found some scent very interesting, so we stopped as he explored it. I was vaguely aware of yelling above me but I was looking back at the Clifton Bridge – so good they've made it impossible to jump off it – and then I heard Sonny yelp, and when I looked back he was lying there… lying there with a huge wedge of glass sticking out of his neck.'

'A vase, you've said.'

'Half a vase, more like.'

'Was the rest of it nearby?'

'Not that I saw,' she said.

'Nor did the police later,' Sun murmured to Moon.

'The yelling – a man's voice?'

She blew her nose. 'A woman's. Giving him what for but I don't know about what. I looked up and that monster was leaning out of his half-open window looking down at us.'

'How did he look?'

'Like a monster. Wild-eyed. Manic. Then he withdrew his head and slammed the window closed.'

'What did you do?'

'Called the police – who were very slow arriving, I must say.'

'And did you know this man?'

'Never seen him before in my life. Are you going to prosecute?'

'He's dead, ma'am. Murdered.'

She said nothing for a moment, then: 'What the murderer deserves.'

Back on the street, Sun said: 'You didn't ask her whereabouts when he died.'

'Because I don't think for a moment that she did it. Anyway, you're forgetting – we don't know yet exactly when he died. Have you got the full report of this incident? What did he say when the police went to interview him?'

'Shall we sit somewhere?'

They went into the Albion. It was quiet. In a corner, Sun got out his laptop. 'Said he was carrying a glass vase and dropped it and it shattered, part of it flying out of the window. Accident. Constable noted there were still shards of glass on the floor.'

Moon's phone rang. He held up a finger and took the call. The pathologist. He nodded and grunted for five or so minutes, then finished the call. Sun looked at him expectantly. 'Anything we don't already know?'

'Clear that it was two days ago but not exactly when on that day. And an odd detail. Fragments of glass in his head and in his left forearm. Cuts there too – older but not healed.'

They looked at each other. 'The vase,' they said together.

'But I'm not sure where that gets us,' Sun added.

'I could do with a sausage roll,' Moon said. 'Let's go down the street to the Bun and Bread and get one and a coffee.'

The small café was popular but relatively quiet when they got there. They ordered sausage rolls and coffee and perched on stools at a window counter, Moon's perch more precarious than Sun's. They asked if the manager could spare a minute.

The manager was a relaxed young woman who came over with their food and coffee. 'Get them whilst they're hot,' she said, pointing at the sausage rolls.

'We will,' Moon said, after they'd introduced themselves. 'But a couple of questions first. Do you have CCTV pointing out at the street. And did you see that row across the street a few days ago?'

'Yes and yes. But if you want to look at the footage for that row you don't really need to, because I can tell you who was rowing.'

'Go on,' Sun said, through a mouthful of filo pastry and sausage meat. He hadn't been able to wait.

'The guy was that crime writer, Terry somebody. Comes in sometimes, used to flirt with all of us until I explained we all dance on the other side of the ballroom.'

'And the woman?'

'Laura Somebody. I think she actually lives at the other end of the street they were rowing on. She's a regular here. Hang on a sec.'

She disappeared behind the counter into the kitchen. When she returned, she said: 'Lives at number 42 with her mother.' He saw Moon's look. 'She had a fling with one of my staff.'

Once they'd finished scoffing, the two detectives walked down to number 42 and rang the bell. A woman in her forties answered. They introduced themselves.

'We were hoping to speak to Laura.'

'Not here, I'm afraid. Why?'

'About an incident that happened down the road.'

'Incident? You mean the row with Terry? I'm her mother, Genevra. You'd better come in.'

'You know Terry Dean then?' Moon said when they were drinking tea around the kitchen table.

'We were an item for a while. And very nice it was. But Terry's Terry. Wandering eyes. Never seen a woman he doesn't want to get into bed. Arrested development? I would say. So we split, much to my regret but amicably.'

'So your daughter – Laura is your daughter? – knew him. Was he her father?'

'She is my daughter and she did know him, but goodness me, he wasn't her father. We got together long after she was born.'

'Do you know what the row was about?'

'Oh, yes. Terry, for all his philandering, is very chivalrous. He does this puerile thing in his fiction of taking revenge on people who've done people he cares about – usually women, of course – wrong. The more ridiculous end such people have the better, as far as he's concerned.'

'And he did that to people who'd done you wrong.'

'You might not think it now, but I was, if I say so myself, a very beautiful woman when I was young.'

'You still are, if I may say,' Moon said, unexpectedly flushing.

She gave him a dazzling smile. 'How gallant of you. I was aware that beauty opened doors for me, people welcome me everywhere but it also made me a target. I put up barriers that only the most resourceful could get past. Unfortunately, Laura's father was such a man.

'He treated me abominably. Abusive verbally and physically. Left me to bring her up alone only a few months after she was born. Never paid child support.'

'You didn't insist?'

'He was Australian. An actor. Couldn't be tied down.'

Moon was wracking his brain. 'He wasn't called Brian Allen, was he?'

'He was. He came to Bristol to see us but never showed up then we heard he'd fallen into the Avon Gorge. To be honest, I was glad to see the back of him. But Laura was not. Daddy issues from the fact he wasn't around during her childhood. She was desperate to get to know him and have him be the father he wasn't capable of being.'

Brian Allen was the drunk staying at the Arvon Gorge Hotel who'd fallen off the terrace. Australian actor known for two things: being very Method and playing psychopaths.

As if she was reading his mind, Genevra said: 'He felt it important to dig deep in himself to find the truth of a character. But he was only convincing as a psychopath and that was, essentially, typecasting. He didn't have to dig at all for that, just play himself.

'I had to watch his American movies – he could do a decent American accent, I'll give him that – with Laura in his absence. So she could feel closer to him. There was one scary one where Laura thought he acted so horribly it showed true acting talent. I was unmoved. I couldn't say, because I've always protected her from the truth about him, that in real life he was far more scary when he used me like a punchbag. He was the Devil.'

'And you told Terry all this?' Moon said gently. She nodded. 'And he took his revenge on your behalf in the novel.'

'Yes. Had him crippled by an ostrich – as I said, he liked ridicule as a weapon.'

'And that's what the row in the street was about?'

'Yes. Laura wasn't a reader, but I left the novel lying round and she flicked through it. Although she thought Terry had killed her dad off. She was furious.'

'She has a temper.'

'Alas, an inheritance from her dad.'

'Where is she now?'

'In Cornwall, surfing with friends, I think.'

'You don't know?'

'Although she lives at home, as most people of her generation need to do, she's free to come and go as she pleases.'

'Newquay?' Sun said.

'Probably.'

'And she has visited Terry Dean's flat?'

'Many times.'

'Can you give us her mobile number?'

As they walked back down the street, Moon said, 'From what she was saying about Laura's father, she's a suspect in the Aussie's death.'

'What do you mean? He was drunk. It was an accident.'

'I was never sure about that.'

'With the greatest respect, sir, can we focus on one real murder?'

'The murder of Terry Dean. I think we'll have that sorted by the end of the day. Let's get a drink.'

Sun had lost count of how many drinks they'd already had

that day. But it helped them think, they told themselves. They went back to the swanky hotel. En route, Moon's phone rang. He listened then told whoever was calling to come to the hotel.

'They've found his diary and cracked his mobile. Some interesting stuff.'

They went into the bar but it was heaving. They went across to the pub over the road. Large video screens had a football match on and there were loud responses from the drinkers, but there was a quieter area upstairs.

Moon had texted the PC about their new location, and he found them upstairs. He was in uniform but Moon slipped him a drink.

He looked at the diary whilst Sun scrolled through texts on the phone. The PC, young lad, probably still a probationer, leaned over the balustrade to watch the match.

When the PC had gone and the match was over, Moon said. 'It's all in here. Everything. Written like a kind of memoir – conversations and everything.'

'Laura isn't answering her phone, by the way. Nothing of interest on his phone,' Sun said.

'Try Laura once more,' Moon said gravely.

The phone was answered but not by her. 'Laura's phone.'

'Is she there?'

'She's missing. Who is this?'

Sun identified himself. 'When you say "missing", what do you mean?'

'Went out with her board earlier, even though the sea was really rough. Hasn't come back.'

'Have you notified anyone?'

'Coastguards, obviously. I'm her roommate. There's a letter on her bed addressed to her mother.'

'I'll have someone come by to collect it.'

'Why?'

'In case.'

Moon sighed. He started reading from the diary/memoir:

Laura called round today. 'I hear you killed my dad in your latest novel.'

'Well—'

'How could you do that to me — did you not think about me for a moment? My feelings?'

'Er—'

'You didn't, did you?'

'Er—'

'You're heartless. It's like whatserface, Margaret Atwood, said. Writers have to have hearts of ice.'

She's a strong girl and she had come off the sofa as her rage mounted and come to loom over me. She roared: did I not think of her when I was killing him off?

It didn't seem the right time to point out that I hadn't, in fact, killed him, just crippled him for life.

She was about two yards away and I saw her look round at something to hit me with — or, as it turned out, throw at me. That's when she threw the heavy, orange glass vase at my head.

Like most cowards, I have quick reflexes. I got my forearm up and the vase shattered on it, shards flying into my head and big chunks out of the open window as what was left of the vase fell to the floor beside me.

Blood streamed down my forearm, pieces of glass stuck out of the shredded flesh.

She stormed off and as the door slammed I heard her shout: 'Bastard. Go swallow a cane toad!'

'Go swallow a cane toad,' Moon said. 'How vivid. Her Aussie dad's influence, I assume.' He read on:

As I was picking the glass out of my arm and pate, I was thinking: no, I didn't think of your feelings for a moment; 'sliver of ice in the heart', not 'hearts of ice'; Graham Greene not Margaret Atwood; I didn't kill your dad, I just crippled him for life; it's not my latest novel, it's a couple of years old.

As I was trying to staunch the blood, I heard a scream out on the street. I stuck my head out of the open window. On the pavement three floors below a woman was kneeling over something. She was sobbing now. She stood and stepped to one side and looked around, bewildered. I now could see a dead dog with half of my orange vase sticking out of it.

Before I could duck back from the window, she looked up and saw me. She pointed her finger at me and screamed: 'Murderer.' I slammed the window. Closed it and sat down again.

Oh yes. Nobody can say I'm not puerile. A lot of crime writers are. We all do it. You know the kind of thing. Some 'orrible murder. Me, I go for the undignified and ridiculous death. I've always thought ridicule is a more effective weapon than a punch in the face. Largely because I'd be useless at punching someone in the face — or anywhere else, for that matter.

I found bandages and was wrapping my forearm when the front doorbell rang. I tied the bandage off quickly and went to the door. I opened it, and a man about a foot taller than me punched me in the mouth.

'That's for Sonny,' he said.

'Who's Sonny?' I spluttered through bloodied mouth as he turned away to head down the stairs.

'My mother's dog,' he called back.

GO SWALLOW A CANE TOAD

I went back to the medicine cabinet and looked for something to staunch yet more blood from my nose and my mouth. Well, this day wasn't panning out very well so far. Surely it could only get better?

Moon skipped ahead.

Call me a predator — when I was younger I was, a disgusting one, scenting a woman's unhappiness or need so I could home in.

Years of which I'm not proud. The drink, the drugs. The blankness. My wake-up call was when a female author I treated abysmally wrote what in her high-falutin' literary circles was called a roman-a-clef, writing about our relationship and excoriating my character. And then that Denise Hunter did the same, although focusing not so much on my character faults as on my physical shortcomings.

Thing is, as a kind of gentleman I couldn't say why we'd split up, and she went for my impotence. Well, yes, with her I sort of was — or became so. See, I realised she was a faker. I've been around the track a few times, and whilst I'm not the greatest lover, I more or less know what I'm doing.

When she started making orgasmic noises within about ten seconds of us starting, it was discombobulating. I mean, I thought I was good, but not that good. Found it increasingly off-putting, so, beautiful as she was — is — I lost interest and, so, yes, couldn't get it up. She made hay of that in one of her novels — Castrated Man, *was it?*

Moon skipped again.

Well, he had to go, that Aussie bastard. For real. Fictional revenge can only take you so far. He was a nasty, dangerous man.

Heard of the dark triad? That's a person who is charismatic, narcissistic and sociopathic. One of the most dangerous creatures on the planet. He was that man.

When I heard from Genevra — we weren't together, but we were on friendly terms — that he was coming to Bristol to see his 'family' — hah! — it didn't take long to figure out where he was staying. A convivial drink or two dosed with GHB, a rape drug readily available round here...

I got the first text message a week or so after I did what I did. 'I know what you did.' The next one: 'You are so fucked.' The next one: 'I'm going to call. Pick up.'

Then: 'Do you ever look up at the skies? Drones everywhere.'

'Really?'

'Especially over Arvon Gorge Hotel late at night.'

Shit.

'How much do you want?'

'Perhaps I only want to see justice done.'

'How much do you want?'

'I'll be in touch.'

I know all about blackmailers. They are a staple of my genre. Once is never enough. They keep copies, etc.

He phoned again. 'Well now. I want you to meet me near the Clifton Bridge with a big wodge of cash in return for the footage.' He gave a time and day.

'And that will be an end of it?'

'That's an end of it — I'm a reasonable man, and I always thought the man you killed was a terrible actor. But if you try some trickery then my footage will go to the police and somewhere else.'

'You won't get any money then.'

'Well, I'm sure there are other ways to capitalise on the footage. Don't worry about me. Worry about yourself.'

Well, we met, the drone hovering above us. It was a blustery night and the drone kept veering. 'Where's the footage?'

'I didn't bring it with me but it's in a safe place. I'll tell you once I get the money. Hand it over.'

He was distracted by drone in the high wind, and I took the opportunity…

I turned off the drone and threw the controls over the edge after him. The drone plummeted down.

The problem was that I didn't know where the footage was. I half expected another call from an accomplice. My phone rarely rang, so when it did, on edge, I barked: 'What do you want?'

'Charming,' Laura said.

'I thought you were someone else,' I mumbled.

'I got a weird note from someone saying I should come and see you, as you had something important to tell me. Oh, and I got a video in the post, but I need to get it converted this morning.'

Shit. 'Come round as soon as you like,' I said as calmly as I could, toying with the ivory-handled knife I kept on the desk as some kind of weird talisman.

The diary/memoir ended there. The two detectives looked at their unfinished drinks, gathered their things, and left them unfinished as they trudged out of the pub.

Donna Moore

Donna Moore is the author of crime fiction and historical fiction. Her first novel, a private-eye spoof called *Go to Helena Handbasket*, won the Lefty Award for most humorous crime fiction novel, and her second novel, *Old Dogs*, was shortlisted for both the Lefty and Last Laugh Awards. Her third novel, *The Unpicking*, is set in Victorian and Edwardian Scotland, and the follow-up, *The Devil's Draper*, set in 1919, was published in May 2024.

donnamooreauthor.com

ANTHRISCUS SYLVESTRIS

Donna Moore

The unaccustomed noises from outside had woken Lorna from her usual fitful sleep. Without turning the lights on, she padded into the living room, pulled the net curtain aside, and peered out. The pile of junk had grown yet again. The two old mattresses stained with pee, half a fake leather sofa in a hideous shade of green and the innumerable bin bags had now been joined by a broken cot and a rickety Ikea bookcase. It unsettled her that someone was here during the night, even if their only aim *was* fly-tipping.

No point in ringing the council. She'd already phoned them several times about the enormous industrial chest-freezer outside her previous neighbour's front door, pointing out that it was a safety hazard. Not only had she skinned her ankle on it several times, but what if a child got stuck inside it? She'd opened the lid and left it open, tucking the little padlock between the back of the freezer and the McLoughlins' old front door. He'd got it from his work, Mr McLoughlin had told her when they were moving out, but it was too big for their new place. The removal men couldn't be bothered taking it back in, so on the landing it stayed. It was part of the council's war of attrition against her. Her most recent nemesis there, Alexander Forbes-Shaw, had told her each time she phoned about it that they weren't interested.

A moth fluttered onto the windowsill and she crushed it under her thumb, leaving a smear of silvery-brown where it disintegrated under the pressure. There was never an identifiable dead moth, just the smear. Lorna rubbed her thumb and fore-finger to get rid of the streaks and looked up and down the deserted street, gradually rotting from the outside in. The once neat squares of grass in front of the six low blocks were over-grown and unsightly, and dandelions poked up from between the paving stones of the few paths that remained. There'd been seven blocks originally, but they'd already knocked down Sapphire. Somebody had clearly had delusions of grandeur back in the 1970s: Sapphire, Emerald, Ruby, Topaz, Diamond, Jade and Amber. Carbuncle was the only gemstone they resembled. Seven blocks, four floors, sixteen flats to a block. One hundred and twelve families had once lived here. You used to struggle to find a parking space. Now, you could drive a whole fleet of tanks in. You'd have to, in fact, given the mountains of rubble caused by the demolition of Sapphire. Yesterday, the monstrous orange excavator had returned and was lurking balefully next to Diamond, ready to destroy on command.

They'd moved here in 1980, her and Robbie, delighted as newlyweds to get a smart, fresh council flat in Topaz. From their fourth-floor living-room window they watched the hills in the distance change with the seasons: green, purple, brown, white.

Lorna had felt all grown up at the age of seventeen, with a new husband, a new home, and a new job at a local factory, packing nuts and bolts and screws. Robbie was at the shipyard and things were good. They were optimistic about their future, and when Thatcher announced her Right To Buy scheme, Robbie had wanted to buy their wee flat straight away. Lorna had been cautious at first: property ownership wasn't for the likes of them, and how would they pay a mortgage when they had children? But, as the years passed and no children appeared, Robbie had finally talked her round, of course; he always did.

And even when the shipyard closed and Robbie lost his job, they'd still managed to pay the mortgage. He got a job at the slaughterhouse and she'd picked up a wee additional evening job at the pub. They had no money for luxuries, but they had their lovely flat. Most importantly, they had each other and they talked about all the things they would do when the mortgage was paid off: 14 June 2010. They'd book a holiday somewhere warm: Spain, or Greece. They'd buy a new car; maybe Lorna could learn to drive, too. A new kitchen and bathroom, new carpets. Robbie insisted that Lorna could give up the pub job, at least.

But, in the autumn of 2009, the asthma that had troubled Robbie from his shipbuilding days started to get worse. His coughing fits became more prolonged, and he was perpetually tired. He became painfully thin but still he refused to go to the doctor. Until he started coughing up blood, and by then it was too late. Asbestosis. Two months before the mortgage was paid off, Robbie died.

Lorna stayed put. Parts of Robbie were still around her – the wonky bathroom cupboard that he'd hung when he'd had a wee bit too much to drink; the giant bluebird he'd painted on the inside wall of the built-in wardrobe; the beautiful window boxes he'd made. She could still hear his voice, sometimes; still catch a glimpse of him from time to time. He was there, in the walls.

Over the years, families moved out and others moved in.

They might speak a different language, or look different to her, but they felt secure and familiar, just as the flat did. When the factory she worked at had shut down, Lorna had taken more hours at the pub. She hadn't been on holiday, or learned to drive, or bought a new kitchen; instead, she'd squirreled the money away for a rainy day.

And that rainy day had come – a monsoon, in fact – about eight months ago.

A rumour had started that the flats were going to be demolished to make way for individual homes and a new community centre. And then more rumours: that the flats were about to fall down anyway. After all, weren't they built on the site of an old coal mine? A couple of tenants moved out, and their flats weren't re-let, adding fuel to the rumours.

Then the council sent out a letter. The flats were system built: factory-made concrete panels which only had a design life of around sixty years, and they'd already been up for fifty-four of those. They were poorly insulated, expensive to maintain, blah, blah, blah, so they were going to be demolished. Lorna wasn't going anywhere and had thrown the letter away.

More families moved out. Junkies squatted in an empty flat in Ruby, and the whole block emptied out pretty quickly after that. On the day the last person in Ruby moved out, the council vans were there and a team of raucous men fixed metal grilles over the windows on the first two floors and over the communal doors, back and front. Within hours, it had become a sport for the local young team to come up and smash the remaining windows. The workers came back and hammered boards over the window frames and cleared away the broken glass from below. Lorna was glad. The darkness inside had drawn her gaze; now she couldn't see it anymore.

Tenants were tempted with the cream of the area's housing stock. Those who'd bought their flats wrote strong letters to the council. *What about us?* they'd asked. *Nobody told us when we bought that these flats had a shelf life.* Lorna heard all the talk, went to all the residents' angry meetings, but sat at the back and said nothing. She wasn't going anywhere. Everyone else moved quickly through all the stages of grief. Anger was replaced by bargaining, and then bypassed depression completely when the council came back with offers for those who owned their flats. Removal vans began turning up at the blocks on a daily basis. It seemed as though everyone had moved straight on to acceptance.

But not Lorna. For the last thirteen years she'd been bouncing wildly, like a ping-pong ball, between anger and depression. And now she was the last woman standing. She'd hardly been outside the flat for a month, other than to take the bins down. The deserted chest-freezer on the landing had got her every time, of course; the emergency light on the landing had flickered and crackled its final gasp, months ago. She'd arranged for grocery deliveries, stocking up on tins, and everything else she needed she bought on Amazon. For company she talked to Robbie. Robbie didn't speak to her so much now, so she made up his answers, too. *It'll be alright, hen. Don't you worry. Everything works itself out in the end.* Nothing special, nothing earth-shattering – pretty ordinary, really, but it was what he'd always said, and he'd always been proved right.

Then the moths started to appear and she investigated ways to keep them away, filling her online basket with all the things she needed to make little bags of lavender, rosemary and peppermint oil. But they still kept coming.

She knew that at some point the council would shut the

electricity off. Her spare room was full of tinned food, bottled water, batteries and other supplies. The internet was great. Typing the words 'survival' and 'prepping' and 'end of the world' had brought up lots of things that she'd never even thought about before: a wind-up radio, foil blankets, a slingshot and ammo, candles and torches galore, camping cookers and gas canisters, emergency bandages and a tourniquet. It was now all stacked neatly on shelves she'd put up in the spare bedroom. And for the end, she had the tablets, of course, tablets that had helped Robbie through his pain and would help her, too.

She'd stopped the Tesco deliveries a couple of weeks ago — she couldn't risk opening the door anymore. The council, in the person of Alexander Forbes-Shaw, kept coming round, unctuous persuasion and incentives giving way to bullying and threats.

It was time to make her final preparations. She unplugged her mobile phone from where it was charging and found the number for B&Q in her speed dial. They knew her there now. 'Sienna? It's Lorna.' She cleared her throat. Days on end of speaking to no one had made her voice rough and crackly. 'Aye, I'm fine, hen. I need some more stuff. I need some of your thickest MDF. Eight-foot sheets. And what are they — about four feet wide?' She double checked in her head the calculation she'd already done several times on paper, hoping her calculations were correct.

She'd only need to do the exterior walls. 'I need about twenty-five sheets.' She looked up at the ceiling. The loft space of the building was a danger. 'Better make that thirty... Aye, thirty. Three zero. And give me four kilos of two-inch nails... Kilos. That's right. I think that's it. How much will that little lot cost me?' She fished out her debit card from her wallet. 'Fucksake, hen; I'm not wanting nails made of gold... Aye, aye, it's fine. I'll give you my card details.' She reached into a cupboard and checked her stash of cash. 'Can you ask the lads if they'll bring it all up? Still no lifts, I'm afraid. The bastards stopped those two months ago. Health and safety, they said. Anyway, tell the lads I'll see them right for their trouble.' She listened and nodded. 'Next Wednesday's fine. It's not like I'm going anywhere.'

Six days. Six days before the next stage of her plan could be put in place. She spotted another moth and slapped her hands sharply, happy to see the telltale smear. As she plugged her mobile back in, Lorna heard slow steps coming up the stairs. She stood completely still and held her breath. She tiptoed over to the door and looked out of the peephole. Just blackness, as though someone had placed a hand over the hole. She placed an ear to the door. 'Mrs Craig? Lorna?' She jumped back from the door and covered her mouth. 'I know you're in there. I know you're *always* in there when I come.' Lorna held her breath. 'You're going to have to leave at some point, you know.' The voice had changed from wheedling to angry in four short sentences. She'd heard every version of that voice before. Forbes-Shaw swore and banged an angry fist on the door. Then the letterbox rattled and she heard steps moving heavily back down the stairs. Lorna picked up the official-looking envelope that had landed on her carpet and went back into the living room. The letters and Forbes-Shaw's visits had become more frequent and more demanding in the last six weeks or so. She took the letter over to the window and lifted the curtain aside. Forbes-Shaw got back into his fancy car and sped off, his departure causing a little flurry of rubbish to swirl in his wake. Now the only things that moved outside were the ever-present gulls and pigeons and a cat lazily licking its arse on top of one of the smaller piles of rubble.

In the early days, the whole town was supportive of Lorna's decision not to move out. Whenever she went shopping, some-one or other would come over to her: 'Well done, missus,' they'd say, or 'Good on you for standing up to those council bastards,' or 'knocking the stuffing out of this place, so they are. Any help you need, Lorna, just you let us know.'

But that had gradually changed, first of all to 'Och, Lorna, hen, why don't you just take their offer?' And 'Aren't you scared staying up there on your own? I heard they're offering you one of those new wee places at the foot of the town; you should take it.' And then she just heard the whispers: 'The woman's mad.' And 'I heard they offered her a nice lump sum. She's just a greedy old cow.' No offers of help any longer. And then people stopped speaking to her altogether. They turned their heads away or crossed the road when they saw her.

She'd tried to work out with the help of the internet what her rights were and what the council's rights were, but everything she found was full of thereins and wheretofores and schedule this and subsection that. The whole process seemed, of course, to be stacked in favour of the council. She'd received a letter which told her that they had applied for a Compulsory Purchase Order and that she had six weeks to make an 'application to the Court of Session in terms of paragraph 15 of the First Schedule to the 1947 Act, as extended by Section 60 of the Land Compensation (Scotland) Act 1973'. She'd cut that bit out and stuck it up on her fridge, attached by a magnet from Blackpool, because it had annoyed her so much.

She'd phoned Forbes-Shaw after that letter. 'How the fuck do you think I have access to whatever the fuck these Acts are? I wasn't born in 1947, and I was practically a wean in 1973. Nobody gave me Acts of Parliament to read along with the

Bunty.' But Forbes-Bawjaws had waffled on about acquisition and vesting and exercises of powers until she'd finally just had enough. 'Listen, pal, you can shove your CPO up your arse, along with Schedules 1 to 15. This is my home and I'm not moving.'

Now, she sat in the armchair and opened the latest missive. Another billet-doux from Forbes-Shaw. This one a notification of a final, increased offer of compensation, plus something new – the offer to pay her rent, if she chose to rent rather than buy somewhere else, for two years. She looked at her watch. He'd be back at the office by now. The council number was stored under the name 'Arseholes'. She stabbed her way through the recorded options, pressing 1, 4, 1, 2, 3 and 1 for a final time when prompted, negotiated Alexander Forbes-Shaw's secretary and was finally put through to the man himself.

'Mrs Craig. How are you? I was just over at your... at the flat. To give you news about our very generous offer. I hope you're happy with the new level of comp—'

'No, I'm not.'

'But, Mrs Craig, it's a generous—'

'Leaving aside the fact that I don't want to move at all, how the fuck is thirty-five grand generous? That wouldn't buy me a fucking shed in *your* back garden.'

'It's far more than—'

'I don't care how far more than anything it is. I've lived in this flat for over forty years, and you want to give me less than a grand for each of those years. That's just insulting. And, as I've told you over and over, I don't want to move. I like it here. My husband liked it here. He died here. And some of his last words to me were that he wanted me to stay here and enjoy it.'

'But, you can't stay there any longer, Mrs Craig. It's not safe, it's not healthy—'

'And whose fault is that? I've been telling you about the rubbish, the rats, the lighting. That fucking freezer… have you seen the size of it?'

Forbes-Shaw sighed and his voice softened. 'Look, Lorna—'

Fake.

'It's Mrs Craig to you.'

His voice turned hard again, the words clipped. 'Mrs Craig, you can't stay there. We have a Compulsory Purchase Order.'

'Which I've objected to. Under schedule fucking fifteen, paragraph 3, or whatever the fuck it is.'

'And which objection has been overturned, as of yesterday.' His voice was smug.

'Oh, well of *course* it fucking has. Which of your wee pals in the Lodge sorted *that* for you so quickly?' She screwed the letter up in her hand. She could feel herself starting to hyperventilate. Another moth fluttered in front of her field of vision and she slapped it down onto her knee.

'Look, Mrs Craig. Thirty-five thousand is our final offer. Plus, as stated in the letter, if you decide that you don't wish to buy another property, we will generously give you your choice of *any* of our available rental stock *and* waive the rent for a period of two years.'

'I was sixty this year, Mr Forbes-Shaw. I haven't paid any rent or any mortgage for the last thirteen years. Now you want to not only throw me out of the only home I've ever been happy in, but I'm going to have to start paying rent in two fucking years.'

'I'm sure you'd be able to get help with that, Mrs Craig. The Government offers a generous level of ben—'

'Fuck your benefits, you smug prick, and fuck the whole lot of you. I'm staying put.'

'The bailiffs—'

She ended the call, wishing, not for the first time, for the days when you could slam a phone receiver back down forcibly on its rest. It was much more satisfying. She rubbed idly at the stain the dead moth had left on her skirt.

It was dark outside when she came to. She must have been sitting there for hours. She stood up and pulled the curtains, before turning on the standard lamp in the corner of the room. She should eat something. She wasn't hungry, but she needed to keep her strength up. She opened the fridge and took out a ready meal – there were still quite a few left from her last big shop, and she needed to use up the fresh food before they turned the leccy off.

Lorna stabbed a fork into the plastic cover over the lasagne, imagining it was Forbes-Bawjaws' face beneath her fork, and set the microwave. She wandered into the spare bedroom to assess her supplies. She had enough here to keep her going for six months or so. She picked up the length of thick chain and the padlock from one of the shelves. They'd have to rip the whole fucking toilet cistern out to unchain her. She'd already planned that.

She walked back into the living room, towards the kitchen. Another moth fluttered in front of her face, as if daring her, and she slapped out at it. She'd noticed the first one two months ago, and she knew that where there was one moth there were more. She'd made up her little bags and, for the first month after she'd seen the first one, she'd obsessively hoovered every square inch of carpet, and gone through her whole wardrobe to try and find more. After the lavender bags hadn't worked, she'd ordered some moth killer spray and traps, along with cedarwood moth rings for the wardrobe and cupboards, but the wee bastards had still kept coming.

During the first few months of Covid, Lorna had finally spent some of her savings. She'd ordered and laid the new wool carpet herself, and she was sure the moths had laid their eggs somewhere in it. She could imagine the larvae, or whatever moths had, busily chomping away at the expensive feast she'd put on for them. She'd also wallpapered the living room and her bedroom at the same time. After years of variations on magnolia walls, she'd gone for a beautiful, summery, yellow silk wallpaper with a delicate tracery of white foliage – *Anthriscus Sylvestris*. It had been Robbie's favourite plant, and he'd always pointed it out on their walks. 'Ravenswing,' he'd called it. 'Cow parsley,' she'd insisted with a laugh. 'A weed.' So when she'd seen the wallpaper on a posh website, she'd had to have it. She'd felt as though Robbie was drifting away from her, and she didn't want that. This would draw him back and she'd see him every time she looked at the walls.

It had taken her three weeks to paper the two rooms, carefully matching up the pattern as she went. At sixty quid a roll she didn't want to waste any. And when it was done, she'd loved it. Then, two weeks ago, she'd splattered two moths in a row. They were resting on the wall and she'd got both of them in one go, one with each hand. They'd left a shimmering dust on the beautiful yellow wallpaper, and she'd been unable to clean it off. The internet told her that a moth's wings were made of delicate scales, easily shed to help them escape predators. They couldn't escape *her*, but in revenge they left this dusty, translucent film wherever she killed them. She could wipe it off windowsills and countertops – although, to be honest, she'd given up bothering – but it wouldn't come off the wallpaper, no matter how hard she tried. It was tainted now. She couldn't see the colour and the pattern any longer. Robbie's beloved *Ravenswing*. All she could see was *moth's wing*. She couldn't see Robbie any longer. She'd loved that wallpaper; and now she hated it.

The microwave pinged and Lorna took out the lasagne and peeled off the curling plastic. She dug a spoon in and took a bite. Tasteless molten lava. She didn't even bother to sit down, just leaned against the kitchen counter and ate her joyless meal straight out of the container. She scraped off the last few mouthfuls and shoved the container into the overflowing bin. She'd need to nip down to the bin shed. The bin men had stopped coming to collect the bins a few weeks ago, so now she made sure the sacks were tied tightly, opened the door of the bin shed, and quickly threw the bag in. God knows what was lurking there.

Five days until the MDF would be delivered. Was this how she was counting days, now? Still, it was surely better than the system she'd been using for the past two weeks: by number of moths killed. That way wasn't very practical – the numbers were gradually increasing, but some days there were fewer than others. Today was already a ten-moth day and it was only four o'clock. Lorna turned on the TV. She hadn't watched it in ages. She flicked through the channels: a DIY programme, people buying a house, people selling their old tat, people doing DIY in a castle, a black-and-white film with Rita Hayworth in, a police car chasing a speeding driver, Judge Judy. She switched the TV off. Out of the corner of her eye she saw a moth. She sprang out of the chair and slapped her hand against the wall. Another shimmering streak on the Ravenswing wallpaper.

* * *

Four days until MDF delivery day. A fourteen-moth day. Somebody rang her buzzer that morning. She crept into the hall and heard the buzzing another fifteen times as whoever wanted to get in tried each buzzer in turn. Whoever it was had buzzed her flat first, though. She waited a few moments to see if any of the buzzers rang again, and then moved quickly to the window. She was just in time to see a white van turning left at the end of the street. She stood at the window and picked at a wee edge of wallpaper that had come unstuck at the left-hand side of the sill.

Three days until MDF delivery day. Twelve moths, two more of them flattened onto the wallpaper. One wall now had four moth streaks – she caught sight of them every time her head turned. Without her glasses on, she'd also killed a screw on the shower cubicle, mistaking it for a moth. Better safe than sorry. And somehow, the wallpaper to the left of the window was now peeling away. Strips of it were piled up on the floor. She couldn't remember doing it, but she must have.

She heard footsteps on the stairs and glanced out of the window. The postman's van was there, but was it the postman? Perhaps it was a ruse and it was Forbes-Shaw and his bailiffs. She'd asked once how the postman managed to get into the flats when the door was locked, and he showed her the drop key that allowed him access to every block of flats, every close, and the outside door of every residential building in the town. The fire brigade had them, he'd told her, and the council, of course. She ran out into the hallway and pressed her hand tightly against the letterbox cover. Just in time. The outside letterbox rattled and she felt a pushing against the cover. 'Go away!'

'Mrs Craig?' The voice sounded like the postman's, but slightly puzzled. 'Mrs Craig? I have a letter for you.'

'I don't want it. Go away!'

There was silence but she could hear him shuffling outside. 'Mrs Craig, are you okay?'

'I don't want the letter. I don't want any more letters. Don't come back.'

'But I—'

'Go away! Don't come back!' She realised that her voice was loud and shrill. What must she sound like? She released her grip on the letterbox cover. Just a wee bit. Enough for there to be a small gap. She put her mouth to it. 'Please don't come back,' she whispered. She heard him go back down the stairs and watched from behind the curtain as he went to his van. He hesitated slightly and looked up towards her window. Lorna pulled her head back and pressed against the wall. She breathed on the wallpaper, her breath moistening one of the torn edges. She slid her nail under and tore off another strip.

Two days until MDF delivery day. Thirteen moths. Unlucky for some. She rummaged in the kitchen drawer. She knew she had a couple of nails left somewhere from putting the shelves up in the spare bedroom; this couldn't wait until the new ones were delivered. She couldn't believe she hadn't done it yesterday. Ah, here they were. She took the three nails, her hammer and a wee bit of wood left over from putting up the shelves, into the hallway. She carefully placed the wood over the letterbox flap and hammered the nails into it. There. She wouldn't be getting any more mail.

As she stood surveying her handiwork, she heard something outside. She peered out of the spyhole. There was nothing on the landing but the enormous freezer. She wasn't sure how long she stood there before going back inside, but she didn't hear anything else.

One day until MDF delivery day. A seven-moth day. Perhaps she'd killed them all. And there had been no sounds outside, either. Last night she'd dragged the cushions from the sofa into the kitchen and slept on the kitchen floor, in order to keep watch. In the living room she looked around her, puzzled. Most of the wallpaper was now off the window wall, a few small strips remaining here and there. Who'd done that? As she tried to work out what had happened, the lights went out.

MDF delivery day. She woke while it was still dark and picked up her phone to see the time. How did she have forty-three missed calls? When did that happen? The little battery thing that told her how much power she had left was red. Four per cent – she'd forgotten to charge it, probably for a couple of days, and now the electricity was off it was too late. She held down the button that powered off the phone and went into the hallway to wait for B&Q. She sat on the floor and rested her head against the wall. When the sun came up, she went into the spare bedroom. She picked up torches, batteries, candles, matches and the powerful little camping lanterns and walked through her flat, placing some of each in every room.

At some point during the morning the buzzer rang, and she went to the window to look out. A big B&Q van sat just outside. You couldn't be too sure, though. She picked up the intercom phone. 'Who is it?'

'B&Q. We've got a delivery for you.'

'Thank you. Could you bring it up and put it all on the landing.'

She put her eye to the peephole. There were four of them. Despite that, it took them a long time to bring all the boards upstairs. At one point one of them knocked on the door. 'What is it?' Her heart was beating hard.

'There's not enough room to put them all here. There's an old freezer in the way.'

She thought for a moment. 'Fine. Put some of them on the landing below.'

'Are you sure? We can bring them inside your flat for you if you like.'

She banged her hand against the door, making the man jump back. 'No!'

'Okay, okay!'

Through the peephole she could see him holding his hands out, as if placating her door, and she struggled to get her breathing under control, to sound calm.

'Thank you, but it's fine. The landing below will be fine. Please let me know when you've finished.'

She sensed rather than saw him shrug and go back downstairs to get some more boards. She went to her stash of cash and peeled off two hundred pounds. Then she quietly prised the nails out of the cover on the back of the letterbox. Eventually, he knocked on her door again and she thrust her hand through the letterbox, waving the notes. 'Thank you. This is for you.'

He took the money and hesitated. Are you sure? This is—'

'Quite sure. Thank you. Goodbye.'

She waited, her back to the door, until she heard them all go back downstairs. The outside door banged, the van doors slammed, and she heard the van drive off. She would start in the bedrooms, then the living room, kitchen and bathroom, and finish up here in the hall. That way she didn't need to bring all the boards in at once.

It took less time than she thought it would to hammer the pieces of MDF over the walls, but hammering them onto the ceiling was more difficult than she'd imagined. The boards were heavy, so getting them up the ladder and holding them in place while she hammered the nails in proved to be impossible. But she had another solution. She would get into the building's loft space and put them on top. It wasn't ideal, but would still stop anyone getting in easily. Then she'd hammer a board over the entry into the block's loft space.

By the evening of the next day, she was nearly finished. Just the living room and hallway to do. Soon every outside wall had a thick MDF panel over it, and every window, too. It would stop them getting in: the council, the bailiffs, Alexander Forbes-Bawbag. She would be able to stay here – not forever, but for long enough. And, once she'd finished this, she would peel off the rest of that fucking wallpaper on the walls that weren't covered with MDF.

Lorna took the last few panels into the hallway. There was only one outside wall and the door here.

She hammered the boards quickly over the outside wall of the hallway. She was getting good at this now. She turned to the door of the flat, hammer and nails in hand, but before she could start, the knocking started. 'Mrs Craig? What's all that noise? What are you doing?' Forbes-Shaw, of course. Who else would it be? Lorna sighed. 'I know you're there! Open this door *now*.'

Lorna leaned her head on the back of the door. She was so close to finishing, to making them all go away, to being able to stay here until the end. She realised she hadn't given much thought to the end. She expected that it would all become clear to her once she'd shut Forbes-Shaw and all his ilk out and it was just her and Robbie again. 'Mrs Craig! If you don't open this door right now, I shall call the police.' But it would still continue, wouldn't it? She'd still hear his annoying, pompous voice. He'd call the police, the bailiffs, and whoever else, and she wouldn't get any peace. She wasn't going to be taken away from this flat. She just needed a few more days to make her plans, that's all.

Lorna let the nails fall to the floor, but she was still holding the hammer as she turned the key in the lock and opened the door a crack. 'Just a few more days,' she croaked, as she peered out. 'That's all.'

Forbes-Shaw stood there, looking triumphant, she thought. 'Oh no, no, no. I've had just about enough of your nonsense.' He held up his phone. 'I'm calling the bailiffs right now. I'll have you out of here by tomorrow morning.' Lorna opened her mouth to speak. 'And I don't care if you've got nowhere to go. I'm recording that you've made yourself intentionally homeless. Let's see where that gets you.' Lorna gripped the handle of the hammer tighter.

Lorna hammered the last board over the door and stepped back to survey her handiwork in the light from the camping lantern. She put the hammer down on the table in the hallway, next to the key for the padlock of the chest freezer on the landing. It hadn't been strictly necessary to close and padlock the lid, but it had seemed neater that way.

Now she had peace and quiet at last. Lorna realised that she hadn't seen any moths today. *See, hen, everything works itself out in the end. I told you it would.* Robbie had been right, as always.

Maxim Jakubowski

Maxim Jakubowski is an award-winning writer and publisher who lives in London. His latest novels are *The Piper's Dance, Just A Girl with a Gun* and *The Exopotamia Manuscript*. A frequent anthologist, he has recently issued volumes of new stories inspired by Cornell Woolrich, J G Ballard and Alfred Hitchcock. He is a past Chair of the Crime Writers Association.

maximjakubowski.co.uk

EVERY DAY I DIE

Maxim Jakubowski

F Scott Fitzgerald wrote a total of 164 short stories in addition to his five novels, the last of which, *The Last Tycoon*, was unfinished at the time of his death. Always short of money, due to an extravagant lifestyle, he spent the latter half of his career, when not toiling in Hollywood, churning out short stories for the well-paying 'slick' magazines, most regurgitating his main themes, reflecting the superficial lives of the rich in what he pictured as 'the Jazz Age' and the everyday emptiness of their affairs of the heart and foibles. Only a few of the stories have become memorable, but every single tale, whether derivative or repetitive, invariably seems to contain a few lines, a paragraph or two, which came from the depths of Fitzgerald's soul, with a sometimes-heartbreaking ring of authenticity. 'The Crack-Up' remains the most memorable, a stark auto-fiction which plumbs depths of genuine despair and truths.

His First Threesome
It was New York in the spring, though not the New York of today, but a city that exists no longer. Still full of second-hand bookshops where you could regularly find bargains and actual

rarities, record stores exclusively stocked with vinyl, the recurring spectacle of beggars and rough sleepers littering the downtown streets, scores of peep shows and porno cinemas within a ten-minute radius of Times Square. Paperbacks still sold for $4.99 or less and Wall Street, in the distant south of Manhattan Island where I seldom ventured, didn't yet concur that greed was good and no one had yet thought of scoring a quick buck by posing as a living statue. A city of lingering, conflicting fragrances, semi-controlled decay and shimmering excitement. It hadn't been sanitised yet and carried a constant air of danger, which I enjoyed. Streets art-directed by Edward Hopper at night and Woody Allen by day. I navigated through both with a sense of both dread and expectation, feeling alive and on the edge, the taste of forbidden fruit hanging like a cloud just a breath away from my thoughts. There was always a fat sliver of temptation around to appeal to my weaknesses.

I wandered, idle.

Close to Times Square, curious about the 'live sex show' advertised in neon letters outside, I'd entered a shady, dark-lit emporium, making my way past the walls of porn mags and VHS videos that formed an X-rated gallery leading to another corridor of malodorous cabins. Inside men jerked off, watching pale, skinny women contort themselves behind the glass or plastic windows of the peep shows, sweating punters frantically feeding coins or tokens into the apparatus to prevent the metal shutter from closing, obscuring their vision, sharply cutting off yet another fleeting glimpse of abominable intimacy; a flash of pink at the heart of the stripper's delta of lust, a hand, a finger dancing across a nipple or sliding its way into her private opening. I controlled my curiosity and walked further on; been there, done that.

Beyond, there was a crowded room and a small stage where a bed had been installed. I handed my stock of tokens to an attendant policing entry to the area. The crowd of standing men quivered guiltily with a furtive sense of expectancy. All ages, races, shapes and sizes were represented. An army of the guilty. Bad disco music was being pumped out through echoey loud-speakers, cutting off any suggestion of conversation; not that anyone here had any wish to speak to or know more of their nervous neighbour. All companions in shame.

Finally, a couple emerged from the shadows and climbed the stage. They were both wearing bathrobes. He was black, shaven-headed, built like a fridge, and she was Latino, curly-haired and almost a couple of feet shorter than him. Once by the bed, they swiftly disrobed and took position on the bed. I didn't even notice whether the bed had a sheet or if they were about to perform on the bare mattress. She settled on her back, opened her thighs wide and her partner lowered himself over her and appeared to penetrate her. From my vantage point, three rows away, it was an indistinct blur of flesh against flesh, black against white, shifting monochrome surfaces. Both participants were silent, he diligently pumping away, she buried under his dark mass. This went on for several minutes. I had to admit it was particularly unerotic. Even porn movies were more arousing; the lighting, the angles, the relative attractiveness of the women, the occasional soundtrack of moans, flesh against flesh and sometimes muzak. I turned around and made my way back to the Times Square area, feeling deflated, my imagination let down by reality.

My senses were unfulfilled. It would be decades before the internet changed dating, sex and all that sweaty jazz; there were no apps, no way of finding a willing partner at the drop of a screen. I picked up one of the free papers you could find in metal dispensers on the corner of most New York streets. Located a phone number. Returned to my hotel on 44th Street, where I had become on first-name terms with the cockroaches, and called out. On the other end of the line, they remarked they liked my English accent and made me an offer of two for the price of one. Allegedly housewives from Long Island who happened to be in town on a shopping trip and felt like being naughty. I didn't believe a word of it, of course, guessing they would be from the Bronx or Puerto Rico or the Midwest, but I was intrigued. I had never had a threesome before. I was curious. Why not? I supplied my hotel details, the room number and agreed a price, then headed for the shower. I just hoped the women wouldn't be too vulgar; a trait that always undermined my libido.

An hour later, as arranged, there was a knock on the door.

With a sense of relief, I noted neither looked like prostitutes, nor were they dressed in extravagantly gaudy outfits, although their accents were definitely not from Long Island. One of them was pale and plain and wore little make-up and even seemed a little shy. The other, taller and bustier, was the one in charge and demanded my payment in advance. Cash, of course. The transaction completed, they undressed. I did too, my eyes swimming across their naked bodies, making mental notes, my cock rising to the occasion.

'Who do you want first?' I was asked.

I was unsure of the etiquette of such an encounter. Did I make love to each in turn? What if I came with the first and had to leave her partner unused? While I was with one, what would the other be doing? Watching? Encouraging my thrusts just by talking dirty?

In turns they took me in their mouths. I remained silent, so many questions zigzagging across my mind. The shorter girl had small breasts and her nipples appeared to harden as she watched her companion busy herself with me. Her eyes were green but absent, and in that moment I knew it was her I wanted to make love to and not her friend. I was no longer interested in a three-some and its problematic geometry, but just her. However, before I could express my choice, the taller, more assertive whore slid under me and guided me into her heat. A slave to my lust, I began moving inside her, feeling a little disconcerted as, behind my back, I could feel the body heat of her partner so close to my skin, and her fingers cupping my balls, their playfulness intensifying my hardness. I tried to lose myself in the moment, to enjoy it more rather than attempt to rationalise the novelty, the strangeness of it all, wanting to become a voyeur at an artless happening in which I was also a principal participant.

I could feel my climax approaching, the whisper of the second girl's breath in my ears as she sat so close to us fucking. Awaiting her turn?

Then, briefly, her hand grazed the back of my neck. The woman I was making love to held her eyes open and, for a second, I glanced something resembling a smile in her gaze. Right then, the piano wire the smaller girl was holding wrapped itself around my jugular and she began to tighten it. I felt it cutting into my flesh. Out of the corner of my own eyes, I saw a steady stream of blood pour out of my throat and spread like dark ink across the breasts of the whore I was rutting with.

There wasn't time enough for pain. My senses were anesthe-tised, sensations fading fast.

My first and last threesome.

A final thought until my consciousness ebbed into darkness

was that they were in for a bad disappointment, as the money I had paid for their services was the only cash I carried, I wore no jewellery and my watch was just a cheap Swatch. Or maybe they only killed men for the thrill?

My breath ceased. In a nanosecond my body would disconnect from my brain.

I died.

Equal Opportunity Lover

I'd never been attracted to men.

It's complicated. As has always been my relationship to sex.

A woman I had a brief affair with, beautiful in her quirkiness, pale-skinned and married, once asked me in bed to do something to her I was not in the habit of doing or had ever even contemplated, and in the process opened the door to a terrible curiosity. I wanted to understand how it felt to be her, to be a woman. Some doors never close again.

Much later, I went with a man.

Took him in my mouth. Neither enjoyed it nor was repulsed by it.

But curiosity leads you onto perilous paths, and eventually I succumbed to the next stage in becoming fully bisexual – if that was what I was – and allowed a stranger I met through the internet to mount me. As if I were a woman.

It didn't hurt as much as I feared. But then neither did it afford me even a distant hint of pleasure. I enjoyed the act in a perverse sort of manner, as if detached from it, a voyeur to my own ignominy. It was easy; without the burden of feelings being involved. I reflected that it was a bit like writing, unenjoyable in the moment but a source of much satisfaction once reflected back on. There was a distinct thrill to knowing I could offer pleasure to others, and I relished the way it released a form of submissiveness that had probably been at my core since childhood but that the adult, public me had carefully been keeping concealed.

I let them fuck me. I never kissed or cuddled them. I had no interest in their faces, their looks, the texture of their skin (an attribute of women that often made me just melt on the spot). All that mattered was that they had a penis and were intent on penetrating my two openings. A one-sided transaction in which I agreed to be unemotionally used. It would have been nice had I on occasion felt some form of sexual pleasure or release from the encounters, but I didn't. I could live with that; it kept things simple. Alongside, I still lusted for and had relationships with women. It was just a different part of the menu. One that did not trigger my heartstrings. An odd convenience.

We make online contact and I drive to the car park by the small wood, which is the nearest dogging site to where I live.

His car is newer than mine. He has dark hair and an Italian accent. And wears a wedding ring. We nod at each other in silent recognition. No names, no questions.

'Your car or mine?'

'I'd rather outside. Doing it in cars is uncomfortable.'

I look up to the sky. It's not particularly warm. End of May. White clouds floating against a grey background.

I reluctantly assent.

We take the small path that leads to the woods, both silent. I feel apprehensive. Something dangerous about him.

The sky is now obscured by the trees. Just the sound of birds in the distance.

He stops. Pushes me down to my knees and has me undo his belt and pull his trousers and boxers down.

'Open your mouth, slut.'

I do. He forces his penis past my lips. He initially tastes of soap. He hardens quickly. Moans. I concentrate on swallowing him, sucking from his mushroom head all the way down his shaft to his balls. His genitalia are shaven. Obscenely large from my kneeling vantage point.

He pushes hard, gripping my hair to get a better hold and dig deeper, towards my throat.

I can't help gagging and retreat momentarily.

'Can't take it, bitch?'

I return to my task, my spit polishing his cock as I apply myself again.

I tire. He tires. He orders me to get up and indicates a nearby tree trunk against which he spreadeagles me and pulls my cargo pants down. I can feel the cold wash like the breeze against the bare, exposed skin of my butt cheeks. I have seen photos of them, taken by other users: I am not very hairy there, white, unsullied skin, shapely like a woman's, not too broad, with my puckered sphincter lying at its centre, like a target.

He is about to push his way into me when a drop of rain reaches us. Then another.

'Damn!'

We pull our clothes up and return hurriedly to the car park.

'A shame…'

'I live only ten minutes away.'

'I'll follow you.'

The moment we enter the house, he strips me bare, places a collar around my neck to which he attaches a leather lead, and pulls me up a set of stairs, leading I guess to a bedroom. The collar is tight. My unease grows.

'Give me your hands.'

He handcuffs them behind my back and forcefully pushes

me down onto the bed. I note the quilt cover is green. He adjusts my position so I am on all fours, strokes my balls and slaps my rump several times. I am no great fan of BDSM paraphernalia and practices, latex gear, toys, whips, canes, floggers, pegs in raw places and all that, but have grown to tolerate minor forms of bondage, so I don't object. My online profile lists pain, marks, blood and water sports as beyond my limits.

There is a moment's silence. I can feel him behind he, his breath rhythmic, watching me exposed, decidedly indecent and vulnerable. The muffled sound of him shedding his own clothes. Then another low-key sound I can't recognise; maybe switching his iPhone on to film himself mounting me?

A finger is inserted deep inside my fundament, as he tests my pliancy, ready to stretch it. I hold my breath, anticipating the moment of penetration.

It comes. But not as I expected. Twice. Three times. More.

Almost simultaneously, the girth of his cock opening me up and plunging deep into my innards, the familiar burning sensation and that ineffable feeling of being filled, but also a sharp pain in my side. Then another, close by.

My whole body feels on fire and I feel short of breath, but manage to somehow half turn my head back in his direction to try and see what he is doing and I catch a glimpse of his hand wielding a large kitchen knife, its blade already bloody, being savagely thrust again deep into my flank.

A surge of irony flashes through my mind, as feelings both fade and intensify. I've entered a bad horror novel, *American Psycho* redux. Whatever final thoughts I manage linger on the alarming evidence that I have – law of averages weighed against risks repeatedly taken – come across a wrong one, the possibly inevitable consequence of anonymous gay sex.

He keeps on fucking me and stabbing me. Studiously multi-tasking.

Everything fades to white.

And then I am dead.

We Won't Get to Albuquerque

She has been a resident at the Manor for two and half years now. The nurses and carers are kind and there is a piano in the downstairs reception area, but no one ever seems to play it. The individual rooms are clean, the common rooms large and well-lit, with massive television screens displaying mostly daytime game shows or property and gardening programmes, which whoever is present gazes at with empty eyes and no sign of understanding let alone enjoyment. The screen is surrounded by a tapestry of cheap and cheerful paper flowers. One resident on her floor, who still has the power of speech, invariably begs any visitor whether they want to play chess, which none ever do. On some days balloons in all colours seem suspended from the ceiling, survivors of a birthday celebration. The kitchen cooks lovely cakes, and hot chocolate is served on the stroke of three.

When I visit, I bring fresh toiletries, bars of dark chocolate and sultanas, which I carefully place in front of her mouth and allow muscle memory to half open her lips in acceptance, the chocolate broken into small pieces or just a few raisins at a time so that she can chew and then swallow them and not choke. I remember the song in which Leonard Cohen's Suzanne would feed him tea and oranges that came all the way from China; I can't compete: my offerings have only made the prosaic journey from the Colindale Aldi.

At mealtimes, which I am not encouraged to attend, the staff feed her. They must do so with patience. As they wash, shower and dress her every single morning.

Whether she has been taken to the common room or has remained in her own room (304), she now seldom opens her eyes more than a quarter any longer, maybe shielding herself from the light or reality, but her look is vacant. She clearly no longer has any perception of where she is. She doesn't recognise visitors. Just sits in the padded armchair or lies in the bed with somnolent indifference.

I speak to her.

But there is no response. I am a ghost to her now.

On every visit to room 304, I water her plants and recall how many orchids she would look after and cherish in the house that we built together. On the sideboard, there are photos of our family over the years, drawings by her granddaughters, but I know all too well she is blind to them. There is also a large-screen TV fixed to the wall, facing her bed, but it is never switched on. A digital radio playing classical music is permanently kept on, its tones soothing, the melodies and eternal orchestrations somehow filling the void.

I bend over her as she lies in the bed staring at the wall or the black TV screen or whatever she actually sees, and kiss her forehead or her lips, and on rare occasions her lips purse as if in memory of a million kisses past.

She is an envelope.

Alive but empty.

The ghost of the woman I loved. In my own way, oh so imperfectly, I am full of guilt. Of all the things I did wrong, of taking her for granted, for small slights which were not apparent to me at the time. The arguments, the infidelities, the good and the bad times. This is worse than death, I realise. A living death. Following every visit, I am shattered – by guilt, pain, regret, anger – and unable to fully function for up to twenty-four hours.

We will never go to Paris or Amsterdam or New York or New Orleans again.

I cannot go to Paris or Amsterdam or New York or New Orleans again, because they are now so full of memories and I am a coward who refuses to face them.

The songs we would listen to together are now a dagger viciously stirring the raw meat of my soul.

> 'And we won't get to Amsterdam
> Or that lake in Africa, Darling
> And we won't get to Albuquerque
> Anytime this year'

Why do others express themselves so much better than I ever can?

I break every hard square of dark chocolate into four pieces. I don't realise she is still chewing the raisins when I place the next piece next to her lips. She shakes her head. It means no, not yet, a final form of communication.

'Bah, bah, beh, bah…' she mutters.

Words rolling off her tongue but mutating into a jumble of confusing sounds.

Her brain desperately hunting for words which have long been expunged. Whether English, Polish or Ukrainian. A babble. A sound-shaped form of despair. Or is it anger, at me for allowing her to be at the Manor, at the world for stealing her soul in such a cruel manner?

'It's okay, my love. I'm here. I'm here. It's me.'

There is no reaction to my words. She reverts to her vegetative state.

She falls silent again while I try and dam the tears welling up in my eyes and the fucking pain buried deep inside my body, my heart, all of me.

Time sitting by the side of her bed stretches mercilessly.

Three or four raisins gripped between two fingers which I bring to the shore of her mouth.

Again, she is not ready.

'Beh, bah, bah, beh, boh…'

The next hour passes in silence as I try to firm up my resolve, alternately feeding her small mouthfuls of chocolate, sultanas and toffee-tasting dried chopped dates.

We are interrupted by a couple of carers who come to change her diapers. She has been incontinent for over two years now, unable to control her body functions. I leave the room and sit on the wooden bench in the corridor while they busy themselves with the unsavoury task. I do not attend, not because of disgust or prudishness but because I cannot bear to be witness to this continuing indignity that has befallen her.

By the time Felicia indicates I can return to her bedside in the room and she has been cleaned, my decision has been made.

I have been contemplating this for weeks now.

How to steal her away from this condition of living death. The logistics of Switzerland are too complicated for me to organise in her present state.

Two for the price of one. Just like that threesome I attempted what feels like a lifetime away in New York.

An image drifts across my mind: a holiday in Phuket. A purple sky at dusk, a festival of some sorts, lighting floating lanterns and letting them drift out across the Andaman Sea.

I go to the tote bag I always bring along, in which I normally carry the book I am reading, a baseball cap and a retractable umbrella.

Find the small, reused medicine bottle I brought along.

I had prepared it months ago.

Waiting for the right time.

A careful mix of ingredients I'd collected in various places, most of which would have little effect on their own, but in the blend that I've concocted are allegedly highly effective if the online research I've been conducting has been studious enough. It's not just sex, arms and drugs you can find on the dark web… I've added and dissolved a copious amount of sugar to the mixture; in the words of Mary Poppins, a spoonful of sugar helps the medicine go down. In this instance, several spoonfuls.

I find a plastic glass by the jug of water on the bedside table and fill it halfway.

Bring it to her mouth.

She tentatively takes a sip, judges the sweetness to her liking, and soon swallows the whole contents of the glass.

If my research and calculations are right, there will be no pain and the process will only take fifteen minutes, or maybe less, in view of the fact she has lost much weight since at the Manor.

I take a deep breath and pour another glass with the rest of what the bottle contained and swallow it down quickly.

No turning back.

Going.

But at least together.

Every day we die.

* * *

The Reverse Side of the Coin

The time for dying was now over, he guessed. Now would be the time for killing. It would make a pleasant change, wouldn't it?

Men? Women? In all fairness, both. He would surely have to be an equal opportunity killer. That would assuredly be politically correct.

He was a crime writer, so, theoretically, knew of myriad ways to commit the perfect murder. But imperfect would do too!

He had read thousands of books on the subject. What to choose?

Piano wire? Mere strangulation or garrotting?

A knife? To the throat? Dug deep into the heart? Frantically buried into the victim's flanks?

Drowning? Burial alive? Poison? Hanging? Simulated accident? Defenestration? Beheading? Disembowelment? Sabotage? A gun; but where could he obtain one? So many options to choose from, so little time to try them all. An embarrassment of choices.

Every day I kill?

No, that would be vulgar, too much.

Just on occasion, on a whim or sometimes a specific agenda. Crime as a leisurely pursuit. The simple art of murder; thank you, Mr Chandler.

But where to begin? And when?

He didn't have to think long. There was an ideal candidate. He grinned.

He knew of the chosen one.

That pesky reader who always complained that his books and stories had too much sex and violence.

Done deal. Gone girl.

Sarah Ward

Sarah Ward is the author of ten crime novels. *A Patient Fury* was the *Observer* book of the month and *The Quickening* a *Radio Times* book of the year. She is currently writing two series – one set in New England and the other in West Wales, where she lives. She has also written *Doctor Who* audio dramas. Sarah is former Vice-Chair of the Crime Writers Association and now helps organise Gŵyl Crime Cymru Festival.

www.crimepieces.com

THE BLACK SPOT

Sarah Ward

The children who remained in the valley called the place '*y smotyn du*' or 'the black spot'. Few remembered where the name originated but it was thought to be around the time of the drought of '76, when the foliage on the tall conifers surrounding the house shrivelled and scorched. The children of that summer became adults and passed the name on to their own offspring and they onto theirs. The valley had already begun to empty out by then, tenant farmers lured away by employment in the mines or ironworks. No one looked back at that time with fondness, and the stone house collapsed from the weight of neglect and the place's history. Only the two who had watched the woman that July evening knew the story behind the name, and they only told one other.

Dwynwen knew as soon as she turned on the news that her reckoning had finally come. It was an innocuous segment informing viewers of plans to carve a logging road through the forest, a new path to scar the ancient ones worked and trodden by her ancestors. The newsreader was a woman she'd not seen before, her blond highlighted hair cut into a sharp crop and wearing a pale-lemon and blue striped blouse Dwynwen would have coveted in her youth.

The day she'd buried Jack she'd also been wearing a multi-coloured blouse made of viscose which had clung to her back as the spade hit the loamy soil. She'd brought her knitting and a flask of water from the house and had attacked the needles with fervour in between strikes of the spade. It had been madness, but then the whole episode in her life been one of lost equilibrium. Her ancestors, though, had come to her rescue. Her great-uncle, sexton at St Teilo's Church, had once confided to her that the trick with burying so many bodies in a small space was to keep the depth to four feet max, not six. Dwynwen had decided at five foot three; if she dug the hole up to her shoulders, that would do. Except it was muscle-cramping work. Within an hour her flask was empty and the tinkling of the stream that fed into the Cothi was a reminder of the water her grandmother had drawn daily before her heart attack on the side of the mountain.

Dwynwen turned her attention back to the programme, but the news had moved on to a story of cuts at a university. She switched off the set, climbed to her small room and opened the wardrobe. Her clothes were still hanging on the sparse rail, their gaudy colours stark against the habitual navy she now wore. The striped blouse, suede A-line skirt and the gillet crocheted by Auntie Joan. Only the wedge sandals were no longer there. She'd thrown them out sometime in the nineties when she'd caught a visitor's children tottering on them after the girls had been rummaging through her things. She guessed their DNA as well as hers and Jack's would be on the clothes. Dwynwen sat on the bed and assessed her options. She'd got used to her life and was reluctant to face another shift in her world. Very soon it would be fifty years since that scorching, back breaking day, and it would be ill luck if the soil threw up its secrets now.

Mallory Dawson crouched over the bones and wondered if her trip was a colossal waste of time. As a civilian investigator, she shouldn't necessarily have been the first port of call after the discovery of the body. Harri, her boss, was on a training course in Aberystwyth, however, and the rest of the depleted CID team were looking for two teenage girls who had boarded a London bound train at Carmarthen for a meeting with a suspected paedophile. Mallory had picked up the call without much interest. The skeleton was old, the forensic lead had told her, but there was something interesting she might want to see before the bones were removed from the site.

'What am I looking at?' she asked the pathologist who had arrived shortly before her. The skeleton had been decimated by the huge yellow digger that had been scooping the vegetation and soil ready for a track it was pounding through the landscape. Mallory had been here the previous year on a case where a young man had threatened her with a gun. Now there was the pong of bananas in the air. The pathologist saw Mallory wrinkling her nose.

'Nitro-glycerine is what you're smelling. An odd scent, isn't it? They've dynamited the ruins of the house that was once here to create the new logging road. They've been doing it in this valley for years. Soon there'll be no old houses left in Wales. This one was called *Llundain Fach*. All now lost.'

Mallory thought this sounded like an exaggeration, although there was something alarming about blowing up houses to support woodland even on this industrial scale.

'What am I looking at?' she repeated.

He pointed with a gloved hand to the skull lying on a mound of earth. It was this that had caught the digger operator's attention. The other bones had been stained a pale brown by their years in the ground and were easy to miss by a worker concentrating on cleaving his way through the land. A semi-intact skull, however, is something to garner anyone's attention, and this is what Mallory and the pathologist, who Mallory suddenly remembered was called Dafydd, were examining.

'This,' said Dafydd, 'isn't a fracture caused by the machinery. There's evidence of a traumatic head injury probably caused by a gunshot.'

'Shit,' said Mallory. 'How old are we talking?'

Dafydd shot her a look. She knew they hated questions like that, but she needed to know whether to call Harri from his course in Aber or leave it to the forensic archaeologists.

'At the moment I can't tell but I don't think we're talking about bones of antiquity.'

Mallory straightened and massaged her sore knees. 'What? I was told they were old remains.'

'Well, they're also not recent, I don't think. Not enough organic matter. Radiocarbon dating will hopefully give us an accurate time frame, but looking at the house that's just been demolished, it could easily be a century-old crime. The most I can tell you at this stage is that it looks like an adult male, but even that will need to be confirmed once I assemble the skeleton.'

'Great. Think it could have been suicide? I heard they didn't like to bury those who died by their own hand in churchyards so perhaps they put him in a grave outside his house.'

'Hard but not impossible to shoot yourself in the back of the head. You can attend the postmortem tomorrow if you're interested, but there won't be any results on the dating of the bones for weeks.'

Mallory groaned.

Dwynwen watched the news every day but there were no more updates on the logging path. After a week, she allowed herself to breathe, grateful but also despairing that the contingency plan she'd been forming wouldn't be needed. It was only on the following Wednesday when Elsa, the cleaning girl came in for the morning, her eyes as round as apples, that Dwynwen's composure crumbled.

'They found some bones at the foot of the hill near Brechfa. Did you see it in the paper?'

Dwynwen, her throat suddenly parched, shook her head. She drew a glass of water from the tap and forced it down.

'They think the bones could have been there for decades. Isn't that near where you're from?'

'I was born in Abergorlech.'

'Near then.'

'Very near.' But Dwynwen had never spoken to her curious cleaner about her childhood at the farm, and the girl would have no way of knowing about the plan she and Jack had hatched to bring the house up to modern standards. Dwynwen now tried to estimate how much time she had left. The police would be analysing the bones which, according to an internet search, would likely date the skeleton to the late twentieth century era. With a heavy heart, she retreated to her room to pack the clothes she would need for the next stage in her life.

The two missing girls were found in Camden. They'd turned up for their rendezvous with the forty-year-old paedophile, who'd failed to appear after the publicity around the teens' disappearance. In the fading June light, Mallory took her boss Harri up to the spot where the bones had been found. The path had been completed and logging begun, with twenty-metre-long tree trunks stacked for removal. There was nothing left of the stone foundations of the house, nor the grave. Harri regarded the spot with a frown.

'You'd never even know a house existed. Do you know what *Llundain Fach* means?'

Mallory shook her head. Place and house names were a particular obsession with Harri.

'It means "Little London". The house would have been on the drovers' path, taking cattle and pigs to England. The drovers, wild tough men, would have stopped here for some refreshment, maybe overnight shelter. Now the history is gone.'

'I've spoken to some of the nearby houses. *Llundain Fach* had been empty since the late 1970s, so any crime is likely to date back to before then.'

Harri shrugged. 'Let's see what radiocarbon dating tells us.'

June blazed into July and everyone resented the stifling heat, even Mallory, who couldn't bear the freeze that spread across West Wales in winter. The caravan where she was temporarily living at the holiday park was hotter than hell and there wasn't enough work to support a civilian investigator, so she was temporarily laid off. A call from Harri in the middle of August changed everything.

'We've had the results back from the body in the woods. Isotope dating of the tooth enamel is coming up with a likely post-1945 birth. Given it's the skeleton of an adult, we're looking at the time of death from the mid-sixties onwards. The last occupants of the house were called Rowlands, who scratched a living from the land, so we need to start with them.'

'If the farmstead was abandoned from the 1970s, anyone could have used the site as a burial place.'

'We've got to start somewhere. In the meantime, I've got a list of missing adult males for the last sixty years. More than I'd have hoped, but we can start to look for connections with the area. Do you want to lead on that?'

Mallory grimaced but took the work. Over the next fortnight, she followed the trail of a man who had gone to a demonstration against the 1969 investiture of the Prince of Wales at Caernarfon and had never been heard of since; a Swansea student in 1972, who went for a walk along the promenade and failed to return to his lodgings; and a 1980s farmer who had inexplicably left his tractor in a field and had walked off to God knows where. If any had a connection to *Llundain Fach*, she couldn't find it.

Harri had better luck and he called her into his office. 'The last registered occupants of *Llundain Fach* were Jeremy and Anwen Rowlands, but according to locals, one of the children had plans to modernise the building and work the land once more. There was a daughter, Dwynwen, born in 1955, and a son, Huw, born two years later. Huw died in 1972, so it's Dwynwen we need to find.'

'Any luck in the usual places?'

'She's got a work history mainly in retail that stops abruptly in July 1976. What I did find was this.' Harri pushed a photocopy of a notice in the local newspaper dated 5 May 1976, announcing the engagement between Dwynwen Rowlands and Jack Rees of Llundain Fach, Brechfa. 'No marriage certificate, though, so at least one of them changed their mind.'

Mallory and Harri went together to visit Jack Rees's brother,

Tomos. He was a big man, still well over six foot in his late sixties with large hands that bore the scars of manual labour.

'Jack's in Australia. He went out there in the 1970s. Told me he was going and was taking that lass of his, too. What do you want him for after all this time? That rough stuff is in the past.'

Harri and Mallory's eyes met. 'Rough stuff?' asked Mallory.

Tomos shifted uncomfortably against the door jamb. There had been no offer of coming inside and his expression suggested he wished he'd not brought up the subject. 'Before he met Dwynwen, he was with Mari Jones, a village girl. A bit of a wild one, if you ask me. They got into some arguments but it all blew over. With Dwynwen he was as good as gold.'

'And they went to Australia?' asked Harri. 'You're sure about that? You've had letters and kept in touch?'

'Well, no, but we weren't close and I was away in Canada for a few years after the trouble with Mari. When I came back, Jack and Dwynwen were gone.'

Mallory took a swab kit out of her bag. 'It's in connection to the bones we found by the ruins of *Llundain Fach*.'

Back at the station, Harri accessed the Police National Computer files.

'Mari Jones made three complaints of domestic assault by her partner Jack Rees between December 1974 and April 1975.' Harri paused, his eyes scanning the screen. 'Christ, it makes for grim reading.'

'Any other reports after 1975?'

'Nothing, although interestingly his work record also stops in July 1976.' Harri ran his hand across his face. 'Take a look at the file.'

Harri turned the screen towards her and she began to read.

The details were sparse and brutal. The third and final attack on Mari Jones had resulted in her face needing stitching back together after being sliced open with a broken bottle. The attending police officer had needed counselling after attempting to hold together the strips of skin hanging from the victim's face.

Harri's eyes were on Mallory. 'Given the extent of Mari's injuries, this attack probably marked the end of her relationship with Jack and he moved on to Dwynwen.'

'You think Jack was killed in retaliation to a domestic violence attack. By Dwynwen?'

'It's possible. Men who attack women with a bottle don't change their personalities. We need to find Dwynwen. Do you know who she was?'

'No, do you? I thought you couldn't find her.'

Harri rolled his eyes. 'I mean the original Saint Dwynwen. She's the Welsh valentine. Unlucky in love, she became a...' Harri stopped.

'What is it?'

'There is a Dwynwen Rowlands on the electoral register, but I didn't make the connection because I've been looking for a marriage.'

Dwynwen regarded the car outside the gate and wondered. Although she was no expert, she thought it was probably over ten years old and the front wing showed signs of a recent repair. There was a man in the driver's seat, watching the gates. The odd thing was that its presence coincided with Elsa's cleaning day. When Elsa drew up in her small Fiat, she could have sworn that the watcher slid down in his seat, his curly head lowering itself from view. Dwynwen took a breath and walked down to the kitchen, where Elsa was blowing a small fan across her face.

'Everything all right?' asked Elsa. 'What a day. Mam says the weather will break soon enough, though.'

'Elsa, do you know anyone connected to the police?'

Else considered the question. 'I know Mallory who I worked with in a hotel on Eldey. Do you need to speak to her about something?'

'You don't know anyone with dark, curly hair. A man.'

Else pulled at her lip. 'Sounds like DI Harri Evans, her boss. My mam thinks they've got something going…'

But Dwynwen didn't care what Elsa's mam thought of anything. She went back to her room, reliving the punch that had lifted her from her feet and propelled her towards the front gate they had recently repaired. Jack had stood there, purple with fury. She couldn't remember what she'd said to enrage him once again. An argument about Australia, probably, and Jack's insistence that the valley held no future for them. She couldn't recall what had made her go back into the house and pick up the gun. Possibly the memory of Mari's patchwork face as she went about the community, or the sight of him coming at her with the knife. He'd turned his head when he saw the raised barrel and the sound of the shot had echoed across the valley. But what accounted for the rustling in the undergrowth? Surely the sound of a shot doesn't make the bushes quiver with fear.

The following day, Mallory sat in Harri's car reading a report she'd downloaded from an academic site. Its finding was that a one-degree increase in annual average temperature was associated with a six-per-cent increase in physical and sexual domestic violence, with an ambient temperature of 34°C serving as a threshold trigger.

'What was the temperature in the summer of '76?' Mallory asked Harri.

'I wasn't born, was I? I'm not that much older than you, Mallory.'

'Can you look it up on your phone?'

Harri sighed. 'You could look it up yourself. Okay, for two weeks in July 1976, the temperature in Wales exceeded 32.2 degrees Celsius, going above 35 degrees for five of those days. Why are you asking?'

'Do you ever wish there was a statute of limitations here in the UK? You know, like in some US states.'

'Not really.' Harri put his phone back in his jacket pocket. 'I prefer to know that a murder that took place in, say, 1983 is still prosecutable now.'

'To be fair,' said Mallory, her eyes back on the gates, 'murder often doesn't have a limitation, but manslaughter does.'

'That's not our call to make,' said Harri. 'Shall we go?'

They got out of the car and made their way to the gate, passing the sign that read 'The Anglican Community of St Benedict'. Mallory, who hated all things religious and most definitely couldn't imagine living with a bunch of women, made a face. As a civilian investigator, she had no powers of arrest, so it'd be Harri who did the talking, which for once she preferred. The gate opened easily, and as they walked up the gravel path, the front door swung open and a woman stood on the steps waiting with a suitcase at her feet. Behind her, seven women dressed in blue stood, her guard of honour. There were no secrets here.

'Dwynwen Rowlands?' asked Harri.

Dwynwen nodded. 'I've been waiting for you.'

Mallory glanced at the bag. 'We won't necessarily be keeping you overnight, and in any case, you can't bring your own things. Leave the bag here.'

'It's got the clothes in it I wore in 1976. I've kept them since I arrived here. I didn't want anyone else getting the blame, you see, if Jack's body was ever found. There's blood on the skirt. Jack's.'

Mallory nodded and snapped on her gloves, lifting the light case while Harri read Dwynwen her rights. She hoped that the people Dwynwen was about to encounter along the long legal process – the desk sergeant, the magistrates, her barrister, the high court judge and jury, the prison staff if that's where she ended up – would show her kindness. Because Mallory thought – was sure, in fact – that if she'd been in Dwynwen's situation, she'd have also gone inside for the gun.

Mari Jones traced the thin scars on her face with her fingertips as she read of the arrest of Dwynwen Rowlands. People had regarded Mari with pity for five decades, but memories had faded and there were some that thought that her disfigurement was the result of a car accident. Auntie Mari was a popular figure now, even if at the beginning it was the children who had been the cruellest. The exception had been her two nephews, who had come to her back in 1976 with a story of what they'd seen from the bushes at *Llundain Fach*. She'd smiled and told them they had vivid imaginations, and in any case, the place was haunted. They'd seen the figure of a female gravedigger but you were never, ever to mention her to anyone, lest she come after you in the future. The boys, their freckled faces pale, had nodded and run off to enjoy more of the relentless sunshine with the instruction that they should tell their friends to stay away from *y smotyn du*. The black spot.

David Penny

David Penny is the author of the Thomas Berrington Historical Mysteries set in Moorish Spain and the early Tudor period. David's work is available in ebook, print and audio, as well as translations into Spanish and German. He also writes the Izzy Wild police thrillers, and the Unit-13 WWII Paranormal Spy Thrillers.

davidpenny.com

THE OCEAN BLUE

David Penny

The rising sun caught the mast of the *Santa Maria* and revealed something tangled in the rigging. For a moment, Thomas Berrington could not make out what it was, then his confusion faded. A body, hanging upside down.

Thomas sprinted across the cobbled dockside. By the time he stood beneath the swinging figure, others had started to gather.

'Help me get him down.' Thomas surveyed the small crowd. Most were sailors, a few traders who had followed him aboard.

'Who are you to give orders?' one of the men demanded.

Thomas took a breath to dampen his frustration. 'I am a friend of Columbus, sent here to ensure the safe departure of these ships. Apart from which, there is a dead man up there – unless you intend to use him as a figurehead.'

The man scowled but began issuing orders. Thomas stepped back and watched as the body was lowered. When it thumped onto the deck, he stepped forward again. The men allowed him to pass. A wise decision. Thomas was a trained physician, but also a solver of crimes. He had hoped for respite, but death seemed to follow him wherever he went.

'He'll have caught himself in the rigging,' said the man who had questioned Thomas. 'Easy to do for someone not used to the sea. Who is he?'

Thomas rolled the body onto its back, discovering that the man had not been hanged, as he first thought, but stabbed through the heart. He drew the torn shirt aside to reveal livid knife wounds on his chest. More welts showed where the ropes had held him aloft, but it was the knife that had killed him. There should have been blood, yet the man's white shirt was unmarked. Hanging upside down, blood – even without a beating heart – should have drained from him.

Which meant he had not been killed here.

Thomas recognised the man and cursed.

Sent to Palos de Frontera by Queen Isabel, Thomas and his companion, the eunuch Jorge Olmos, were tasked with appointing barber-surgeons for the voyage into the unknown. A task Thomas had undertaken to the best of his ability, which was good enough. Doctors had been assigned to the smaller *Niña* and *Pinta*. There had been a dozen applicants. Thomas had dismissed half on the first day, assigned two, and had chosen his man for the flagship but had not yet informed him.

Now he lay dead.

Thomas would have preferred to choose Moorish physicians, but there were few left in Spain since the fall of Granada at the start of this year of 1492. The Moors had fled, been killed, or expelled – even those with skills Spain needed. Thomas, who had trained in the Moorish infirmary of Málaga, was allowed to remain because he was a man of England.

'Someone find me a cart,' he said. 'And I need two men to carry the body.'

'Carry him yourself,' said a sailor. 'It is bad luck to touch the dead before a voyage.'

Thomas had grown used to the surplus of superstition among these men of the sea. He could not blame them. Soon, they would sail west into the unknown, perhaps never to return. Some claimed they would sail over the edge of the world and fall endlessly.

Nobody moved, so Thomas lifted the man, slung him over his shoulder, and staggered down the precarious walkway to the dock. Several carts stood ready with supplies for the three ships. The largest was the carrack *Santa Maria*, sixty-two feet in length and capable of housing forty men. She was heavy and slow but more stable than the two smaller caravels.

Thomas dropped the body into an empty cart, ignoring the complaints of its owner. He would return it once he discovered more about the man who had been killed.

The house he shared with Jorge stood on the edge of the dock, facing west across the River Tinto to where Portugal lay. It did not look like land anyone would envy. Seagrass, scrub and dunes stretched far inland, whipped by a constant wind. Fishermen's cottages huddled together on the far shore. A caravel with furled sails floated next to a small dock. It flew no flag.

Jorge sat at the table eating bread and some unidentifiable meat. When he saw what Thomas had brought in, he rose and flung the food through the back door.

'I need the table,' Thomas said.

'In that case, I have an urgent appointment.'

Thomas smiled. 'Who is she?'

'I do not know yet, but at least I will be away from you.'

Once Jorge had left, Thomas removed the man's clothes. No, he thought, not 'the man'. He knew his name. Augustin Montras.

He was unmarried, as were all the barber-surgeons waiting to be told if they had been selected for the voyage. The journey had many dangers, and Queen Isabel had not wished to see widows and fatherless children left behind. Augustin's skills were good enough for a long voyage. He could pull teeth, stitch wounds and deal with minor ailments. Anything more serious would likely be fatal.

Thomas had told him only the day before that he was his choice to sail with Columbus. Now he would have to find a replacement.

He took a small blade from the leather satchel that always accompanied him. Thomas cut Augustin's clothes away, washed the body and leaned close. The knife wounds on his chest were clear to see, but Thomas would assume nothing until he was finished. He palpated the flesh, but no blood appeared, which confirmed what he already knew. The man had been killed elsewhere and taken to the Santa Maria. It must have been done in the deep of the night not to have been seen. Even so, Thomas had questions he would need to ask.

Would the carrack have watchmen? Would there be traders unloading their wares? What about those on the dockside? He made mental notes for later. He would write them down when he could. Memory was a fragile thing, particularly when it had too many calls on it.

He turned Augustin's body over and examined his back, buttocks and legs, but found nothing unexpected. When he checked the neck for any injury, he discovered hair had been torn loose and there were abrasions on the back of the head. Thomas wondered if Augustin had been struck from behind before being stabbed. He went to a set of shelves and returned with paper, quill and ink. He noted the number of strikes: five.

He noted bruising around the wounds and recorded that as well. It might indicate rage, the hilt of the knife slamming against flesh, or a punch for good measure. Someone had wanted Augustin dead. But why?

Thomas pulled a sheet from his bed and shrouded the body. He left it on the tabletop and went outside, to discover Jorge standing in the street.

'Do not go back inside,' Thomas said. 'The body is still there.'

'Then I will come with you. Where are we going?'

'To tell the Hermandos there has been a killing and ask them to find someone to bury the body. Then to Augustin's house, to see if there are any indications of what happened.'

'He is one of the physicians you chose?' asked Jorge, who had been with Thomas during the process because he saw into people in ways Thomas never could. It was a skill that had served them both well over the thirty years they had known each other. They had not always been friends but were now.

The house Augustin had used was set away from the docks. One of a row of a dozen, each assigned to an applicant for surgeon to the voyage. When Thomas tried the door, he found it locked. He went along the road and took a narrow alley, then came at the house from the rear. But that door too was locked.

He handed Jorge a thin metal tool, one he used in his own work, but which would suffice for a different purpose now. Jorge went to one knee and picked the lock. How he knew how to do so he had never revealed, and Thomas had stopped asking.

They entered a small kitchen. When Thomas held his hand over the embers in the fire, they were cold. An iron pot hung above the grate but it, too, was cold. Nothing showed that a meal had ever been eaten here. This was a temporary home.

The single room on the ground floor had a staircase to one side. Thomas walked the room, staring at the floor.

'What are you looking for?' asked Jorge.

'Blood.'

'Of course. How foolish of me to ask. Do you see any?'

Thomas shook his head. He climbed the staircase to the room above, which was only half the size. Here he found blood. It had pooled and dried, no doubt some draining through gaps in the floorboards. It would have been a great deal of blood. The fact it had dried told him the man must have been killed before midnight, but the fact it was dry also made it difficult to know how long before. It could have been an hour, or ten hours. Thomas had spoken with Augustin shortly after noon yesterday, so after that.

Augustin's death would have been quick, which was a blessing. Not as much as if he had not died, but a blessing all the same. Better than taking hours to die with every moment an agony. Other than the blood, nothing in the room told him more. Augustin had died here, taking any knowledge of his attacker with him. He was too recent an arrival to have made enemies, so had it been someone he knew? And why was he killed? Something he had done? Someone he had crossed? Some information he possessed?

As he descended the stairs, Thomas saw some hair caught between its treads. When he examined it more closely, he found more blood. It told him the body had been roughly dragged down these stairs, hence the marks on the back of Augustine's head. It would have been easy enough for one man to drag him that way. Did that mean a lone killer?

Thomas and Jorge left the way they had come. Out on the street, Jorge asked, 'Did you find what you were looking for?'

'I found what I was expecting, but not what I was looking for.'

'Which was?'

'Who killed him.'

'Ah, but you are Thomas Berrington, so you will. Since you so rudely interrupted mine, can we break our fast now?'

'You can. I need to question people.' A thought occurred to Thomas. 'I also need to select another physician. Go and eat. I will find you later at the house.'

'Not if that body is still there.'

Augustin Mantras could not have been hoisted into the rigging without someone making note of it. Thomas returned to the *Santa Maria* but was unfortunate to find Christopher Columbus standing at the wheel. The man came down to greet him.

'My friend.' Columbus clapped Thomas on the shoulder. 'Come the morning tide we will be on our way. You will see us off, yes?' He looked beyond Thomas. 'And that friend of yours, of course. I had hoped the queen might have come.'

'She has many calls on her time,' Thomas said. 'Has no one told you what happened here overnight?'

'Not more thieves,' said Columbus. 'We lose a quarter of what is delivered. I told men to stand watch, but they are worked hard and often fall asleep.'

'Not thieves,' Thomas said. 'A dead man was hoisted into the rigging. I am here to question your men, in particular those who were meant to be on watch.'

'A dead man? Do you know who?'

'Augustin Mantras, chosen to be physician for the *Santa Maria*. I will have to find another man today. There are still a few here in case of sickness or cowardice.'

Columbus stared at Thomas. 'You are sure you can find someone? By this time tomorrow we will be sailing into the wide ocean.' He smiled. 'Of course, you could always come in Mantras's stead. I trust your medical skill over that of any other man.'

'The queen wants me in Granada when I finish here, but I will bring you someone before sunset. First, I need to speak to your crew. Are most on board?'

'Bar a few more barrels of water and biscuits, we are ready to sail. I allowed the men to spend their last hours ashore enjoying themselves. They will have sore heads come morning, but memories to last the voyage. You are welcome to question those here, or you can hunt through the taverns and brothels to find the others.'

'Those here will suffice,' Thomas said.

An hour later he returned across the docks, having learned nothing. He could scarce believe no one had seen or heard anything, but all those he spoke to told the same tale. They slept soundly, or if they were on watch they saw no one. Unless one of them had killed Augustine, but Thomas did not think that likely.

No witnesses. No murder weapon. He was blocked. Thomas had to put his frustration aside because there were other matters to attend to, and little time.

Three physicians remained in Palos de Frontera, unless any had left after not being chosen. All had volunteered, despite the danger of crossing an unknown ocean with no guarantee of returning home. They had been promised a small fortune if they did. It was incentive enough.

Thomas went first to the man he favoured most, though he admitted Luis Santo had not been considered until now. He was a competent physician, better than the barber-surgeons chosen for *Pinto* and *Niña*, but not as skilled as Augustin. When he knocked on the door of his lodgings, he got no response, and a bad feeling came. Had more doctors than Augustin been murdered? The door was unlocked. Thomas performed a quick search of the ground floor but found nothing unexpected. A coat hung beside the door. A cold iron pot hung over the fire, as in Augustin's house. Upstairs there was nothing useful. The man's tools of his trade were in an aged leather bag similar to the one Thomas used. Other physicians had their own choices, but always something they could grab quickly. Thomas scored Luis Santo from his list and moved on.

José Volta opened his door on the first knock. Thomas explained about Augustin's death, but neglected to tell it was murder. He did not want the man thinking someone was selecting physicians as targets. Once he was on board and out at sea it would be too late to change his mind.

'I am surprised you came to me,' said José. 'I know I am not your first choice, or perhaps even your last. I am packing my things to leave tomorrow. Have you asked others before me, and they turned you down?' José did not seem concerned. Thomas admitted he had been to see Luis Sanso, but the man had already left.

'I spoke with him not an hour since,' said José. 'If he has left it was sudden. Do you need an answer now, or may I have a little time? I know the voyage is important, but not without its perils.'

'I can wait until noon, but no longer. You should know I also intend to speak with Juan Girabel.'

Luis offered a nod. 'He may be a better man for the task than myself.'

'Give it some thought,' Thomas said, and left.

Juan Girabel was Thomas's third choice, but in reality, no choice at all. He was close to forty, experienced but too old. The voyage would be hard on him. There was still much discussion regarding how large the world was and how wide the great ocean. Thomas believed he knew, but few wanted to hear a truth that did not suit them.

Juan was drunk when he admitted Thomas after some wait. His shirt was tied askew, and his long hair stuck out in several directions. Juan glanced at the staircase before asking Thomas if he wanted wine. He declined.

'Do I still get payment for turning up in this forsaken town?' asked Juan.

'You were told it was twenty silver coins for coming here. Ten times that if you take the voyage.'

'Spanish silver or that Moorish stuff?'

'Silver is silver.' Thomas wondered if the killing might have something to do with money. There was a great deal washing around in Palos de Frontera, and not all of it ended up where it was meant to. He knew he was being paid too much for the small amount of work he was doing but would be a fool to turn it down.

'Have you come here for a reason?' asked Juan. 'If not, I am busy.' He glanced upwards, as if that was explanation enough.

'I need a doctor for the *Santa Maria*. Would you be willing to do the work?'

'I might. When would you want me?'

'Tonight. They sail early tomorrow.'

'Tonight will do, but late. Do I come to the ship?'

'I will return here if you are needed,' Thomas said. Then, 'Do you know Augustin Montras was murdered?' He watched Juan for any reaction, but he showed neither surprise nor guilt.

Of course, if he was guilty, he most likely would not. Thomas's experience told him killers could present the face of an angel to the world, however dark their deeds. Not that Juan's face could ever be mistaken for that of an angel.

'I will be here,' he said.

From upstairs, the voice of a woman threatened to start without Juan if he did not come up right now.

'She would, too,' muttered Juan, turning away and climbing the stairs unsteadily. 'Shut the door when you leave.'

Left alone, Thomas checked the room without knowing altogether what he was searching for. Whatever it was, he did not find anything incriminating.

When Thomas found Jorge, he was talking with a woman he recognised as the wife of the captain of the *Pinto*. She was young, handsome, and hung on every word and gesture Jorge made, who enchanted all without ever seeming to try. Thomas once asked him how he did it, but Jorge said he did not know. He simply did.

When Jorge kissed the back of the woman's hand she flushed. He would leave her dissatisfied without knowing why. At least she would have one last night with her husband, and might offer him greater attention, thanks to Jorge's unsettling.

'Have you found your killer yet?' asked Jorge as he fell into step with Thomas, who headed towards the Santa Maria once more.

'I am no further forward. A new doctor needs to be found, so I have spoken with the three remaining. None are as suitable as Augustin Montras was.'

'Except they are alive,' said Jorge, which made Thomas scowl. 'I expect you will catch your man. Or it might have been a woman, yes?'

'I doubt it. Augustin was not a small man, and whoever killed him had to carry him from his house to the ship and then get him up where he was found. So, a man. Other than charming Vicente's wife, what else have you been doing?'

'Talking with people on your behalf. It is what I do best. I cannot fight like you, but I can unearth secrets when no one else can.'

'What secrets have you teased out today?'

'Several, but few that apply to your task. It appears Augustin Montras was deeply unpopular. A bully, and arrogant. He pressed himself on women whatever their status or who their husbands might be.'

'None of which would preclude him from being physician to the voyage.'

'It would not, but he might have angered a husband enough to kill him. I would suspect a local man, or one of the administrators. Not necessarily doing the deed themself, of course. Money flows as plentifully as the water of the Guadalquivir in this town. Over one million maravedis spent so far. Not all has ended up buying what it was meant to. A man with his fingers in that pot could afford to hire an assassin, or even a score.'

'Agreed,' Thomas said. 'In which case, why hang him from the rigging of the *Santa Maria*? If they wanted him out of the way, better to toss him in the river to float out to sea.'

'They wanted to show he had been punished. It would have been part of the contract taken out, and the *Santa Maria* was his intended home for the voyage. It had meaning for someone. Which is why I have spoken with the administrator's office.'

Thomas waited. They reached the *Santa Maria*, and he took the gangway for the third time that day, suspecting it would not be the last.

'And?' he asked.

'I spoke to those who were the bravest, but even sheep would make them look like cowards. They work with numbers and dockets, with silver and notes of promise. We are no further forward.'

'No, *we* are not.' Thomas was starting to suspect the killer was beyond punishment. If he was a hired man, he would be on his way to one of the big cities to disappear forever. Thomas knew he had too little time, and even less information.

He stared across the river to the far bank, where the unknown carrack remained at anchor. He turned to Jorge and said, 'Go back to the administrators and ask them who might want to stop this voyage. Tell them there is no wrong answer. Press them for ideas.'

'What will you be doing?'

Thomas glanced at the sky, noting the position of the sun. Already it sank towards the west. He juggled priorities in his head before saying, 'I will be making sure Columbus's new doctor is aboard the *Santa Maria* before dark. Only then can I think about Augustine's death, but already I believe we will never discover who killed him, or why. Sometimes you have to let things go and move on.'

'Isabel wants you to return to Granada,' said Jorge. 'She has plans for you.'

'She wants me where she can find me, that is all.'

Thomas made his way to Luis Sanso's house to see if he had returned. The man was his only choice, so was relieved to find him sober and his belongings packed ready for a voyage.

'Do we go now?' he asked after Thomas told him what he wanted.

'Not yet.' Thomas glanced at Luis's right hand, which was bandaged. 'Are you fit enough to serve?'

Luis laughed as he lifted his hand. 'This? It is nothing. I burned it in the fire. It will heal in a day or two. I assume all food and water are provided. I need only my clothes and the tools of my trade, which are here.'

'You will be paid on your return,' Thomas said. 'That is acceptable?'

'I have no one to send money to, so yes.'

Thomas helped Luis settle into a small cabin beneath the prow of the carrack. At least it was his own, and he did not have to share. Space was at a premium, much of it taken up with provisions. Barrels were stacked as high as they could go. Sacks of grain and biscuits filled every available crevice, including beneath and to the sides of the crew's hammocks, which would alternate between watches. On deck, more barrels were being tied down, containing enough water for the start of the journey. Thomas knew Columbus intended to break the voyage at the Azores. A speck of land in the middle of an endless ocean, but the man was confident he could navigate there, as he had done many times before. It was claimed sea water ran through his veins and the stars guided his way.

Luis accompanied Thomas on deck. He looked around, then kicked one of the barrels, which made a dull sound.

'These hold water?'

Thomas nodded.

'Is it enough for a voyage no one knows the duration of?'

Thomas told Luis of Columbus's plan to replenish supplies, which seemed to offer him satisfaction. He shook the man's hand and left the *Santa Maria*. He found Jorge in the small administration building, which was jammed tight with scribes and clerks frantically completing deals and making payments. Columbus was there, and Thomas told him he had found a doctor for the voyage.

'I wish it was you, my friend.'

'I am a poor sailor. Besides, the queen is expecting me.'

'There are rumours you are too close to her,' said Columbus. 'Take care, for the king is a jealous man.'

When Jorge approached, Thomas wished Columbus a safe voyage, which made him laugh.

'So,' Thomas said, once they were outside. 'Did you learn anything more?'

'My head aches with too much information. I may know something but cannot prise it from all the detail. Let us find somewhere to eat and drink and I will see if it settles my mind. Did you get your doctor aboard the *Santa Maria*?'

'I did.'

'Is he any good?'

'No, but I hope he will prove good enough. It is no longer my responsibility.' He thought of Augustin Montras and wondered if his death was still his responsibility. Would it matter if his killer was never found? In a few hours, the three ships would sail, perhaps never to be seen again. Time had run out. There was nothing more he could do. As the realisation settled through him his tension faded. One day, and then he and Jorge could ride east to Granada to resume their lives.

Thomas woke in darkness, not knowing what had roused him. He lay in his narrow bed, listening, but the night was as quiet as a buried coffin. He stared blind-eyed into the dark as doubt filled him. He thought he had set the murder aside. Good food and wine had seen to that, but as he slept his mind had continued working. He knew he would not find sleep again so he rose, dressed, and walked into the night.

On the dockside, lamps burned on the three ships and men

moved on deck. In a few hours they would follow the river estuary east, before turning west. The unknown awaited each vessel. Just as an unknown mystery eluded Thomas.

Why had Augustin Montras been killed? For something he knew? Something he had done, or not done? Or something he intended to do? Thomas had not considered the latter. Now it rose to the fore.

Augustin's house remained empty. He lit a lamp and searched again. He had already done so, but something nagged him to do it again. This time he went slowly. There was no rush. The time for haste had passed. Only curiosity made him continue until, when he took down the pot that hung over the fire, he found what he had missed before. As he held up the lamp, he saw a faint residue in the bottom and scraped a little onto the table. Leaning close, he saw a pale ochre granular dust. His mind worked through possibilities. Rust, dye, paint, wood detritus? He discarded them all until a darker thought rose.

Poison.

He licked the end of his smallest finger, touched it to the dust, then put it to his tongue. There came an immediate burning and numbness. Thomas ran into the yard behind the house and used the pump to wash his mouth out, swilling and spitting until sure he was safe.

Mandrake root. He had mixed it himself for medicinal purposes, but in stronger doses it was a potent poison. It acted quickly, and there were few antidotes. Those Thomas knew of were poor at best. This was meant to kill.

If Augustin had prepared mandrake, to what purpose? The small detritus left would be enough to kill a man. The whole pot would kill how many? The crew of a ship? Or three ships? Except Augustin had been the one killed.

Outside, Thomas discovered dawn had arrived, and he saw the dock empty of ships. He ran to Luis Sanso's house and took the iron pot from over the fire. When he peered inside, he saw more of the ochre dust, and everything became clear.

A single man stood on the empty dockside, staring across the river. The carrack on the far bank was still there. A Portuguese ship.

'When did they leave?' Thomas asked.

'Before dawn. The tide was right, and Columbus did not want to wait for the sun to rise.' He offered a smile that barely broke surface. 'On their way to...' – a shrug – '...who knows where?'

'I need to cross the river.'

'I can row you across, sir, but why? You know the far bank does not belong to Spain.'

'There is a caravel there and I have to follow Columbus. Wait here, I will only be a moment.'

When Thomas returned with a small, heavy sack, the man sat in a skiff, oars ready. Thomas climbed in and they set off across the river, which flowed fast with the outgoing tide. He feared the caravel would be abandoned, but as they approached, men appeared on deck. Fortunately, some spoke Spanish.

'Where is the captain?' Thomas called up.

'Standing before you, sir. What do you want in such a hurry?'

'May I come aboard?'

The man stared down, then nodded. 'Aye, if you wish.'

On deck, Thomas asked, 'Can you gather enough crew to sail?'

'To where, and why?'

'After Columbus. I fear all three ships and their crew are in danger.' Thomas held out the canvas bag. 'Take me, and this is yours whether we catch him or not.'

The man looked inside before grinning. 'Aye, this will do.

You are fortunate Columbus sails in a carrack. It is stable, but slower than a caravel. It will take us time to catch him, but with a fair wind and good fortune, catch him we will.'

'Why have you sat at dock here all this time?' Thomas asked, and the man laughed.

'My king sent me to watch the Spanish set sail to their doom. You seem a clever man, so will know there is no love lost between Spain and Portugal.

Men flung ropes ashore. A rising wind from the east caught at the sails and the boat heeled over. The captain spun the wheel with easy expertise as they sailed out into the river. When they reached the sea, there was no sign of the small fleet they were chasing. Not before noon, nor even into the night. Only as the following dawn rose did they catch sight of a sail in the distance. Beyond, the wide ocean threw waves in their faces, but they were gaining. Thomas judged himself fortunate the captain and ship had been sitting there. He suspected no one but this man could have brought him so close.

The *Santa Maria* dropped her sails when they sighted the pursuit. The two smaller caravels did the same. As they came close, a rowing boat was lowered. Thomas climbed into it, hanging on as waves threaten to turn it over.

'Have you decided to be my surgeon after all?' asked Columbus as he pulled Thomas aboard.

'Where is Luis?' Thomas asked.

'I have not seen him this morning. He is a poor sailor and threw up half the night. Shall I send someone to fetch him?'

'I know where he is.'

Thomas went below. He did not knock on the door to Luis's cabin, but when he opened it, the man was not there.

Thomas went on deck as fast as he could.

'Where do you store the water barrels?' he asked.

'Up here,' said Columbus. 'All of these, both sides. Enough to take us to the Azores.'

'Tell your crew not to drink from them.'

Thomas moved along the deck, opening each barrel. The first dozen were untainted. When he removed the top on the thirteenth he saw a wash of pale grains beneath it. He moved on, found another, then another. And then, as he neared the stern, he saw Luis Sanso. He had the lid of a barrel open and was pouring something from a canvas sack into it.

'Is this why you killed Augustine?' Thomas asked.

Sanso spun around so quickly he dropped the sack. Thomas pushed him aside and threw it overboard. Sanso swung a length of wood at him, but Thomas knocked it away easily.

'Why?' he asked.

He expected no response, but Luis said, 'The French king offered us a great deal of gold to make sure the voyage failed.'

'And you wanted it all for yourself, yes? How did you expect spend it with everyone dead? Can you sail a carrack single-handed?'

'There is a ship waiting for me. It was promised.'

'There will be no ship, French or otherwise.' Thomas stepped closer, aware of several crew watching. He reached out and ripped the bandage from Luis's hand to find what he suspected. A deep gash made with a sharp knife.

'Did he come to kill you, or you him?' he asked.

'He attacked me,' said Luis, then smiled. 'But in all honesty, I went to his house with the intention of killing him.'

Thomas half-turned. 'Fetch me a rope to bind this man. I will take him away once I have checked your water barrels. With luck not all are tainted.'

'The *Niña* and *Pinta* can help us if needs be.' Columbus said, before embracing Thomas. 'The queen will reward you well when she hears of this.'

Thomas smiled. 'She will not hear of it from me.'

'Sir!' one of the crew shouted, and Thomas turned to see Luis Sanso climb onto the transom. He hesitated a moment, then, as he saw Thomas start towards him, threw himself overboard. Men gathered and looked down to watch him drift away into open water.

'Send a boat after him,' ordered Columbus, but Thomas raised a hand.

'Let him swim until this ship he thinks is waiting for him comes. Which will never happen. I hear drowning can be a better death than the rope. He will discover the truth of it in a few hours.'

'Less in this sea,' said Columbus.

'I am no seaman, Christopher. I take your word on it.'

Columbus looked across the ocean blue, judging the height of the waves and their force.

'Yes, less than an hour. You are sure you want this?'

'I am sure, and tired.'

Back in the Portuguese caravel, Thomas asked if the captain could set him ashore. 'I will find a horse and return overland. I hate the sea.'

As Columbus's small flotilla raised their sails, Thomas looked across the water but saw no sign of the killer who had jumped overboard. He felt no satisfaction. Now two men were dead, both as guilty as each other. He wondered if all the doctors had been offered the same bribe. He suspected they had.

He went to the prow and gulped in a great lungful of spray, hoping he could keep from throwing up before they reached landfall.

Vaseem Khan

Vaseem Khan writes two award-winning crime series set in India. In 2021, *Midnight at Malabar House*, the first in the Malabar House novels set in 1950s Bombay, won the Crime Writers Association Historical Dagger. His latest is *The Girl in Cell A*, a psychological thriller set in small-town America. Vaseem is also the author of the upcoming *Quantum of Menace*, the first in a series featuring Q from the James Bond franchise.

vaseemkhan.com

THE STALKER

Vaseem Khan

I first realised that I was being followed on the day after my thirtieth birthday.

I was on my way back from work, a late finish at Morgan's tourist-tat store on Kennedy Street, a stone's throw from the beach. Darkness had descended on the little seaside town of Salting, a few miles west of Brighton. You might be forgiven for thinking that a week before Christmas, at the height of winter, the streets would be deserted. But one of the first things I discovered after moving here, six months earlier, was that Christmas in Salting is as popular as summer, the winding lanes full of flushed day-trippers, trussed up against the biting wind that whips in off the English Channel and puts the fear of God into the homeless.

Salting isn't a wealthy place. Like many seaside towns it's been on death row for decades, the slow slide into economic ruin, the steady march towards stagnation. And you can see it, if you take the time to walk even a little way off the main drag. Boarded-up houses; whole sections of rundown streets cordoned off, ready for the bulldozers. Shapes huddled in doorways. Why do people still come here? Because Salting is the sort of town that exerts a powerful force over our imagination; this is the England we think we know, the England we grew up believing in: piers and arcades and Ferris wheels and fish and chips by the sea. The problem is that nowadays people only come here for a day, never to stay. They spend money on the beachside stalls and the tourist shops, squeak excitedly at the seagulls, and then they go back to their cosy city homes, honking their oversized SUVs out of town and back onto the motorway.

The people who arrive here for the long haul – people like me – are those with few options.

In the run-up to Christmas, Morgan's stays open till eight.

Most of the shops were still open, and all the restaurants, so there were still plenty of people – mainly families – trudging up and down looking for the cheapest eatery, or just intent on squeezing the last dregs out of their day by the seaside. The pavement is narrow and you have to step into the road to let women with prams pass by, or the elderly, who clop along brandishing cheap NHS walking sticks, flashing dirty looks at anyone who doesn't resemble the sort of person they think should be living around here. And there are a lot of those types in Salting now.

It's about a mile to where I live and most of that route is along the high street, which always surprises visitors by being much longer than they think.

I noticed the man as a shadow on the edge of my vision, a blip on an internal radar that murmured the hairs along my inner ear. I suppose you might say that after years of watching my back I have become hyper-attuned to the presence of potential danger.

He was a black man, tall, probably in his fifties, with a short, greying beard and thick, silver-rimmed glasses. He wore a long puffer jacket, navy, and heavy trainers below jeans. Rings on almost every finger. A fisherman's beanie covered the top of his head. He had the look of a fading rapper. There was nothing immediately menacing about him, not out on the street, but then I popped into Sainsbury's to buy a bottle of milk and suddenly he was there again, just a few yards away, rigidly still, staring at me.

Our eyes met and I felt a curious ballooning of fear in my stomach. Something about his expression was off. Predatory. He looked away and began fumbling with a pot of yoghurt on the shelf.

Of course, I knew about the dangers in a place like Salting. Street crime was rife. Pickpockets, for the most part. Mobile phone thieves on mopeds. Drunken brawls after dark. Drugs. A seaside town attracts the type. Habitual users sent here to dry out. Attacks on women were rare, but not unheard of.

I paid for the milk and hurried out.

The rest of the way, I kept looking over my shoulder, poised to run at the first sign.

I didn't see him again.

My landlady, Mrs Taylor, was still up, watching a reality TV show in the living room.

Gladys Taylor is a sixty-year-old widow who survives by renting out the three spare bedrooms in her larger-than-average home. Her husband had made a killing out in the Gulf, and had bought the place a long time ago. They had moved in a decade earlier. A week after settling in, he had suffered a massive heart attack, fallen out of his newly purchased boat, and drowned. Mrs Taylor hadn't remarried.

'What an idiot,' she said, not lifting her eyes from the television. 'Silly slut actually thinks it's him.' The series was called

I Wanna Marry Harry, a short-lived dating show where women tried to woo a Prince Harry lookalike. Mrs Taylor was obsessed by it, as she was by all things monarchy related.

I mumbled something non-committal, then clumped upstairs to my room.

Kicking off my clothes, I quickly showered, the pipes groaning thunderously.

Afterwards, wiping steam from the mirror, I looked at myself.

I am a petite white woman, mousy blonde and brown-eyed. Having turned thirty the day before, I could easily have passed for younger. But not if you looked in my eyes. If you look into my eyes, you might see a woman who has lived several lifetimes and maybe doesn't want to live many more.

I dressed in track bottoms and a hoodie, then went downstairs to cook.

Mrs Taylor doesn't provide meals. Nor towels. Nor a cleaning operation. The rent here is low because she does precisely nothing, except sit around smoking all day and passing comments on the TV.

As I busied myself in the kitchen, she wandered in, her customary fag jittering between her fingers. 'Man came around looking for you earlier.'

My hands froze, fingers clenching around the knife as it hovered above the loaf of bread.

'Big black guy. Didn't much like the look of him.'

'Did he say who he was?'

'No. I asked, but he just sort of stared at me, then left.'

'Did he ask for me by name?'

'Helen Cassidy.'

My spine turned to water. He knew my name. *Who was this man?*

'He sound familiar?'

'No. I don't know who he is.'

'Well, you know the rules. No men on the premises.' She walked into the room. 'Show me your arms.'

'What?'

'Your arms.'

I stared at her. Her jaw was set in that way she got when her temper was up. A cold temper.

I pulled back the sleeves of my hoodie.

'All the way up.'

I complied and watched her check out the crook of my elbows. 'Fine. But I catch you using and you'll be out of here so fast your arse won't touch the floor.'

I glared at her, yanked my sleeves back down, went back to making my sandwich.

She eyed me a little longer, then walked back to the living room.

Later that night, I found myself at my bedroom window, peering from behind the curtain to the street below.

Did I imagine a face lurking around the corner, eyes gleaming in the dark?

Sleep came uneasily, and I drifted in and out of dark dreams, reliving moments of my life that left me bathed in a cold sweat, awake, and unable to cross the river back to the other world.

The next day I turned up for work to find my boss, John Morgan, in a foul mood. John was the grandson of the original Morgan, a fact by which he set great store; he was also a man too full of spit and vinegar for a customer-facing role.

I hadn't seen my stalker again that morning. I had toyed with the idea of taking an Uber to work, but in the end had decided against it. Instead, I armed myself with a fruit knife from Mrs Taylor's kitchen. Probably not the wisest course of action, but I wasn't thinking clearly.

Now, in the cold light of day, surrounded by the early morning bustle of the high street, my fears seemed foolish. Whoever this man was, he wouldn't be silly enough to try anything. Not after announcing his presence at the guest house.

John was having his usual moan about the immigrant crisis. He was the sort of man who went out of his way to make it clear his objections were rooted purely in economic rationality. He was no racist, merely a pragmatist. He had seen the writing on the wall a long time ago. You couldn't sustain such an influx. The mocha-drinking liberal elite had no clue, living in their London mansions. John had told me many times that he had voted for Brexit purely because he saw no other way to save the town. As far as he was concerned, Salting was sinking into the sea, weighed down by the needs of those who didn't belong here.

I had always stopped myself from asking whether he thought *I* belonged here.

I suppose I should be grateful that he had offered me paid employment. I had been so long out of the job market that finding such work was anything but straightforward. But John, for all his faults, was a decent human being. And who among us is without sin? Certainly not me.

It was a busy morning, and we did a brisk trade. I cleaned up the store, stacked shelves, navigated my way around customers desperately looking for the cheapest thing they could get away with that might satisfy their whining, entitled kids. *Little barracudas*, as John called them. *Little shits*, when he was feeling less charitable. Most of the stuff Morgan's sells is garbage. Cheap tat made in China or Bangladesh or Vietnam and stamped with the Cross of Saint George. The hypocrisy in this has never seemed to strike John.

Lunchtimes are as unpredictable as the weather. John usually lets me wander off around one o'clock. My routine is the same each day. I take my backpack, with my homemade lunch, and wander down to the beach. I sit on a bench and eat, looking out to sea.

I love the sea. I grew up in a concrete jungle, inner city London, a place so compressed by poverty and dying dreams that it was almost impossible to breathe.

But here I can look out onto a horizon so vast I can barely encompass it.

In the middle distance, a line of wind turbines poked up out of the dark expanse, marching along the coastline. Boats bobbed on the chop. A few hardy types floated in the water, dressed in wetsuits. Joggers ran behind dogs. Families stood carefully back from the water's edge, taking in the sea, drawing in lungfuls of air as if it might vanish and they needed to get as much of it locked away as possible before they went home to their polluted Edens.

It was then that I saw the man again.

I turned my head and there he was, about a hundred yards away, standing beside a food truck. He wasn't quite part of the queue; he stood quietly to one side, hands tucked into his puffer, eyes on me.

Fear slithered up my spine. I was gripped by conflicting impulses. I wanted to walk up to him, confront him. At the same time, my instincts were telling me that would be a bad move. In moments like this, you doubt yourself. Of course you do. The human reaction, when faced with danger, is to flee. More often than not that is the right thing to do.

It's a lesson I have learned the hard way.

He began walking towards me.

I stood up. A gull perched on the edge of the bench, waiting for scraps from my sandwich, flapped into the air, squawking angrily.

Paralysis gripped my legs. He came closer, flashing in and out of view as he passed behind pedestrians on the seafront.

I shook myself awake, turned, and walked away.

Behind me, I saw him pick up pace. I moved faster. Soon I was running.

It was only when I got back to Morgan's that I realised I had left my backpack on the beach.

Over the next two days I saw him again, several times.

I had started taking an Uber to and from work, an expense I could ill afford. And I hadn't gone back to the beach for lunch, instead eating in the little storeroom at the back of the shop. Not that this sudden change in routine seemed to alert John to the fact that something was going on with his only staff member. The man was too wrapped up in himself and his ever-widening list of grievances, against the state, the local council, his fellow Salting residents, his family, God.

But I couldn't entirely cocoon myself off from the world.

On the Tuesday, I walked out of Sainsbury's with a bag of groceries to find him barrelling down the road towards me. I turned and shot off. On the Wednesday, I saw him just as I got into my Uber, a dark ghost floating ominously along the crowded pavement, a mobile phone tucked under his chin.

I waited for him to pay another visit to the guest house, but, for some reason, he didn't.

The sensible thing would have been for me to go to the local police station and register a complaint. But that wasn't an option, for many reasons, not least of which was that I knew, with utter certainty, how useless such a complaint would have been.

Until recently, stalking was barely considered a serious crime. On the list of police priorities it ranked a distant low behind more pressing concerns. After all, as I had heard time and time again, until a man actually *does* something, he hasn't really committed an offense. And unless you can prove a pattern of harassment – the constant bombardment of unwanted and abusive phone calls, emails, text messages, or persistent surveillance – it was hard to gather enough evidence to take stalking over the line.

The truth is that you need your stalker either to be visibly batshit crazy or to actually hurt you before the police will take an interest. The technical definition of the offence is for the offender to behave in a way that makes the victim feel scared, distressed, or threatened. Intimidation and life invasion.

The fact that I *did* feel that way counted for nothing.

Not with my past.

Four days later, he finally caught up with me.

For the past few days, he appeared to have vanished. I had no sightings of him. By the time Sunday rolled around, I had all but convinced myself that he had left. Whatever his motive had been in tracking me down, in following me around, he had, ultimately, decided to leave me alone. My relief was palpable, though edged with the feeling that this wasn't over. How could it be? He had asked for me by name!

I decided to walk to church. Religion had come late into my life. I had been born Catholic, but my single mother had been scathing rather than practising. I had long ago lost touch with her, but, in so doing, had found my way to God.

The little church in Salting that I went to was a red-brick affair, with an elderly priest who had been around for decades. Entering the confessional with him was a straightforward matter. He had heard it all, and took a perfunctory approach to the absolving of sin. I sensed that he knew he wouldn't last much longer and was merely trying to get through to the end without making a mess. He didn't seem to much care for his flock; but that suited me fine. I had no wish for a priest who wanted to take a magnifying glass to either my past or my soul.

After the service, I began walking home.

I turned a corner, and there he was.

For a moment, I said nothing. I imagined my startled expression said it all.

He raised a hand, muttered something, but I was already turning to flee.

I heard him chasing, flapping behind me. A cry rose inside me, but nothing emerged.

And then, without warning, I tripped. I fell, hit my head on the pavement, found myself momentarily stunned.

And there he was, looming over me.

'No, no!' I raised my arms, warding him off.

'Helen.' His voice was thick and urgent. 'My name is David Mills. I'm Tanya's father. I just want to talk to you.'

Tanya.

The world went away. I felt the pavement melt beneath me, turn to water; I sank and began to drown.

Fourteen years ago, I murdered a girl named Tanya Mills. A mixed-race girl who went to a rival school. I was sixteen at the time, part of a group of girls who called themselves a gang. We grew up on an estate. We were tough and we made sure everyone knew it. We took no shit from anyone.

Tanya and I got into it at the local multiplex. Two rival girl gangs having a go. Preening. Egging each other on. A bitter war of words that soon turned into a raging fire.

A few days later, Tanya hacked into my social media, posted a load of insulting videos. An open challenge.

A fortnight after that, we came across each other again. Only this time Tanya was on her own. And I was armed with a blade.

She died on the pavement.

The judge told me that my crime was wicked. That there was now a zero-tolerance policy to this sort of knife crime. That I had taken a beloved daughter from her family and that young thugs like me were a menace to society.

I spent fourteen years in prison, almost as long as I had been alive at the point that I committed my crime.

I changed. I became a whole other person, one that I never believed could even exist.

At the time of her death, all I knew about Tanya was that, like me, she had grown up in a single-parent home, with a white mother. Her father had been out of the picture for a very long time.

And now here he was.

We sat in a café.

'I don't want to hurt you,' he told me. 'I just want to know about my daughter. I— I walked out on her when she was a baby. I never really knew her.'

'Why now?' I asked him.

'Why not?' he replied.

He had taken off his glasses. There was a sadness in his eyes, and something else, something I couldn't begin to fathom.

'There's nothing I can tell you,' I said. 'I didn't know your daughter. She was just a girl I came across. The girl I... killed.' My stomach fell away. My eyes drained of light.

He reached a hand across the table, placed it over my own. It pulsed warmly. 'It's okay,' he said, in a voice as gentle as a falling leaf. 'It's okay.'

And I began to cry and thought I might never stop.

Jane Petersen Burfield

Jane Petersen Burfield is an award-winning author of short fiction. She loves to show the darkness that lurks behind the facade of sweet domesticity and respectability. Her story 'There Be Dragons' was a finalist for the Crime Writers of Canada Award of Excellence for Short Stories.

THE RAMA CABIN

Jane Petersen Burfield

Amelia leaned back into the seat of Rob's car, watching wet snow bead on the windshield before being swept away by the wipers. The drive from Toronto to Orillia this late at night was soothing. Few headlights on the other side of the highway interrupted the darkness. Her brother, Rob, was an excellent driver and knew the way to the cabin on Lake Couchiching. She hoped she could find peace there as she had when she was a child. It would be a good place to remember their grandfather, and for her to get better.

She woke up briefly when streetlights along Highway 12 interrupted the darkness but fell back asleep as they headed north on the Rama Road. It was still dark when they arrived at the cabin. Rob brought their bags in and built a fire in the woodstove. He guided Amelia up to her old room, where she used the commode, swabbed her face with bottled water, swooshed out her mouth, and fell asleep in her bed, fully clothed.

Rob fed more wood into the stove, looked for leaks from the rain, and went to bed as early light lit up the eastern sky. They would deal with all the challenges in the morning.

* * *

On Saturday, Amelia woke first when sunlight flowed into her bedroom through dirty glass. Reluctantly, she got up, shivering in the coldness of a late April day. She smoothed out her short red hair in front of the bedroom mirror. Outside her window, she saw Lake Couchiching, small waves dancing where the ice had thinned. After putting on slippers and a green housecoat, she went quietly downstairs. In the chilly kitchen, she stirred the coals in the stove and added more wood. Percolating coffee on the stove filled the small space with a lovely aroma.

Despite the cold, Mia opened the front door for fresh air. The soft odour of spring earth under the wet snow was delicious. With a mug in her hand, Amelia sat wrapped in an afghan and thought about her grandparents. They had been anchors in her chaotic childhood. She couldn't believe Grandpa was gone. She wished she had made more time to visit him this past year.

She glanced around the downstairs rooms filled with memories. Worn blankets were folded on the blue armchair near the stove. The linoleum kitchen counter was tidy but covered in fine grit. When she turned her head to look for her favourite sketches on the wall behind her, she was puzzled to see they were missing. 'Find sketches' was the first item on her list of what needed to be done.

Finishing her coffee, Mia found the broom and dustbin. She wet the bristles in snow outside the cabin door and began to sweep the kitchen and lounge. A mask kept most of the dust from her congested sinuses. She swept away the spiderwebs attached to the ceiling and walls near the window. And then she sat down beside the stove, exhausted by her work. She wondered how much longer her cold – picked up, no doubt, on her flight home from England – would last. And she fell back asleep.

* * *

Three hours later, Amelia came into Rob's room with a coffee and a smile. 'Time to get up! We have a lot to do,' she said.

Rob buried his head in his covers. 'We were up so late, Mia. Just another hour.'

'Not on your life, brother dear. We need to get this place civilised. It needs cleaning, repair and I don't know what else. Drink your coffee. It'll make you feel better.'

Rob sat up, stiffly. 'When are we getting power and water? It's cold in here.'

'Monday morning,' said Amelia. 'I phoned the utilities companies yesterday. We'll have to cook on the stove and use bottled water till then. I'll see you downstairs in a few minutes.'

Half an hour later, Rob came down the stairs to find the warm kitchen full of the smell of toast and coffee. Amelia was frying eggs in Grandma's cast-iron pan, and the table was set with bottles of juice, jam and butter.

'This reminds me of the power outages when we were kids. The grandparents always managed to make great meals on the woodstove,' Rob said.

'I miss them. Grandma died more than ten years ago. Now Grandpa is gone too,' said Amelia. 'I wish I had a few more days with him. I have so many questions I never asked.'

'Are we all set for the Celebration of Life service on Tuesday?' Rob asked.

'I still have a few details to arrange,' Mia said.

'Don't push yourself too hard,' he said. 'How are you feeling today?'

'Tired. Congested from the dust.' She put the scrambled eggs on two melamine plates and brought them to the table. 'I'm looking forward to feeling warm.'

Over breakfast they planned what they had to do in the cabin and at Grandpa's business up the road in Garden Park. Rob wanted to work on the outside of the house, repairing the roof, fixing some shaky railings and rotten wood in the porch. Amelia planned a preliminary clean of the rooms and then sorting generations of stuff inside the cabin. With luck, they should have finished their tidy-up and could go home to Toronto by the weekend.

The day flew by while Amelia, protected by a mask from the haze of dust, wiped every surface in the kitchen and swept the floor. She made tea several times that morning and then got back to work.

Outside, Rob put a tarp over a leak in the corner of the roof and assessed the supplies he would need after measuring the porch and steps. He emptied the commode in the old outhouse and filled two buckets of snow to be boiled for cleaning. At noon, Rob drove to Orillia to pick up building supplies and a takeout lunch for them, along with ice for the cooler. Mia hugged him when he produced the chicken soup, appealing to her diminished appetite.

After a necessary nap, Amelia began sorting the stacked paper on the kitchen shelves. She was disappointed to find mostly old recipes, newspapers from different decades and some letters and bills. She did find a notebook of Grandpa's thoughts and daily life. Amelia looked for more of the old, buff-coloured notebooks, hopefully some with her grandma's sketches in them.

Later in the afternoon, she sat, deeply tired, in the kitchen armchair, taking a cold pill with a bottle of lemonade. Her throat was starting to hurt again. Rob invited her to town for dinner, but she asked him to bring her takeout instead.

After scrubbing off dust and dirt in warmed water, Rob reminded Amelia to lock the door behind him. He was surprised to feel uneasy at the cabin, a place of refuge in the past.

* * *

At the bistro, Rob was directed to a booth near the back. He read the local paper while he waited for his meal. Grandpa's service was in the announcements next to the Obituaries. When the waitress brought his pasta, he heard someone call his name.

'Hey, Rob!' Tim said as he came over to the table. 'I'm so sorry to hear about George. A good man. He taught me how to fish.'

'Tim! Good to see you.' Rob waved at Gina and Ben, other high school friends at Tim's table. 'Thanks for your thoughts. Grandpa was special, wasn't he?'

'He was. I'm going to write a story about him for the paper on Saturday. I'll interview some people at the service if that's okay. Do you have a photo we could use?' Tim asked.

'Sure. I didn't know you worked for the local paper, Tim.'

'I own it,' Tim replied with a smile. 'Do you want to join our table? Are you here on your own?'

'Another time. I'm up with Amelia,' said Rob. 'She's getting over a bad cold and stayed at the cabin. I don't want to be too long. We're sorting out paperwork and cleaning, and it's bringing back the years after our parents were killed, when we lived with our grandparents. Without them, I don't know where we would have gone.' Rob was silent in memory.

'Your cousin, Gerrie, comes to Orillia sometimes. No one likes him much. Do you hear from him?' Tim asked.

'Rarely,' Rob said. 'I should eat my dinner and get back out to the cabin.'

'Do you need help cleaning? I could come out tomorrow,' Tim said. 'I'd love to see the cabin again.'

'I think Amelia needs quiet time. She's upset. Can you visit later in the week?'

'How about lunch in town tomorrow?' Tim asked. 'I know Gina and Ben would like to see you both.'

Tim thought for a few moments. 'I can come. But I'd rather let Mia rest up at home before the service.'

'Sounds good. See you tomorrow. And we'll see Amelia at the service on Tuesday. A lot of the town will be there,' Tim said. He put his hand on Rob's shoulder. 'You look like George, you know. Same blue eyes.' Rob smiled while Tim went back to his table.

Rob ordered soup and a chicken sandwich for Mia, finished his coffee and drove back to the cabin. He wondered how Mia would feel about meeting Tim again. Their romance had lasted for much of high school.

As he pulled into the driveway, the sun was going down in the west, illuminating the ice in the lake through the skeleton tree branches. He shivered when he looked down at the shore.

Amelia heard the car and met him on the front porch. 'This place is beautiful at sunset,' she said. 'After difficult days, it always soothed me.'

'It scared me. Maybe Grandpa's stories stirred up some primitive fears,' he laughed.

Amelia had supper and set the enamelled kettle on the stove for tea. As they listened to a portable radio, Mia searched for the two sketches. She looked in the lounge in the back of the cabin but didn't see them there. Tiredness, physical and emotional, made her decide to go to bed early. One more day, and she could have a hot bath.

She turned as she put her foot on the first step. 'Rob, do you remember the sketches of the lake through our trees? They were on the wall in here. I loved them. I think they were done by a visiting artist a long time ago. I can't find them.'

'I remember but I haven't seen them, Mia. Maybe Gramps put them away? I remember the two of them, similar in style.

I liked them too, and I remember how much Grandma loved them,' Rob said. 'We'll look tomorrow.'

Mia nodded and headed with a lantern up the stairs.

Downstairs, Rob sat staring at the flames through the stove grate. Memories from childhood at this cabin overwhelmed him. He looked around the kitchen, a place of safety for Mia and him throughout their early teens. After reading the first few pages from an old novel and stoking the fire, he locked the door and climbed the stairs.

Rob glanced out his bedroom window at the nearly full moon and then at the shoreline. Grey mist at the water's edge reminded him of his childhood dread. He felt a familiar frisson of terror, and knew the primitive fears of the child would always be there. He drew his curtain.

Downstairs, the cabin returned to its silence. And outside, there was a sense of anticipation, of waiting.

Early Sunday morning, dust motes circulated in the sunlight coming through Amelia's bedroom windows. She rolled over and buried her face in her pillow, knowing she wasn't ready to get up. Her throat hurt, her backed ached from yesterday's activities and she felt rather ill. She reached for her small radio on the bedside table and put on the seven o'clock news. The usual reporting about politics, American presidential candidates and economic woes preceded the weather. Another sprinkle of snow was predicted for the Orillia area.

Out her window, she saw diamond shards dancing on the water of the lake near the shore. Ice breakup should happen soon with the warmer temperatures.

In slippers and warm robe, she went downstairs to make a much-needed morning tea. Too much dust yesterday had assaulted her lungs. She'd wear a better fitting mask today. After freeing the coals from a covering of ash, she stirred them up before putting more wood on.

And tomorrow, with electricity and water, life would become much more pleasant! A hot bath would ease her congestion and her muscles. Rob would look less like a lumberjack when he shaved.

Mia pulled four boxes of documents towards the blue chair. She knew she could sort at least three of them before Rob awoke. Growing heat from the stove made her sleepy. She closed her eyes and rolled into thoughts of the past, both good and bad. She thought of Grandma's loving hugs, of the stories she heard at the dinner table. She remembered helping Grandpa keep the garden pretty, of his short fishing trips with her in the old canoe. And then she thought of Gerrie, of his grasping hands, and she woke up with a shudder.

To lighten her mood, Mia decided to wake her brother up in her favourite way. Picking up a pot and a wooden spoon, she climbed upstairs and banged the pot mightily beside his bed. And like yesterday, he alligator-rolled over to bury his face in his sheets, but after breathing in, he began to cough from the dust.

'These beds desperately need cleaning, Mia!'

'I know. I'll vacuum the mattresses tomorrow when we have power. Betty is coming next week to clean. I want this week here for us, for our memories.'

'Betty was with Grandpa when he had his stroke,' Rob said. 'I called her to find out what had happened. She called an ambulance, but it was too late. She said Gerrie had visited that afternoon and left Grandpa very upset.'

'I didn't know that. I don't ever want to see him again!'

'I want to thank Betty again for everything she's done,' said Rob.

'Look at that sunshine,' Mia said, pointing to his window. 'Another glorious day! Time for us to get going.'

Mia decided she would clean the windows, wet-wipe the lounge shelves and sweep the upstairs floor. In the afternoon, she would tackle more paperwork. Like yesterday, she made herself a coffee while she got started.

Rob came downstairs to see clean windows in the kitchen and lounge, coffee hot on the stove, and a toasted bagel on the table. He sat, waiting for his brain to finish waking up.

'Good morning, Little Miss Sunshine,' he said, with a grimace.

Mia smiled back. Maybe memories were affecting him as well. She moved to take a pot of hot water off the stove. 'I'm looking forward to cleaning the curtains and rugs. I may take them into the laundromat in town later this morning. Remember how we used to wash them in the lake?'

'Yes. They often smelled a little fishy. I'm going to town for an hour or two at noon. I can take you.'

'Thanks, Rob. We could have lunch.'

'I can't join you. I have a meeting. But there's a restaurant right across the street from the laundry,' Rob said. 'You can have lunch and charge your phone between washing and drying.'

Mia looked curious but didn't want to cross-examine Rob about who he was meeting. He needed his privacy, she thought. 'Okay,' Mia said. 'We can stop at the grocery store on our way back to the cabin. We need more ice and cleaning supplies, and we can pick up supper.'

In town, at the diner, Mia felt eyes on her. She looked around and saw Gerrie sitting at the counter, staring at her. As he got down from his stool, the waiter came to her table with the bill. She left money on the table and walked quickly out the door. She hoped Gerrie didn't see her ducking inside the laundromat.

Rob picked her up and they drove back to the cabin after a quick stop at the grocery store. Amelia sat in the rocking chair, surrounded by storage boxes. She sorted the paper into piles: bills, bank, correspondence, photographs, notes and discards. As she worked, she realised what a vivid picture the collection gave of life in earlier days in this region. Logging, fishing, business and town politics.

Could she transform the cabin into a museum experience for the local schoolchildren? She must talk to Rob over dinner.

Papers flew through her fingers, getting put into piles. She crowed in delight at one box. When Rob came in from working on the canoe, he sneezed from the dust released by the sorting. 'Any treasures, Sis?' he asked.

'I found them! The sketches. They were in a box with some journals and other papers. Betty left a note that Grandpa asked her to hide them.' She held them out for Rob to see.

'They are wonderful,' he said, looking at a sketch of the lake seen through a foreground of pine trees. The other sketch showed the view north towards Washago. There were no signatures.

'Grandpa talked about artists visiting the cabin on the way to Algonquin Park,' Rob said.

'I also found notebooks with sketches and paintings,' Mia said. 'Do you remember Grandma teaching art in the summer? You were off working in the store or fishing with Grandpa. I stayed here, sitting near the classes, working on my own sketchbook. I found several books, including mine. I'd forgotten how much I enjoyed drawing.'

'Can I see yours?' Rob asked.

Mia looked hesitant but passed it to Rob when he gave a beckoning wave. Rob looked through a few pages in some surprise.

'You were good!' he said. 'Lake views, canoes, people. You must keep these, Mia.'

Mia smiled. 'I will. I've also found some of Grandma's books. Her mother was an artist, and Gran's drawings are good.'

Rob seemed to be in a good mood, Mia thought. She took a breath and launched her idea.

'I'm getting some great information about the practicalities and experiences of living here in the old days. I think there's information in the papers and books going right back to the first decade of the 1900s. What I want to do, Rob, is turn this place into a history experience for schoolkids. I could live upstairs and have them visit downstairs for a half-day of classes. They could learn about early life in the bush.'

Silence was not the reaction Mia had hoped for. He sat in his chair, shaking his head a bit.

'I don't know, Mia. I was hoping to sell the land. It's worth a lot. How would you pay for the upkeep, for taxes, for your living expenses?'

'I think I could get a teaching position in town. And I'll write a book about life here at the turn of the twentieth century. The logging and quarrying for railroads. The growth of Orillia. Local families. Stories, legends, even ghost stories.

'Grandpa's business in Garden Park continues to bring in a good income. I heard it was still doing well from the lawyer. Are you interested in taking that? It's on picturesque land on the lake,' Amelia said. 'We could have both properties appraised, and make sure we each get an equal portion. And you could always come up to the cabin to stay.'

Rob got up to walk to the window and back. 'You surprised me with this, Mia. Let's think about it and talk another time. Now, let me get our supper warmed up.'

'And tomorrow, hot water!' Mia said. 'I can't wait for a bath. Luxury!'

'And an electric stove. Coffee pot! Cold beer,' Rob said.

'Vacuum cleaner,' Mia added with a smile.

On Monday morning, Mia was delighted to find the power had been turned on. When she turned the kitchen tap, water poured out. She left it running to clear out rust from the pipes. What a luxury it was to fill the electric coffee pot and turn it on.

Smelling the enticing coffee aroma, Rob came downstairs in his robe. 'My, my. We are back in the twenty-first century!' He poured two cups, and they sat to talk.

'I've been thinking about your idea for the school, Mia. I have some concerns. I think it will take more money than the estate has. Your expenses will creep up and eat your capital.'

'I can do this,' Mia said.

'Let me finish,' said Rob. 'You must be practical about this idea. Can you talk to the school board before you make this decision? See if they like the idea and have funding for it?'

'I'll call and make an appointment,' Mia said. 'Are you reluctant to let me do this for other reasons?'

How could he tell her about the sense of menace he felt outside, near the shore. Rob was embarrassed to reveal this sense of dread.

'I want you to think about the financial demands of your idea. How will you like being isolated here on the lake? What will you do with your condo in the city? There are so many questions. And if it doesn't work, you won't have a job or money.'

'I'm going to talk to our lawyer and financial advisor.'

'I think you've been through some painful times in the last few months. And I don't want you to have to go through more, Sis.'

Mia smiled. A younger brother taking care of his older sister. She felt cherished.

Rob went to the kitchen counter and got a toasting fork and bagel. He turned to her, noticing the new spray of lines on her face and dark circles under her eyes. 'What happened in England, Mia?'

She swept her hand up the right side of her face. 'I had a tough ending with Peter. He had another girlfriend. I saw them together at a restaurant, and it was obvious they were a couple. When I asked him about her, he got rough.'

Rob crossed to the chair and hugged Mia. 'I'm so sorry. You deserve better.' He opened the stove door and held the bagel near the flames.

'We do have an electric toaster,' Mia said, looking at the rapidly browning bagel, 'but that smells good.'

Rob laughed. 'The other toasting fork is waiting. Shall I stab a bagel for you?'

'Yes, please,' she said.

By late morning Mia had sorted another dozen boxes. She found notebooks filled with random notes her grandmother had written. And she found several more of Grandpa's journals which had tantalising hints about painting. A grainy black-and-white photo pictured two men in the canoe holding a large muskie aloft as they neared the shore.

Mia phoned the Orillia library to ask for research help. She booked an appointment for that afternoon. After a quick lunch, they drove into town with the two sketches, notebooks and photo. Hillary Kershaw, the archivist and librarian, greeted them in her office.

'There's a family story,' Rob said, 'that Tom Thomson and other artists stayed at our cabin with our family back around 1913. We think these sketches might be by Thomson.'

'If they are, they'll be valuable. Let's see what I can find.' Hillary searched the 1912 to 1914 town newspaper files and other sources, but didn't find anything.

'Do you have evidence Thomson stayed at the cabin, Mia?' Hillary said. 'Any family stories, photographs?'

'We were told he and other artists visited. Great-Grandmother Fraser was a known artist and quite the hostess, we were told. Artists liked to visit on their way north. Many of them worked on a new form of Canadian painting, showing nature the way they saw it.'

'We have looked at some of the papers stored in boxes and on shelves at the cabin,' said Mia. 'There's still a lot of documents to examine. I remember Grandpa using papers to start fires in the woodstove, but he would have been careful not to burn important ones.'

'Try to find direct references to the visitors, Mia,' Hillary said. 'A friend knows about the painters in this area. We could ask him about your sketches.'

'I wish I had asked Grandpa when I was here last summer. He knew about so much! He used to tell us stories at the dinner table,' Mia said. 'I can't remember much about those stories now.'

'Do you remember how Grandpa loved to scare us with a ghost story about a girl who drowned in the lake?' Rob asked. 'If she found you on the shore at night, she would pull you into the water. It sure kept us from going down to the shore on our own when it was dark.'

'I've heard that story,' Hillary smiled. 'I'll keep looking through the library documents. I suggest you contact the Owen Sound Thomson Gallery. They may have more info there.'

'Thanks,' said Mia. She looked at the sketches she had brought in. 'My grandparents drew the lake and the bush as well. Their work seems darker, more filled-in and not like the defined lines in these two sketches.'

'We still have a lot of papers to go through,' Rob added. 'We'll look for any mention of Thomson in the family journals.'

'Could you lock these sketches up here, somewhere secure?' Mia asked.

'I can,' Hillary said. 'Let me know what you find. Let's meet again in a few days. If these are early Thomson sketches, they're very valuable.' She walked them to the door. 'We should keep this quiet for now.'

Mia and Rob discussed the art and took advantage of the Wi-Fi while at a nearby café.

'Google shows Thomson began sketching at Algonquin Park the summer of 1912,' Mia said.

'That's when he may have stopped into Fraser's Outfitters. The store sold sketching supplies and journals like the ones Grandpa kept. Thomson died just five years later, when he was canoeing at the park.'

Mia sipped her coffee. 'I'll spend the rest of the day at the cabin, searching. Grandpa wrote his journal regularly. In the two 1920s notebooks I've looked at, his subjects jumped around from what wildlife they had seen on a hike to what he thought about life. I'm hoping to find his journals from 1912 to 1915, where he might have written about visitors.'

'I'll work on repairing the cabin in the mornings this week and help you in the afternoon,' Rob said.

They drove back to the cabin in late afternoon. As they pulled into the drive, Rob and Mia looked at the open door in dismay. The lock had been pried open, and the downstairs rooms were in chaos. Who had done this? Had they found any of the journals or the art?

They spent the next hour talking to the police and then trying to tidy up. Rob warmed up a quick supper. An hour later, Mia went up to bed while Rob figured out how to keep the cabin safe until he could replace the lock in the morning.

He pushed the kitchen table against the front door and sat up reading for several hours. Around midnight, Rob looked out the window one last time. Down by the lake, he saw mist that reminded him of his childhood ghost. Rob shivered as he went up to bed.

The next morning, Rob went to Canadian Tire to get a new door lock and dropped by Ontario Provincial Police headquarters to ask about the investigation. Sergeant Sean Murray, another school friend, answered some of his questions and said a police car would drive by the cabin regularly. When Rob got back to the cabin, he found Mia dressed for the Celebration of Life and hurried to get ready. After a quick bite, they left for the funeral home in town.

They waited in the Serenity Room, while other members of the family gathered. Mia was talking with their aunt when Lynn and Gerrie appeared. 'My God!' she heard Rob say. They greeted Mia with tight air kisses.

'We are sorry, Mia, to be getting together for Grandfather's death. How are you doing?' Gerrie asked.

'We are sad, of course, Gerrie,' said Rob. 'I understand you visited him the afternoon of his death. I'd like to know more about that. Right now, Mia and I look forward to celebrating his remarkable life.'

'Are you staying in town?' Lynn asked. 'Could we get together for breakfast?'

'We are out at the cabin,' Mia said. 'So many memories help us through this time.' She used the handkerchief, embroidered by her grandmother, to wipe away a few tears.

'I'd love to see the cabin again,' said Gerrie. 'Can we come out to see you?'

'Not now. We must finish sorting everything this week. Perhaps we can talk for a few minutes after the service today,' Rob said.

When people started to arrive, Rob and Mia sat on the sofa to meet their friends. Gerrie and Lynn stood further back in the room, looking at the photographs on the table by the flowers.

The afternoon passed quickly. Relatives they had forgotten pressed their hands and spoke in funereal cliches. The more enlightened asked how they could help. The guests enjoyed party sandwiches and wine, an unusual pleasure on an Orillia Tuesday afternoon. At three, Rob asked the crowd to raise their glasses in memory of George Fraser's life. Late-arrival friends lined up to give Mia their condolences. By four, they were both glad to see the crowd thinning out.

Leftovers were bundled into small cake boxes and bottles of wine were sent home with Mia and Rob. On the way out, Mia gave a bottle to Lynn and Gerrie, hoping she wouldn't have to see them again. At last, they were alone in Rob's car, heading back to the lake cabin.

'Gerrie looked older today,' Mia said. 'I was hoping we wouldn't see him. Grandpa wouldn't have wanted him there after his embezzlement.'

'He was a mean guy. Remember how he bullied us,' Rob

said. 'He made life at school horrible. I hope he isn't going to challenge Grandpa's will. Despite the past, he might expect a portion of the estate. I'll call our lawyer tomorrow, just in case.'

'He's dangerous, Rob. I never told you. He grabbed me when we were alone in the cabin. I was sixteen.' She wrapped her arms around herself. 'He tried to pull me into my bedroom. I screamed, and Grandpa ran up the stairs. He threw Gerrie out and came up with the embezzlement story to cover Gerrie leaving.'

'Why didn't you tell me, Mia?'

'You were just thirteen at the time. Be careful of him, Rob. Don't trust him.'

'I could cheerfully kill him,' Rob said quietly.

Mia knew he was serious.

As they rounded the slight curve in the Rama Road, they saw the OPP had posted a police car to keep the cabin safe during the service. Thanks, and party sandwiches, were given to the officer.

Creaking groans coming from the lake indicated the ice would go out very soon.

After dinner, Rob read aloud Grandma Ellen's journal entries about visitors. Mia listened, fascinated by this glimpse into that time. The artists would stop on their way north, getting off the train in Longford Mills and travelling by horse and cart up to the cabin. They slept in bunk beds in the shed and had meals with the family. At night, they had great discussions about art, books and philosophy. And Grandpa, as a small boy, had loved it. Taking the canoe out, the guests travelled to small coves on the lake where the fishing was good, and the drawing was exceptional. Several times, winds had blown up suddenly, flooding the canoe, but they managed to bail it out before returning home.

When Rob saw Mia yawn, he suggested they get some sleep before watching the ice flow.

Upstairs, now warm, they slept in their clothes for several hours before a strange noise alerted Rob that the ice was about to break apart. He went to Mia's room and woke her, and they both went down to the cliff above the shore to watch the magical spectacle. Moonlight on shards of slowly moving ice reflected like dim diamonds. White mist swirled below. They didn't hear the car pull up at the cabin and were surprised when Gerrie climbed down behind them.

'Watching the magic, eh?' he said. He came closer.

'Stay back, Gerrie. I swear I could kill you!' Rob said.

Mia moved behind Rob, grabbing his arm to restrain him. 'There's nothing for you here, Gerrie.'

'I think I'll stay. We need to talk about the art, and my part of it,' Gerrie said.

'You have no right to anything,' Rob said, trying to move closer to Gerrie.

'I think I do, Rob. You two have taken everything from the grandparents. I've gotten nothing. I want my share.' Gerrie's dark tone made Mia whimper.

'You are owed nothing. Not after what you did to Mia,' Rob said. 'Get out of here, or I'll…'

'You'll what? Hit me? I used to beat you, easily. Don't you remember?' Gerrie asked.

Rob picked up a tree branch. 'Your last chance to leave.'

'I think not,' Gerrie said. He pulled a gun from his coat pocket. 'I want you to sign an agreement to split the money from the Thomson art. On second thoughts, the hell with that!

I want you to sign over your rights to all of it.' He walked towards them slowly. 'And Mia, we are going to finish what we started almost twenty years ago.'

A sudden loud *crack* from the ice made Gerrie turn his head to look. Rob jumped at him, and the gun went off. As Gerrie tried to shoot again, Rob pushed him backwards off the cliff. The thud of his body against rock and water was hidden by another great groan as the ice started moving, and Gerrie was dragged away with it.

'We should try to get to him,' Mia said, pulling Rob's arm.

'It's too dangerous to go down there now. We can't.' Rob watched white mist form and swirl around the rocks below.

Mia turned into his shoulder and cried. They heard the ongoing moans of the ice as it cracked and flowed. After moving Mia back from the cliff edge, Rob called the police.

In the warmth of the cabin, Mia and Rob told Sean Murray what had happened. Mia was wrapped up warmly, drinking sweet, hot tea by the stove. After an hour of questions, the police left, saying they would interview them again at the station in the morning.

Rob sat up with Mia, talking gently about the past and her idea. He realised they would have support from many friends in Orillia. He could work remotely and travel to Toronto when he needed to. By morning, they had decided they would stay on the lake.

Gerrie's body was never found. And in future times, Rob could swear he heard the tinkle of laughter coming from the shore. The maiden ghost was pleased with her latest conquest.

Ruth Dudley Edwards

Ruth Dudley Edwards is a journalist and prize-winning historian. In her twelve satirical crime novels, she ridicules political correctness: her targets include academia, gentlemen's clubs, the House of Lords, literary prizes and conceptual art. As well as the CWA Non-fiction Gold Dagger for *Aftermath: the Omagh Bombing and the Families' Pursuit of Justice*, she won the CrimeFest Last Laugh Award for *Murdering Americans* and CrimeFest's Goldsboro Last Laugh Award for *Killing the Emperors*.

ruthdudleyedwards.com

DUST TO ASHES

Ruth Dudley Edwards

'I hate that bloody cat,' said Roger.

'Not as much as I hate bloody Cressida,' said his wife, Tracy.

They'd been together for almost thirty years, and this was the first time they had jointly taken a violent dislike to either a human or feline so quickly. They had always got on well with neighbours and were expecting graduall——y to develop friendly, slightly distanced relationships with anyone in the small apartment block to which they had just moved, with the hope of finding a few cooperative types for mutual help in minor domestic emergencies. And maybe, in semi-retirement, even acquiring some congenial companions.

For the first few weeks, they had mainly been focused on the logistics of the move, doing up the flat, finding their way around the locality, and speculating about various neighbours.

Friendly, but unobtrusive, they were already on nodding, smiling and exchanging-basic-information terms with a few, whose first names they now knew, and had been thinking of inviting one or two for a drink. And then came the formal invitation to have a glass of sherry next door.

'Hand delivered with the envelope saying just "The Residents at Number 13",' announced Roger. 'It's an actual at-home stiffy from number 14! "Sherry, 6–8. RSVP". Friday fortnight.'

'Who does that anymore?'

'Mrs James Gribbinshaw-Smythe does.'

Tracy leaned over and took the card. 'Do you reckon she's the sour-faced one we saw getting into that Bentley in the car park?'

'Possibly.'

'Sounds like she's some kind of throwback. Didn't Belinda say she was a bit antisocial? If so, what's she doing inviting us?'

'I suppose she'll tell us if we accept.'

Roger retrieved the card. 'Judging by the design and typeface, this could come from a museum of the 1960s.'

'Intriguing.'

'But she might be a liability? Do we risk it? If she's antisocial, why can't we just say no? Or just not answer?'

Tracy shook her head. 'That would be plain rude, Rog. And we'd end up having to dodge her. Anyway, it might be a laugh. Everyone's been nice but a bit beige so far. Maybe we need some spice.'

'What are you anticipating? A septuagenarian nudie troika.'

'I don't know. Haven't seen her properly yet. But anyway, we shouldn't get on the wrong side of our next-door neighbour.'

He sighed. 'You're always so damn nice!'

'Someone has to be. Anyway, maybe she's a sweet, old-fashioned thing who will happily take in parcels.'

She wasn't.

Cressida had been a cross baby, who grew into a bully who used every weapon she had to achieve dominance. It wasn't all her fault. Her parents were conscientious but humourless and both nursed resentments at having gone down in the world socially – her father because he was a failed businessman, her mother because she was a flibbertigibbet who had married a bore, expecting a luxurious future that didn't materialise. Their attempts to make a lady of their only child with piano and ballet lessons were an expensive disaster they could ill afford, and added to the multiple blows from fate which they complained vociferously about to their daughter. Cressida had tried and failed as an actress, and from what they could see, her only talent appeared to be putting things in rows and dusting them. 'She's seems fit to be a parlourmaid and not much else,' complained her mother. This not being a suitable job for a Gribbinshaw, and Cressida having no aspirations to which her parents could relate, they did not protest when she became a clerk in the civil service. At least the job had promotion prospects and was pensionable, respectable and could be talked up.

As a child, she had found it difficult to live up to the grand-ness of her first name, let alone the forbidding surname – but it wasn't for want of trying. She had, in fact, compounded it by forcing her meek husband James Smith to adorn his surname and add hers.

But James Gribbinshaw-Smythe – who had made this ill-advised marriage because of his weakness for blue-eyed, bossy blondes – had quickly realised he was married to a scold, and before she could have the wherewithal to play the pregnancy card, he had left the marital bed and extracted himself from the marriage. Cressida had raged and threatened, but he had slid out of her life with the minimum damage to his finances.

She hung on to the phoney surname, talked a lot about the Gribbinshaws of north Norfolk and hunted assiduously but vainly for a classy husband. But her looks had faded quickly, her affected accent went out of fashion, her increasingly disagreeable personality was reflected in facial expressions that mainly indicated anger, contempt and superciliousness, and though she beefed up her origins for dating agencies, she had initially few, and ultimately no, takers. Nobody's fool when it came to money, even when she got some after the deaths of her parents in their sixties, there was no chance of her parting with any to a suitor with a sob story. Their demise in a car crash was a relief to her, for the thought of nursing either of them appalled her.

At work she had risen to be a middle-ranking, bullying bureaucrat who escaped the sack because she was meticulous with her paperwork, and was a ruthless barrack-room lawyer to boot. She was left to moulder in a corner of Human Resources updating health and safety legislation.

As a young woman, she had revelled in flaunting her body in front of the less well-endowed. In middle-age, possessions became her weapon. Her family were nobodies in the great scheme of things, even in north Norfolk, but her parents had left her enough to buy an expensive car she hoped would incite envy in others. Uninterested though she was in anyone except herself, it had not escaped her notice that some of her male colleagues craved cars far beyond their means. So she chose a Bentley, and delighted in seeing colleagues in the car park gazing at it. If asked any questions, she said it had been a present from Daddy. And when loneliness drove her to seek feline companionship, of course she bought a status symbol – a pedigree Siamese – which was chosen spitefully. Like many of its breed, it was wedded to the indoors, howled annoyingly when left alone and bit the few people who came to the flat and foolishly tried to stroke it. She called him Lucifer.

'He's so wicked,' she would explain to anyone who would

listen, 'what else could I call him?' Cressida took her disdain for people-pleasing to such a level as to make herself utterly dislikeable, was cold-shouldered socially, and had no surviving relatives or workmates who could stand her.

'I'd love to get rid of Lady Pain-in-the-Arse,' said one of her line managers, 'but the old bat would make our lives a misery and probably win at the tribunal by presenting sackloads of ammunition about her diligence and punctuality. And being a thundering snob who goes on and on about posh origins and could bore the universe about her bloody cat is – sadly – not a firing offence.'

So her life had continued uneventfully until the department was relocated. She refused to move and she couldn't get another job. She and Lucifer were on their own.

Their relationship was that of two cantankerous oldies who tolerated each other since they had no option. Sometimes, when Lucifer vomited or gave in to his mysterious cravings for wool, she wondered about having him put down. But though she was irritated by his clinginess, she appreciated having some company and she repressed her violent instincts.

And she was uncharacteristically tolerant of his propensity to vomit.

One of Cressida's workmates, a cheerful soul whom she had particularly despised, had used the medium of crochet to create cuddly messages about love and friendship and looking on the bright side which she distributed widely. She had given Cressida '*No act of kindness, no matter how small, is ever wasted – Aesop*' but never repeated the gesture after it was returned with a curt, 'It is on me.'

It was, however, inspirational, since after she became unemployed, Cressida began relieving her feelings by crocheting in depressing colours one-liners that demonstrated her contempt for humanity in general and her antipathy to individuals who particularly annoyed her.

She arrayed these on the walls of the smallest bedroom with uplifting messages like '*Kindness is a weakness exploited by the wicked*', '*Life is a cruel joke, and you're the punchline*' and '*The grass is always greener on the other side, and it's probably full of snakes too.*'

Often she personalised them with the names of people who had got on her nerves, as in '*I'm sorry I hurt your feelings when I called you stupid, Marcia, I really thought you already knew.*'

The invitation to sherry was not an act of kindness. Cressida's health was not as robust as it had been, not least because – like Lucifer – she took no exercise and had got extremely fat. It had occurred to her, when the hospital told her after a minor accident that she couldn't go home for three days if there was no one to look after her, that being on bad terms with everybody had its disadvantages. She couldn't think of a single neighbour with whom she had anything that remotely might be called a friendly relationship. Mostly they avoided her like a bad smell, which was apposite, since one was burgeoning. Hence the decision to find the at-home cards and see if she could exploit the newcomers. Unfortunately, she had long since lost any social skills she had ever possessed, as she had ceased to see the point of cleaning, either her or the flat. It was a long time since she had fallen out with the cleaning lady by telling her she was a slattern. And increasingly, Lucifer was losing control of his sphincter muscles, or indeed his inclination to use the litter tray.

'Christ, Trace, that old bat is Hyacinth Bucket on speed,' said Roger, after they extracted themselves. 'Talk about "Tuppence ha'penny looking down on tuppence". Pitying you for having been lumbered with such a common name was refreshingly blunt.'

'Poor old thing. I found her more of a Miss Havisham.'

'Without the wedding dress.'

'But heavy on the decaying grandeur. What a mess. And I don't think Miss Havisham had a malevolent feline about the place.'

'You can laugh. That's a foul animal! I was being friendly and that bite was deep. It hurts.'

'Pharmacist, heal thyself.'

'I'd rather strangle the bloody cat.'

'You shouldn't hold it against the cat. Siamese are like that. But it's done for fun. And at least it gave us the excuse to leave early.'

'You and your bloody silver linings. '

'Wasn't it T S Eliot who said, "Let's not be narrow, nasty, and negative".'

'Just embroider it and put it through Cressida's letterbox. Even I was rocked by the venom she displayed towards the neighbours.'

It was reciprocated, they discovered, when they cautiously raised the subject with Belinda, who invited them to meet at hers that night for what turned into a hatefest with two other couples. There was no lack of material. It was one thing to be an unfriendly neighbour, but worse to be dragging down property values. It was three months since Roger and Tracy had had their flat valued, but it emerged that the stink had caused the cancellation of two offers for number 12.

Cressida became ever more demanding as she made such a mess of ordering shopping that Tracy found herself having to take over. As the flat became a complete dump, social services were called and sent in a cleaning firm that refused ever to return on the grounds of the danger to their health and safety.

Cressida roamed the communal garden in the evenings, which made it effectively unusable by anyone normal. There were innumerable urgent phone calls about lost keys, visits to the vet and shortages of cat food. And everything was made more of a problem because Cressida wouldn't give Tracy a key. She claimed unconvincingly to have valuable family heirlooms with which no one could be trusted.

'I'm going mad,' said Tracy a few months later. 'I've tried every organ of local government and they rebuke me and recommend kindness, which she has exhausted. I've completely changed my mind on assisted dying. I'd assist her death in a heartbeat. Can we afford an assassin?'

It was just two weeks later that silence from Cressida's flat caused Tracy to call the police. 'It's very suspicious that the cat hasn't been howling for the last few days,' she told the constables, who then broke down the door and reeled from the stench.

The discovery of morphine tablets in the bedroom explained the deaths. 'I fear poor Cressida must have hoarded drugs,' said Tracy.

Officialdom had no interest in a difficult old woman inadvertently taking an overdose and a cat that had starved to death. None of the neighbours had seen or heard anything suspicious.

Later that month, after the medical report had found accidental death, Roger and Tracy opened a bottle of champagne in the garden and toasted Cressida and Lucifer.

'I feel kinder about them now,' said Roger.

'Me too.'

'It's true that sometimes you just have to be cruel to be kind,' he said.

'Excuse me while I crochet that,' said Tracy.

Nadine Matheson

Nadine Matheson is the author of the Detective Inspector Anjelica series. Her debut crime fiction novel, *The Jigsaw Man*, was published in 2021 and received recognition by being shortlisted for an International Thriller Writer Award and included in the *Evening Standard*'s list of 'The Best Crime Novels to Read in 2022'. The latest title is *The Kill List*. Nadine has dedicated twenty years of her career to criminal law, both as a solicitor and lecturer.

nadinematheson.com

CARL

Nadine Matheson

Carl did his best to stop the smile from snaking across his face as Detective Constable Simon Abbey stepped into the front office. The years had not been kind to Simon. The muscles in his stomach had slacked and his once-chiselled jaw had disappeared into the heavy flesh on his face. Carl pursed his lips as he caught a glimpse of his reflection in the brass panels of the main door. Prison had been kind to him. Daily access to the gym, morning runs in the yard. He'd left HMP Brixton with a first-class degree in Marketing and two stone lighter; he'd actually lost three but had put on a stone in muscle. Carl had been escorted into prison with the knowledge that he'd been well and truly fucked over, but four years inside had given him time to think. Much to Carl's surprise, he'd been kicked out of prison two months early due to overcrowding and his good behaviour, but ex-con was not what people thought as they watched him walk confidently on the street. His sister's neighbour had asked him if he'd just come back from holiday. It's amazing what a bit of tinted moisturiser and a fresh trim could do for you.

Carl remained in his seat as Simon took a step towards him.

'I didn't think that you were going to make it,' Simon said as he rubbed at the thin patch of red scaly skin on his chin. 'Punctuality was never your strong suit.'

'What can I say,' Carl replied as he remained seated. 'I'm not the man I used to be.' He smiled. '*I'm not the man I used to be*,' he repeated. 'I'm pretty sure that was a song.'

'Fine Young Cannibals, and despite what people think, it never made it to number one. Eight weeks in the chart and it never got higher than number twenty.'

'Eight weeks and stuck at number twenty.' Carl blew out a whistle and shook his head as though the impending thought in his head pained him. 'They must have been well pissed off. All that work but no award. Can you imagine having to watch other people pass you by? Imagine being good but not quite good enough. I suppose that it's a bit like being a detective constable for ten years and watching all these little upstarts passing you by as they make their way to sergeant, inspector and chief inspector.'

Simon eyes flicked to the side as a woman burst through the doors and ran to the front desk, the strong autumn wind and fallen leaves following her.

'They stole my bag. The fucking little shits stole my bag,' she screamed at the police officer who sat behind the security glass. 'You need to do something about it. They've taken everything.'

'It could be you sitting at that desk,' said Carl as Simon stepped away and closed the door. 'He's a constable. You're a constable,' he continued as he kicked away a piece of dirty tissue. 'The difference is that he probably has ambition. I doubt that he'll be sitting at that front desk for much longer. Give it an hour and he'll probably be making the biggest arrest of his career.'

'That was always your problem,' Simon said as he returned

to his previous spot and tapped the blue folder he'd been holding in his right hand, against his leg. 'So easily impressed by titles and what's on the outside, that you remained oblivious to what was going on around you.'

'That was the old me,' Carl said as he picked up his black overcoat from the bench and stood up. 'I'm a changed man. A new man.'

'I doubt that,' Simon replied. 'Leopards never change their spots.'

Carl limped towards Simon and stopped until they were almost nose to nose. Carl smirked as Simon sniffed. He could already see it. The hesitancy and anger in Simon's grey, rheumy eyes, the pupils slightly dilated, his cheeks bloated and the eczema on the corner of his mouth. The telltale signs of someone trying to stay ahead of their gram-of-cocaine-before-breakfast habit.

'Have you found her, then?' Carl asked as Simon stepped back and pulled his warrant card out of his pocket.

'Not here,' Simon replied as he pressed his card against the reader and the door unlocked. 'You came here voluntarily, but this is still an official police interview. Follow me.'

'Hospitable as always,' Carl replied flatly as he limped behind Simon.

'What happened to you?' Simon asked as he stopped at the door of a consultation room.

'Don't act like we're two mates catching up after finding each other on Facebook. Seeing you has never been my idea of a good time,' Carl replied as he followed Simon into the room.

'Typical. All mouth but you're quite pathetic really. Sit down,' said Simon.

'I didn't have to come here, you know. As you said, voluntary,' Carl said as he carefully lay his coat on the back of chair and sat down. 'I've been inside for four years, and they let me out early because I was such a good boy. There was nothing hanging over my head when I was sent down and I have no scores so settle. I could have brought my lawyer with me, but I figured that if I did, then maybe the invitation of a trip to Charing Cross Police Station would have been taken away and you would have rocked up at my front door instead.'

'Have you quite finished?' said Simon as he took a seat on the other side of the table.

'I'm just letting you know that you shouldn't mistake the absence of my lawyer as a sign of either stupidity or naiveté.'

Carl sniffed the air. The lingering smell of cannabis was thick. 'It's a bit strong in here, innit? Did CID have a party. Is that why I'm here? Are you upset because you need a friend?'

'There was a drugs raid in Soho this morning,' Simon said as he leaned across to his left and pushed open the window. 'Some bright sparks thought it would be a good idea to sit in an eight-by-eight room interviewing people for hours whilst extra-large exhibit bags full of weed sat festering against the radiator.'

'Well, no one ever said that the Old Bill was clever,' Carl replied as he clasped his hands and placed them on the scarred table. He bit his inner cheek as the sleeves of his cashmere jumper rolled up, revealing the faded scars that had been left behind by handcuffs. Carl adjusted his sleeves, hiding the reminder of his first meeting with Simon.

'Are you ready?' Simon asked as he opened the blue folder and removed a single sheet of paper.

'Ready for what exactly?' Carl asked as he leaned forward, squinting his eyes as he attempted to read upside down.

'As I told you on the phone,' Simon said as he turned the sheet of paper over. 'This is a voluntary interview, which I understand is an alien concept for you. I doubt it's a record, but twenty-two arrests. Hardly anything to be proud of.'

'Twenty-seven, actually,' Carl replied as he leaned back and stretched out his legs. 'I had my first arrest at the tender age of fourteen, when an interview was recorded on two cassette tapes, and then we moved on to CDs and now…' Carl waved his right hand in the air. 'It's all up in there, innit. Saved on the cloud. I wonder what it will be next.'

'This is a voluntary interview,' Simon said, ignoring Carl as he took a pen from his inner jacket pocket. 'Also referred to as a caution plus three, which means that you are being interviewed under police caution, you are entitled to legal advice, and you are free to leave at any time.'

'Are you trying to tell me that I can walk out right now, and you won't chase after me?'

Simon sniffed as a smile thinned out his lips.

'I didn't think so,' Carl replied.

'You do not have to say anything. But it may harm your defence if you don't mention now, something which you later rely on in court. Anything you do say may be given in evidence.'

'Well done,' Carl said as he leaned back and clapped slowly. 'You get a gold star for learning the caution by rote. Where would you like me to put your little gold star? On your shirt, or have you got a chart upstairs on your office wall?'

'A lot of time has passed, Carl,' Simon said as he placed his phone, screen down, on the table. 'Four years inside. Six months on remand before that, and in all that time you didn't say one word. Didn't answer questions when you were interviewed, and you didn't stand in the witness box and speak up in your defence.'

'It's hard to speak up in your defence when the police are setting you up.'

'Is that what you think happened?'

'I know for a fact that's what happened. It's very small, this criminal world of ours, and I learned quickly that there are four reasons why people get caught. Stupidity, greed, they talk like a bloody parrot on ecstasy, or they're set up by someone who has something to hide or to protect. Now, you and I both know that I'm neither stupid, greedy or a fucking parrot.'

'We've been keeping a close eye on your family since you went inside,' said Simon. 'Your sister, for example. She lives very well for someone on a teacher's salary. Nice holidays with the family. A new car last Easter. A loft conversion. Those aren't cheap.'

'It's not just a loft conversion. It's gone an en suite, too, and overlooks the park.'

'Expensive and she's single.'

'Single but she divorced well,' said Carl as he straightened up in his chair.

'And then there's your mum,' Simon said as he pulled out a photograph from the folder.

'Aw, she looks nice there,' Carl said as he turned the photograph around and tapped his finger on the woman getting out of a black cab.

'Retired, and the only income I can see is her pension and the rent that her lodger pays.'

'Marco. Lovely kid. Studying musical theatre at the Trinity Laban. Have you heard of it? It's a specialist university. Dancers, musicians, actors. One of their graduates won an Bafta, and the other day, Princess Kate visited and—'

'I don't give a fucking shit about Princess Kate and your mum's dancing lodger,' Simon said as he slammed his hand on the table.

'What do you give a shit about?' Carl asked gently as though he was questioning a five-year-old about his missing shoe.

'Where is it?'

'Where's what?'

'You know exactly what I'm talking about?'

'Shall I tell you what I do know,' said Carl as he sat up, turned his head to the left and cracked his neck. 'You've done all the right things. Sat me in this room. Told me more than once that this was a voluntary interview. Cautioned me and told me that I was free to go at any time. But you failed to do the most important thing.'

Carl stood up and took his time as he walked over to the water cooler in the corner of the room and poured himself a glass of water.

'Twenty-seven police interviews. Every single police station in London and, this may surprise you, three voluntary interviews with the City of London police in Bishopsgate. City Police. They're a bit sharper over there and much nicer refreshments,' said Carl as he walked back to the table. He remained standing as he sipped his water. 'So, thirty interviews in total. Cassette, CD and the cloud.'

Carl walked behind Simon and tapped the blank monitor on his left. 'You did all the right things, but you didn't turn this on.'

Simon's shoulders inched up to his ears, his breathing laboured as Carl returned to his seat.

'You've done a good job of making it look legit,' Carl continued. 'You've invited me here for a voluntary, met me at the front desk where everyone could see, including that woman who you probably paid to come into the station and make a scene. You bring me into this room, and you caution me and then you start asking me questions, but you're not recording a second of it, which makes me think… actually, no, I don't think. I *know*. You want something from me. You're desperate.'

'Desperate?' Simon asked, his voice slightly hoarse.

'Charlie will do that to you,' said Carl. 'Fuck your voice up. That's the problem with cokeheads: they think that no one else knows. That all they have to do is put on a nice suit, comb their hair and string a coherent sentence together to cover up the fact that at lunchtime, they'll be in the loo snorting a line off a dirty toilet seat.'

Simon pulled a tissue out of his pocket and wiped his nose. 'Quid pro quo,' he said.

'What was that?' Carl said, leaning forward and cupping his right ear.

'Quid pro quo,' Simon repeated.

'Something for something.'

Simon nodded.

'The only problem with that is there's nothing I want from you,' said Carl as he pushed aside his coat and pulled out a blue asthma inhaler from his pocket. 'This room isn't conducive to my health,' he said as he put the inhaler to his mouth and pressed the pump three times.

'Before you went inside, you were a suspect in a missing person investigation,' said Simon.

'It wasn't just a missing person investigation,' Carl said as his eyes darkened, and he slowly shook his head. 'Your mate, the dodgy one that just got twelve years for supplying drugs and theft, arrested me for murder.'

'You were a suspect in a missing person investigation and then we released you. You were never charged with murder.'

'You make it sound like you did me a favour. My face was all over the papers when you arrested me and paraded me about like a prize cow at the county fair, but no one gave a toss when you released me. Hangs over your head a bit when you've been accused of murder and your wife is still missing.'

'As I said. Quid pro quo,' Simon said as he leaned back and picked up the single sheet of paper. 'You give me what you owe me – what you stole from me – and I'll—'

Simon paused as the aged pipe in the corner of the room rattled.

Carl tapped his fingers against his leg in time to the sound of a detainee kicking the pipes in their cell somewhere in the bowels of the police station. Simon slid the single sheet of paper towards Carl.

'Did you find a body, or did you find *her*?' Carl asked once the banging had stopped.

'Would you like to take a look?' Simon replied as he lifted the flap of the blue folder and pulled out another small stack of photographs.

'Not until you answer my question. Did you find a body, or did you find *her*?'

Simon groaned as he shook his head. 'Why are you making this so fucking difficult? I'm giving you answers to questions that have been rattling around your head from the second I arrested you nearly five years ago.'

'See, this has always been your problem. You make assumptions, and you know what they say about assumptions,' said Carl.

'And what would I be assuming?' Simon asked.

'That I give a shit about my missing wife. She was a liar and a cheat.'

'I thought that was the way you liked them,' Simon smirked.

'I don't the mind the danger, but I do mind when my missus is screwing bent coppers.'

Carl smiled as the smirk quickly disappeared of Simon's face. 'Did you think that I didn't know?' he asked.

'You think that I was sleeping with your—'

'Oh, I don't *think*. I know,' said Carl as he reached again into his coat pocket, pulled out his phone and tapped the screen. 'That's the problem with voluntary interviews, no one ever pats you down and checks you. Here you go. Have a gander.'

Simon's face paled as his eyes swept the screen.

'That's you, innit. Screwing my wife the night before she disappeared. In my bed, no less?' asked Carl. 'I had to burn the sheets when I got home.'

Simon swallowed.

'What did you do with her?' Carl asked.

'What makes you think that I've done anything with her.'

'No, you're right. You haven't done anything with her. I reckon she's done something to you. Ripped you off. Put you in an awkward position with people you owe a lot of money to.'

'She didn't take my money. You did,' said Simon as the colour returned to his face. 'Five hundred grand, you stole from me.'

'So you say.'

'Quid pro quo. You give me my money and I'll give you your wife. Something for something. It's all there,' Simon said as he tapped the piece of paper in front of Carl. 'All the information you need to find her.'

'As I said. Assumptions,' said Carl as he folded his arms. 'You're assuming that I want her back.'

'Why won't you?' Simon asked. 'It's either you take her back or the five-year missing person investigation finally turns into a murder investigation and then the inevitable charge, trial and life in prison – but all of that goes away once you give me back what you stole from me.'

The lines around Carl's eyes deepened as he laughed hard. 'Wow, you really are desperate,' he said as he wiped the tears from the corners of his eyes.

'You fucking little shit,' Simon said as he grabbed Carl's collar and pulled him towards him.

'Get the fuck off me,' Carl croaked as Simon stood up, dragged him off his seat and threw him across the floor.

'For fucking years, I've had to sit and wait,' Simon said as Carl gingerly got to his feet.

'And you thought it would be easy,' Carl said, straightening his collar as he limped towards Simon. 'You thought that I would just simply roll over because you threatened me with a murder charge. Do I look like a mug?'

'I want my money.'

'I'm sure that you do. In fact, I'm sure that you both do.'

'What the fuck are you talking about?' Simon asked as he turned his back, planted both hands on the table and shook his head with frustration.

'I'm talking about the fact that the pair of you have been rattling around in whatever hovel you've been living in, coming up with this stupid plan to have me hand over whatever it is you think I took from you. I bet it really rattled your cage when you arrested me all those years ago, searched my lockup and found that it was empty.'

Simon raised his head and locked eyes with Carl. 'How do you know that?' he asked with surprise.

'Never ask a question that you don't know the answer to,' Carl said as he perched himself on the corner of the table.

'Fuck off,' Simon grunted.

'Oh yeah, I forget that I can do that,' said Carl as he picked up his phone. 'Free to go at any time, you said. Even though this interview wasn't even official police business. You just thought that it would be the safest place to go fishing. Hey, Si. Look up.'

Simon straightened up and looked at Carl. 'What have you done?' he asked as Carl held up his phone and he saw the voice memo app with a single recording on the screen.

Carl pressed *play*.

'*I didn't think that you were going to make it. Punctuality was never your strong suit.*'

'No, no, no,' Carl sung as Simon lunged at him and attempted to grab his phone. 'It's a little bit too late for that. This recording has already gone and right about—'

'What the fuck have you done?' Simon asked, his eyes wild, as he looked at the door and then towards the window, searching for an exit. Panic seeped from his pores as an alarm sounded in the building.

'I hedged my bets,' Carl replied as he picked up his coat, the single sheet of paper and the blue file. 'Exactly what I did with your side of the deal just before I took my little trip inside. Hedged my bets. Eighteen-to-one. It's a lot easier to play when it's not your side of the deal on the table.'

Simon swallowed. 'All of it,' he croaked as the door swung up and the police officer who'd been sitting at the front desk and Simon's boss, DCI Mateta, stood at the door.

'Every single penny on the 3.28 race at Epsom Downs. Placed first. Quid pro quo,' Carl said as he saluted Simon with the blue folder and walked out.

Zoë Sharp

Zoë Sharp has written for a living since the 1980s. She is a neuro-diverse autodidact, fascinated by criminal instinct and the way characters react to stress. She is known for writing strong female protagonists, and giving occasional self-defence demonstrations. Her work has been nominated for numerous awards, been used in a Danish school textbook, inspired an original song and music video, and been optioned for TV and film. Fun fact: Zoë owns six chainsaws.

ZoeSharp.com

John Lawton

John Lawton divides his time between an eyrie atop an Etruscan necropolis and a garlic farm in the north of England where he now counts Schengen instead of sheep. His latest novel, *Smoke & Embers*, the ninth book in the Troy series, is published by Grove Press. It is available to all discerning readers for a modest sum.

ONCE UPON A TIME IN NEW JERSEY

Zoë Sharp & John Lawton

2025

Joe found something new to hate about growing old almost every day – teeth, guts, hair (what was left of it)… you name it.

Today, knees.

He'd dropped a stack of envelopes, two fat, one thin, reaching into the safe behind his desk. To squat was easier than to bend – back ache, fuckin' back ache – but once squatted he couldn't get up again, as though whatever hydraulics were in knees had just seized up.

'Consuela!'

Nothing, just the hum of the air-con.

'Consuela!!'

An age rolled over… perhaps two minutes. Then footsteps behind him.

'Con…? Oh shit.'

Not Consuela… worse… the bitch he'd married. Whatsername.

'While you're down there, see if there's anything else you can do. A little dusting maybe? Scrape up some of last week's dogshit?'

'Fuckit, Marcia. Just help me up.'

She wasn't a big woman. All the same, she dropped him back in his chair as though he weighed about as much a bag of potato chips.

'Y'okay now?'

'As if you cared.'

'Fuck you, Joe. Get it together. Julian just called. He'll be over in five. I'll be out.'

'When are you ever in?'

She walked off.

He stalled her in the doorway with, 'Which one is it this time? Bob? Jim? Randy?'

'Joe… they're all called Randy.'

And she was gone.

The picture window – rolling lawns and neatly tended flower beds, courtesy of Consuela's husband Juan Carlos – Joe saw Marcia bundle the twins into the back of the Lincoln and pull out as Julian pulled in. She was a lousy driver, but managed not to lock fenders with Julian's crock-of-shit Tesla. She was lousy at most things. Unfortunately, she'd been a great fuck. As Bob, Jim or Randy was about to find out. She'd drop the kids at her cousin's in Union City and then gigolo away an entire afternoon God-knows-where.

But he did know where. Joe had made it his business to find out all there was to know about Bob/Jim/Randy. This was where Julian came in.

Julian said, 'Are you feeling alright, Joe?'

The English and their insufferable politeness.

'Yeah. I've just been overdoing the yoga exercises. I need a shot. Bring over a glass. Bring two if you're joining me.'

'Really, Joe? Brandy? After yoga? At ten in the morning?'

'It's okay. It's Tibetan vegan brandy. I have it imported from Lhasa.'

Julian raised one eyebrow. A little Roger Moore.

The man was a humourless fuck – but so what, he was the best PA Joe had ever had.

'*Basta, basta*. We need to get down to business.'

Joe set out the envelopes he had retrieved at such cost.

He picked up the thin one.

'Name, address.'

He picked up the fat ones.

'Payment. And a few more if you have to up the ante. Keep 'em separate. I ain't made of moolah.'

'Timing, Joe?'

A pause while Joe knocked back half a large shot and felt a spreading warmth that in a lesser man might have induced a sense of bonhomie.

'Don't let this one get strung out, Jules. Four weeks, maybe five at the most. Let things go… cold… let any trace of a trail evaporate and then just get it done.'

'How often would you like to hear about it.'

'Just get it done. I don't need progress reports.'

Meeting at a hamburger joint in East Orange would not, and would never have been, Julian's choice. His choice would have been somewhere with real crockery serving real coffee that did not resemble the water they'd just cleaned the windows with – even more than he hated stranded prepositions, he hated weak coffee.

Ricky was fine with transparent coffee in a paper cup. Fine with a thrice-fried brown mess in a sesame seed bun. If only he'd learnt not to speak with his mouth full.

'Sho?'

'Oh, merely business as usual. *Semper idem.*'

'Whatever. You kill me sometimes, Jules. You remind me of that English comic… somebody Fry. Human dictionary.'

'Yeees… I keep getting told that. It just so happens that his *Oscar Wilde* is my favourite film. Not that I copy him, of course. Now, to the task in hand.'

He pushed the thin envelope across the table. Sat with his palm across the fatter of the fat ones.

Ricky slit the envelope. Read the page. Stopped chewing.

'Sheesh. For real? I mean, he's—'

'Ricky. You know the rules. I don't know the name of the hit. You don't know who's paying for the hit. I am the very model of a modern middleman.'

'What's that? More Stephen Fry?'

'Gilbert and Sullivan.'

He pushed the fat envelope over.

Ricky didn't touch it.

'Fifty?'

'Fifty.'

'Since you don't want me to tell you who the hit is, you kinda gonna have to trust me here. This guy is too risky for fifty. Way too risky.'

Julian reached into his inside pocket and took out the last envelope.

'Another twenty-five. I'm afraid it's a take-it-or-leave-it, old man. I am not empowered to negotiate.'

Ricky hesitated.

Looked at the money, not at Julian.

Then he scooped up both envelopes.

'I'd say I'll let you know when it's done, but fuckit, you'll know anyway. If this doesn't make the front page of the *Post*, you can call me Ernie Bilko.'

Murder had been a wise career move. Meeting Stan had been pure chance, but he'd seen something in Ricky: the qualities of an assassin – ruthlessness, an acute detachment from the personal, no sense of justice, not a shred of guilt or regret and a profound sense of fair play. A job was a job was a job. Ending a life was no different from serving up a burger or stacking shelves in a mini-mart. It just paid better. That was where 'fair play' came in. And with the profits of fair play, they'd bought a cute-beyond-cute red-brick house on leafy Washington Street in Hoboken.

They'd been a good – no, the perfect – double act. They saw themselves as Gig Young and Robert Webber in *Bring Me the Head of Alfredo Garcia*. The best-dressed gay hitmen on the East Coast. Okay, Ricky was still a bit of a slob and would eat or drink anything put in front of him, but Stan was working on that. He'd 'sophisticise' him sooner or later. For now, he was content to see Ricky in an Aquascutum overcoat, occasionally – the kid had thought Aquascutum was a waterworld theme park – and a Canali suit, occasionally. Cordon bleu could wait. After all, since the accident he'd had time on his hands, and what better use for it than to come to terms with Julia Child. He'd had all the counters lowered to wheelchair height. Treats were in store.

'You've been eating garbage again. I can smell it.'

Ricky cupped one hand and breathed into it. He could smell burger, he could smell East Orange. Fuckit, he could even smell Julian's cologne. Did the dude really use *Miss Dior*?

'Okay. I stink, I admit it, but we got the job.'

'Fifty?'

'Seventy-five.'

'What's so special about this one that our little English buddy pays over the odds?'

Ricky gave Stan the thin envelope.

'Is he fucking with us? Jesus H. Christ… Giuseppe Braconi? Ricky… you should have passed on this one. Do you have any idea who this is?'

'Sure… I listen to you… I remember what you tell me.'

'For fuck's sake, Rick… this is a made man!'

'As I said… I remember what you tell me… and if memory serves, he *was* a made man.'

'Dammit, kid. There's no such thing. You can't un-ring a bell.'

'Hold on there… you told me they were through with him… he was in… exile? Exile, that's what you called it.'

'Ricky – Braconi is in the Piccinini family. His mother was a Piccinini. Fat Mickey's his uncle. So's Utterly Obese Angelo. Pretty Boy Al is his cousin. That's why he's in exile and not six feet under. He stole from the family. You do not steal from the family. You do not piss on your own doorstep. If he'd been a plain Joe McDoakes comin' up from behind the eight-ball, they'd never have found a body. He'd have vanished plain and simple. But – he's Alessandro Piccinini's cousin. Money's green, but blood's red. Geddit? If we do this job, we might as well put up a billboard on the New Jersey Turnpike with our names and addresses and a caption saying "Whack Us Now".'

'Shit'

'Yep, shit.'

'What do we do?'

'It's like this. No one who knows who Braconi is would take this job. So what we do is find someone who doesn't know and pass on the job and the fee.'

'Who wouldn't know?'

'Someone too old, too young or too stupid.'

'It's a lot of money to give away.'

'We take a commission. A finder's fee. In fact, let's keep the twenty-five. Whoever we find will think fifty about right, whereas seventy-five attracts suspicion, and there's a bonus. One more layer of immunity… we move further from the hit as the chain gets longer.'

'You got someone in mind?'

'Right now I can think of two or three guys. Let me make a few phone calls.'

Lorraine Malinowski might not have been the wisest choice. She wasn't too young, too old or too stupid. But – three guys who might have been had all said no.

She didn't bat an eyelash, fake or real, at the name on the page. A silent 'never heard of him'.

All the same, Stan knew she was lying. But… but… unlike 'Shemp, Moe and Larry'… she was here. In a 'fifty-kinds-of-bread-you-never-knew-existed' breakfast bar at Warren and West Broadway in TriBeCa. Artisan this, artisan that. If 'artisan' were now the coolest adjective, then he and Ricky might have to consider rebranding as 'artisan assassins'.

He had eggs benedict – his favourite crazy thing to do with an English muffin. One day he'd manage to make it without curdling the hollandaise.

Lorraine stuck with coffee.

Stan had known Lorraine since she was a kid. She was the daughter of a seventies 'great' among hitmen, Tad Malinowski. Maybe ten or twelve, when they met, and Stan would be twenty-one, twenty-two, which would make Lorraine about forty-five now. She looked seventy. Lips a mess of vertical grooves from the 3.8 million times she had drawn on a Camel Menthol. Hair a shapeless grey bun. Glasses chipped and smeared. She looked two or three stages away from bag lady. Enough to remain ordinary. What was ordinary ought not to be memorable. If it was a disguise, it was a great disguise. 'Ol' Rainie' was beneath suspicion. Effective, efficient as she slipped under anyone's radar.

Clearly she regarded this meeting as work.

The li'l old lady act didn't slip.

Back home on Franklin, Lorraine slipped off her wig. Shook her hair free and looked in the mirror. Not bad, she thought. Still red at forty-three. If anything a touch redder than it had been at thirty-three.

The fat suit was itching. She shed it like snakeskin. Ran her hands across her belly and uttered her favourite line from her favourite movie, *Midnight Cowboy*: 'Twenty-eight years old and one hell of a gorgeous chick.'

Well. Maybe.

It hadn't been hard to invent Ol' Rainie.

It hadn't been hard to convince Stan Cukor that she was Tad's daughter, picking up where three bullets to the chest had forced Tad to leave off. The guy had a very selective memory. Names without faces. All she'd had to say was 'Surely you remember me?' and Stan had launched into anecdote, nostalgia and reminiscence that told her everything she needed to know about Lorraine Malinowski, and she could go on being Judy O'Rourke and just take Lorraine out of the closet when she was needed. Lorraine's death had been unfortunate – she hadn't meant to kill her – but why waste an identity?

Once or twice, Stan had seen her for 'real'. An expensive

dress, heels, maquillage… he hadn't recognised her.

Judy shared her apartment with a cat, a dog and a python. Cat and dog got on well together. The snake was rarely allowed out of his terrarium. It was her practice to consult all of them about the big decisions in a hitwoman's life.

The cat sat on the table, the dog stood with its front paws on the edge and the snake slept the sleep of the just.

Judy shuffled her tarot cards. Turned over the first three.

Sun.

Hermit.

Dead skunk.

The cat stretched out a paw to land on dead skunk.

Judy dealt the next three.

Fool.

Devil.

Dead skunk.

The cat gently set a paw on dead skunk.

'Oh shit, kitty. Bad as that?'

With two matches, best of three was pointless. Whatever the cat might have chosen next, the cards had spoken: Do Not Take This Hit!

She showed the card to the dog. The dog backed away. She tapped on the glass wall of the terrarium. The snake slowly stirred, stuck out its tongue, and went back to sleep.

Shit. She'd have to pass this job on. A pity, the fifty K would be good just now.

Then: 'Fuckit, does it have to be fifty? Why not just forty?'

Then: 'Why not thirty-five? I earned my cut already.'

To those dumfuck Russians out at Brighton Beach thirty-five was a fuckin' fortune. They killed for nickels and dimes.

* * *

'Ivan Ivanych Ivanov,' the big Russian said, indicating his own chest with a meaty thumb. His voice rumbled like an eighteen-wheeler on the freeway.

'Of course it is, hon.' Lorraine leaned forwards and patted his arm. It was like patting a side of beef – if the bull had gone on the rampage in a cheap tattoo parlour instead of a china shop.

Ivan Ivanych Ivanov was not his real name. That was a given, Lorraine thought. Or she hoped so, anyway. In this business, nobody but *nobody* gave out that kind of info. The ones dumb enough to do so were long since embedded into construction projects. Some bridge supports she could name were standing room only.

Still, he was all muscle and she began to regret her Ol' Rainie disguise. But… business was also business. Maybe – if the boy did good – she'd come back out to Brighton Beach in full warpaint and give him a bonus he wouldn't forget.

If he wasn't too dumb to get the job done.

Giving him a speculative glance through her smeared glasses, she said, 'Didn't you used to work with a couple of other guys – Sidorov and…? Now, what was his name?'

Ivanov grinned. 'Petrov,' he said. 'They died. Very sad.'

She allowed herself a small smile in return. The three most common Russian names. So, there was something other than muscle between his ears. That was good… unless… unless he was too smart to take the job after all?

They were sitting out on the boardwalk in the area known as Little Odessa. She slid the thin envelope, now a little crumpled at the corners, across the café table, keeping her fingers on it, and it wasn't just so the breeze coming off the Lower Bay didn't whisk it into the sand.

He took the envelope, opened it.

'Хорошо,' he said, expressionless. 'Когда?'

Lorraine knew enough Russian to understand 'Okay' and 'When?'

'Good. As soon as you can. Within the next three weeks.' She'd left herself a buffer, just in case.

Ivanov's eyebrows came up. He pursed his lips, rubbed one thumb across the tips of his fingers – universal language that needed no translation. Lorraine retrieved the fatter envelope from her capacious purse and slid it across the table. He didn't open it – not in front of her. That would have been an insult.

'How much?'

She told him. He tried to hide the gleam in his eye, didn't quite succeed.

'Хорошо,' he said again.

'I never met a lady hitman. What was she like?' Ivan's lover demanded. 'Was she pretty?'

They were in the upstairs room of an illegal gambling joint in Mount Vernon, Westchester County, run by the Albanians. Since Ivan's lover was Albanian, that didn't cause a problem. Unless anyone found out about it... *then* it would be a big problem.

Ivan would burn that bridge when he came to it.

Now, he rolled onto his back, stared up into a pair of impossibly blue eyes. 'She was a hag,' he said, running his fingers through glossy hair, black, with the sheen of a raven's wing. 'But her money was beautiful.'

Andrijana laughed. She was the daughter of Alban 'the Finger' Lucaj, an ethnic Albanian from Montenegro, who'd come over to fill the vacuum after the whole Rudaj Organisation got taken down by the Feds in the early 2000s. Lucaj had earned his nickname by the trophies he took from his enemies.

Ivan could imagine what would be taken from *him* if anyone found out Lucaj's only child was in bed with the Russians – even before the old man discovered she was *literally* in bed with one of them. And it wouldn't be a finger, of that he was quite certain.

Which was another reason for Ivan to take a few little jobs on the side. Their running-away fund. One day…

'And who is—?' Andrijana began, but Ivan silenced her with his own finger across her lips.

'Better you don't know.'

'But… it's not… dangerous, is it? For you?'

Ivan reassured her with light words and heavy kisses. Andrijana was twenty. Ivan, twenty-eight. Sometimes that eight-year gap seemed a lifetime in experience. The girl was slender, almost delicate… definitely not cut out for the sharp end of the family business. The Finger was sharp enough to know that. So Andrijana was in college, majoring in business, finance, accounting – some shit like that.

Ivan wasn't nearly as dumb as people often assumed – and he played the Russian heavy to the hilt – but when Andrijana got to talking numbers, she blew him into the weeds. She could glance down a column of figures and point to the skim in a second. And her old man knew the value of that. Any dumfuck could beat the shit out of the skimmer, after.

An hour later, Ivan stepped into the alley at the back of the building, just as the headlights of his Escalade turned in at the far end, right on time.

Only, when Ivan opened the rear door, the back seat was already occupied.

'Uncle Radimir! I—'

'Save it,' Radimir said. 'Get in.'

Ivan did as he was told. His uncle was the one who'd plucked him from the slums of Tolyatti – a cess pit in the arse end of Samara Oblast. Who'd rescued him from an entire working life at the Lada factory, from the endless grey no-hope existence of his parents.

The big SUV accelerated out of the alley and rejoined traffic. Uncle Radimir let him sweat in silence for six blocks.

Then: 'Did you think we wouldn't find out?'

Ivan sighed. 'No, господин.' Best to call him sir, to mind his manners. 'Do you mind if I ask... how...?'

Radimir, a big man with permanent shadow on a chin like a sledgehammer, did not look at him directly. 'The Finger... reached out to us.' A grim smile. 'You might say, it beckoned.'

'Ah.' Of course. Andrijana's father, putting temptation out of his daughter's way. 'What now?'

'You are going home.'

Somehow, Ivan knew his uncle was not talking about the two-bed condo overlooking the boardwalk in Little Odessa. He swallowed. 'To... Tolyatti?'

'No.' Radimir reached inside his Scabal overcoat, noting the way Ivan tensed automatically. His smile was filled with contempt. When the hand emerged, it held an envelope. For just a second, in Ivan's imagination it was the one containing the contract. Did they know about that, also?

It took him longer, after he opened it, to realise the significance of the official documentation inside.

'What is this?'

'You have the honour of being called upon to fight for the glory of the motherland.'

Ivan's mouth fell open. He'd watched the news reports about the war in Ukraine, feeling only pity for the poor bastard recruits drafted to die there. And winter was coming. They would die faster now.

He closed his mouth, swallowed. 'I am twenty-eight. Too old to be conscripted into the army—'

'Things change. All citizens eighteen to thirty are now subject. You leave in three days,' his uncle said, unsmiling. 'Congratulations.'

'What about… the job?' Andrijana whispered, leaning across the table. It was not the question she wanted to ask. Fuck, it wasn't in the top ten… twenty, even.

They were in a high-backed booth in a Korean BBQ joint on the corner of West 32nd and Broadway. Neutral ground. She gripped her glass tight for something to do with her hands, so she didn't reach across the table. With the number of eyes on them – both sides – that would not be wise.

Ivan muttered a curse under his breath. 'Forget about the fuckin' job, Andri. Last thing on my mind right now is a goddamn two-bit contract for—'

'Ssh,' she told him sharply. 'A deal is a deal. You should know that.' She put her head on one side, took a breath, struck a pose. '"We're not negotiatin'. I don't like to barter. I don't like to dicker. I never have fun in Tijuana. That price was non-negotiable."'

It took only a second for the puzzlement to lift from his face. 'Ah. *True Romance*. My favourite movie.'

'*Our* favourite movie,' she corrected. 'So, you'll know that—'

'"My peace of mind is worth that much."' His smile backed and died. 'But I don't have time to—'

'Relax,' she said. 'We don't have to let go of all the money, do we? And I know just the guy.'

* * *

His name was Gojak. He'd been her personal driver, gofer, fixer, since Andrijana was six years old... although, at first, he'd been more babysitter than bodyguard. Gojak was a quiet, stocky man, from a family of peasant farmers in the north, on the border with Serbia. Uncle Gojak to her, then and still.

He was old enough to remember when Montenegro had been part of the Socialist Federal Republic of Yugoslavia. Old enough, also, to remember the disintegration after Tito died. And nowhere near old enough to forget the things he'd seen and done during the bitter civil war.

Gojak's family had no TV set growing up. So, when Lucaj first brought him to America, Gojak was fascinated by the number of TV channels and all they had to offer. He gorged... a crash course in speaking Yank.

To begin with, his thick accent had people mishearing his name. They looked at him funny, said things like, 'Where's your lollipop?'

Only after he stumbled across re-runs of the old seventies' cop show did he realise they thought he was saying 'Kojak'. Entranced, he shaved his thinning hair to resemble the lead actor, Telly Savalas... drew the line at those damn lollipops.

But the swagger, the slang, those Gojak took to heart. And when his little Andrijana came crying to him about some contract her dumfuck boyfriend had staked his name on, and was now trying to weasel out of? Well, how could he resist those big eyes?

But he knew better than to step out on his boss. So he took a ride with The Finger, laid it out for him. And when the man who'd saved him from scratching a living in the Montenegrin dirt said, 'Pass on it – and pass it on,' Gojak went trawling the Bronx for some snot-nosed Dominican kid. Didn't matter to him what gang the poor shmuck – a good American word, Gojak learned – was a member of. Dominicans Don't Play, the Trinitarios… who gave a fuck?

Andrijana had passed him a crumpled envelope that seemed too loose for the fifteen K it held. He took ten off the top – like a broker on Wall Street. Doing business the American way, yes? After all, the Dominicans were not artists, with blade or bullet. Five large was more than enough for some scrawny street kid, out to make a name for himself.

The next day, he told his little Andrijana he had it all taken care of. She flung her arms around his neck in gratitude.

'You are the best, Uncle Gojak!'

He smiled, winked. 'Who loves ya, baby?'

Marcelino Rodríguez's mother had sweated blood to keep her youngest child out of the gangs. She had already buried her elder son, hacked down by machete-wielding rivals outside a bodega on East 183rd.

Marcelino's sister was in the ground, too – out on Hart Island – after that *hijo di perra* she hooked up with forced her to whore for him. But if she had eased the pain inside with a needle in her vein, who could blame her for that?

Marcelino was a skinny runt of a kid, despite his name, which his mother always told him meant 'young warrior'. The only time he felt like a hero was in the old Roxy movie theatre he snuck into. They showed very little that was new, but it was warm and comforting, and out of the rain. And Marcelino fell in love with all the old movie stars – Barbara Stanwyck, Cary Grant, Katherine Hepburn, Humphrey Bogart. He could hide away there all day, in the dark, watching those movies back-to-back.

In school, he was the kid who got his books trashed, his lunch tray tipped over, his body bruised and his money stolen. He was not brave, nor quick – in body or mind… A dreamer. Before he skipped out permanently, he'd always been towards the bottom of every class. The kid nobody noticed, or paid attention to… unless as prey.

So, what else was there for him but the gangs?

He'd still been in school when they first lured him in. He recognised the colours they wore, even as he heard the warning voice of his *mamá* in the back of his head.

They'd taken him in, protected him, made him feel a part of something. At first, he was just a messenger or a lookout. They'd made him swear an oath – to abide by the rules in the book they'd given him… even if he was too ashamed to admit he could barely understand the words.

As time went on, they demanded more – and he wanted to give. Wanted to prove himself finally worthy, even if the thought of it made him sick to his stomach.

Marcelino answered to his *primera*, José, who was eighteen – almost an old man. When José drove him out to New Jersey, Marcelino asked no questions. Just slumped in the passenger seat and tried to look cool, like he rode a Benz rather than a bus, every day.

The suburb they reached was loaded, he could tell. Sprawling houses with yards full of trees and grass, flowers and shit … and new cars that were on the driveways, not on bricks on the lawn.

'See this place, *compañero*?' José asked as they cruised past the latest mansion.

Marcelino kept his head still but slid his eyes right. '*Sí.*'

'I need you to kill the *hombre* who lives here.' José spoke so casually that for a second the meaning bounced off.

Then: '¿Qué carajo?'
What the fuck?

Swear-to-God, Marcelino had never been so shit-scared in all his life. It did no good telling himself to be Bogart in *Casablanca*, or Jimmy Cagney in *Public Enemy*. Those guys looked so cool up there on the screen, doing what they did. You never saw them shaking and sweating with the sheer terror of it.

José had told him to case the joint first, so for a while Marcelino lurked nearby and gave it the eye. He was a good lookout – been practising since he hit thirteen, but that was in the kinda neighbourhood where a Latin kid could hang without attracting attention. This was something else, man.

He tried looking casual on the street, but people slowed as they drove past in their fancy European cars, and he knew that sooner or later one of them was gonna call the cops.

Marcelino had never been around houses this fancy, or so far apart. But there were enough trees and bushes in the front yard to mask him as he crept closer. He shivered among the dirt and leaves for a couple of hours… saw the gardeners tidy around the place, the wife and kids drive off. It turned colder, started to rain.

The thought of killing made Marcelino wanna hurl. But José had given him a down payment of five hundred, with the promise of another five after…

Marcelino patted the pocket of his hoodie, feeling the hard outline of the gun. There had been a machete under the car seat, the rust pared from the edge of the blade, but Marcelino wouldn't touch it. Not after what had happened to his brother. José didn't push him on that, just blew out an annoyed breath and jerked his head towards the glove compartment instead.

Marcelino knew enough to tell the gun was a revolver, but no more than that. He'd picked it out carefully, saw the butt-end of bullets gleaming in the cylinder.

'There you go, man,' José said. 'No safety. Point and shoot. You feel me?'

'*Sí.*'

'*Bueno.*' José nodded. 'Bring proof.'

That last order gave Marcelino the idea. It simply took a while for him to work out exactly how he was gonna do just that.

Getting in wasn't a problem. Marcelino had robbed plenty. A slightly open window was all the invitation he needed. That led into a pantry off the kitchens. And whaddya know? Even rich folk ate Cheerios in the mornings.

His dirty sneakers made a slight squeak as he moved across a tiled hallway the size of Queens, trying not to gawp at a curving staircase like something outta *Gone with the Wind*.

He paused with one hand on the newel post, like Clark Gable, heart trying to punch right outta his chest, straining for any sound. Then he heard a low coughing off to his left, followed it.

When he pushed open the double doors, resisting the impulse to knock first, he found an old man sitting behind a desk. The old man looked up when Marcelino came in, but did nothing – no start of surprise, or fear, or anger. Nothing. He fumbled the gun out of his pocket.

'Hey, *jefé*, I gotta… a proposition for ya, so listen good. I been paid to whack you, yeah? But I figure, what's a guy like you wanna die for? You gotta big fuckin' house, *una bella esposa*, two *preciosos* kids. So, here's what I'm gonna do.' His voice was too high. He cleared his throat. 'You lay on da rug, I spill a little red paint over you, take a few pictures – I show 'em to my *primera*, job done. You pay me a… a kill fee, you get me? And then you get to fuck your *esposa* another time, and everybody happy, yeah? Whaddya say?'

Marcelino grinned. Bogart himself couldn't have delivered it any better.

The kid just stood there grinning. A stained hoodie. Ripped jeans, also stained. If the hoodie was an attempt at a disguise it was wasted on Joe. He never could tell one greasy kid from another.

The gun, held at arm's length, wavered, left right right left. If he squeezed off a round right now, he'd miss by a mile. Despite the stupid grin, the kid looked shit-scared. For fuck's sake, Julian! A goddamn amateur?

'What kept you?' Joe said.

'Whaddafuck?'

Joe stood up behind his desk.

'Siddown!'

'No. I paid for this, so I call the shots. Literally. You, ya slimy shitsucker, are late. I expected you weeks ago. I pay a guy seventy-five grand, I expect him to be on time.'

'Seventy-five? What fuckin' seventy-five? All I got was five fuckin' hundred.'

'Then you got scammed. Royally scammed. I paid seventy-five Gs for this hit.'

'Whaddafuck?'

'I said, I put out seventy-five for you to whack me.'

'I don't get it.'

'Yeah, I guess you wouldn't. So stop shaking and listen. You heard of double indemnity?'

'Sure, das a great movie. Barbara Stanwyck and da guy from *Flubber*.'

'No, you fuckin' idiot. I mean the idea double indemnity. If I die of natural causes, my insurance pays out two mill. If I die in an accident, four mill. That's double indemnity. But… but… I got quadruple indemnity. If I get killed as a result of criminal activity – you being the criminal – my kids get eight mill. They get set up for life. My wife gets diddly.'

'*Qué?* Diddly?'

'Yeah – she's an undeserving bitch. She's had the gardener, the pool guy… even the guy who services the air-con… God forbid we should ever get a visit from the cable guy… if she were here right now she'd probably fuck you.'

'Should I wait around for her?'

'No. Just pull the fuckin' trigger!'

'I still don't get it.'

'You don't need to get it – I got it. Lung cancer. A quick hit has to be a thousand times better than coughing myself to death. Now, to quote Eli Wallach in my favourite movie, which, by the way, is *The Good, The Bad and the Ugly*, filmed in 70 mill in 1965, great soundtrack, and if you ain't seen it you're really missing out… to quote Eli Wallach, "When you should be shooting, shoot – don't talk."'

Lindsey Davis

Lindsey Davis is best known for Roman detectives Marcus Didius Falco and Flavia Albia. She has also written standalones and a Quickread. Her books are translated and dramatised on BBC Radio 4. Her awards include the Premio Colosseo (from the city of Rome) and the Crime Writers Association's Cartier Diamond Dagger. She has been Chair of the UK Crime Writers Association, President of the Classical Association and is a Fellow of the UK Society of Authors.

lindseydavis.co.uk

A WALL STORY

Lindsey Davis

Couch potatoes may remember *The Trowel 'Tecs*, that rip-off archaeology programme from the Bandwagon TV Channel. When it failed to live up to its more famous precursor, the series failed to attract a celebrity presenter. Initially they remained stuck with their reject from *Pets in Peril*: that Darren, the one the goat once bit. Then Darren turned to his own series about alpaca-farming; cute little kids, both hoofed and his own (or, as has been revealed on social media, his sister's) are helping him overcome his fear of being bitten, while on what he persistently calls his journey.

Bandwagon soldiered on. Rick 'Plummy' Duff had seemed settled as the molasses-voiced team leader, until he sent a sick note (having his hernia fixed, he claimed, though why in Tangiers?) For glamour, they retained the reliable Xenobia Smith, their very attractive, intelligent woman in shorts, who knew her stuff and had always been liked by viewers. Although hints were dropped, Ed the producer refused to move on; he stuck it out because the only way he could live with himself was to see himself as indispensable. Petrina, the intense intern, had been dumped by her Italian boyfriend but still did a lot of running around for the team, while she wondered how to change direction. With Flavio off the scene, Ed had her in his grimy sights.

A decree had been issued. *Trowel 'Tecs* was under threat of being axed due to miserable ratings ('Let's face it, Ed, there's no line on the graph for your lousy figures. You don't have the sex appeal of *Game of Thrones*; well, the problem is, in your projects you just don't have any sex'.) Ed decided to make a living-history series, based around Sensible Martha, a stern woman who could slaughter pigs. She generally came with two male helpers in moleskin weskits who would try anything; well, they would try it once. Ed now wanted to put the lads in hairy tunics, to live as incumbents of the *canabae* next to a Hadrian's Wall fort; Petrina had told him the *canabae* would be a squalid military village, so very telegenic.

Sensible Martha backed out because she had been misinformed that the new series would be at an ancient farm, the one with those round houses that are always used for telly; from there she could have nipped away to London at weekends to get blathered on fifteen G&Ts, instead of forcing down endless elderberry bloody wine. Once she skipped, her whiskery helpers decamped to do bare-chested ploughing on a drama saga.

Ed's rethink was a cracker (he said): *Something Ancient to Declare*. It would still be set on Hadrian's Wall. Now he thought of it, a fortified border seemed bravely topical. Following tradition, this was called 'an exciting new premise'. The idea was that in the first century, traffic with the northern tribes had been controlled by Roman officials much as it is nowadays at airports; Ed would depict this like the daytime TV customs franchise where border officers who are Australian, American, Irish, Canadian – 'so, why not bloody Roman?' – work politely and with interesting language issues, as they interrogate vague crooks seeking illegal work and suspected human drugs-mules, or recoil from dangerous reptiles that have been hidden in socks in suitcases and pathetic dead beetles in packets of forbidden snacks. The young look dirty and are generally high on drugs, the old plead ignorance, the crooks act angry, the baffled will faint or snivel. It must have been the same, claimed Ed, in history's greatest bureaucracy, those Roman buggers, two thousand years back.

Ed had set Petrina to work out details: how would 'my mother packed my suitcase' be mumbled by a Pict in a cart, plus what is officious Latin for 'Sir, this may come as a surprise, but we weren't born yesterday.' Secretly, the crackpot director dreamed of subjecting someone to an intimate body search, *'too right, I mean on camera!'* A hapless reenactor would do, though if she was up for it, he aimed to use Petrina; he guessed she would accuse him of being a predator ('Took her long enough to realise,' everyone was saying at the snack waggon). Ed's plan was devious, however: if the goofy girl resigned, he viewed it as marketing gold: an ensuing Me Too protest would throttle up a social media frenzy, leading to hugely inflated ratings for *Something Ancient to Declare*, until the finance boys would have to insist that Bandwagon Management green-lit a second series…

So far, Management were only saying, 'This may come as a surprise, Ed, but we weren't born yesterday.'

Ed, who was as adaptable as olive oil and twice as slippery, swung into his next rethink; he set about finding a celebrity presenter. His top pick was Dr Martyn Morello, sometimes called the thinking woman's bannock, although in Classical Civilisation circles he has other names.

Morello, who will go anywhere if his fare is paid, came north, wearing his trademark corduroy jeans, Hamlet scarf and fuchsia-pink gilet ('He thinks he's the rust guy on *Antiques Roadtrip*, or a bloody disgraced politician.') His appointment certainly got up the nose of Xenobia Smith, who knew she ought to have the job. She fought back, accusing the network of sexism because they preferred jutting-jaw Martyn to a woman, especially one in clean-cut shorts who actually knew about archaeology. Bandwagon played deaf, so she flashed up on her socials how Morello had stupidly revealed that the bastards would be paying him significantly more than her.

An admin mole at Bandwagon, trying to help, whispered to Xenobia that she needed a trademark, like other heritage presenters who were so easily identified: 'The red coat and parasol have been done to death – and *per-lease* don't get me going on hair slides – but it doesn't matter what you say, you absolutely have to be tossing masses of hair. I'm longing to promote someone with a pixie-cut, but it's not the time, Xen. Get yourself a wet-to-dry styling brush with multiple accessories.'

Xenobia thought bitterly, *Well, you try digging a trial trench across a muddy field, with corkscrews billowing in your eyes!* Long lengths might survive in the pot-washing tent, but luxe smoothness and shine as portrayed on the shopping channel would be doomed, outside in the sun and rain.

She knew how things worked. Make a fuss and they call you neurotic. Best to accept the situation, let the falsie in fuchsia begin to feel comfortable – then stick the knife in. It is fair to say that as she pressed the pleats in her shorts with a travel iron and brushed off her desert boots, Xen was already plotting. Somehow, she wanted to do for Morello.

Lean and keen, the thinker's bannock had opted to begin his northern stay at a good hotel with a Scurf and Barf bar, from which he would be collected by taxi. Iskander was the driver who ferried people to the film set on account. No one knew he was on a government watch list. Though all his family were born and brought up in Leamington Spa, his elder brother had gone to a war zone in the Middle East; he sent nightly emails urging Iskander to blow up some famous heritage site, to symbolise rejection of corrupt Western values. Unfortunately for big bro, Iskander had taken one look at Hadrian's Wall and felt the barren and beautiful upland sweeps of landscape calling to him like their grandparents' homeland. He liked the Wall. He was being urged to download build-a-bomb manuals, but instead had signed up for ancient history evening classes.

When his brother found out that Hadrian's Wall had originally been built by a gay man, the incoming texts went ballistic. Too late. By then Iskander was a Roman groupie. He would only go to a battle site if he was asked to drive Dan Snow. He had also palled up with his anti-terrorist caseworker, with whom he was enjoying discussions about how far could Alexander the Great have really gone, if he had imposed a postcode system and had access to satnav? His caseworker suspected this was a smoke-screen, but he/she/other was too preoccupied with the question of what he/she/other wanted to be, supposing he/she/other ever managed to acquire a personal life... Up so far north, it became keenly obvious why legionary commissariats had begged for more beer to pacify their restless troops and, especially, why Roman soldiers had written home to their mums begging for warm underpants. Soon he/she/other classified Iskander as not in need of monitoring, and rushed back south to GCHQ. Spooks – well, those kinds of spook – like a civilised life. This is a wide-ranging story; we shall meet the other kind.

When Iskander picked up Dr Martyn Morello, the presenter sat hunched like a paperclip over his top-of-the-range mobile phone. Iskander talked to him anyway. He knew who he had in the back of his cab because whenever he was stuck at a traffic light, he nosily googled the customer he was driving. He eased his way in with Martyn by explaining why phone reception was notoriously wobbly anywhere that had stony crags and sheep farms. His hope was that this famous personality, so well-known for his cheekbones and corduroys, would engage in debate on the politics of walls. Martyn Morello did 'do' walls. He liked to stand photogenically in front of them with a fresh-faced lad who could use a drone; they would reproduce some ancient building in 3D, to show viewers what the bloody hell some ruined place they'd never heard of had once really looked like.

'As I see it,' stated Iskander, 'nothing changes.' Despite the lack of reaction, he calmly continued. 'The presence of a border between the barbarian and imperialist worlds prompts the population to make a comparison, which unfortunately does not always turn out in favour of imperialism.'

As he lost his Wi-Fi yet again, Morello looked up. He soon keyed into conversations where he might grab something useful for a script. As well as being filmed against backgrounds of remote territory, his trademark was to spit out soundbites. He was a well-rounded professional. Soundbites equalled insights. So, he fact-checked the driver, sounding disingenuous. 'Where d'you get that from?'

'Wikipedia, basically.'

'No!'

'Berlin. Ossis and Wessis. Must have been the result here too, is what I am saying. The West Bank. Mexico—'

'China,' chimed in Morello, quickly getting it. He had been to China, naturally. That documentary was recent enough for him to regurgitate the spiel. 'You are so right, my friend: stick up a wall. Apart from defence – the obvious – you achieve border control, which means customs duties on goods, careful regulation or encouragement of trade, plus manipulating people movements. All very similar to here: on the Great Wall they too had watch towers, troop barracks, access points against incursions, signalling between garrisons, plus the fact that the path of the wall served as a slick transportation corridor on the home side.'

'A military road,' Iskander agreed as he drove along part of this one. Symbolic importance if you bombed it, his brother would have said. In fact, Iskander knew, the B6318 was a relic of General Wade fighting Bonnie Prince Charlie and had caused immense damage, being constructed in great part upon the Wall's Roman foundations.

Delayed by a flock of sheep, the taxi was overtaken by what appeared to be a man, trudging. His rather short red tunic caused Dr Morello to wind down the window. He did have a thread of human kindness running through his lithe limbs; at least, he was always on the scrounge for ideas to pinch. 'We are heading for the film set. Are you one of Mick's Merrie Menne? Want a lift?'

So, the figure hopped in and introductions ensued. Since the newcomer named himself (in rather thin tones) as Junius Delta, that seemed to confirm he belonged to a historical re-enaction group. Ed the producer had hired one to waft around as background; they were bringing their own camp, complete with blacksmiths and women who made herbal possets, they had a fine reputation for accuracy, and were fully insured. Their commercial name was Pax Romana Education Inc., because they specialised in research into ancient artefacts. Mick's Menne was a nickname they had acquired due to the forceful self-promotion of their lead centurion.

'Been doing this long?' asked Iskander, assuming their pick-up was one of Mick's meek followers. He had a sense that his new passenger smiled acknowledgement, though neither he nor Morello picked up the truth of why Junius looked translucent and his voice sounded far away. The new passenger had in fact *been* a Roman for two thousand years. He was a ghost.

'Junius Delta' had been Ed the producer's jokey name for a bunch of bones the Trowel 'Tecs had dug out of a trench when they were looking for something else. Junius (not his real name, therefore) had been dumped in a ditch after he was murdered by two thieves who had left his skeleton wearing only socks, pants and a puzzled grin. His own quest now was to find the thieves and obtain justice. A so-called investigator called Falco had materialised to hear his plea for help, but that apparition said it was hopeless and rejected the case. Junius was on his own.

He knew one thing: the killers were Tungrian auxiliaries who had been coming north for wall-building. Following them would have been a long march, but he had been a soldier himself, and spirits can whoosh from place to place, once they put what is left of their minds to it. Junius had acquired some clothes at the Treasurer's House in York, or Eboracum as he called it. This building is famously haunted by Roman ghosts; they were first spotted by a workman in the basement who saw dispirited soldiers march through the room, clad in armour, shields in hand, and even leading horses. They were visible only from the knees up, since the Roman road under the Treasurer's House had been about fifteen inches lower than the cellar floor.

Junius found those spirits a miserable, mud-stained lot; they were not from his century, in either the time sense or in Roman troop nomenclature. However, he ran into Mick, whose versatile Merrie Menne were doing a stint as Vikings at Jorvik at the time. Old friends from the Trowel 'Tecs' filming at

Mordaunt Castle, these men of vision had always been partially aware of Junius; for decency, Mick lent him a Roman tunic plus boots from their costume van. The Treasurer's House soldiers owned no boots to lend, since in the apparition world, if your legs don't show while haunting, you are not issued with footwear. There is budget-control in the afterlife, though, of course, no justice.

'I will have my vengeance!' Junius was unwittingly quoting one Maximus Decimus Meridius, a character supposedly possessed of a classic trianomina, yet oddly unable to announce his three names in the correct Roman order. Still, he was from a film, so of course not real.

When Iskander's taxi drew up at the set, Junius jumped out with Morello, who complained, 'Is this it? How are we supposed to make a groundbreaking documentary from a line of robbed-out footings?'

His outrage was lost on Junius, who could visualise the Wall as it had been, in its various manifestations. Morello's disgust puzzled Iskander, who like Mick's Menne was driven by a mission to educate, so he prepared to launch into many facts he had learned: 'Forget the idea slaves built it; this was constructed by soldiers. Took six years originally, with changes later. It was eighty miles long, with twelve fully garrisoned forts whose names we know from ancient tourist mementos that show the Latin. It was twenty feet thick at the base with milecastles and gated turrets. I believe,' he imparted, 'your producer—'

'Bloody Ed?'

'—wishes to reconstruct a milecastle.'

Morello snarled cynically. 'Don't tell me – he's got runners visiting garden centres looking for cheap stone?'

'Just don't ask anyone local about the bloody tree,' Iskander advised. 'They are getting most thoroughly pissed off.'

'What's your view?'

'I don't drink.'

'Poor you. The tree was from a garden centre?'

'No, it grew of its own accord, in Sycamore Gap.'

'Could form the basis of a good piece...' Morello imagined himself staring to camera with those water-grey eyes that have seen several deserts and, indeed, many pavement café desserts, while he brooded fetchingly about the famous tree in the famous gap, that used to look so good on carrier bags. 'From pointless destruction, maybe shoots of hope may follow...'

'They are cloning it,' grumbled Iskander. 'Bloody weed, my mum says. She does gardening. She's got a sycamore; it came with the house. She hates it. Drips resin all over her patio chairs and she has to haul up thousands of bloody seedlings every year. Worse than the chestnuts that squirrels plant.'

'Still, this is all about romantic emotion, isn't it? Couples had got engaged under the tree.'

'People can act like idiots anywhere,' opined Iskander.

Junius Delta took no interest in this conversation. Pairing himself to the past, not only was he aware of how the Wall had been, when teeming with the noises of men and smells of horses, he could see all its variations, as turf wall and squared stone in two widths, and its accessories: the Stanegate, the defensive ditch in front with its vertical sides, and the wide vallum behind. Junius visualised other borders thrust forward into Caledonia at different times, and the network of forts, often short-lived, that had formed part of a complex defensive frontier. Iskander had made himself a pie-chart to show this, but Junius had no need of visual aids.

Where would he find his killers? He ruefully acknowledged that even though he was hard on their trail, there was no point asking witnesses the usual crimey questions of who, when, with what and why? All anybody who came here was bound to ask was: where the bloody hell is Tungria?

'Belgium,' Iskander informed him, sensing the query even though the hollow-eyed essence of Junius had not spoken. The Roman slow-nodded mystically. Belgica, south of Batavia; it was birthplace to Roman auxiliary troops who were used in the conquest and subsequent colonial suppression of Britannia, which was Junius's own native land. Britons could also become auxiliaries, though less was made of it. He had taken the pay because it was better than pig-farming, they trained you in many useful skills, you got to encounter different women (ones who didn't know your mother) – and the SPQR officials held out a promise of citizenship. If you survived.

Just his luck that he hadn't. But he would pay back the culprits, when he found them.

Though no passive victim, he still felt he needed help. There existed – that shyster called Falco had told him, as *he* bunked off back to relaxing in the afterlife – a famous crime investigator from Belgica. 'Never managed decent shaving. Minces about spotting middle-rankers' jealousies. Bit prissy for you, Junius. Stick to working solo.'

In his miasma of solitude, Junius resumed thinking bitterly about the Tungrians who murdered him. There were many ways he might have died prematurely, though ending up in a ditch had not been a death he expected: knifed at an inn by Continental thugs, who pinched his armpurse, its contents, his uniform and his precious pocket multitool. It was the loss of his Roman Army Knife that grieved Junius most. It had had a three-pronged fork, a spoon, a spatula, a pick, a spike and an iron knife. Each tool was hinged to fold it out as needed or to neatly tuck it away. Junius was — had been — a gadget man. Besides, someone special had given it to him. He felt that was true, even though after two thousand years his memory of who it had been was shaky.

'A First Cohort of Tungrians was stationed at Housesteads from around Common Era 205,' Iskander imparted helpfully. *Vercovicium*, thought Iskander, too polite to point it out. 'Best preserved fort, and most dramatically sited on a crag. Another Cohort of Tungrians left inscriptions at Birrens from about 159 to 184—' *Blatobulgium*. 'I read online that a Fourth Cohort was based in Abusina during the second century, but I suspect Abusina was somewhere outside Britain.' *Raetia*, you slave. Back of beyond, the bloody Danube. Enough to give any legionary the shakes.

Junius Delta decided this was going nowhere useful so dematerialised himself.

He gave practical time to hunting his personal adversaries, realising the task would be tricky. It took more spectral energy than he had to spare, first placing himself as an apparition in exactly the right timewarp. Whichever fort the two Tungrians were attached to, their daily assignments could have taken them anywhere: not just stuck in barracks, on guard, or with fatigues like killing rats in the granary or polishing armour. Perhaps they were, as Ed surmised, deployed on gates to issue Britunculi with Nothing to Declare certificates, in quadruple sets as was the Roman clerks' way. But if the Tungrians had been sent out on patrol beyond the Wall, they might roam as far as a hundred miles, monitoring tribal meetings, flogging wine, or delivering cash 'incentives' for quiet behaviour. He might never find them.

Meanwhile, back on the Wall, there was a great deal of training. Then, as the social types Junius knew them to be, the Tungrians were quite likely to be pesky regulars at the shops and bars in that part of the military zone that civilians had made their own (since it was understood that soldiers were well paid and too dumb to resist having their salaries taken off them by merchants, trinket-sellers, beer-vendors and goodtime girls).

Daunted, Junius Delta slithered mistily back into modern times and planted his posterior carefully, lest his ectoplasm sink through the camp chair; he sat alongside Xenobia Smith, who said, 'Hello again!' with a troubled look, as if aware of how on a previous site she had handled his excavated bones.

Xenobia was listening while Martyn Morello held forth. They had disagreed on issues such as: did shreds of paint on the squared stone suggest the Wall had been deliberately coated in white so it stood out as a more dramatic barrier? Was there a walkway along the top? What's your poison: Hadrianic or Antonine?

Sensing that Xenobia knew more than him, Morello was viciously fighting back; he chose to reveal that Ed the producer was not intending to dig a previously unexcavated turret, as Xenobia had believed. Instead, Ed would knock up a quick tower reconstruction for a hideous new series of paranormal investigations, to be fronted by Morello. A team of supposedly scientific psychics would film in murky light, with sudden loud noises and dangling orbs of opaque green and pink, while Morello pretended to be terrified as he asked imagined spirits what they wanted. 'Do you mean us any harm?'

I bloody do, thought Xenobia.

So you bloody ought to, thought Junius.

'Of course, a turret will be location-building on the cheap.

In fairness, Ed would prefer a milecastle; they were much bigger, with buildings inside; we could have filmed me looking in anxiously from a verandah, hoping for communication with the Beyond, while over my shoulder the camera picks up eerie figures… I assume you believe in apparitions?' Morello asked. Junius smiled gently.

Since nobody stopped him, the presenter launched into a lecture on fourteen different kinds of haunting (as invented by the psychics, those determined young people who would help to fake his series). Junius, a corporeal spirit, was full-bodied enough not to cause suspicion that he might be too misty to be caught on camera. According to Morello's definition, he was a Class Five apparition from whom pets would run away in fear; his curriculum vitae, or curriculum mortis, listed his work skills as teleportation, telekinesis and pyrokinesis; he was an intelligent and interactive spirit who could walk through walls, even lift small items like coins if he bothered to concentrate, although as a one-time legionary he preferred not to pay for things. In theory he could communicate with clairaudient parapsychologists, but since ghosts are capable of judgement, he never did because he thought they were all deluded frauds.

Morello was totally unaware that a genuine spirit sat with him. He simply saw Junius as an odd bloke who kept suddenly appearing and disappearing; in fact, Junius was trying to rest what remained of his spectral energy, so he faded out his aura until Morello thought he had gone again. Supposing himself alone with Xenobia, Morello invited her to bury the hatchet with drinks, back to his Scurf and Barf hotel.

Xen told him no. She and Petrina had heard what might happen if anyone went to his room. There were stories. Whispers of Morello greeting innocent girls in his underpants, and asking them to help adjust his cord trousers… Standing up for herself, she told him precisely why she refused to go.

'I have total respect for women!' the impenitent slimeball lied to her. 'Otherwise I'd be asking, Ms Smith, are you wearing knickers under those shorts?'

It was so subtly done. He could claim that his question was merely hypothetical and misunderstood by a middle-class hysteric, yet Xenobia knew he meant it. She jumped up and walked off. A silent transmission reached the faded-out Junius as she departed: *He's a bully and a pervert but he is ratings gold so the authorities ignore it. If we say anything, we're done for. I need my job. Petrina certainly needs hers. What can we do?*

Junius Delta gathered his forces to rematerialise. 'Menopause,' Morello shared with him. 'Mentally unstable, if you ask me. Can't see what the viewers see in her.'

He neither knew nor would have understood that Junius had a special affection for Xenobia Smith. After all, she had led the team of undergraduates who dug up his long-buried bones. As a modern archaeologist, Xenobia believed in showing respect to disturbed bodies. She had kept Junius carefully intact, apart from one portion of dense skull bone from near his left ear, which was now in a laboratory, awaiting DNA tests.

Nor did the bannock grasp that at that moment it had been decided that the Tungrians could wait. Let them play with his Roman Army Knife, even if they bent its implements. They had tarried for two thousand years; that could continue a day longer. Junius had something else to do.

There were rules. A ghost was not supposed to interfere, not enough to alter history. Certainly not to affect a human being's fate. Junius would have to lure Martyn into danger through the man's own stupidity. But the Roman had thought up a way. It was no problem for him to communicate with the Beyond – including place memory. He had a very special weapon in mind.

The haunting was to happen that evening. Morello was working on his laptop, while he waited for Iskander to come and fetch him for the ride back to his hotel. Iskander failed to appear. Unknown to the would-be fare, it was the night of his evening class. The history group were to have a special speaker: Xenobia Smith. Petrina was coming too, because while discussing male abuse, she had realised the calm, apparently confident Xenobia ought to be her role model. Ed the producer was tagging along, with most of the crew, since they had all heard there would be finger food and liquid refreshments afterwards. Xenobia would speak tellingly of why, in our dark present and with the fear of a perilous future, it is important to understand the past. In a warm hall, people would share their love of enquiry, their pleasure in results, the hopeful struggle for historic understanding, some cheese rolls and, if they were lucky, plastic cups of lukewarm merlot.

Afterwards, of course, if any suspicion of unnatural death was raised, all who were at the talk would have alibis.

Back at the site, came movement. Once he grew bored, Morello had emerged. He found the film set deserted. Nobody witnessed the het-up celebrity ranting horribly about admin's failure to arrange his transport. He could have punched a hapless underling, even though he was aware that if he did, he might be forced to move to a minor channel and make podcasts.

Out in the wild country where an emperor once placed his frontier, it had grown extremely dark. *What is that?*

The bannock had stumbled across a full-sized stone tower,

two storeys of it, forty feet high, apparently crenelated, well-made gate facing him. Morello was astounded that Ed, whom even he saw as incompetent, had managed to build the necessary replica so fast. He presumed it was constructed not from roughly squared local limestone, but a few batons and sheets of MDF. But the result in fact had three-foot walls and looked passable – so much so, it even carried the air of being part of a much more imposing structure. You could imagine a whole mighty wall, a statement of power, striding away into the night in both directions, so solid it needed no buttresses, rolling over crags and along rivers, providing defence and announcing rulership...

Morello felt something tickle him behind his left ear, just at the spot where thick bone would yield most DNA (Junius Delta could be playful). He smelt unfamiliar perfume – the musky niff of a bath house unguent, some cheap pastiche of more expensive patchouli, as used by hippies and ancient royalty. Cold air seemed to waft around him, though Morello presumed that was classic Northumbria.

Someone seemed to be there. The paranormal investigators must already be setting up fake effects, because an orb of light rushed past him, drawing his attention after it. Clever tech. This was promising. He felt he had to follow. Mist seemed to become a human form. An arm (bare and hairy) was beckoning from an internal doorway. He imagined he heard disembodied voices. Pretending to be terrified was easy when you were genuinely nervous. He called out, 'Who are you?' Nobody answered. Yet he knew sentient beings were there ahead of him. He climbed the stone stairs.

Forty feet above the ground, for an instant he felt he was standing high above an escarpment. He was standing on one of many turrets, positioned every third of a mile, two between each of the milecastles. A pair of new spectral figures appeared to be playing a board game, one trying to win something that the other had. Watching, seemingly unnoticed by them, was the figure that had lured Morello up the steps.

Junius Delta was smiling to himself. It is said, normally as an excuse for incompetence, that plans can go awry; the truth is, well-laid plans don't. Junius had foreseen all this. He was going to retrieve his Roman Army Knife and Xenobia Smith would obtain the public position she deserved. Without a word spoken, he had persuaded the Wall, with its ancient memories, to become the presence that he needed.

The Tungrians had left their weapons leaning against the parapet while they played draughts instead of pursuing their phantom task of 'keeping our border safe'. Soon Junius would sleep in peace where Xenobia had reburied his bones. In the pile of stashed equipment were two short military swords, but he was only going to need one.

Meanwhile, Martyn Morello felt more fear than he had ever intended to act out in his paranormal series. There was no time to retrace his footsteps. For once in his life, he saw his error. The Wall's ghostly substance supported him until he knew that he was damned, even though, as a man with no conscience, he would never understand why. He stood there at the top of a turret for an instant. He felt briefly overwhelmed by unlooked-for knowledge of how the Wall had grown and been used, and what it had been like in life. He heard many voices, smelt unfamiliar odours, felt the zing of sometime pain and occasional pleasures. In his mind there was marching, digging, stripping of turves, chipping of stone blocks. For forty miles before and beyond, the original inhabitants had dispossessed, so round houses stood deserted in their enclosures – yet those who would do so had made a life in civilian places. Among the hard male voices came the lighter ones of women and children. There had been a world here; it had left its mark. Place memory, yes.

The bannock had made his communion with the Beyond. Momentarily, as a saying from another era had it, the trumpets – tuba and cornu, Mick's Menne would know them – sounded for Dr Martyn Morello on the other side. He wanted to scream out in protest at being taken, but he was gone before he could do it. The Wall was subsiding back into more centuries of rest. The turret where he had stood was gone again into incorporeal nothing.

He fell, and there was silence.

Simon Brett

Simon Brett has published over a hundred books, including the Charles Paris, Mrs Pargeter, Fethering, Blotto & Twinks and Decluttering series. *A Shock to the System* became a feature film, starring Michael Caine. Bill Nighy plays Charles Paris in the books' Radio 4 adaptations. In 2014, Simon was presented with the Crime Writers Association's highest award, the Diamond Dagger, and he was made an OBE in the 2016 New Year's Honours 'for services to literature'.

simonbrett.com

ENTRIES AND EXITS

Simon Brett

Diary of Charles Davenport. 15 April 2015.

I've just met this absolutely terrific girl! Went to dinner with a frightfully nice couple I met at a charity auction. He, Rollo, is a… hedge fund manager or something… money, anyway. Spends it in large quantities, from the look of their house in Belgravia… and the quality of the wines he dished up. She, Jools, is something in fashion… designer, I don't know.

Usual kind of crowd there. No one else I knew, but lots of people with whom it turned out I had mutual chums… same schools, that kind of thing. Conversation fairly predictable, what a waste of space Milliband is, what a shrewd statesman Cameron is, usual guff. Can't say I listened much… *because of this girl*. The *placement* sat me next to her, which was really good luck, and we… just clicked.

Her name's Vinnie. Lavinia Trumpington. Blonde, thin… but still with enough, you know… womanly curves sort of thing. Late twenties, maybe. Stunning. I don't believe in that 'love at first sight' garbage, but this evening I feel like I've been run over and processed by a combine harvester. She gave me her phone number, and I don't think I'm going to be able to concentrate on anything till I see her again.

She didn't say anything about it, obviously, but I just knew she was getting the same kind of tingly vibes for me as I was for her. I think I made an impression.

Diary of The Honourable Lavinia Trumpington.
15 April 2015.

Went to a terribly dreary dinner party this evening. Rollo and Jools, who spent most of the time, as usual, boasting about how much money they've got. Jools had sat me next to Rollo, quite deliberately, I'm sure. While our affair was going on, he swore she never knew a thing about it, but Jools isn't stupid. She had thirteen years to find out. I think she just chose not to make any comment, confident that he'd never break up the marriage, and come slinking back to her in time. Which, of course, is what he did, like the creep he is.

Sitting next to him, I felt nothing. Even when he put his hand on my thigh, there was no electricity. I removed it. So far as I was concerned, Rollo was just another braying idiot. I was amazed that I let the affair go on as long as I did. Looking back, it was just thirteen years out of my life, thirteen years wasted, when I could have been getting married and having babies like most of the girls I was at school with. At forty-three, the ticking of the old biological clock is getting rather deafening.

I'm afraid the chances of Daddy ever having the male heir he so wants to pass the estate on to are getting slimmer by the minute. Maybe I should just reconcile myself to nothing happening on that front, and take up bridge. Oh, and sitting the other side of me there was a rather dreary little man called Charles Somethingorother. We had some mutual acquaintances – clearly he went to the right schools and that sort of thing. At the end of the evening we exchanged telephone numbers. God knows why.

Diary of Charles Davenport. 16 April 2015.

Round lunchtime I finally plucked up courage to phone Vinnie. I can't believe it – she's agreed to meet me for dinner at Rules next Friday! Don't know whether I'm more excited or scared. How will I manage to survive till Friday?

Diary of Charles Davenport. 21 April 2015.

Just back from the most wonderful dinner at Rules with Vinnie. The perfect venue – and we just clicked. Conversation flowed. I felt like I'd known her for ever. I think this could be the real thing!

**Diary of The Honourable Lavinia Trumpington.
21 April 2015.**

Dinner at Rules with Charles Davenport. Typical of him, I discover, to have chosen such an unimaginative venue. Conversation very sticky, went in fits and starts. Seems he doesn't work, lives on some family trust fund, shared with his brother Julian. I've agreed to see him again. God knows why. Hope he goes for somewhere more exciting than Rules next time.

Diary of Charles Davenport. 28 April 2015.

Dinner with Vinnie. At Rules again. She clearly loves it there. We found out more about each other. Apparently, she's an 'Honourable'. Father's Lord Trumpington... not the genuine article, only a Life Peer, so the title goes when he snuffs it. I seem to think I've read something about Lord Trumpington in the papers, can't remember exactly what. Taking a potshot at some animal rights activists, was it?

Anyway, *much more importantly*... afterwards I took Vinnie in a taxi back to her place, nice little townhouse in Pimlico. I was all set to do the decent thing – quick peck on the cheek and tell the cabbie,

'Knightsbridge and don't spare the horses!'… but she *invited me in for a coffee*! Once we were inside, no messing about with coffee, straight up to the bedroom. Sensational 'little old roll in the hay'!

Vinnie and me is forever!

Diary of The Honourable Lavinia Trumpington. 28 April 2015.

Dinner with Charlie at bloody Rules again. Invited him back to my place for the inevitable sex. Messy as ever. And not great. I'm afraid shitface Rollo's set the bar rather high in the bedroom department. Still, I'm in no position to be choosy. Thank God Mummy's no longer around to know how near the bottom of the Debrett's barrel I'm scraping.

Diary of The Honourable Lavinia Trumpington. 19 May 2015.

Still no visit from Auntie Flo. Tempted to try a pregnancy test, but I'll give it a few more days.

Diary of The Honourable Lavinia Trumpington. 23 May 2015.

Pregnancy test positive. It's what I wanted, and I suppose Charlie Davenport's no worse than any other man. I haven't told him yet. But I will very soon. It'll give me an excuse not to have any more of that sex nonsense for a while.

iPad Diary of Julian Davenport. 2 June 2015.

Call from little brother Charlie today – and a big surprise. He's asked me to be best man at his wedding! I suppose even someone as stupid as Charlie can always find some woman gullible enough to marry him.

Lavinia Trumpington, she's called. Daughter, it turns out, of Lord Trumpington, the one who's always banging on in the Lords about how we Brits should be allowed to carry guns like the Yanks. Sensible fellow. Of course, he's not the genuine article. Born Reginald Trumpington. Just some jumped-up Northern industrialist who bribed that shyster Tony Blair to give him a life peerage.

Dripping with loot, though. He's got that amazing spread in Somerset, Chestings, stately home, huge lake, acres of woodland. I've actually been shooting there. I remember the weekend well – cost me a bloody fortune.

So… my little idiot brother seems to have landed on his feet.

Diary of Mr Challis. 17 June 2015.
As the solicitor administering the Davenport Trust, I had an appointment today with Charles Davenport, the younger of the two brothers who share equally in its proceeds, and who are beneficiaries of each other's wills.

By arrangement, Charles Davenport brought with him his fiancée, Lavinia Trumpington, daughter of Lord Trumpington. With her father's agreement, she wishes to make a new will, leaving her estate to her soon-to-be husband and any issue of their marriage.

She made no secret of the fact that, though not yet married, she is already pregnant – a situation which seems increasingly prevalent among today's young people… not that it would be my place to pass any comment on the morality of such arrangements. But I believe this to be one of the reasons why the couple are getting married very soon, in what was known in my young day as 'indecent haste'.

The proposal that Charles Davenport put forward seems to

me to represent sensible estate planning, so I agreed to draft Lavinia Trumpington's new will as requested.

Diary of Charles Davenport. 30 June 2015.
Today I actually tied the knot with Vinnie in the family chapel at Chestings! I couldn't be happier. I feel like all my birthdays and Christmases have come at once... in spite of a couple of rather off-colour remarks about my intelligence that Julian put into his best man's speech. Still, I suppose it was all in good fun.

Otherwise, the whole day went swimmingly. Vinnie's father was very good about it all, given the circumstances. He seemed just very relieved to know that she's pregnant... as he kept saying in a manner that was rather... He is a bit of a rough diamond...

Mind you, it's wonderful to think that a child of mine will inherit Chestings and all the rest. Vinnie and I went for our wedding night to a very shooshed-up country house hotel. She was feeling queasy and had to leave halfway through dinner.

When I got to the bedroom, she was asleep, which rather disappointed me. We haven't had a, er, 'little old roll in the hay' since she found out she was pregnant. Still, I feel I must respect her wishes in this. The health of the baby is what matters.

We have a whole lifetime together to catch up on 'little old rolls in the hay'.

Diary of The Honourable Lavinia Trumpington.
30 June 2015.
Got through the wedding. God, I'm now Lavinia Davenport... how dreary. Still, the baby will be legitimate, which is all that matters. Managed to avoid wedding night sex by pretending to be asleep. Think I can play that card right through the pregnancy.

Then maybe let Charlie have his wicked way in a few years' time if we need a spare to go with the heir.

So… do I feel any different as Mrs Davenport? No. Charlie still bores the pants off me. Do I feel anything for him? Absolutely not. Still, the Aged Parents never felt anything for each other, and their marriage survived more than thirty years, till Mummy's cancer let her off the hook. Heigh-ho.

iPad Diary of Julian Davenport. 30 June 2015.
Did Charlie and Vinnie's wedding. Got a couple of gibes into my best man's speech about how thick he is. Everyone roared, though, as ever, Charlie was too thick to realise he was being insulted.

Spoke to Challis on the phone a couple of days before the ceremony. Just to clarify things. It seems that if Vinnie pops her clogs prematurely, Charlie and the child cop the lot. Wonder if my little brother remembers that, under the terms of the Davenport Family Trust, he and I are still mutual beneficiaries of each other's wills. Interesting.

Anyway, good thing about my now being allied to the Trumpingtons… means I'll get invited to Chestings for the shooting… and won't have to pay. I'll ensure I get invited for the first Saturday in October. Trumpington always throws a big shooting party then. It's an ill wind…

Diary of Charles Davenport. 24 September 2015.
Lord Trumpington has all his cronies coming down for the shooting next weekend. Chance to show the great and the good his new son-in-law. No pressure, then. Actually, makes me feel a bit nervous.

Vinnie very uncomfortable in the hot weather. Seen her quack, who says there are some worries about the pregnancy. Vinnie thinks separate bedrooms would be a good idea. She knows best. The baby's what matters. I'm so happy to have such a caring wife.

Diary of The Honourable Lavinia Trumpington.
24 September 2015.

Daddy insists I've got to be around at Chestings for his bloody shooting weekend. Can't wait to show off his pregnant daughter to all those tedious old farts he usually invites.

Doctor's appointment this morning. Gender confirmed – male. Told Daddy, he was ecstatic. And all fine with the pregnancy. But I told Charlie there were complications, which means I've managed to get him out of my bedroom for the duration… so that's progress.

Suddenly remembered, I forgot to tell Charlie about the baby's gender… Must remember to do that some time.

Had a call on the mobile from Rollo… Sounding quite keen again. Talked of booking the usual room at the usual hotel for next Wednesday afternoon.

Obviously, I told him to forget it… till after the baby's born. I don't want him seeing my body in its current condition – but I can't deny I was quite tempted. Just get this bloody pregnancy over… not to mention Daddy's bloody shooting weekend… and we'll see what happens…

Diary of Lord Trumpington. 24 September 2015.

Don't believe in this diary-writing nonsense myself. Just another form of navel-gazing, and I haven't made the money I've made by gazing at my bloody navel. Still, the ghostwriter who's doing my memoirs said I must keep a record, so that's what I'm bloody doing.

And at least today there's something worth bloody reporting. Had a call this morning from the daughter Lavinia. Sprog she's carrying's a boy – bloody great! She's finally done something to pay me back for all the money I spent on her education.

Have to see to it the boy carries my name, though. I'm not having Chestings and everything else owned by someone called 'Davenport'. No, I will order my son-in-law, the halfwit Charlie, to change his bloody surname. He won't argue. Never does. He's a streak of piss, if I ever saw one.

I'm looking forward to the bloody weekend more than ever now. Shooting should be great, and I'll have some good news to pass on to all the bloody freeloading toffs who'll be here stuffing their faces at my expense.

Report from Detective Inspector Timpson.
3 October 2015.

Had a call from the commissioner this morning asking me to investigate an incident at a stately home called Chestings in Somerset. I realised it must be serious. The Somerset and Avon boys'll do anything to stop Scotland Yard muscling in on their patch, so it must be very serious.

Turned out the 'incident' involved a prominent member of the House of Lords. Trumpington. After the fuss the old boy's made about law and order issues, relaxation of gun control… no wonder the Commissioner wants the kid gloves on for this one.

I got briefed on the phone in the car down to Chestings. Trumpington was hosting a weekend shooting party, and out on the estate on Saturday he apparently tripped and took the full blast of his shotgun.

Accident, of course. No one's mentioned the word 'murder'. And I will be very careful that I don't.

Commissioner wants me to nose around, though, get the SP. There's quite a militant anti-shooting lobby lurking about in the undergrowth. 'Shoot the Shooters' they're called. A rumour was picked up that they might be targeting Chestings this weekend. Doing away with Lord Trumpington'd be just the kind of stunt they'd like to have pulled off.

Commissioner wants me to find out as much as I can, try to have a coherent response before the press get hold of the story. I must tread carefully.

Phone of Micky Lipton. 3 October 2015. WhatsApp Encrypted Message to 'Shoot the Shooters' Group.

Wow, what a result at Chestings! Death of a capitalist mogul like Lord Trumpington's just the kind of high-profile story we need. Congratulations to whichever brother did the deed!

Usual procedure, though. No direct claim for responsibility, just start the rumour-mill churning that STS might have been behind it. That'll get a few more of the animal-murdering lobby quaking in their boots.

Keep up the good work, and soon shooting will have gone the way of fox hunting.

Solidarity, brothers!

Diary of Charles Davenport. 3 October 2015.

At Chestings. Still in shock about what happened to Vinnie's old man. Ghastly. They keep trying to make shooting safer, but you can never really account for human error.

Apparently, there's some police detective from Scotland Yard down here, asking everyone lots of questions. I suppose they have to go through all that, even with an accident.

Vinnie's taken the news pretty well, really. Never quite sure whether she actually felt anything for the old monster. Still, just as well she's not too upset, what with the baby coming.

Had a chat with Julian in the Rose Garden this morning. He asked if I realised that, now old Trumpington's off the scene, Vinnie will inherit the lot. I hadn't, actually.

He also told me that, if I was questioned by this detective inspector johnny, I should say that, during Saturday's shooting, Julian and I were never out of each other's sight. He said it'd simplify things.

I agreed to do it. Rather an odd thing to ask, though, I thought.

Report from Detective Inspector Timpson.
4 October 2015.
I've finished questioning all the guests at the Chestings shooting party. If this was the appropriate place for me to pass comments on the habits and behaviour of the filthy rich... but it isn't.

Nobody seems to have been anywhere near Lord Trumpington when he died. He was quite deep into the woods. Why he was so far from the rest of the party, no one knows.

The people who seem to have been nearest to him geographically were two brothers, Julian and Charles Davenport. The latter is the deceased's son-in-law and apparently now calls himself Charles Trumpington. Anyway, with all the guns that were firing, both brothers denied hearing the fatal shot... which would have come from behind them rather than in front. They also claim not to have been out of each other's sight all day, and not to have seen anything suspicious.

The younger one, Charles, is... well, he seems to be on the verge of educationally subnormal – or whatever the current politically correct term is for 'thick as two short planks'. Julian is a lot cannier, quite bright I think, under his languid upper-class exterior.

But, like everyone else I questioned, they didn't see or hear anything relevant to my investigation, so, with some reluctance, I must exclude them from my list of suspects.

Next thing I have to do is find out more about these animal rights protesters, 'Shoot the Shooters'. Some were apparently spotted climbing over a wall into the Chestings estate on the Friday night.

No doubt they'll be the usual line-up of niffy, dreadlocked loonies and losers.

iPad Diary of Julian Davenport. 4 October 2015.

Back in the Barbican after my eventful weekend at Chestings. Wasn't allowed to leave until I'd been interrogated by a rather tiresome little policeman called Thompson or something.

He just went round the same questions again and again. Did I see anything? Did I hear a gunshot from behind in the woods rather than in front of me? No and no. But there does come a point when you feel you've said 'No' enough times. I thought I'd never get this Thompson character off my back.

By the end I was quite glad Charlie had insisted I say he and I hadn't been out of each other's sight all day. I suppose that provided what they call an 'alibi', and did, finally, get me off the hook.

Came back to find another letter from the bank, whose tone can only be described as 'threatening'. Oh dear.

Phone of Micky Lipton. 5 October 2015. WhatsApp Encrypted Message to 'Shoot the Shooters' Group.

Had a predictable interrogation from the pigs today. Detective inspector called Timpson. Needless to say, about Lord Trumpington. Needless to say, I couldn't help him.

This is where the 'Shoot the Shooters' cell system works like a dream. I know the Chestings assassination was our hit, but I literally don't know who did it. Perfect.

So, however much the pig pressured me, I didn't tell him anything because I didn't know anything. Eventually he had to give up – yeah, result!

Had a WhatsApp from an STS brother this morning, in which he suggested the hit on Lord Trumpington might have been *done* by one of us but *contracted* by some toff who had a grudge against him. Mutual result – we get the publicity we're after, toff gets rid of someone who's bugging him.

And the contract fee goes into our fighting fund. Don't know if there's any truth in the suggestion, but it's a cool idea.

Solidarity, brothers!

Diary of Mr Challis. 7 October 2015.

Julian Davenport came to my office this morning for an eleven o'clock appointment. He claimed he wanted to check the provisions of the Davenport Family Trust. I ran through the details for him and confirmed that currently he and his brother Charles are mutual beneficiaries of each other's wills.

Though it is not my place to make recommendations in such situations, I did draw his attention to the likelihood of his brother Charles redrafting his will to reflect his changed circumstances. In fact – although I did not confide this to Julian Davenport – I am surprised his brother has not already taken such action. I can only think that he has been distracted by the death of his father-in-law and his impending fatherhood.

Or maybe he is planning to make a new will once the baby has arrived. It is not my place to anticipate the actions of my clients. Julian Davenport also asked me about the health of the family trust, and I was not able to give him any very encouraging response. So much capital has been taken out of the fund that the remaining investments are producing virtually no income.

I think my client was aware of this, and merely required confirmation from me. Very soon his only assets will be his flat in the Barbican and his Range Rover. Whether he sells those to raise capital and moves somewhere cheaper, or whether he takes the unfamiliar option of getting a job, it is not my place to speculate.

Diary of Charles Davenport. 4 February 2016.

Absolutely marvellous day! At 3.17 this morning my son, Reginald Trumpington, was born here at Chestings. He's a complete stunner! I'm already calling him 'Reggie', though to be truthful, he doesn't really answer to it as yet.

Everyone's on top of the world… well, except possibly Vinnie, who it seems didn't have a frightfully good time. But I'm sure she'll soon perk up, and we'll be back having 'little old rolls in the hay' – yippee!

One thing I have decided… I've been about to buy a speed-boat for the lake, you know, water-skiing and that kind of stuff… and I'm going to name the vessel, in honour of the old one and the new one – the *Reginald Trumpington*! Gosh, I'm absolutely over the moon!

Diary of The Honourable Lavinia Trumpington.
15 April 2016.

I'd forgotten till Charlie reminded me, but it's exactly a year since he and I first met. He said we should celebrate, suggested we should go out for a swanky dinner and come back here for what he insists on calling 'a little old roll in the hay'. I told him to keep his bloody hands to himself.

God, when I think what that baby did to my body! I don't see the creature much, there are nurses who feed it and do all the other disgusting things that have to be done to babies. Charlie keeps saying I should show more interest in what he insists on calling 'Reggie'. I told him I hardly ever saw my parents when I was growing up, and it hasn't done me any harm.

I've been working out like mad at the gym ever since the little blighter appeared, and I think – thank the Lord – I have more or less got my figure back. I'm going to put it to the test, anyway. Next Wednesday, I've told Charlie, I have to go to London to do some shopping. Next Wednesday, I've told Rollo, I'll see him at the usual time in the usual hotel.

I'm not about to put my life on hold because of some bloody baby.

iPad Diary of Julian Davenport. 16 April 2016.
Had a call from my idiot brother this morning, inviting me down to Chestings for the weekend of the 27th to the 30th. Said it was because we haven't seen each other for a while, need to catch up, but it's really that he wants to show off this new speedboat he's got for the lake.

Seems to have become very keen on water-skiing all of a sudden. Funny, Charlie never knew a thing about boats… whereas I've always known quite a lot about them.

Report from Detective Inspector Timpson. 29 April 2016.
Call from the commissioner this morning. Another incident at Chestings, down in Somerset. Since – as he rather gleefully reminded me – we never found out whether Lord Trumpington's death was an accident or not, he wants me to check whether

there might be any connection between this latest incident and the 'Shoot the Shooters' group.

Accident involving a speedboat this time. Two dead. Names: Lavinia Trumpington and her infant son Reginald.

Diary of Charles Davenport. 29 April 2016.

I can't believe what's happened. I'm devastated. It seems there was some malfunction with the engine that made the boat explode. Why on earth did Vinnie agree when Julian suggested she take Reggie out in it?

God, this is terrible!

Report from Detective Inspector Timpson. 30 April 2016.

Talked to Julian Davenport. He was very interesting on the subject of his brother's marriage. Apparently, all was not well there. Lavinia Trumpington had not allowed her husband any… conjugal rights, since she first got pregnant.

Also, apparently, she's recently revived her affair with a former lover. I'll have to check that out.

And Julian told me that, shortly before Lavinia Trumpington set out on the lake, he saw Charlie in the boathouse, tinkering with the engine of the *Reginald Trumpington*… which he thought was strange, given that his brother had never shown any interest in boats before.

Another interesting piece of information from Julian… Apparently, brother Charlie keeps a regular diary. I think I might need to look at those diaries as evidence.

Notebook of Charles Davenport. 5 May 2016.

Forced to write in this bloody notebook, because that bastard policeman has had the nerve to take my diaries. I can't believe it! He can see the state I've been thrown into by Vinnie's and Reggie's deaths. Surely he can't be suspicious that I had anything to do with them?

Really strange thing happened today when I was shopping in Taunton. As I was stepping off the curb outside W H Smith, a car seemed to drive straight at me at high speed. Fortunately, I just managed to jump out of the way in time. It was a Range Rover.

Afterwards, given the state I'm in, I wished the bloody thing had hit me, put an end to this utter misery.

Call from Julian this evening, inviting me weekend after next to a shooting party some friends down in Hampshire are organising. Not proper shooting, obviously, this time of year, just lamping for rabbits after dark… you know, air rifles with powerful flashlights attached. It's not really sport, more like shooting fish in a barrel.

Still, Julian said I needed to get out of myself. I said I don't think I'll ever get out of myself. I just feel so… crushed and hopeless. I appreciate the thought, though. That's what brothers are for.

I told him I'd think about it.

Notebook of Charles Davenport. 20 May 2016.

Against my better judgement, I did go on this Hampshire shooting weekend with Julian. Soon as I got there, I knew it was a bad idea. Full of braying oafs, whose only aim seemed to be to see who could get the most pissed. I suppose there was a time when I would have been just like them, but… after what's happened…

As soon as I arrived on the Friday evening, I was tempted to turn straight round and go back to Chestings, but Julian persuaded me to stay for that night's shooting at least.

And a very strange thing happened… We were all wandering

around in the woods, smashed out of our skulls, crashing through the undergrowth, frightening off any wildlife there might be out there, and too bladdered to focus our lights on a rabbit, anyway… when suddenly I was aware of a light shining directly in my face, you know, like someone was aiming straight at me.

It was only for a second, because then another member of the party came stumbling towards me and… this is the strange thing… as his light waved past, it caught Julian's face, almost as if Julian was the one who'd been focusing his light on me. Obviously nonsense. Funny, the tricks the mind can play when you're in an upset state.

Anyway, I'd had enough, left first thing Saturday morning. Didn't really get a chance to have a word alone with Julian, just say goodbye. But when I did say goodbye to him, he seemed really, I don't know… tense, angry. I suppose it was his way of sharing my grief.

Julian and I may not always have seen eye to eye over the years but, at bottom, he's a good bloke.

Report from Detective Inspector Timpson. 23 May 2016.
I've read the complete diaries of Charles Davenport – or Charles Trumpington, as he now calls himself – covering the past two years, since before he met his late wife… and the conclusion I have reached… is that when the brains were handed out, he was way at the end of the queue.

He certainly hasn't got the intellect to work out something as complicated as the murder – and I'm still convinced it was murder – of Lord Trumpington.

What is interesting from the diaries, though, is the respect – almost hero-worship – that Charles has for his elder brother Julian… who is an altogether more sophisticated operator.

I think the next stage of my investigation will very definitely have to be a visit to Mr Julian Davenport.

iPad Diary of Julian Davenport. 23 May 2016.
Back at the Barbican from Hampshire. Not the most productive weekend of my life. And I return to a message that I am soon to have a visit from the odious DI Timpson. It seems I've been clever, but not quite clever enough, and he's on to me.

Pity. Just bad luck, really. Charlie never suspected a thing. I'd got an alibi set up with my mate down in Hampshire, and if only that bloody drunken oaf hadn't appeared when I was about to shoot, no one would have questioned that Charlie had been the victim of an unfortunate accident.

Just as nobody questioned that Lord Trumpington had been the victim of an unfortunate accident.

Just as no one suggested that I might have been involved in the deaths on the lake of my sister-in-law and my nephew.

Incredible, bloody bad luck. So now... I'm not quite sure if there's anywhere left for me to go. I think I only have one option left.

Report from Detective Inspector Timpson. 23 May 2016.
I went to visit Julian Davenport at the Barbican this evening. No reply, I had to get the porter to let me into his flat.

I wasn't surprised to find him dead. In the bathroom. He'd put the shotgun in his mouth – hell of a mess.

Once the Scene of Crime boys had gone through their usual ritual, I checked out the stuff on his tablet.

He'd kept a pretty thorough record of his misdeeds. He was still the beneficiary of his brother's will, nobody had bothered to change that. If Charles Trumpington's 'accidental death' in

Hampshire had gone ahead as planned, Julian Davenport would have inherited Chestings and everything that went with it.

Tomorrow I have to go see the surviving brother, return his diaries to him, and generally eat humble pie… huh, never my dish of choice.

Diary of Charles Davenport. 24 May 2016.

DI Timpson came to Chestings around midday to return my diaries. He was all set to tell me about Julian, but I said I'd heard the news. I didn't offer him lunch.

He apologised for his suspicions of me… which I suppose provided some level of satisfaction…

…though not as great a satisfaction as that provided by all my plans working out.

I was waiting for Julian in his flat when he came back from Hampshire yesterday. In the bathroom, wearing gloves, with his shotgun.

Then… what do they say… 'a brief scuffle ensued'?

I was always stronger than him. I got the barrel into his mouth, pulled the trigger, and got out before the splatter hit me.

I did it in the bathroom, so there wouldn't be any blood on his iPad. So sensible of Julian to write his diary on that, rather than in longhand… no one can tell who's actually made the entries.

I knew the dates which were relevant, and I didn't actually have to make many changes. Getting him down to Taunton on the right day, bit about him fiddling with the engine of the *Reginald Trumpington*, that kind of thing.

Then just type up the final entry, wipe the keyboard down for fingerprints, and make my exit.

Now I'm safely back at Chestings… which, of course, I own.

Not bad for the 'idiot brother', is it?

Did rather regret having to do away with young Reginald, but then I'd never have been absolutely certain that he was mine rather than Rollo's, so…

And now… what shall I do with the rest of my life?

Diary of The Honourable Serena De Vere Townsend.
15 April 2017.

I've just met this absolutely terrific chap. At a dinner party. Called Charlie Trumpington. Widower, poor fellow, wife died tragically. Quite a lot older than little *moi*.

But he was fascinated when I told him about Daddy being a Life Peer. He's really nice… kind of simple, straightforward, honest. Not terribly bright, but generally that's a good thing with men.

I think this could be the real thing!

Adrian Muller

Adrian Muller graduated from the Reinwardt Museology Academy in Holland. After moving to Bristol, he worked at Watershed Media Centre. As a journalist, he specialised in interviewing crime writers, and edited four annual Crime & Thriller Guides for *The Times*. Adrian organised events for London's Crime in Store bookshop, was a co-founder of Manchester's Dead on Deansgate festival and the International Thriller Writers organisation. Having co-hosted Left Coast Crime's 2006 Bristol visit, the hosts continued the US convention as CrimeFest.

AFTERWORD AND ACKNOWLEDGEMENTS

It was with sadness – but great pride – that Donna Moore, my wonderful and patient co-host, and I announced the sixteenth CrimeFest would be the last.

With ongoing support from our wonderful headline sponsors, Dame Mary Perkins and Specsavers, sponsor H W Fisher, and benefactors Jane Petersen Burfield, and Barry Ryan at Free@LastTV, finances were not an issue.

For Donna and I (and, before he retired, Myles Allfrey), CrimeFest is a labour of love, and we decided to go out on our own terms and whilst we were at the top.

CrimeFest was a spin-off from the same organisers as the highly successful one-off 2006 UK visit of the American crime fiction convention, Left Coast Crime.

When CrimeFest began in 2008, there were just two major crime fiction events in the UK. Now, readers don't have to travel far to find a wide choice of crime fiction events, varying in scale.

Regardless of how they define themselves – festivals, conventions, etc. – the format, in most cases, is largely the same: featured guests and authors give interviews and appear on panels. A quiz and an award ceremony are frequently also part of the itinerary.

CrimeFest remains unique in the UK, because it followed the egalitarian American format: everyone – with exception of the few featured guests – registers to attend, and authors with a commercial British-based publisher are offered a panel as part of their registration. Which goes someway towards explaining why CrimeFest had a very loyal attendance, with most delegates – be they authors or readers – returning year after year and, together with the CrimeFest team, warmly welcoming annual newcomers.

In her first Gala Dinner speech, Dame Mary perceptively recognised that special quality, which she named the 'CrimeFest family'. It is an atmosphere that past and present organisers have always strived for, and an accolade we deeply value.

But, how to deliver a final CrimeFest to live up to the last sixteen years?

With many delegates already registered, the first thing we did was gather as many of our favourite authors as possible to celebrate the joint achievement that is CrimeFest. 'Joint achievement' because we are fully aware we could not have done so without the wonderful range of delegates that have attended over the years.

Lee Child and Jeffery Deaver have been headliners at all the key CrimeFest moments, from Left Coast Crime onwards. Inviting both was a no-brainer. (Whilst Jeff wasn't physically able to be at the final CrimeFest, he is present through his story in this anthology.)

AFTERWORD AND ACKNOWLEDGEMENTS

Others enthusiastically signed on and, with an exemplary list of participating authors, Donna, in her inimitable way, worked her usual magic scheduling another wonderful itinerary with the wonderful mix of panellists and guests.

Yet, somehow, organising a final CrimeFest didn't sufficiently seem to mark the occasion. Donna and I wanted to do something to thank everyone for their support over the years. Then a mad thought struck.

Thanks to a generous donation from our Canadian benefactor Jane Petersen Burfield, we celebrated CrimeFest's 10th anniversary by giving all delegates a complimentary copy of *10 Year Stretch*, an anthology of short stories commissioned especially for the occasion. Sales of retail copies went to our designated charity: The Royal National Institute of Blind People (RNIB).

We'd had a year and a half to put that book together. Could we do it again, but this time in less than six months?

First port of call was the wonderful Ion Mills, who published *10 Year Stretch* through No Exit Press in 2018. Dubious at first, he thought it would be very, *very* tight, but agreed that it *could* be done.

Due to prior commitments, Martin Edwards, co-editor of the previous anthology, was unable to return. However, multi-talented and long-time CrimeFest supporter Maxim Jakubowski generously agreed to come on board. (Prior contractual obligations required him to merely be acknowledged as 'advising editor'. However, like Martin before him, Maxim was more than an equal, bringing decades of long and invaluable editing experience to this collection.)

Then Donna, Maxim and I put together a wish-list of authors who had previously attended CrimeFest. We wanted to invite back those from the previous publication who had a noteworthy connection to the convention, but also recognise other long-time supporters by bringing in new contributors.

Despite the deadline – which included the break for the end-of-year festive season – we were incredibly moved by all the positive responses. The list of superlative names made it easy for Ion to persuade Jamie Hodder-Williams, the new owner of No Exit Press, to agree to publish the anthology. We are grateful to have their support.

Jane Burfield kindly agreed to top-up the remaining 10th anniversary funds to make the publication possible. Now a published author in her own right, we are delighted to have her as one of the contributors.

And, as previously, proceeds from this book will once again go to the RNIB.

This anthology is, at its heart, put together by those who have been a continued and integral part of CrimeFest. It's an acknowledgement to them, and to all of you who made CrimeFest possible.

Now, *that* is the way to celebrate the close of an event like CrimeFest!

All that remains is to dedicate this book to all who attended CrimeFest; to absent friends, such as Toby Gottfried; and to members of the CrimeFest family who are no longer with us: Heather Cressy, Bill Gottfried and Thalia Proctor.

Adrian Muller

CrimeFest Co-Host & Director

Over the years, many others have supported CrimeFest in various ways. These include:

Audible UK • Stephanie Bierwerth • Simon Bewick • Camilla Bolton • Bristol Blue Glass • Anita & Jo at the Bristol Business Centre • Bristol Cultural Development Partnership • Amanda Brown • Lauren Brown • Edwin Buckhalter • Jane & Miranda Burfield • Ann & Clair at Cause UK • Lee Child • Martina Cole • Beverley Cousins • *CrimeTime* • Crime Writers Association • Jenny Dunbar • H.W. Fisher & Andrew Subramaniam • Martin Edwards • Barry & Judith Forshaw • Gianna Faccenda • Nev Fountain • Alastair Giles & Rob Garraway at Agile Marketing • Nicky Godfrey-Evans & Tours of Discovery • Daniel Gedeon & Goldsboro Books • Maggie Griffin • Peter Guttridge • Liz Hatherell & Myles Allfrey • Lizzie Hayes & Mystery People • David Headley • Sarah Hilary •Fiona Holbrook • Kerry Hood • Imprint Academic • Patsy Irwin • Maxim Jakubowski • Ali Karim • Janet Laurence • John Lawton • Steven Mair & Claire Watts • Philippa McEwan • Angela McMahon • Ann Mackinolty • Ann & Adrian Magson • Naomi Miller at Bristol Ideas • Ion Mills • Max Minerva's Marvellous Books • Jennifer, Eleanor &

CrimeFest Co-Host & Director

Gabriel Muller • June Muller • Tony Mulliken • NORLA • Ayo Onatade • Jonathan Peacock at VWV Solicitors• Dame Mary Perkins & Specsavers • Barbara Peters, Robert Rosenwald & the Poisoned Pen Press • Nicci Pracca • Lucy Ramsey • Red Herring Games • Richard Reynolds & Heffers • Mike Ripley • Andy Roberts at Aspyre Accountancy • Barry Ryan & Free@LastTV • S.A. Events • Bill Selby • Zoë Sharp • Kathryn Skoyles • *Shots* Mystery Magazine • Mike Stotter • Louise Torm • Stanley Trollip • Sue Trowbridge & Joe Mallon • Anne Ulset & the Norwegian Embassy • Waterstones Bristol-Galleries & Edouard Gallais • Julia Wisdom • any other individuals, companies or organisations who were unintentionally overlooked.

Thank you.